WITHDRA

59372088887289

D0345572

WORN, SOILED, OBSOLETE

GINGER
SNAPS

GINGER SNAPS

• A NOVEL •

Webb Hubbell

BEAUFORT
BOOKS

ISBN 978-0-8253-0777-5

A CIP record for this book is available.

For inquiries about volume orders, please contact:

Beaufort Books
27 West 20th Street, Suite 1102
New York, NY 10011
sales@beaufortbooks.com

Published in the United States by Beaufort Books
www.beaufortbooks.com

Distributed by Midpoint Trade Books
www.midpointtrade.com

Printed in the United States of America

Interior design by Neuwirth & Assoicates, Inc.
Cover Design by Michael Short

To:
Suzy, Will and Jake, Mary and Allen, Lila,
Rebecca, Frances, and George

AUTHOR'S NOTE

The story is set in Little Rock, Arkansas. Although I know all of its schools, parks, and neighborhoods, lovers of Little Rock (of which I am definitely one) shouldn't expect to recognize its topography, or to find the Russell Robinson Courthouse, City Park, Butler Field, the Armitage Hotel, the Kavanaugh Home, or Ben's. They also shouldn't believe that the fictional characters or events have any connection with reality—they exist only in the imagination of the author and his readers.

FRIDAY

April 18, 2014

1

AN AXE CRASHED through the solid oak front door. Nelson, the big Calico cat who lay sprawled on the sofa, enjoying the warmth of the April sun, flew up the stairs, his paws barely touching the floor. Not even a ten-year-old could mistake the dozen men who charged into the house. Wearing dark blue flak jackets with blaring yellow DEA initials, the agents entered with guns extended. Fanning throughout the house, they played their clichéd parts, calling out "all clear" or "area secure." Two guys in suits brought up the rear.

The agents soon tired of the game and took up the real job of tagging, packing, and boxing almost every single item in the house — the art, the silver, the dishes, the knick-knacks, even the lady's lingerie and nightgowns. They took detailed photographs of each item they didn't or couldn't box up: the crystal chandelier in the dining room, the marble fireplace, the designer window treatments, even the Thermidor appliances in the newly renovated kitchen. They gave up on the cat, who had found refuge behind the old chimney in the attic's cedar closet.

Curiously, several agents were rooting around in the back garden pulling up all the plants and stuffing them into pre-labeled bags. They followed the same procedure for the hundreds of seedlings in the flower shed. Under an old tarp in the garage they found a reconditioned Austin-Healy 3000 and a 1961 F-100 pick-up. A tow truck and a moving van arrived and, within a couple of hours, the house, garage, and shed were almost empty except for the dishes in the sink, the seasonings and cereal boxes on the pantry ledge, and one terrified cat. The yard and house were cordoned off with bright yellow tape, isolated by brusque signs informing all comers that the old house was now the property of the U.S. Government.

Assistant U.S. Attorney Richard Bullock, one of the two suits, frowned. "Is all this necessary? Really? An axe through the door, carting off all their furniture and underwear—aren't we going a bit too far?"

U.S. Attorney Wilbur "Dub" Blanchard grinned like a kid in a candy store. He had all but begged the marshals to let him swing the axe.

"Professor Stewart is a threat to our nation's security. He doesn't deserve to be treated gently. We're sending a message to would-be terrorists."

"It's me you're talking to, not the press," Bullock cautioned. "You sound like you believe your own bullshit."

"Of course I believe it," Dub said with a smirk. "Stewart smells as bad as any Middle Eastern jihadist. And your job, Mr. Bullock, is to help me convince everyone, especially the press, of exactly that fact." Of course, Blanchard had leaked the bust to the press; reporters and cameramen were already in place on the front lawn, gravely informing the public of the developing situation.

Bullock didn't respond. He was worried his boss's ego might compromise an airtight case and a financial windfall for the U.S. Government.

At about the same time, three armed agents in full battle gear barged into a chemistry classroom at the University of Arkansas-Little Rock, shoved the professor to the floor and handcuffed him. A pair of more appropriately dressed agents were politely explaining to the University's President that the school's most distinguished professor had been arrested, and that his office, computer, and chemistry labs were off-limits.

His students sat in stunned silence as one of the agents pressed a gun barrel against Dr. Douglas Stewart's head and read him his rights. For a moment, time seemed to stop.

"Do you understand these rights? Can you hear me?" the agent shouted, and the balloon of silence burst. The room filled with the noise of slamming books, scraping chairs, and a general rush to the door. Stewart's voice came through loud and clear.

"Of course I can hear you. I want my lawyer. I want to speak to Jack Patterson."

2

◇━━━━◇

MICKI LAWRENCE HAD spent the night with Dr. Eric Masterson. Eric didn't have rounds this morning so she slid out of bed quietly, slipped into her running clothes, and jogged off the front porch into the still quiet, tree-lined streets of Little Rock. Last night's thunderstorm had cleared the air of pollen, and she soaked in the cool spring air and the fresh smell of greening lawns and trees.

As she picked up the pace, she didn't notice a black Infiniti slowing down a block behind her. The driver, a skinny man on the long side of forty with a bad comb-over, the kind of a man parents warn children about, sat low in the seat, but not so low he couldn't keep Micki in his sights, admiring her stride. A "Mr. Smith" had recently hired him, although he'd never met him in person. He figured from Smith's accent that the man was Oriental, but he didn't care. He wouldn't care if the man was another Osama, as long as he got paid.

He leaned forward a little as he watched her run—short sun-bleached hair, broad shoulders, tanned legs that seemed never to end. The man allowed himself a smile, a little gurgle of anticipation. "This job could be fun."

Micki broke into a full sprint when her office came into sight. Sweat poured down her face, and her shirt was soaking wet.

HER OFFICE—A TWO-STORY home in the Quapaw Quarter, Little Rock's historic district, was a turn-of-the-century Victorian that a real estate agency had restored. Azaleas and dogwoods now in April's full bloom adorned the property. When the Quarter's tax breaks expired and the real estate bust hit, the agency happily sold Micki the property for her solo law practice. The neighborhood wasn't thrilled with her criminal clientele, but they much preferred the daily comings and goings to an unoccupied building.

Micki entered through the rear door. She had transformed one of the back offices into her personal space, complete with a day bed, an updated bathroom with a shower, and assorted exercise equipment. She kept a full array of clothes in the closet. The door to this room was the only one in the building equipped with a heavy-duty deadbolt. One chilly morning she had found a homeless man sleeping in her lobby. The alarm was still set, and no one could figure out how he had gotten in. She didn't take any chances after that.

She relaxed under the tingle of the high-pressure shower as she washed away the sweat and what remained of Eric's scent. They'd met a few months ago at a Pepsi 10K and quickly discovered a mutual love of running, cycling, and full body massages. Now she kept several pairs of shoes and other clothes at his house in Hillcrest, and she'd cleared out a closet at her ranch just outside of town for his things. As the shower did its work, Micki mused about their relationship, trying to imagine where it might lead. They'd had their first major tiff a couple of weeks ago because she'd gone out for a beer with her former boss and friend, Sam Pagano, the Pulaski County prosecutor. She'd turned his tantrum into a night of athletic sex, but even good sex couldn't shake her resentment. His possessiveness left a bad aftertaste.

It didn't take Micki long to get ready for the workday. She slipped into a pair of jeans and made coffee in the little kitchen down the hall. Unless she was going to court, she simply dried her hair with a towel, not bothering with make-up. She grabbed a Diet Coke from the fridge and walked into the former living room that now served as her office. Her antique desk faced a large bay window, and the old fireplace and comfortable furnishings were warm and inviting. Debbie Natrova, her office manager, always made sure the flowers on her desk were fresh, either from the farmers market or Kroger, depending on the season.

First thing every morning Micki read her e-mail and texts and listened to her voice messages. Then she unlocked the front door and picked up the *Arkansas Democrat-Gazette*, always in the same place on her porch, the result of a generous December tip. After she'd scanned the entire paper, including the funnies, she turned her attention to the day's schedule. This morning she'd seen nothing of great interest, and so far none of her clients had left a message. Unless an emergency walked in, she looked forward to leaving the office early. She had plenty to do at the ranch while Eric worked the weekend shift at the ER.

Debbie bustled in the front door. Debbie's dark red hair came from a bottle, but the short bob suited her round face and small pouty lips. She wore heavy eye make-up and blush, and the fabric of her flowery jersey top stretched tight across her ample chest, a look left over from her former occupation. Her short skirt revealed–well, it was way too short in Micki's opinion. Micki knew she couldn't change Debbie's heavy Eastern European accent, but she was determined to change her sense of style.

Debbie had literally dropped on her doorstep not long after Micki left the public defender's office. She had arrived in the States when she was barely sixteen, intent on becoming a pastry chef, confident she would meet the perfect man and realize the American dream. Her parents were skeptical, but grew to trust the man who promised to make her dreams come true. She spoke English fairly well and longed for adventure, ready for new freedoms in a new country. Her sponsor, Novak, greeted her warmly and treated her well at first, buying her clothes and make-up, even sending her to a hair stylist for a new look. He had put her to work busing tables in one of his nightclubs, promising a promotion after she learned the ropes. It didn't take long for her to discover what "the ropes" meant–a heroin addiction and serving more than drinks to customers. One rainy spring morning Micki found Debbie curled up on the front stoop of her old office downtown, beaten and barely alive, clutching a matchbook with Micki's name and number scrawled inside. She couldn't resist thinking that someone had left her a bedraggled and half-starved kitten.

Micki had spent months battling the authorities to keep Debbie from going to jail or being deported. It didn't help that Novak had confiscated all her immigration papers the day she arrived. To keep an eye on Debbie's recovery, Micki hired her as a receptionist. Once free of drugs and her sponsor, Debbie had quickly proved to be a capable, if quirky, employee. Micki soon promoted her to office manager, and the office now ran as smooth as silk.

Now, Debbie gushed, "Did you see all the DEA agents at that purple house on Elder? They're hauling everything off, and the house is taped off like a crime scene. The moving van blocks the whole street, and you wouldn't believe the press and the rubberneckers. Wonder if it's a meth lab? Maybe there's a client in it. Do you want me to send Mongo to check it out?" Debbie brought Micki a homemade carrot cake muffin. Debbie hadn't become a pastry chef, but she was a truly intuitive baker.

"I ran a different route today, so I missed it. I bet the neighbors called the cops."

"Maybe. But neighbors don't usually want to get involved. Novak ran one of his casinos in the Quarter for the longest, and nobody complained, remember? He ran high-stakes poker games downstairs while we worked upstairs."

Micki remembered all too well. After discovering Debbie on her doorstep, Micki had vowed to end Novak's reign. Unfortunately, Novak's clientele had more power and influence than she did. Her efforts to shut him down ran up against a political stonewall. Eventually he moved the casino to Maumelle, but Micki's only real success had been keeping Debbie clean.

"Look, Debbie, I want you to use a fine screen on any walk-ins today. I'd like to get to my horses early. No *pro bono* clients who have a trial on Monday, okay?"

Not that Micki was averse to walk-ins. She took on more than her share of *pro bono* clients and hard luck stories, but no matter how big her heart was, she had to limit the number. It was the occasional wealthy client, a big personal injury case, or drug dealer whose assets haven't been confiscated that enabled even the very best criminal defense lawyer to keep the doors open.

She nibbled on her muffin and set about responding to e-mails, reviewing court pleadings, and organizing the rest of her day. Micki tried to keep the creaky sliding doors to her office closed to the reception area, but she had a solo practice office, not a big law firm: clients dropped in to pay down their bill with wadded-up fives and tens, or just to get a cup of coffee. Walk-ins stopped by with problems that might need a lawyer, or usually just a sympathetic ear—she never turned them away.

Mongo, another of Micki's "projects," fulfilled the multiple roles of receptionist, part-time bouncer, and occasional investigator. Debbie and Mongo handled the first interview for all the walk-ins and screened Micki's calls, but former clients needed to be greeted with a warm hug and at least a few minutes of Micki's time. She gave her legal interns almost free access to her office and was always available for their questions, either about the law or the personal. Debbie was constantly back and forth with messages and reports. The huge, sliding oak doors constantly rumbled along their tracks.

Micki really didn't mind, or even notice. She wanted no part of a traditional big law firm. Sure, she could make lots of money, but at what cost? She'd heard about one DC firm that kept cots in the basement, sort of like a dorm, so young lawyers could prove their worth in billable hours. Not knowledge or appreciation of the law, not empathy for their clients, just cold, hard time, billed to the client. Micki loved life and working with real people too much for that sort of drudgery, no matter what the pay. The day passed quickly, and she relaxed, contemplating a sunset horseback ride. Debbie's insistent voice broke through her reverie.

"Sorry, Micki, but there's a random woman I don't know waiting in the front office. No appointment, says she only needs a few minutes. I'd say maybe late forties, casually dressed, lots of messy blonde hair. I don't think she's a nutcase—she smells of money. Wait till you see the rock on her finger. She drove up in a brand new Mercedes convertible. It's out back, if you want a peek. She won't tell me why she's here. I bet it's a divorce. Oh—and Marshal Maroney wants you to call, didn't want to leave a message."

Micki bit her lip. A call from Maroney always made her nervous. Hopefully he didn't have one of her clients in lock-up.

"I need to call Bill first. Tell Ms. Blonde I'll be right with her."

Micki was punching in the marshal's number when she noticed the black Infiniti parked across the street.

She hollered out. "Mongo, check out that car across the street, will you? I saw it there this morning."

The Infiniti's driver had recognized both the Mercedes and its driver. He called Mr. Smith and told him that Liz Stewart had just gone into Micki's office. Amazed that Smith had been dead-on about Stewart's choice of counsel, he pulled away from the curb as instructed and sped off just before Mongo opened the front door.

The U.S. marshal got right to the point. "Micki, sorry to bother you, especially on a Friday afternoon, but we've got a man in custody who's asking for his lawyer." Micki instinctively knew her sunset ride and probably her whole weekend were blown.

"This morning the DEA arrested a professor at UALR—a Dr. Douglas Stewart."

The name meant nothing to her.

"The crazy son-of-a bitch insists that his lawyer is that Jack Patterson fellow. Do you know how I can reach Patterson? The marshal's office in DC gave me his law firm's number, but the firm says he no longer works there. They either can't or won't give me a new number. All I need to do is confirm Patterson doesn't know this pothead."

"What are the charges, Bill?" Micki asked.

"Oh, he's in a shitload of trouble—possession, cultivation, and distribution of marijuana, a lot of marijuana. Dub held a press conference about the bust this morning—called him a terrorist, no less. If you want the details, Dub's already got the case on his website. The DEA seized his house, cars, and most everything else. Come to think of it, I think Stewart lives over near you."

Micki mulled it over a bit. Jack Patterson didn't practice law in Arkansas, nor did he represent drug dealers. His DC antitrust clients stole their money using more sophisticated schemes. Last year, Jack had reluctantly returned to Little Rock to help his boyhood friend, Woody Cole, against the charge of murdering Senator Russell Robinson. After the case, Jack had returned to DC, and she couldn't recall the last time they'd talked.

"Bill, tell the professor that Jack's not a criminal lawyer. I'd come down there and tell him myself, but it's Friday afternoon, and I have a horse that hasn't been ridden in more than a week."

"Hell, Micki, we've told him that. The fellow won't give an inch, keeps insisting he's entitled to speak to his lawyer, and that his lawyer is Jack Patterson. He told one of my deputies he used to work with Patterson's wife. Didn't she die a few years back?"

"She did. Look, maybe this guy does know Jack. Let me call him. I'll get back to you as soon as I can."

She sat tapping a pen on her desk calendar, allowing her mind to drift to Jack. His six foot three inches weren't Hollywood handsome, but he was still a good-looking man, the athletic type. His face was etched with lines of both grief and laughter. She missed his sharp mind and their easy rapport.

She dropped the pen, stood up abruptly, and walked into the reception area. The mystery woman, clad in black leggings and a long pullover that hung off one shoulder, was lounging crossways in the old, overstuffed armchair Micki had meant to recover. Micki guessed her to be in her early fifties—very well preserved. She'd clearly spent a lot of time at the gym and probably with some damn fine surgeons. An abundance of frothy blonde hair dominated her appearance. Micki extended her hand, and the woman jumped up from the chair with a guilty grin. Micki caught the flash of several gold bracelets.

"Sorry to barge in on you unannounced. I'm Liz Stewart. You've probably know why I'm here. It's all over the news. I'm afraid I've gotten my husband into a bit of trouble."

Micki appraised her coolly for a few seconds, but she didn't turn a hair.

"Well, you could say this is a bit of coincidence. Marshal Maroney just called to tell me he has a Dr. Doug Stewart—your husband, I assume—in custody. Apparently he's demanding to speak to my friend Jack Patterson. Let's talk in my office." She could see that Debbie and Mongo were bursting with curiosity.

Liz accepted her offer of ice water, and Micki motioned her to a chair across from her desk. She watched Liz settle herself, laughing breezily.

"Isn't that just like Doug? Jack's not going to fly to Little Rock for such a minor matter. You and I can deal with this mess without bothering him. Let me tell you what happened—I'm sure you'll know exactly how to fix it. Those bastards have locked me out of my own house over a few measly ginger snaps."

Micki wasn't sure what to think. Either Liz didn't have a clue or she was running a very good con. Debbie came in with tall glasses of water, and Micki handed her a note:

No interruptions and plan to stay late.

"The whole thing's very innocent, but first things first," Liz put her glass down on a side table and reached for an oversized handbag. "I need to write you a check. Is ten thousand enough?"

Ten thousand. Most of her clients had a hard time paying her at all, much less coming up with a retainer. She murmured that it wasn't necessary, but Liz ignored her, tearing out the check as she continued her running monologue.

"My good friend, Judy Farrell, has breast cancer. She's gonna be fine, I mean it's not really a bad diagnosis, no lymph nodes, but still, she was having a really tough time with the chemo. So I made her a batch of ginger snaps." Liz smiled. "You know what I mean, don't you?"

Micki felt sure she did, but asked anyway. "I assume you mean they were laced with marijuana?"

"Exactly!" Liz exclaimed. "Ginger snaps are so much better than the brownies we had back in college. Well, they did the trick—Judy couldn't stop thanking me. I told her not to tell anyone, but damned if she didn't tell her whole book club. Can you believe it? Now it's all over town, and the police have Doug locked up. How do we deal with this? For God's sakes, I'm supposed to host a cocktail party for my garden club in two weeks. I'm in the Armitage Hotel for now, but I really need my house back."

Micki watched her carefully, trying to keep a straight face.

"Did you sell ginger snaps to anyone?"

"Heavens, no!" Liz exclaimed. "They're not Girl Scout Cookies. I was simply trying to help a friend. Two women from her book club have asked me for the recipe—can you imagine? Her friend Claire wouldn't take no for an answer. I had to hang up on her. Maybe she got mad and told the police. Her husband's a lawyer at the Roma-towski law firm, you know."

"I'm sorry. But I can't imagine the DEA or even our pathetic U.S. attorney getting worked up over ginger snaps. Marijuana is still illegal in Arkansas, but a batch of marijuana-laced cookies hardly justifies seizing your house. Besides, the Feds have backed off going after marijuana users since Obama said it's not as dangerous as alcohol. Maybe they arrested your husband so he'll give up his source—trying to get him to roll on his supplier who probably is selling a lot worse stuff. Where'd he get the marijuana?"

Micki expected Liz to hesitate. Most of her clients did at this point; fearful their source would retaliate.

But Liz blurted, "Oh, Doug didn't buy it. I just went out in the back yard and picked some."

With a sinking feeling Micki asked slowly, "You mean you had a marijuana plant growing in the backyard?"

Liz didn't flinch. "Oh Lord, not just one. We have a whole garden full."

3

GINGER SNAPS, *my ass,* Micki thought. *This floozy really had me going.*

Even now, Liz looked comfortable, her expression clueless. Watching her touch up her lipstick, a flashy coral shade, Micki wondered whether she should throw her out on her ear. Now ten thousand dollars didn't seem like much of a retainer, and she had to assume the Feds had frozen the Stewart's bank accounts by now. She felt sure Liz was just another crook who'd been caught red-handed and come up with a very creative story.

Almost all her clients lied to her, at least at first–part of human nature. She wondered what kind of relationship, if any, the Stewarts had with Jack. One phone call would put that question to rest. She decided to be direct.

"Liz, what exactly is your husband's connection to Jack Patterson?"

"I'm sorry–I thought you knew. My husband worked with Jack's wife, Angie, at the National Institutes of Health. To some extent, Angie's cancer is why we moved here. After she died, Doug decided to leave NIH. He wanted to have the freedom to engage in pure research, independent of any government grants or control. UALR's offer of an endowed chair was perfect.

"Angie told Doug if he ever needed a lawyer to call Jack, day or night. At dinner one night she made Jack swear he'd represent Doug. Jack said, 'sure, okay,' but I don't think he was really listening. I thought at the time her insistence was strange, almost as if Doug and Angie knew something the rest of us didn't." She paused, staring out the window.

If Liz was telling even half the truth about the relationship, Micki owed it to Jack to get as much information as she could, whether she ended up representing Dr. Stewart or not. She began to probe Liz about their marijuana garden, gently making it clear that Doug was in serious trouble.

Liz babbled on and on about organic fertilizer, grafting, cross pollination, and watering techniques, most of which Micki let go in one ear and out the other. But she did glean one bit of good news: Liz had money in her own right. Maybe that explained her devil-may-care attitude. Micki couldn't turn down a paying client, lying or not. Liz seemed unconcerned at the possibility that the legal fees could run much higher. The loss of a weekend seemed a small price to pay.

Micki had a hard time squaring her priorities with Liz's. Micki wanted to meet Doug, learn about the charges, arrange his bail, and prepare for an arraignment. Liz wanted to get her make-up and clothes back before a Saturday night cocktail party. She seemed annoyed when Micki told her the marshal would probably release her personal items sometime the next morning—Liz had her regular hot yoga class at 9 o'clock. Could he have them delivered to her hotel tomorrow afternoon?

Micki played cat-and-mouse for a while longer, but Liz didn't give an inch. She finally sent her to Debbie to fill out paperwork. She had to call Jack before he left his office, and besides, she was fed up with Liz's act. As they both rose, she closed with the one question she'd avoided for the last hour.

"Liz, you don't seem to need the money, and your husband's an endowed professor. Why on earth was he growing that much marijuana? I mean—why a whole garden?"

Liz looked confused.

"Why, for his work, of course. Wait, you didn't think he was selling the stuff, did you?" She blinked. "Oh my God, how could you ever think such a thing?"

WASHINGTON, DC

FRIDAY AFTERNOON

April 18, 2014

4

I WAS HAVING a bad week.

A letter from Montgomery County had arrived on Monday advising me that my property taxes had doubled. I couldn't argue with a new valuation—real estate in the Chevy Case was booming—but double? Maybe with the extra money the county could manage to pick up the garbage on the right day and turn off that damned camera on Connecticut Avenue that always claimed I was speeding. Probably not. Why kill a cash cow?

Tuesday, Sophie had gotten tangled in the leash during our morning walk and gone down hard. She limped all the way home, so we headed for the vet. The Burnese Mountain Dog had been a gift from a well-meaning friend after my wife's death. I'd named her Sophie after Angie's mother, fully intending to find her a new home, but for some reason I never got around to letting her go. The vet discovered a hairline fracture along with worsening hip dysplasia. Nothing would do but surgery. I'd always raised a skeptical brow at my friends who spent inordinate amounts of money on their pets, but now I found myself in the same boat. How could one damn dog cost so much money? I told the vet to go ahead. How could I say no?

As a favor to a former colleague, I had agreed to help a young lawyer who had brought an antitrust suit against certain drug companies conspiring to keep new products off the shelves until they could maximize their profits on the old drugs. The case was turning out to be a real pain in the ass. Big law firms use their clients' deep pockets to overwhelm a solo practitioner with mounds of paperwork. I had already spent way too much time answering stupid questions posed by lawyers who enjoyed spending their clients' money. My job as president of Walter Matthew's new charitable foundation kept me busy enough without spending days and nights responding to their futile attempts to overwhelm me.

To top off the week, I was stuck in a conference room on a beautiful Friday afternoon, trying to pay attention to a group of well-meaning men and women who droned on and on about how "misguided" our foundation's goals were and how under my leadership the foundation was "destined for failure." They suggested, ever so politely, that my background rendered me woefully unqualified to head a major foundation. They were ever so sorry, but they really felt Walter should hire someone else. I tried to keep my eyes open.

Rose, my administrative assistant, stuck her head in the door. "Jack, I'm sorry to interrupt, but Mr. Gates is on line one." A few heads turned, and I tried not to smile at our carefully crafted signal. *Deliverance at last.*

I muttered an apology and slipped out the door. The speaker continued without even glancing up, as if my presence weren't important, which I thought odd since he had called the meeting to discuss me and my "misguided plans."

"Sorry to interrupt, Jack, but two guys from the FBI are waiting for you in the lobby, and I have Micki on line three—she says it's urgent."

"The FBI? Great. Show them into my office. Offer them coffee or something. I'll take Micki's call first." I picked up a phone in the office adjoining the conference room.

"Micki, it's great to hear your voice. Your call has saved me from a fate worse than death. What's up?"

"Pack your bags, Jack. You have another client in Little Rock. This one didn't kill anyone, but he's in a heap of trouble."

I had no idea what she meant, but it was sure to be much more interesting than the FBI or the snore of a meeting I had just escaped.

"Okay, I'll bite. Who's the mystery man?"

"I'm kidding about packing your bags, but the client is real—a Dr. Douglas Stewart. He was arrested for growing marijuana, lots of it. The DEA has already confiscated everything he owns. So far, he's refused to talk except to say, 'I want to talk to Jack Patterson.' I've met with the wife—in fact, she gave me a nice retainer. I've got to hand it to you, Jack—you have some interesting friends."

I remembered Doug Stewart. He used to work with Angie at NIH. Angie had really admired him, thought he was a genius. Doug had grown up in Mena, Arkansas, a little town near the Oklahoma border. He was named a Rhodes Scholar while at the University of Arkansas, and, after several years in England, returned to the states to teach chemistry and engage in research at the University of Michigan. He'd won tons of awards, including the DeWitt, for his work in molecular biochemistry. He came east to work at NIH, where he and Angie became good friends and colleagues. He was so crushed by her illness that it was hard for me to be around him. After the funeral, he tried to be a friend, but I was acting out my hermit role. Over time, I lost track, as I did with most of Angie's friends. It just hurt too much.

I pictured him in my mind—tall and lanky, long brown hair, perfectly typecast as Ichabod Crane. I was surprised to learn he'd been a walk-on football player for the Razorbacks. He never played a down, but practiced all four years on the scout squad. Angie told me his office at NIH was filled with Razorback memorabilia, even one of those bizarre plastic Uncle Heavy's Hog Hats. His Chemistry awards and diplomas sat in a box in a corner of his office, but his hog hat was front and center on his desk.

Well, I'll be damned. I had no idea Doug and his wife lived in Little Rock, my boyhood home. Doug, the Rhodes scholar, arrested for dealing drugs? What next? Watching your good friend murder a U.S. Senator on TV took the cake, but Doug ending up a drug dealer was right up there. I asked Micki to tell me what she knew.

"Well, not much. So far, the marshal won't let me talk to him— direct orders from the US attorney. Stewart's no help at all since he insists you're his lawyer. Gotta be more to it than just grass. Maybe it's meth—after all, the doctor is a chemistry professor. The Feds have backed off marijuana busts since Colorado legalized it and other states are headed that way. His wife is either a ditz or a con, but she knows her husband is in serious trouble. Of course, word's gotten out that Doug's asked for you, and the local press is foaming at the mouth. I'm surprised you haven't heard anything."

"The FBI is waiting in my office. What a pleasant surprise," I said dryly.

"He'll be arraigned on Monday. His wife has hired me, but before I show up in court, I thought I better make sure I've got the whole story. Liz says you made some kind of promise to Angie to take care of Doug if he got in trouble."

"I wouldn't know the first thing about defending a drug case."

"No, and this doesn't look like that exciting case we dreamed about working on together. It looks like a pretty cut-and-dry bust, and I don't see much hope for your friend. He was growing over fifty plants in his backyard and had hundreds of seedlings in the garage. He's looking at serious jail time even if he comes clean, cooperates, and that's the end of the story. He told his wife he was growing for his work, and she either bought it hook, line, and sinker, or she's a hell of a liar. I told Marshal Maroney I couldn't imagine you'd consider representing a drug dealer. That is, assuming you haven't gotten so bored with foundation work that you want to join my detested lot—Little Rock's criminal bar." She left the question hanging.

I didn't remember any promise to help Doug and was sure Angie had no idea he was growing pot, but the prospect of seeing Micki again and spending some time in Little Rock carried some appeal. Anything beat sitting in a conference room with a bunch of foundation types. But my lawyer's caution kicked in.

"Well, I've got a lot of irons in the fire here . . ."

In mid-excuse, I wandered off-course, talking and thinking at the same time. Doug had been a friend, uncommonly supportive of Angie in those last months. The least I could do was make a quick trip to see if I could help. My regular weekend golf game had been cancelled because the club was hosting a charity tournament. I could enjoy a little golf in Little Rock with old friends and try to figure out why Doug had gone bad. *Angie would want me to go*, I told myself.

"Oh what the hell, Micki, I don't have any plans for the weekend. I'll have Rose check flights and let you know when I'll be there. Try to get word to him that I'm on my way."

"You're shitting me. I don't see any reason why you should get involved." Micki was clearly dumbfounded.

"Well, I know that, but I really don't have anything better to do this weekend, and he's asking for me, right? He was a good friend to Angie, especially when she was so sick. Maybe I can help by telling him to trust and cooperate with you. I need a mini-vacation, and I haven't seen you in ages. I'll see Doug and then you and I can catch up over dinner."

Micki's silence was a dead giveaway. Usually she could think and talk and stay two beats ahead of the game. Finally, she said, "Well, uh, dinner might be a little awkward. I'm seeing someone, Jack, and well, you know . . ."

I was glad she'd put a halt to any expectations before things went further.

"No problem. I'll stay at the Armitage and take Liz to dinner."

"Thanks, I knew you'd understand. E-mail Debbie your flight schedule, and I'll make an appointment for you to see Doug. I don't understand why you're coming, but I'd love your read on this one. The wife is a handful."

I put the phone down, told Rose to get me an early morning flight to Little Rock and walked into my office where two burly FBI agents were waiting.

"Gentlemen, what can I do for you?" I asked extending a hand that they declined to shake. I relaxed into the chair behind my desk, leaving them standing.

"Mr. Patterson, we understand you represent Douglas Stewart."

"You understand incorrectly." I already didn't like these guys.

They looked at each other, and the taller of the two asked. "How do you know Dr. Stewart?"

"He worked with my wife at NIH." I didn't offer more, and again they exchanged glances.

"Dr. Stewart has been arrested. He claims you're his lawyer. If that's not the case, we'd like to explore your relationship with him and what you know about his activities."

"Then make an appointment. I'm in the middle of a meeting and don't appreciate being called out of it for this."

"I'd suggest you cooperate, Mr. Patterson. Your wife's friend is a terrorist."

A terrorist—horseshit. I dealt with the FBI for years when I worked at the Department of Justice. I thought I knew all their tricks. But morphing a respected scientist into a terrorist?

"Sorry, but I decline to be interviewed until a meeting has been scheduled and my attorney can be present. By the way, he will also arrange for the interview to be transcribed."

"We don't participate in recorded interviews, Mr. Patterson. You know that."

I smiled, indeed aware of their position on recorded interviews. They didn't want any records to exist that could dispute their recollection of what was said.

"Then you're refusing to cooperate with me. Good day, gentlemen."

I left them staring and returned to the conference room. Most people are afraid to say no to the FBI, rightly afraid of their power to destroy a person's life. I'd represented way too many clients who had fallen into their traps. Never, ever meet with the FBI alone—you'll find words put in your mouth you never said.

Thankfully, the foundation meeting was breaking up. After a few empty and insincere remarks, I wished them all well and escaped into Maggie's office to tell her where I was going and that I'd be back on Monday. Maggie Matthews had been my assistant, paralegal, and right arm when I practiced law at the firm of Banks and Tuohey. Her new husband, Walter Matthews, was the president of Bridgeport Life Insurance Company and chairman of the foundation where I now worked—The Walter and Margaret Matthews Foundation. As part of my arrangement with the foundation, I have a small antitrust practice on the side. Maggie continues in her role as my assistant and paralegal, although she's technically my boss at the Foundation. Don't ask, it works.

I told her about Micki's call and my brief meeting with the FBI.

"I remember Doug. He and Angie were extremely close. Don't look at me that way. They were professional friends. That's all. You probably don't remember, but he came to your house a lot at the end. You should definitely go. It's about time you got out of the office. It'll do you good. Take the plane—it's just sitting on the tarmac. Do you need me?"

When I went to Little Rock last year, I didn't think I needed Maggie, but she came anyway and I was glad she did. I knew less about this situation than the previous one, but I couldn't imagine needing her. I would see Doug, assure him about Micki's abilities, play some golf, and come home on Monday. I was interested in what could have happened to Doug. How did he go from being a research chemist to a drug dealer? That answer alone would be worth the trip.

"No, not this time, but I'll call if things get messy." I winked.

Rose poked her head through the door. "The press is calling; the guy from the *Arkansas Democrat* is getting to be a downright pest. He's holding on line one now."

I told Rose to give him to Maggie. Maggie pretended to frown, but said she'd take any press calls if I promised to keep my phone turned on. I didn't quite know where it was at the moment, but felt sure it was on wherever it was. After checking my calendar, I spent a good hour on the phone with my close friend Keith Stroup, founder of the National Organization for the Reform of Marijuana Laws, or NORML, for folks who like an easy acronym. He gave me a quick update on the laws regarding marijuana cultivation and civil forfeiture. Arkansas still didn't recognize medical marijuana, much less recreational use, but it was bound to soon. The South always seemed to be an election or two behind the curve. Keith felt there had to be more to Doug's arrest than growing marijuana.

"The Feds are leaving growers and users to the locals. Your friend must be part of a cartel or maybe he's laundering money."

I wondered.

I drove home feeling good about the prospect of a spontaneous mini-vacation. I poured myself a glass of wine as soon as I walked in the door, noticing I'd left the phone on the bar. I smiled, thinking it really was okay to be beyond its reach every now and then. It rang almost immediately—I almost jumped out of my skin. I saw Maggie's name and number on the screen.

"Sorry—I left my phone at home." She didn't respond. "Maggie?"

"I'm not calling to scold. Turn on CNN."

Oh, jeez—surely not again. The last time I'd turned on CNN in response to someone's command, I'd seen my friend Woody put a gun to a senator's head and pull the trigger. I quickly found the remote.

The banner running across the bottom of the screen read: "World-renowned chemist busted. Dr. Douglas Stewart accused of masterminding campus drug operation and terrorism." The host, a Friday evening sub, was interviewing none other than "Dub" Blanchard. Dub smiled gravely as he railed on about kids, drugs, school grounds, terrorism, and drug cartels. I knew him to be a media-hungry hack: now he was on his high horse, relishing the spotlight. The host smoothly fed him softballs, and he hit each one out of the park. Finally, he asked if it was true that the drug kingpin's lawyer was the same Jack Patterson who had defended Woody Cole. Dub spit out his response.

"The last time Jack Patterson came to Little Rock he cooked up some of his 'Yankee stew' to manipulate justice. He'll find this U.S. attorney doesn't appreciate either his cooking or his tricks. If he thinks he's welcome at my table, he'll soon find his placemat in the outhouse." The host found all this hilarious, as did Dub, who drooled a bit while he laughed. I couldn't help a laugh myself.

Maggie had been holding the whole time.

"Maggie, don't pack your bags, but you might want to get them out of the attic."

SATURDAY

April 19, 2014

5

No matter how many times Maggie explains the economics, I still feel guilty every time I use Walter's plane. But I couldn't deny it was a heck of a lot more comfortable than Delta. Stretching my long legs into the aisle and leaning all the way back, I remembered the last time I'd flown to Little Rock. I'd sworn never to return to Little Rock, but here I was, returning for the second time in two years.

This time, as the pilot began his approach, I felt none of the trepidation, but mulled over the same question that had nagged me before—why? Why would a renowned chemist get involved in a drug operation? Angie had the greatest respect for Doug and believed that one day he'd bring home the Nobel Prize in Chemistry. Neither he nor his wife, Liz, lived an exorbitant lifestyle. They didn't have children. I remembered they both played club tennis, but as far as I knew he had no other outside activities except watching college and professional football. Angie told me that if the Razorbacks lost on a given Saturday, he'd sulk until Tuesday, but he never exhibited any erratic behavior. Liz, the daughter of a wealthy Memphis cotton merchant, radiated self-confidence and good health, a woman who clearly loved life. Whether at charity events or on the tennis court, she loved to organize everyone else, and no one seemed to mind or had the courage to object.

The plane taxied to the Hodges Air Center, and as I peered outside the window I recognized my ride and its driver. Clovis Jones, a former All-American linebacker, leaned against a large, black Tahoe, boots crossed, regarding me with some degree of apprehension. Clovis had provided our protection during the Cole case. He owned a successful security company and provided consulting and investigative work for Walter Matthews' insurance company. When he was in DC, we usually found time to catch a Nationals game or drive up to Cantler's for crabs and cold beer.

"You didn't have to meet me," I said as we gave each other a man-hug.

"Do you really think I'm going to let someone else drive you around? Maggie'd read me the riot act if I let you set foot in this town without being by your side. You still got folks madder than a wet hen that you defended Woody, and now rumor has it you're here to represent Mr. Wizard. Dub's got em convinced he's their kids' drug dealer, the scum of the earth. You're not far behind. Situation normal." He chuckled.

"I'm not here to represent Doug. He's a friend, sort of, but I have no idea why he's calling for me. I'm gonna pay him a visit, set things straight, have a few beers, play some golf, and go home. I don't need protection."

Nobody talked like this in DC. They all took forever to say anything, probably because they could charge more the longer they talked. It felt good to be in Little Rock.

"I hear you, but Maggie's already pulled rank. I've been hired, and you might as well get easy with it. Besides, the press is camped out at the Armitage. You'll need me to run interference at any rate."

With that pleasant bit of news, he shoved my bags and golf clubs into the Tahoe, and we headed to Micki's office.

Her receptionist stuck out his hand and gave me his name, Mongo Stankovitch. I saw a muscular man with multiple piercings and tattoos, wearing jeans and a tight t-shirt, definitely not who I expected.

"Mongo–really?" I had to ask. Turned out his mother loved the movie *Blazing Saddles,* and she named him after her favorite character. Better him than me.

Micki rushed in suddenly, clutching a fat ginger cat, which she deposited on the window ledge. Her sandy hair had grown out some, but she still wore her usual plaid shirt and jeans. She followed a welcoming hug with a quick kiss.

"Sorry–I'm fostering Doughnut for a friend. Yes, the cat's name is really Doughnut. I see you've met Mongo. Debbie is out running errands. Where's Clovis?"

She rolled open the door to her office, as I explained that Clovis was trying to sneak my bags in through the back door of the hotel.

"Right—I can just imagine," she laughed. "Listen, thanks for understanding about dinner and not staying at my place. Eric is as old-fashioned as you. Besides, I just might not be able to keep my hands off you. You're a sight for sore eyes."

"Hey, no fair," I protested. "I want to hear more about Eric, but first tell me what's going on with Doug."

Micki went over what she had learned from Liz and what she had found out from her own sources. No formal charges had yet been filed, but both the DEA and the U.S. attorney claimed very publicly that Doug was growing at least a hundred full-grown plants in his backyard and hundreds of seedlings in the flower shed and garage.

"The good news is there's no indication they're going to charge his wife. I'm surprised. Dub not's above indicting Liz, or her cat for that matter, to put pressure on Doug. The other lawyers in the U.S. attorney's office are completely out of the loop. A tight little group of DEA agents and lawyers from Main Justice are in control. Dub's also taking pot shots at you—a badge of honor, I'd say." Micki grinned.

"I saw him on TV last night. I'm not sure I understand his wit, but he seems anxious to tee it up. Listen, Micki, defending drug cases is your bailiwick. I'm happy to talk to Doug, but I'll take my lead from you. My thought was to meet with Doug, find out what in the hell this is all about, play some golf, eat some real barbecue, and head home."

"Well, you have an hour with him at three. Liz and I'll meet you at the Armitage for drinks at six. Eric was okay once I told him she'd be there. I wish he could join us, but he's on call this weekend. Liz is spending the afternoon looking for someplace to live. As long as Doug insists you're his lawyer, Dub refuses to talk to me, much less let me see Dr. Stewart. I'd say something big is up, but Dub's just acting the same as always—an arrogant ass."

THE BLACK INFINITI had pulled into a spot along the curb a little bit further down the street. For now he was content to watch the comings and goings at Micki's office. He'd seen Clovis drop Patterson off and knew he'd have to leave before the bodyguard returned. Clovis would draw a bead on him in a heartbeat. Patterson's arrival was unexpected. Like everyone else, Mr. Smith knew the professor had asked for the DC lawyer, but nobody thought he'd actually show up. Too bad for him. No chance Mr. Smith would let Patterson interfere with their client's business.

MICKI AND I spent what little time we had talking about what Doug and Liz faced. If the charges held up, the government would demand the maximum sentence and throw away the key. Dub was sure to argue that all the Stewarts' possessions were fruits of his criminal enterprise, including their house, furniture, and their extensive art collection. They would target every asset they could find, including their bank accounts. It would all be forfeited and auctioned off, with the proceeds going into the U.S. Treasury. I could never get over the fact that even if they never filed a single charge, the government could still bring a civil forfeiture proceeding against what they believed to be illegal gain from an alleged crime. It reminded me of a Kafka story except it wasn't fiction: in America it happens every day.

Fortunately Liz had money in a trust fund created by her grandfather that the government couldn't touch. Micki hoped she could convince Dub to return the house or at least her personal possessions by arguing that the money for the house and clothes came from Liz and not Doug. Whatever belonged to Doug was as good as gone.

Liz continued to insist that all of the marijuana was intended for Doug's research, and that the government couldn't prove he'd sold even a dime bag. Well, maybe, but Doug was still in serious shit. The press accounts, fed by Dub, claimed his large backyard had been knee-deep with well-tended plants and his double garage had contained hundreds of small seedlings under grow lights. The Feds might have ignored a few plants, but this was a different story. The penalty for cultivation was based on the number of plants and seedlings with a root ball, not the weight of the marijuana or how much was actually harvested. Besides, despite the legalization effort all over the country, Federal law still doesn't recognize using marijuana in research or for medical use as a defense for possession or cultivation. Doug was up a creek, without any kind of paddle.

Micki hoped she might be able to cut a deal if the research story panned out, but she worried that Dub's malicious theatrics might make a plea bargain impossible.

Rodney Fitzhugh, her friend and the deputy U.S. attorney, had warned her, "Don't get your hopes up. This is clearly no ordinary drug bust. I haven't seen this much secrecy since 9/11. I've heard wind of a lot of chatter between Dub, the DEA, and Washington, but nobody in the U.S. attorney's office knows what's going on except Dub, and he is atypically closemouthed."

Nor could Micki figure out why Dub hadn't involved Sam Pagano, the local prosecuting attorney. The DEA almost always turns drug busts over to the locals. Sam told her he'd been told to keep his head down and his office out of the way.

Sighing, she shook her head. "Well, whatever—our immediate problem is that Dr. Stewart wants you to be his lawyer, even though his wife has hired me. Of course, if you're bored, I can spare an office."

"What would Eric think?" I retorted, and she frowned. Her signal was clear: no teasing about Eric. I let the moment pass.

"My presence would only make things worse. Dub's itching to use my involvement in Woody's case to draw press attention. No, thank you, I'll spend a little time with Doug, then get out of your hair." One corner of her mouth turned down skeptically.

I'd seen the Tahoe pull up to the curb, and now Clovis walked in, holding the door for a young woman who had to be Debbie. Nothing in our phone conversations had prepared me for either her getup or make-up. I rose automatically, and she blushed and smiled coyly as she took the hand I extended. Micki scowled, giving her a "hands-off" look. She flounced out without a word.

"What was that about? A little possessive, are we?"

"Don't even think about it, Jack."

Clovis saw my confusion and jumped in, direct as ever. "That one will get your throat cut. A thug by the name of Novak thinks she belongs to him. She's terrified of him, and you should be too."

I had no idea what they were talking about, but I had a date at the courthouse, so I let it lie.

"Time to go." I turned to Clovis, but Micki pushed back from her desk and stood, this time scowling at me.

"Why *are* you here, Jack? And don't tell me it's because I called. Last time, you came running because you owed Helen Cole. This time your bags were packed before I was halfway through asking. Doug Stewart grows and sells marijuana, pure and simple; there's no reason for you to drop everything and come running half way across the country. This guy isn't your best friend like Woody. You hardly remember him. Is there something you're not telling me?" Micki's eyes bored into mine. Hip cocked to one side, she waited for an answer.

I shrugged my shoulders and walked out the door. Truth to tell, I didn't have an answer. I had come back to Little Rock looking for one. Maybe I was tired of my work at the Foundation, maybe Little Rock had a greater hold on me than I realized, or maybe, just maybe, I owed Angie a promise long forgotten.

6

You would have been hard put to find anyone in the business section of downtown Little Rock on a Saturday, much less at the Federal Courthouse. Unlike the stately, turn-of-the-century county courthouse, the Russell Robinson Federal Courthouse and Office Building was a 1960's five-story building with absolutely no charm. The afternoon skies had darkened and the thunderstorm broke just as we arrived. To my surprise, the press and their cameras were huddled under umbrellas outside the front entrance. Fortunately, Clovis had arranged for a deputy marshal to meet us at the back door and escort us to the holding area where Doug was waiting.

Doug's stooping posture bore witness to his life in academia: too many hours spent leaning over microscopes or staring at computer screens. I vaguely recalled a clean-cut guy in polos, but today he wore a blue prison jumpsuit and canvas slippers that dwarfed his feet. The deputy removed his handcuffs, ankle shackles, and the chain belt connecting them both. We greeted each other with a handshake and awkward hug. His voice was deeper than I remembered.

"Thanks for coming, Jack. I'm sorry to drag you here, and I know it looks bad, but you're the only one I can trust." Doug said as he sat down across the table.

I wasn't sure what to say so I took the easy route.

"We can talk about why you're here in a minute. I haven't seen Liz yet, but I'm sure she'll want to know you're physically okay. So, tell me. How are they're treating you? How'd you get that shiner?" I asked fearing Doug had already met unfriendly cellmates.

"I'm fine. One of the DEA agents gave me the black eye when he stomped on my face. I'm a lot safer in a cell with fifteen other prisoners than I was with them. We take turns sleeping on four bunks and share a toilet in the corner. Other than the lack of privacy, I really am okay. Actually the shiner helps. My new friends are giving me advice on how to claim police brutality," he deadpanned.

The Feds didn't have any lockdown facilities of their own other than a few holding cells in the courthouse, so anyone they arrested landed in the county jail. So far, Micki's concern for Doug's safety seemed baseless.

"Unless you're a sex offender or a snitch, you're probably safer in county jail than in Little Rock's high schools. Of course, it helps that my cellmates all know why I'm in. I've had some interesting business propositions," he snickered.

Doug appeared to be in surprisingly good spirits, not intimidated by his circumstances. I told him what to expect at the arraignment, and that Micki and Liz had been working to make sure he'd make bail and be out by Monday afternoon. A quizzical eyebrow went up at Micki's name.

"Doug, I'm no expert on drug cases. I'm an antitrust lawyer. Liz has hired Micki Lawrence, a criminal defense attorney. She worked with me when I defended Woody Cole. She's top-notch, and I can't think of anyone I'd rather have on my side."

"You don't need to justify her to me; I assumed you'd need local counsel. Work with Liz on the money issues, but I'm prepared to pay whatever. You know what's at stake."

This conversation was headed down the wrong path. I wasn't about to defend Doug. I had to set Doug straight immediately.

"Of course, I realize what's at stake. You're likely to spend a long time in jail and lose your home. The Feds claim you're a drug dealer and a terrorist who preys on kids. Every newspaper and newscast leads with the story. Your entire future and reputation are on the line. That's why I'm glad Liz hired Micki. She's as good as it gets. You don't need me; you need an experienced criminal defense lawyer."

Doug stared down at his hands clasped between his knees.

"I'm sorry, Doug. Maybe I shouldn't have come to Little Rock at all.

I didn't mean. . . ." He reached out his arm to stop my babbling—a trick I myself used more often than I'd like to admit.

"No, I'm the one who should apologize. I thought Angie had told you everything. She obviously didn't. Remember when she made you promise to defend me, and you agreed? I thought you knew why."

"What does Angie have to do with this?" I jerked my arm away. I heard my voice change, raspy with a little hard edge. I couldn't help it. "You're likely to be charged with possessing, growing, and selling boatloads of marijuana. What does any of that have to do with Angie? Don't try to drag my Angie into your problems."

He remained calm, oddly the one in control. Had I fallen down a rabbit hole?

"Jack, if you don't want to get involved, I understand. Angie warned me I would probably be arrested. She said you'd be my only hope at that point. We both knew I was taking a terrible risk, and I went forward with my eyes wide open. Don't feel guilty. I have no right to hold you to a promise made a long time ago that you don't remember."

That stung–I struggled to remember. He continued.

"I told them about my research before I planted the first seedling. But I understand why you don't want to defend a 'drug dealer.' You have a reputation to keep."

That stung deeper.

He smiled. "Thanks for coming, Jack. I appreciate it. Liz will be glad to know how much you respect Micki. I'm disappointed, but I understand." He looked down at his hands again, lost in thought, finished with me.

Suddenly that night became crystal clear. Angie had been adamant. Over cocktails, she'd gotten me to agree to represent Doug if he got into any trouble. Wondering what kind of trouble this mild-mannered chemist could get into, I'd gone along, more to lighten the mood than anything else. I brought it up with Angie when we got home, but she'd turned prickly, said she needed a hot bath. I figured she'd cool off, but she never brought up the subject up again. That evening's promise retreated in the face of cancer, the increasingly hopeless treatments, and the awful pain.

I felt like a jerk. I didn't want to get caught up in a lost cause, but the least I could do was be polite. I took a deep breath.

"Doug, I'm sorry. I'm overly sensitive when it comes to Angie. I do remember that night, but unfortunately Angie never gave me any details. To be honest, she got sick and I forgot about it. I still don't think I'm the right lawyer for you, but I want to know what this is all about. Why don't I just listen for a change?"

Doug smiled wryly.

"Angie talked about you all the time. She'd say, 'every now and then, Jack gets ahead of himself, talking before he thinks. When that happens, I've learned to keep quiet. It only takes a minute. Pretty soon he'll stop and think. You'll see.' Watching you shift gears, I can almost hear her."

I had to clear my throat before I could reply, "I'm all ears, Professor. Why don't you tell me what's really at stake, and then we'll figure out if I can help."

At that very moment, the deputy stepped in.

"I'm sorry, counsel, but it's past four o'clock, and I have to get the prisoner back to the County Jail before dinner. The marshal says you can see him again tomorrow at one o'clock."

The deputy's offer was more than reasonable. I couldn't complain, especially after he agreed to let Micki come as well. As he brought out the handcuffs and shackles, I turned to Doug.

"I promise to do the listening tomorrow, but is there anything you want me to tell Liz?"

"Liz doesn't know much about this. Just tell her I love her, I'm okay, and things will get better now that you're here. I'll tell you everything tomorrow, but here's your takeaway for today: it's not about the marijuana."

7

As Clovis and I walked the empty halls of the courthouse, I wondered what Doug meant by—"it's not about the marijuana." What in the hell else could it be about? I also thought about Doug. Just now he had seemed very solid, undaunted by the circumstances, certainly not the image of a drug dealer, yet his backyard was full of marijuana.

Maybe Doug had been tending his garden a little too often. Dub had already convinced the press he was a major drug dealer and terrorist. Micki would really be up against it if Doug was delusional.

The deputy was now blocking the back door so we couldn't sneak out that way. When we reached the front entrance, I saw a bank of microphones already in place on the steps. I hesitated at the door.

"Well, we can either try to hustle our way through or I can walk up and answer their questions. Where's the car?"

Clovis shrugged. "Still out back. Your call, but they need a story. If you don't give them one, Dub will."

"Aw, hell—they already know I'm here, I might as well get it over with. But if I start to make a fool of myself, rescue me, okay?"

I made a beeline to the mics, catching the press a little off-guard.

"My name is Jack Patterson. I assume you think I'm here to represent Dr. Stewart. I'm not. He's a friend and a former colleague of my late wife. I don't normally talk to the press regarding a pending legal matter, but I hope that by answering a few questions I can dispel any further misconceptions. Fire away."

"Do you represent Dr. Stewart?"

"No, Dr. Stewart's wife has engaged Micki Lawrence to represent him." Micki was going to shoot me for letting this information out before arraignment.

"Is the professor connected to Woody Cole in any way?"

"No. To my knowledge Dr. Stewart and Mr. Cole have never met."

"Dr. Stewart told U.S. Attorney Blanchard that you represent him. If you aren't going to be his lawyer, why are you here?"

Micki had asked the same question, and I wasn't sure of the answer. So I did the Texas two-step.

"As I said earlier, he and I are friends, and he worked with my wife. I don't know why he told Mr. Blanchard I was his lawyer. I have the utmost confidence in Ms. Lawrence, and I'm here to offer the Stewarts my support. I can't believe his arrest is anything but a misunderstanding."

I heard a few muffled snickers. They were justified. Someone in the rear shouted,

"When will charges be filed?"

"I have no idea. I'm not privy to the U.S. attorney's plans. One more question." It was time to leave.

"Dub Blanchard says Dr. Stewart was a major supplier of drugs to Little Rock's school children and a terrorist. How can you suggest his arrest is a misunderstanding? He had over a hundred marijuana plants growing in his back yard." Fair question.

"The Dr. Stewart I know is a world famous chemist who has devoted his life to serving humanity and science. I'm sure your questions will be answered in due course, but I hope you will all give him the presumption of innocence our Constitution guarantees."

Hiding behind the Constitution never works, but it was all I had. I'd given the press some copy and not done too much damage to Micki's defense. I gave Clovis the high sign and we walked around back to his Tahoe, ignoring their shouted questions. The reporters were unhappy, but at that point, so what? A lawyer's job is to win his case in the courtroom, not become a media darling.

"Clovis, Doug Stewart threw me for a few loops today. The deputy marshal shut it down before I could get many answers, but Micki and

I get to see him again tomorrow. I sure hope he can explain why he grew all that grass."

"You getting involved after all?"

"I hope not. I don't know him well, but he seems like a stand-up kind of guy, and I know Angie thought a lot of him. But I run a foundation that doesn't need me to get mixed up in a drug case. He seems to be okay with Micki, but maybe I can help a little from the sidelines. You up to doing a little investigative work? Just for the fun of it?"

Clovis chuckled. "Shit, I knew trouble was landing when your plane touched the ground. Tell me what you're thinking."

"Well, I'm curious. Dub insists Stewart is a major league drug dealer. I know Dub's a blowhard and inclined to put his foot in his mouth, but he wouldn't get this far out on a limb unless he had some sort of solid proof. Besides, Main Justice wouldn't let Dub get involved with a local grower unless he was part of a cartel or selling other big-time drugs. Liz told Micki that Doug only used the pot for research, claims he never sold a single leaf. So, nothing adds up. I'd like some answers before I get back to my never-ending board meetings. That's all."

The corner of his mouth turned down skeptically as he brought me back to reality.

"No offense, Jack, but I'd cool it for at least a day. Maybe he'll tell you what he was doing with all that grass. Maybe it'll all make sense, but the facts seem pretty straight to me. If Micki can deal with Dub, he'll be out on bail by Monday. You need to put the brakes on that engine of yours."

He had a point.

"The professor got caught with some weed, it's that simple. Micki handles these cases in her sleep. People grow marijuana for two reasons: to make money or to use it themselves, usually both. Don't let your imagination get the better of you."

Clovis and I had been through a lot the year before, so his blunt words of advice came as no surprise. Besides, he was right. I was sticking my nose in Micki's business because I was bored with my own. I gave it up and was well into a mental checklist of friends I hoped to see when Clovis muttered, "I'll be damned."

"What?" I looked up.

"I've been lecturing you about not getting worked up, and damned if we ain't being followed. Shit, Jack. Can't anything you do be simple?"

I instinctively turned around.

Clovis said, "It's the black Infiniti a few cars back."

"Really? You sure it's not some old girlfriend following you?"

8

THE MAN DRIVING the Infiniti instinctively knew he'd been made. He made a quick right turn. Damn that Clovis Jones, he thought. He shouldn't have taken the risk. Keeping an eye on Liz and Micki was a piece of cake, but he'd gotten sloppy, and now he'd have to throw Jones off his scent.

He parked the car on a side street and called a cab. A new car would be waiting for him tonight in a lot downtown, the Infiniti long gone. As he waited, his phone beeped the arrival of an incoming message—the report on Patterson's meeting with the professor from Smith's source inside the courthouse. He knew Patterson could quickly become an irritant, but right now he was more worried about Jones.

"HE'S GONE," I said. "Maybe it was a false alarm."

"No, he was tailing us," Clovis said, as his eyes moved rapidly back and forth from the rear-view mirror to the road ahead.

"It's pretty simple. Someone's worried about what the professor might have told you. In the drug world, the first guy caught rats everybody else out up and down the chain. Someone's worried you've come to town to make a deal. Every doper in town knows Micki won't let her clients plead out by fingering their cohorts. She drops them like a hot potato. If we'd gone to Sam's office after talking to the Professor, you could bet the rats would be deserting town tonight."

"Well, maybe I should go see Sam," I kidded.

Sam Pagano was the first friend I'd made when I moved to Little Rock as a kid. He was Pulaski County's public defender for years before he was elected prosecuting attorney. Maybe he could shed some light on Doug Stewart.

We pulled up to the Hotel Armitage, and after changing and cleaning up, I went to meet Micki and Clovis in the hotel's bar. I felt my heart miss a beat or two when I entered the familiar room. I loved its dark oak paneling and its comfortable musty smell. The only sounds were quiet strains of jazz and the low rumble of voices, no blaring racket from big screen TV's. I found Micki and Clovis seated at a quiet corner, far removed from the bustle of the late afternoon crowd. She had changed into slim white pants and a shimmery blue silk blouse. I noticed a hint of mascara and the sheen of lip-gloss, unusual for her. I took a breath and asked for a Bombay Martini, extra dry with olives.

"I hope you got dressed up for me." I knew I shouldn't flirt, but couldn't resist. She didn't seem to mind.

Smiling smugly, she retorted, "Well, no—I'm meeting a client. The rule for the female professional is not to overdress, but not to diminish your client by dressing down. You know what? I bet when Liz appears, I'll feel underdressed."

The waiter brought our drinks, and I filled Micki in on my meeting with Doug. She agreed that Doug was delusional if he thought it wasn't about the drugs. Dub's office had been fairly cooperative in allowing Liz to get her clothes and some basics. The calico cat was enjoying life at a neighbor's, and Liz had found a place to rent near her spa.

"Clovis told me you want him to do some investigative work. Sounds like I have my partner back. What's up? "

"I don't want to get ahead of you, but I have a few ideas. What you do with them is up to you."

"I remember your 'shower thoughts,'" she said with an easy laugh. "Fire away."

"Dub has a slam dunk against Doug on the growing charges, but instead of playing it straight, he's going to great lengths to trash him, accusing him of selling to kids and being a terrorist. He's on a media blitz, appearing on every TV show he can. I don't see the point, but we shouldn't underestimate him. Dub learned how to sling mud with the best when he worked for the Senate Judiciary Committee. He knew just how to play the press when his senator wanted to kill a judicial nomination. He may be a media hound with zero legal skills, but he has a doctorate in character assassination."

"So what do you think he's up to?" Micki asked.

"He's brought in all these suits from Main Justice, not to mention the DEA—why? He's kept his own staff and the local authorities totally out of the loop, even Sam—why? Why all this secrecy and firepower for a local drug bust? I smell a skunk. Clovis, this is where you come in."

"Happy to do what I can—what do you have in mind?"

"Well, if Doug were really a major supplier in Little Rock, somebody had to have known it. And why is Dub so hell-bent on discrediting Doug? If he's no more than your garden-variety dealer and pusher, why all the hoopla? It doesn't make sense. Nose around a little, see what you can find out."

I asked a few teasers about gambling and underworld connections in both Little Rock and Arkansas in general. It wasn't long before Micki and Clovis took over, tossing information and ideas back and forth while I listened, enjoying my martini and trying to absorb what I heard. It seemed my old hometown had quite the dark side. The name "Novak" came up more than once. From what I'd heard about the man, it seemed he had a lot bigger fish to fry, but then again, Doug had grown a whole lot of grass.

My thoughts had begun to drift when Clovis laughed at something Micki said, and she put her hand behind my head, surprising me with a firm kiss.

"I'm not complaining, but what brought that on?" I asked, grinning.

"Because it's so damn much fun working with you. I wish you were staying."

I wished Eric were leaving.

Clovis chortled, "I'm not about to kiss you, Jack, but it is good to have you back. With your permission, Micki, I'll get my people to work, starting tomorrow. I'll give you an estimate. If it's a problem, we'll work something out."

"You're on. I'll run it by Liz, but money doesn't seem to be a problem."

Speak of the devil—my eye caught Liz posing in the doorway, dressed in a bright red St. John suit. Unmistakable, even to me. I hadn't seen her in years, but she was hard to forget. Same confident manner, same undisciplined blonde hair, but not a man in the bar was looking at her hair. Her glossy red lips were as shiny as her jewelry, and she wore incredibly high heels. *How do women walk in those things?* She crossed the room deliberately, clearly aware of the impression she made. Reaching the bar, she ordered a double Manhattan and sauntered to our table.

Clovis and I stood. She gave me a quick hug and planted an unexpected kiss on my cheek. I introduced her to Clovis. She greeted him like they were high school sweethearts, leaving a smear of lipstick behind. Micki nearly choked on her wine and for the first time since I'd known him, Clovis turned brick red.

The bartender brought over her drink, and I took a deep breath.

"Liz, it's really good to see you after so long. You look terrific! I sure wish the circumstances were different. I spoke with Doug this afternoon. He said to tell you he loves you and he's doing okay. They didn't let me stay long, but I'll see him again tomorrow."

"Of course he's okay. He's right at home with a bunch of guys watching basketball on the tube, while I'm doing all the work. I almost missed my Pilates session because the real estate agent took forever to draw up the paper work." Liz took a large sip of her cocktail, asked the waiter to bring the table some "munchies," and went on with barely a pause.

"You'd think this Dub character would have some sympathy. After all, the woman does have cancer. But enough shop talk. Jack, you look as handsome as ever, and I'm dying to know all about Clovis here." Liz squeezed closer to Clovis on the banquette.

Clovis looked as nervous as a hooker in church. I bit my lip trying not to laugh. Micki was not amused.

"Liz, what's going on here? Are you okay?"

"I'm fine. Look, I took a few hits while I was getting dressed, but I'm not stoned. Joel, he's my Pilates instructor, worked us extra hard today—I could hardly move. A couple of hits always help me loosen up. What's the big deal? I've got a medical use card."

I watched the scene in silence. Micki kept a poker face as she carefully explained that Arkansas did not recognize medical use, nor did the Federal Government, which currently had her husband locked up for cultivation, possession, and distribution. Perhaps Liz would consider whether she would enjoy watching sports from inside jail as much as her husband did.

Turning to Clovis, she said without a trace of humor, "Mrs. Stewart is going to give you the key to her room. Please dispose of whatever unnecessary products you may find there. We'll wait to order dinner until you return." Liz gave her a truly dirty look, then took Clovis by the arm and whispered in his ear. He blushed again and left the table abruptly. Liz shouted across the room for another Manhattan. It took all my self-control not to laugh outright.

A sulking Liz listened as Micki carefully explained the risks of her misbehavior. I could almost read her mind, already trying to figure out how to get around Micki's code of conduct for unindicted spouses. Clovis returned, but chose to pull up a chair rather than slip in beside Liz in the booth. I suggested we get dinner–Liz clearly needed some food. I had hoped to try out the newly re-opened Bruno's, a great Italian I remembered as a kid. But as Liz threw down her second Manhattan and ordered another, I opted for the hotel restaurant.

We were seated at a good table where we could hear each other rather than the noisy bar chatter or the racket of waiters and dishes. I tried to lighten the mood.

"Liz, I had no idea—when did Doug leave NIH? Why, for that matter? And why did you two move to Little Rock, of all places? Did you know I went to high school and college here? I would have thought he'd return to Ann Arbor. How'd you land here?"

Liz perked up, slightly. "Oh, it was all Doug's idea. After Angie died, Doug told me he needed to find someplace where he could have the freedom to do pure research. He loved teaching at Michigan and the students loved him, but there were too many strings attached to their job offer. Lots of schools recruited him, but Doug loved the idea of coming back to Razorback country. I finally gave in, so he contacted Fayetteville, Stafford, and UALR.

"They all wanted him, but a wealthy alum heard about Doug's interest and donated big bucks to create a special chair in Chemistry at UALR. Doug was given carte blanche and full funding for his research; he only has to teach a couple a classes a semester. Plus, he gets to own his own patents and his research. He loves Fayetteville, but I think the ownership issue was what finally swayed him. UALR wasn't too happy about the terms, but agreed in the end."

"What kind of research?" Micki asked.

"Don't ask me. I barely eked out a 'C' in high school chemistry. Whenever we have to go to one of those faculty receptions, I hang out with the grad school bartenders. They're a lot more fun than a bunch of professors trying to impress each other. Doug hates those things as much as I do. He'd much rather go to a sports bar."

I watched her idly as the waiter brought our salads, wondering how much of her bravado was an act. The few times Angie and I had gone out with Liz and Doug, she didn't play the role of the devil in the red dress, but she could be outspoken, and I remembered how quickly a room could turn silent when she got rolling. Doug had a way of touching her arm or hand lightly if she went too far, and she'd immediately tone it down. Not a word passed, but a clear message was conveyed.

They were such an unlikely couple. She'd grown up in Memphis, my hometown until the tenth grade, but our paths never crossed. Her family was in cotton—which means her dad, and his dad, and his dad before, had been cotton brokers. If you were a doctor in Memphis, it was natural to be asked about your specialty–pediatrics, orthopedics, etc. If you practiced law, you might be asked about the area of prac-tice–antitrust, tax, and personal injury. But if you were "in cotton," no further questions were asked—it meant money, very old money. If you had to ask what it meant to be "in cotton," you didn't need to know.

Surprisingly, Liz didn't go to either Ole Miss or Tennessee. She rebelled against the wishes of both her father and Memphis society, and left for Arkansas. In her senior year, a sorority sister fixed her up with a jock who turned out to be Doug, and the rest is history. Liz can almost look him in the eye, and is as effusive as Doug is reserved. Yet somehow it works. I didn't buy the "C" in chemistry story. Doug told Angie that Liz graduated summa cum laude from Arkansas with a double major in psychology and philosophy. While Doug was at Michigan she also earned a Masters and a PhD. In DC, she worked for a small, below-the-radar think tank—something to do with the application of psychology to public policy. In reality, there were two Dr. Stewarts. Both blended into their environments in different ways, but hidden behind Liz's affectations was a very intelligent woman.

WE WERE ALL ravenous and ate our meals in friendly silence.

Finally, looking sheepish, Liz pushed back her plate and said, "Okay, y'all, I'm sorry. I apologize. This mess has me totally bummed out. I'm behaving badly, and I know it. To tell you the truth, I've never fit in in Little Rock. Now my husband is in jail, my so-called friends won't return my calls, and I can't even go to my own bed and have a good cry." She took a sip of the Cabernet I'd ordered for her.

"Jack, I can't believe you're here. Thank you. Micki, I promise to behave. No more dope. I promise. Damn this suit–it itches and pulls in all the wrong places." She squirmed.

I was ready to kiss and make up, but before we could take a deep breath Liz morphed back into the siren.

She grabbed Clovis by the arm. "You know, you are one gorgeous hunk of man. I'm a married woman, but you better watch yourself if I don't get my husband back pretty quickly."

Liz had found Clovis's Achilles' heel. He had no idea how to react. An amused Micki rescued him as we waited for coffee and dessert.

"Liz, Jack and I both think there has to be more to the story than your unique garden or a batch of ginger snaps. Doug may not have been selling dope, but he clearly grew a whole back yard of the stuff, and thanks to Dub Blanchard, most people think he was selling it to school kids. We want Clovis to do a little investigating. He'll give us a cost estimate, but I need your approval."

"I keep telling you, do what it takes. My husband would never have sold drugs to his students or anyone else. I know the man, and I know he's telling the truth. Doug doesn't even smoke the stuff. I use grass to make a few ginger snaps and to calm down, but that's hardly anyone's business. Hell, if he thought what he was doing was illegal, why did he tell the Feds he was growing?"

"What?" Micki's voice rose in surprise. Doug had told me the same thing, but I hadn't been listening.

"Doug wrote all kinds of government agencies to let them know he was growing for his research. I know he wrote to the Drug Czar, the DEA, the FDA, and the Department of Justice–maybe more. He showed me the letter before he sent it. I thought I told Debbie."

Liz dug into her flourless molten chocolate cake.

I asked, "When was that? Did they respond? Do you have a copy?"

"You really need to take a bite of this cake." She stuck a loaded fork in my mouth. I didn't resist; it was chocolate heaven.

"It's a little fuzzy, but it must have been as soon as we moved here, maybe even before. He started growing seedlings in the flower shed and the garage almost before the moving van left. He's a regular Gregor Mendel. Every afternoon, he's grafting, pruning, and planting. He was always trying to develop new strains of the plant. I have no idea if anyone responded to his letter. He must have kept a copy of the letter—it's probably with the files the government seized. I'm telling you, the Feds have known about Doug's research all along."

9

LIZ'S CASUAL REVELATION was a stunner. Alerting the authorities before committing a crime doesn't make it any less of an offense, but neither did it make it the crime of the century. I stared at Liz blankly as she ordered brandy for the table along with another piece of cake. I was too dumbfounded to argue. Maybe the cake would keep her on her feet a little while longer.

We peppered her with questions, but she either had no answers or chose to give none. I glanced at Clovis as Liz downed her brandy. Time for her to go to bed. She made no objections as Clovis stoically offered to walk her to her room. Better him than me.

"What do you think? It looks like Doug knew he was crossing the line before he started. I wonder what he was up to," Micki mused, twirling her brandy.

"I haven't got a clue. But I'm sure of one thing—the next few days should prove interesting. Besides all the obvious questions about why he notified them and what he actually told them, we have to wonder why they waited until now to shut him down. And what was he doing with all that grass if he wasn't selling it? Liz has to know more than she's telling us. Either she's a fine actress, which means we're getting conned, or she's a well-educated airhead. I don't know which is worse. Speaking of Liz, Micki, you've got your hands full."

"Not just me. Did you see Clovis's face? He looked like a preacher in a strip club."

Right on cue, Clovis returned to the table, shaking his head.

"That woman is big trouble. I'll admit it: she's more than I can handle. She was asleep before I could open the door. If she'd shown up in this bar alone, stoned and thirsty, there's no telling what would have happened."

"I take it you don't want to be her bodyguard?" I joked.

Clovis shot me a look I hoped I wouldn't see again. He and Micki left me to finish my brandy and pay the bill.

I wasn't sleepy when I got back to my room, so I turned on the TV in time to hear that Dub would make the rounds of the Sunday morning talk shows. I texted Maggie to record tomorrow's shows, turned the channel to *Saturday Night Live,* and tried to let go, but my mind wouldn't settle.

I hoped Doug would clear everything up tomorrow. Angie was such a great judge of character—it was a struggle to believe Doug had become nothing more than a glorified dope dealer. But Angie had died almost four years ago. Maybe something had snapped in Doug's brilliant mind. He wouldn't be the first scientist who burnt out early in life.

After med school at Georgetown, internships, and residency, Angie had chosen to work in cancer research at NIH. Like many others in her field, her hope was to find "the cure," but the disease got her first. The last year of her life was consumed by chemo, radiation, exhaustion, and pain. Sitting alone in my room, memories of those dark days thundered in my skull. Thank God for friends like Maggie and Walter, and Angie's indomitable spirit.

Meeting with Doug this afternoon and remembering the promise I had made brought Angie back front and center. When the cancer got to be too much, I tried to get her to quit work, to devote all her energy to fighting the disease, but she would have none of it. Despite the exhaustion and pain, she glowed with enthusiasm. I could hear her say, "Hey! It takes time, but we're making progress." I should have paid more attention, asked her to tell me more about her work, but I didn't. I was afraid that if I pushed her into explaining what she meant by progress, we'd both have to face that any "progress" would be too late for her.

One night when we were curled up on the sofa she'd tried to explain. "Most days I don't have the strength to do what I need to do, but I've come to grips with that. I'm not the person I used to be, but I've had my hard cry, and I'm thankful I can keep working, even for a little while. Don't pity me, Jack. I have you and Beth and I have my work—I've had so much life. I'm going to do what I can do for as long as I can. You can never understand, but I am a happier person now than before the cancer." God knows, she was right: I would never understand. I just knew I was going to lose her.

I closed my eyes and took a deep breath as I reminisced: our first meeting, our first date, and the wonderful years together before cancer's poisonous bite. She was always only a moment away; I could bring her back in an instant. I could still see her, hear her voice, and speak to her from my heart—her spirit surrounded me. I finally managed to put my memories back in the box where I kept them, and let my mind drift to Little Rock and how odd it was to be here again—again with a friend who needed help, and again with so many unanswered questions. Suddenly sleepy, I clicked the TV off and fell fast asleep.

SUNDAY

April 20, 2014

10

WHEN I CAME down for breakfast, Liz was already seated at a table by the window, looking fresh as a daisy in workout clothes, part of her hair hidden beneath a Michigan baseball cap. The waiter had just brought her oatmeal, scrambled egg whites, and some kind of green smoothie.

"Come sit down," she smiled, patting the chair next to her. I sat across the table and asked for coffee.

"I have a full morning, Pilates and hot yoga—then a massage—I'll need it. After that, I'm meeting with the decorator. It'll take a lot of work to get the rental livable, especially if the government won't let me have my furniture. Doug and I will have to stay here at the hotel for a while. Like it or not, I still have a party to host. Maybe it would be simpler to just have it at the Club." She tossed back the green concoction as though it were a shot of tequila and asked, "So how long will you be here?"

My poker face deserted me. How could she be so blithe; why no hangover?

"I don't know yet. A lot depends on what we learn from Doug this afternoon. You seem to be in pretty good spirits, all things considered."

Stirring her eggs with a fork, she didn't respond immediately. When she looked up I could see tears brimming in the corners of her eyes.

"It's all an act, Jack. My whole life has been turned upside down, but I have to keep it all in, never let it show. Southern women raised you. You know what's expected. I'm scared to death. What will I do if he goes to prison? I have no idea when the next shoe's going to drop. But it was drilled into me—no matter what, don't let it show—act like tomorrow is just another day.

"So, I'll do my duty. I'll act the airhead, work out like Jane Fonda, furnish a house I can't imagine living in, and meet with a caterer to plan a party for a hundred of my dearest friends, friends who're all talking about me behind my back and probably would rather drop dead than be seen with me. My mother would be proud."

I couldn't argue with any of it, so I retreated, asking her to meet me at the hotel around four o'clock.

She rose, gave me a cool kiss, and walked away, leaving her eggs untouched.

I ordered breakfast, glanced at the *Democrat*, and dropped it on the seat next to me. Anything I'd read about Doug or my press conference would piss me off. I turned to the *New York Times*, which thankfully didn't contain a word about Arkansas, much less about Doug.

My thoughts turned to what Liz had said. My mother was a Vietnam War widow. Until she remarried and we moved to Little Rock, we lived with my Grandmother Louise in Memphis. I understood exactly what was expected of Southern women. And yet, when I think about women from stark New England, American Indians, or British women in World War II, I think of their stoicism, their strength. Women in general, come to think about it. Maybe it's not the place—maybe it's just the ingrained strength of the fairer sex.

I noticed Clovis peering around the door into the restaurant. I couldn't help but smile as he gave a sigh of relief and strode in, ready for the day. He reported that his folks were hard at work, and I brought up my one "shower thought."

"I'm not too current on the regulations regarding government surveillance and wiretapping, but I do know that the mere mention of 'terrorism' or 'national security' allows the Feds to throw the Fourth Amendment to the wind. I think maybe a little bug inspection at Micki's office is in order."

"Great minds think alike," Clovis said. "I'll check your room and Liz's too, while I'm at it."

"Good thinking. Clovis, if Doug is in fact a major grower and distributor he's bound to have enemies and associates who might wonder what Liz knows. You know, I still can't believe the Feds haven't charged her—or even brought her in for questioning. We need to think about getting her some protection. How about you? You two seemed to hit it off."

"Not funny. I ain't about to fall on that grenade. If you think she needs protection, I've got the perfect person."

"I wouldn't wish that duty on anyone, but you've piqued my curiosity. Who's the sacrificial lamb?"

"I'll introduce her when and if the time comes."

The server brought us coffees to go, and we left for Micki's office. She'd already been on a five-mile run and was dunking one of Debbie's pastries into her second cup of coffee. Munching on a cinnamon roll, Clovis took advantage of a pause in our small talk to tell her his people would come by later to sweep her offices. She played with the pastry, looking resigned.

"What, no protest?" I asked. "Usually you think you're exempt from the government's intrusion."

"Well, maybe not this time. I spoke with a friend at the U.S. attorney's office last night. He confirmed what Fitzhugh told me, that a special task force comprised of special agents from DEA and Homeland Security is running this gig, with Dub in charge and only answering to the Drug Czar himself. No one else. Dub's only obligation to Main Justice is to keep the Criminal Division informed."

"That doesn't bode well."

"Not one bit. He may think he covered his ass, but Doug Stewart's in a world of trouble. Growing plants in your backyard and baking ginger snaps doesn't warrant an interagency task force. Dub's not even using his office at the courthouse. He got a special appropriation to rent office space downtown and hire a completely separate support staff. And he hasn't brought on a single agent or attorney from his U.S. attorney's office. Everything's hush-hush. The way they're going after Doug, he might as well be Al Capone."

"Well, forewarned is forearmed. That seals it. I've got a friend at Justice who might be willing to talk. And, Clovis, Liz needs full-time security. The last thing we need is for the cops to charge Liz with possession or for her to get smacked with a DUI. You've got someone in mind to babysit, right?" Clovis and Micki exchanged amused looks.

"Oh, hell, Micki! I'm sorry. This is your case. I'm sorry. Why didn't you stop me?" I asked.

"I will, when I disagree. Normally, I'd say you're being overprotective, but I've known my source in that office for years, and he was scared to talk. He warned me more than once, 'Micki, be careful. Watch your back.'"

11

THE SKINNY MAN now sat behind the wheel of a dark gray Volvo SUV. He'd assured Mr. Smith that he could handle Patterson and Micki Lawrence just fine, glossing over his worry about Clovis Jones. Last night, Jones had personally tucked the Stewart woman in before driving Micki back and securing her office. Worse, Jones' people were on campus asking questions. He had a moment now, while Lawrence and Patterson were huddled in Micki's office, and Liz Stewart was off getting a massage. So he turned his attention to his primary problem—how to neutralize Jones. Mr. Smith had made it clear he didn't tolerate mistakes.

LEAVING MICKI AND Clovis to hash out security with Mongo, I perched on the edge of Micki's desk and searched for Peggy Fortson's cell number in my contacts. Peggy and I had joined the Justice Department at the same time. I had left for a private practice after a few years, but she'd stayed the course and was now the deputy assistant attorney general for the Criminal Division. We were still very good friends, so I didn't feel bad about calling on a Sunday. She answered on the second ring.

"Jack! I wondered if I'd ever hear from you again. Are you finally calling for that dinner you owe me?"

No beating around the bush from Peggy. I owed her a lot more than dinner, but I got to the point.

"No, I wish I were, but, well, I'm in Little Rock, and I've got some questions."

Her naturally cheerful voice took on an edge.

"I know where you are, Jack. I also know why you're there. Let me shut this down before you start. I've been specifically instructed by the attorney general to have absolutely no involvement in the Stewart case. He said if you called I should tell you that the appropriate person to speak to is Dub Blanchard. Other than that, I'm not to give you the time of day. I'm sorry, Jack. When will you be back in town?"

I couldn't imagine why the attorney general had hogtied Peggy. She was a career senior deputy, not some new intern. But she was also my friend, and I knew not to cross the line.

"I'm not sure, but I'll call you for that dinner as soon as I get back. I promise. I'm sorry to have bothered you on a Sunday."

"Wait, Jack. Look, please be careful. I mean . . . well, just watch your back." She sounded miserable. *Watch your back*—it was becoming repetitive.

Sliding the door closed with her foot, Micki eased carefully back into the office, juggling a stack of papers and two cups of coffee. I took one from her, helped her with the papers and said, "No luck with Peggy, they've put a muzzle on her. I have no idea what's behind all this, but she's been told 'hands-off.'"

"Don't go all conspiracy on me, Jack. Dub knows you two are close, and he's made sure you can't go around him. Once Dr. Stewart announced you were his attorney, I bet he called Main Justice even before he called the press." She was tapping the eraser end of a pencil on her desk.

"What about the late-night call from your friend at the U.S. attorney's office? Don't tell me that doesn't bother you."

"Let's not box at shadows. Doug's probably going to tell us he was growing all those plants because it's his right under the First Amendment. As if I haven't had a dozen clients try that one on me."

She turned to Clovis and asked, "Find out anything at UALR?"

"Not much yet. The kids in Stewart's classes are pretty freaked out, don't know what to think. But the faculty rumor mill is working overtime. Did you ask Mongo and Debbie? They probably have more insight into Little Rock's drug scene than my people."

She bit her lip. "I did, and neither has heard a thing—Stewart as a major drug supplier seems pretty unlikely. Look—I'm a little hesitant to involve them. They've invested a lot in getting and staying clean. They run with a different crowd now, and they're trying hard. For Debbie, drugs mean Novak and a lot of bad memories."

"I'm with you, but they do have good sources. Let me give them a couple of harmless suggestions. I promise not to get them in a situation they can't handle," Clovis reassured her.

"Okay. But if Novak turns up again, he's all yours."

"Rumor has it he's left Little Rock for good, but I'll have my radar up. I'll be sure both Debbie and Mongo can reach me any time." He left before Micki could object.

That was the second reference to Novak I'd heard. He sounded like Russian mafia, or some sort of Boris and Natasha wannabe. I asked Micki to explain. Her revelations about Novak and how she'd gotten involved in Debbie's liberation and rehab gave me a jolt. Debbie seemed so bubbly, almost without a care in the world—I wondered how she felt underneath. I knew this sort of thing happened, but not, I'd thought, in Little Rock, or to anyone I might know.

Micki clearly took him very seriously. "I know in my heart Novak's going to make another run at Debbie. She seems pretty solid right now, fairly content, but it just takes one slip—she's still vulnerable. He sees her as a source of income and a means of blackmail for his well-heeled clientele. And he has an image to think of—escapees can be dangerous in his business. He's capable of anything. She's my responsibility now. I need to keep her safe."

Debbie's story made me feel guilty. Several of the better restaurants I enjoyed in D.C. employed an ever-changing bevy of beautiful Eastern European servers. The young women were attractive and hands-on friendly. I ignored the rumors and occasional lewd glances from some of my fellow diners. Several colleagues had even encouraged me to go with them to one of the Russian restaurants that catered to professional ice hockey players and high rollers. They said "the view" was worth the expensive drinks. It never crossed my mind that these cute women might be victims of the sex trade. Human trafficking was a rapidly growing problem across the country and had spread well beyond major metropolitan areas. But Little Rock?

I knew enough from my days at Justice to know how difficult it was to pinpoint the money behind these operations. I'd lay odds that Novak was just the front man for some Russian or Chinese mafia. I hated the way society used the phrase "the sex trade," like the oil trade or international trade, as though it were just another economic market. How any decent human being could participate or condone the abuse handed out to these young women was beyond me. Having met Debbie, I knew I wouldn't be so polite or listen so quietly the next time my buddies hinted at being more than friendly with those young women.

My mind returned to Novak. What could he have to do with Doug Stewart? He may have used drugs to tame Debbie, but that didn't make him a competing drug dealer or Doug's business partner. In fact, it didn't connect him with Doug at all.

My thoughts were interrupted as Clovis returned to the office looking pleased. "Whenever you need to downsize, Micki, I've got a job for those two. They caught on real quick."

"Don't you go stealing my employees, Clovis Jones," she laughed.

Clovis left to run a few errands before he drove us to the courthouse. Micki and I dug into the basics of the case. Much of the daily grind of lawyering is dull as nails: court preparation, forms, unending paper work, and an undervalued commodity–thought. Our need to make some sense of all this, hung over us like a fog. Still, we had to get Doug ready for the arraignment and what we hoped would be a successful bond hearing.

Micki asked the question I knew was coming.

"Are you going to enter an appearance tomorrow? I need to know."

"I know you do. Can we put that decision off until this evening? We'll have met with Doug and know how he's going to plead. You're handling the arraignment and the bond hearing anyway. I'm just helping you prepare, throwing in my two cents. I'll meet with Liz after we see Doug. Why don't you join us? We can decide then."

12

DEBBIE, GOD BLESS her, had gone to get lunch, She returned with a large box of fried chicken and potato salad from a place called Lutie's's—one bite and I was in heaven. The chicken was crispy on the outside, juicy on the inside, skin coated with just a hint of breading, salted to perfection.

Consumed by pressure, hunger, and the guilty pleasure of fried food, we all dug in. Bones picked clean, I was sure I couldn't eat another bite, when Debbie pulled out little fried peach pies that were still warm. Clovis gave a moan as he bit in. We lingered in contented silence until my eyes drifted to the face of my watch—time to go to the courthouse.

No press on the steps—the first tickle of apprehension. Sure, it was Sunday, but the Lord's Day never kept a good reporter away. Clovis had arranged to meet the deputy at the side door, but the door was locked, and no one answered his insistent knocks. He called the deputy's cell, but only got his voice mail. They'd probably been delayed in transit. We waited a few minutes, but after no one appeared, Clovis called again. No answer. The tickle turned into a sinking feeling.

Micki's face was grim. She'd had plenty of experience with deputies who played games with her clients just for kicks. She punched in the U.S. marshal's cell number.

"Micki, how can I help you on this beautiful Sunday afternoon? Everything okay?" He sounded sincere, a nice enough guy.

"Bill, I'm at the courthouse. We're supposed to meet with Dr. Stewart, but the deputy isn't here and doesn't answer his phone. The courthouse is locked tighter than a drum. Is my client still in the county jail? We can be there in fifteen minutes."

"Randy was supposed to have the prisoner there at one. I'll track him down and get right back to you. Shouldn't be a problem, so far as I know."

Clovis had walked around to check the other doors, but the building was deserted.

"There's a bad smell here—I'd bet it's the stench of Dub Blanchard." Micki said harshly.

I tried to stay positive. "The deputy couldn't have been nicer. Maybe they're just running late."

Micki's cell rang. As she listened a deep flush crept up her neck and her teeth clenched.

"You tell that arrogant son of a bitch he can kiss my ass! I . . . here . . . talk to Jack!"

Micki threw the phone at my head and went storming off. I ducked and picked it up from the shrubbery, no worse for the wear.

"Marshal, this is Jack Patterson. What's going on?"

"Mr. Patterson, this is Bill Maroney. I'm real sorry about this. Randy, my deputy, just told me that Dr. Stewart was involved in some sort of altercation last night. He wasn't hurt, but in a move of caution he was moved to a different facility."

"Okay, so where is he? We'll come to him." I waited as he audibly swallowed and cleared his throat.

"Um . . . well, apparently he's in Oklahoma City at the Federal Prison Transfer Facility."

"Oklahoma City—you mean the federal prison at the airport." I struggled to keep my tone neutral.

"Yes, sir. I don't know why they didn't move him to the Faulkner County jail. That's only about thirty minutes from here. Or even to Forrest City—it's not much further. But, well, um, no, it looks like they flew him to Oklahoma City."

"What do you mean 'they?' You're the marshal."

"Well, that's certainly true, but the Justice Department detailed some deputy marshals from Fort Smith to Mr. Blanchard's task force, and last night they took jurisdiction over the prisoner. I didn't know until just now. I mean I didn't even know they could. One minute the guy's in county jail, the next thing I know he's in Oklahoma City. The guy that told me all this, said it was done on Dub's orders: my only responsibility is to keep Dr. Stewart safe when he's in the courthouse. He was pretty strong; said that mostly I should just keep out of the way. When I said you were supposed to meet with the prisoner this afternoon, he said that was too damn bad, and what they did or didn't do was none of my, uh, well 'fucking' business anymore. I'm repeating his words exactly. As soon as we hang up, I'll try to get DC to tell me what's going on, but for now, my hands are tied."

"Any more good news?"

"He said if you have a problem, you're to take it up with Mr. Blanchard. I'm really sorry, Mr. Patterson. I have a number if you want it. I don't treat people this way. Micki will never trust me again."

"Oh yes, she will. What she thinks of Dub Blanchard is another matter. You might warn your courtroom deputies to be ready. Anything's possible."

"I wouldn't blame her if she kicked him in his fat balls. Most folks know better than to try to jack Micki around."

"Okay, Bill," I sighed, ending the call after getting Dub's number. No sense going off on him.

Micki had returned from her walkabout, still fuming, ready to let loose on anyone. I put my hand on her arm, and she jerked it away.

At last Clovis ventured, "So, where now?"

"Micki, did your friend say exactly where the new task force is head-quartered?" I asked.

"No, but it's bound to be downtown. It can't be too hard to figure out."

I punched in the number Maroney had given me for Dub.

"Dub Blanchard, please."

"May I say who is calling?"

"Jack Patterson." No need to elaborate.

The woman came back on line in seconds. "Can he call you back? He's in a meeting."

"No, he needn't bother. I'll be at his office in five minutes."

I hung up.

"Clovis, pick the newest, most expensive building downtown, if there is one. Five'll get you ten that's where they've set up shop. Micki and I will try to get past security while you call Walter's pilot. Find out if he can be ready to go to Oklahoma City in thirty minutes. The transfer facility is right there at the airport. They even have those jet ways a plane can pull up to just like at a regular airport terminal."

WE PULLED UP to the only new building in downtown Little Rock, twelve stories of glass and steel. I knew we had the right building because a guy who clearly wasn't a banker stood outside the entrance talking to two armed men wearing blue vests labeled "U.S. Marshal." These guys have no reason to be discreet.

As we got out of the Tahoe, I held Micki back. "I know you want to deck someone, but you catch more flies with honey. Let me try it my way, okay?"

She gave in with a scowl. "I'll be good, but if this doesn't work . . ."

I smiled, kissed her cheek, and whispered. "Did I ever tell you how much I love you when you scowl?"

"Jack..." A glimmer of a smile crossed her face.

I walked up to the clean-cut, fortyish-looking man—with his white Oxford shirt, loose tie, cuffed, dark slacks, and running shoes, he could have been a Mormon missionary–and stuck my hand out.

"Hi. I'm Jack Patterson. I'm here to see Dub." I tried to walk forward but one of the burly marshals stepped in to block my way.

"He's in a meeting, unavailable," Mr. White Shirt said without a smile.

"I know that. I can wait."

"Sorry, he's simply not available."

"Neither is my client. That's why I'm here. I need to prepare him for tomorrow's arraignment, but I understand he's in Oklahoma City. I can be at the federal prison in less than an hour, but I want to make sure he'll be available when I get there. Marshal Maroney said I should take this up with Mr. Blanchard. Since he won't take my calls, I thought I'd take it up with him in person." I smiled kindly—like I would to a cable guy who was five hours late.

He didn't budge an inch.

"You're correct; the prisoner isn't here. He was moved because we're concerned for his personal safety. Mr. Blanchard will tell you tomorrow when you'll be allowed to see Dr. Stewart, not before."

Micki couldn't hold back. "We have a right to see our client. What do you mean by 'allowing us to see?'" she demanded hotly. "You—"

I held out my hand to catch Micki's arm. "I didn't catch your name." I asked.

"Jim Bullock, assistant U.S. attorney." He stood a little straighter.

"Well, Jim, you're denying me access to my client. I've told you I'm willing to charter a plane, but you tell me that even if I do, I will be denied access to my client. Is that correct? I want to get this straight. Assistant U.S. Attorney Jim Bullock is telling me I may not talk to my client either in person or by phone?"

I hoped by getting personal I'd at least get an audience with Dub. Most junior lawyers would back down to the point of checking.

His eyes narrowed. "I repeat that Dr. Stewart is unavailable today. Mr. Blanchard will inform you when and under what circumstances you may see the prisoner. Mr. Blanchard has meetings scheduled all afternoon. His schedule is quite full just now. This building is closed and our offices are off-limits to uninvited visitors. Do I make myself clear?"

"Very clear. May I at least inquire as to the condition of my client? I understand there was an altercation last night. Is he okay? Is he isolated from the other prisoners?"

Jim knew he had the upper hand. "When the prisoner left Little Rock he appeared to be unharmed. Any other questions concerning his condition or the nature of his housing should be made through channels to the Bureau of Prisons."

Now it was Micki's turn to hold me back.

"I wish I could say you've been helpful. But in fact, you've been a real pain in the ass. Tell Dub I'll see him tomorrow. I hope he's ready."

Bullock finally managed a real smile.

"Oh, he's ready, all right."

13

I OPENED THE door of the Tahoe for Micki. She was seething. I was just plain pissed. Clovis had the sense to keep quiet.

"Jack, one of these days you're going to hold out your hand to calm me down one too many times, and I'm going to chop it off. That bastard couldn't even look at me? Misogynist pig! How in the hell are they going to get Doug back for the arraignment? Dub is jerking us around. He's not in Oklahoma City. They've probably got him at a safe house near the courthouse. I can't begin to imagine what this is all about—what on earth are they up to?"

I had a feeling I knew exactly what they were up to.

"Micki, if it's okay with you, why don't we drop you off at your office—you've got a lot of paperwork to prepare. I need to tell Liz what happened. Clovis, if I promise Liz will behave, will you join us for dinner?"

"Only if you promise." He was dead serious.

"Micki, I'm sorry about the hand thing. Old habits die hard, and those marshals were hoping you'd light into Bullock. Assault an assistant U.S. attorney, and you *will* land in jail."

She didn't like it, but knew I was right. She reached over to squeeze my hand, and I realized the time had come to fish or cut bait.

"If it's okay with you, I'd like to be your second chair, at least for now."

She gave me a sweet smile as she opened the door.

"As you said to me once before, no second chair. We're partners. But don't get any other ideas."

"Of course." I could see Clovis trying not to laugh. *Right.*

"What about Liz? Does she need security tonight? What with everything else you've got to tell her, is this a good time?" he asked, as we watched Micki go into her office.

"There won't ever be a good time. You're going to join us for dinner. Why don't you ask her bodyguard to come as well? She's here waiting, right?"

"What makes you think it's a she?"

"Liz makes you nervous. You don't think you can trust Liz around another guy. I figured if you'd found just the right person, she had to be a female. Besides, earlier you slipped and used the word 'her.'

"Look—my gut tells me Doug's arrest is bigger than drugs—he said as much. I'll bet you two doughnuts he's not in a safe house: they really did fly him to Oklahoma City. They want him miserable, scared, and willing to say or do anything. Oklahoma City is the Federal Transfer Facility. The Bureau has adopted the Federal Express approach to inmate transfer. Prisoners are handled like chain-wrapped packages. Almost every federal inmate who is moved from one jail to another goes to OKC and then out again. Prisoners aren't there long enough to get phone privileges or mail. The Bureau of Prisons won't even acknowledge who's there. That's why Bullock referred me to them. Your cellmate can be some poor guy who's in for a minor drug offense or a skinhead doing life.

"A lawyer friend of mine, convicted of a petty, white-collar crime, went through exactly this ordeal. He told me about it over a beer— called it 'diesel therapy.' He barely escaped with his life. I remember he said, 'One more night, and I wouldn't be telling you a thing; I'd be dead.' It's a terrible way to treat anyone. Thank God, it's never happened to any of my clients."

I dreaded breaking the news to Liz.

14

"I'M ON TIME," Liz announced brightly, jumping up from a couch as we walked into the hotel lobby.

"That you are. Come on, let's find a table in the bar." Clovis opted to stay in the lobby, muttering that he needed to make some calls.

I asked the waiter for a couple of Diet Cokes, but Liz interrupted, insisting on a Silver Patron margarita. Ah, what the hell. So far nothing had gone right, and it clearly wasn't about to get easier. So I ordered a margarita, and we made small talk until our drinks arrived. She told me about her decorating efforts and the hassles she'd had with the caterer for her party. She'd been able to get the club, but . . .

"Enough with the party, Liz, I need to tell you about this afternoon. As far as I know, Doug is okay."

"What do you mean, as far as you know?" Her breezy attitude vanished.

"I didn't get to see him. The marshals have moved him to a prison transfer facility in Oklahoma City."

I braced myself, ready for some kind of outburst, but nothing happened. She bit her lip, and her face began to quiver. Gripping her drink with shaky hands, she closed her eyes and took several deep breaths.

Finally she looked up and said quietly, "Tell me everything."

I explained what had happened at the courthouse and outside the office building. I gave her the highlights of Micki's call to her friend at the U.S. attorney's office. I didn't want to frighten her about conditions at Oklahoma City, but I didn't sugarcoat it either. She took it all in, asking questions about how this might affect the arraignment and whether Doug could still get out on bond. She took it without crying or hysterics. I started to compliment her, but she stopped me abruptly.

"Thanks, but don't. Order me another margarita. Don't worry—I won't lose it. I told you at breakfast. Southern women don't make scenes in public. Don't kid yourself: I'm scared to death. You think Doug will be in court tomorrow. I don't. You say he's safe. I'm not so sure. The only reason I have to think this might turn out all right is that you're here.

"I thought Doug was being dramatic when he warned me that things would get really bad. But he also thought you would show up, and you two would figure it all out. Everything Doug told me could happen is happening, so maybe, just maybe, I'll get through this." She produced a weak smile.

It didn't seem like the best time to ask her what else Doug had told her.

"Liz, I don't know how you're going to feel about this, so please listen. I'm not just worried about Doug. I'm concerned for your safety, too." I told her that we'd been followed, that Clovis was checking for bugs in all of our hotel rooms and Micki's office, and I reiterated the warnings from Peggy and from Micki's friend. I explained that Clovis had arranged for her to have a bodyguard for the next several days.

I was determined to be serious and stern, but failed utterly when she squealed, "Will he look like Kevin Costner?"

I told her the best we could do was Costner's sister.

"You know, Clovis is a stick in the mud. The least he could do is give me a hunk. I don't mind a bodyguard, but I'm not about to have a babysitter."

I laughed, thinking that a babysitter was exactly what we had in mind.

I asked her to meet us for dinner at seven She could meet her bodyguard and we would map out a strategy. She left for her session with a massage therapist who was a "genius." He apparently helped her get "balanced," whatever that meant. I saw Clovis slink in—he'd been hovering around the door waiting for her to leave.

"That woman is going to be the death of me. On the way out, she called me a wuss and said her bodyguard better be ready to party."

"Clovis, Liz hasn't got a single friend in the world right now. Cut her some slack. What you're seeing is an act."

"I'm not so sure. Anyway, I've got some things to tend to before dinner. You need me?"

I waved him away, paid the tab and went back to my room to call Maggie.

"I thought you'd fallen off the map," she answered.

I brought her up to date, and she filled me in on Dub's performances on the talk shows.

"He's making your friend out to be another Bin Laden. He also had a few choice words for you and Micki, calling you as much a part of Doug's criminal enterprise as street pushers."

"Nice. I have a few choice words for him, too, but I'll save them for the courtroom. What about the foundation—any backlash?" I knew that neither Maggie nor Walter would volunteer any rumors of discontent, but I was sensitive to the fact that I was the president of their foundation. Lawyers can usually get away with representing bad guys. It comes with the job description. But foundation presidents don't have that luxury.

"None," she answered. "You know Walter. He'd love nothing better than to have somebody try to tell him how to run the foundation. Don't worry."

"I do worry."

"I know. But no one here gives a fig. We know you wouldn't be in Little Rock if you didn't have a good reason."

"That's the problem. I'm still not sure why I'm here. I haven't had enough time with Doug to understand what it's all about."

We talked a little about having the plane available to go to Oklahoma City. I asked her to email me a few things I hoped I wouldn't need and said I'd call her after the arraignment. I detected a little melancholy in her voice. Tomorrow would be the first time I'd been in court as a private attorney without Maggie.

I also called a number at the Justice Department and left word for an old friend. He returned my call immediately, even though it was Sunday. I told him what I needed, and he said he'd have it to me by the end of the day.

I cleaned up and sank into the sofa for a good while, just thinking. I wasn't at all sure I should be part of Doug's defense. Given Dub's attitude, my presence might hurt rather than help. I didn't sense any personal danger, but foresaw plenty of surprises. I mulled over what had transpired so far, but my mind kept wandering back to Angie and her plea to help Doug. What had she known over four years ago? What could have been so important? One thing was certain: I wouldn't figure it out from this couch.

15

CLOVIS AND MICKI were sitting at a quiet, corner table in the bar, but neither had a drink, and Micki's lips were set in a thin line. She gave me a look that would chill a polar bear.

I pulled out a chair and asked casually, "What's up?"

"Ask him!" Micki said hotly. "I'm not speaking to either one of you!"

I looked at Clovis. "What happened?"

"She left her office to go to Eric's after we left and spotted a dark sedan following her. She's convinced Dub ordered the tail."

"Well, I don't see how that's your fault, or mine either for that matter."

"I told her she should have protection when she left the office, and . . ."

"Hello—I'm right here," she interrupted, "and I'm not helpless. I don't need a guard. And I might just go see Dub myself!" Her leg bounced angrily under the table.

Ah, jeez—why did everything have to be so hard? Clovis waited patiently for me to respond.

"Look, Maggie hired Clovis to protect me, but you're the lead dog. The fact is we don't have a clue what's really going on here. We've got a client charged with God-knows-what, a vengeful U.S. attorney, some crazy Russian mob guy, and now you've got a tail. Be reasonable. I have no idea how to defend Doug without you, and we can't stop Dub from tailing any of us. Let Clovis do his job. We can't afford the luxury of your temper."

I finally sat down, now in a bit of a huff myself. We all thought about it for a minute as I calmed down.

"Clovis, is this Dub's doing?"

"Well, I guess it could be. But why? What would be the point? At any rate, I've asked Paul to be on stand-by."

"Where's Paul right now?" I asked.

"He's waiting outside to stop Micki before she does anything to Dub she'll regret." Micki was having a hard time holding her frown.

"Okay, I'm sorry, you're right, I'm through pouting. I guess we do need to talk about this. But first, I need to call Eric. I'll be right back."

I looked at Clovis. We raised our glasses in silent relief, the tension slowly dissipating.

"The wildcat sure has her claws out." Clovis said, using his nickname for Micki. Needless to say, neither of us used it in front of her.

I said, "Don't let that bravado fool you—she's worried. Probably more about Debbie than about herself. She's also worried how Eric's going to react."

Clovis asked, "You don't seem too surprised. You thought this might happen, didn't you? What tipped you off?"

"If this case is simply about Doug growing pot, why the hard line by the Feds? Why have they denied him access to his attorney, whisking him off to Oklahoma? Why is Dub involved at all? A simple drug case is a matter for a rookie U.S. attorney or the locals. What on earth is the terrorist charge about? Shoot, it looks like they want to lock Doug up and throw away the key. There's got to be more to it than a backyard full of marijuana, and Micki is the one person who stands in their way. When you knock a team's ace pitcher out of the game early, you clearly have a better chance of winning. Someone is trying to rattle her, throw her off her game. Maybe it's not the Feds; maybe it's someone else. Dub's good for a lot of big talk, but why would he have Micki followed? Even he's not that dumb."

"I don't know—he hasn't shown much between his ears so far."

"Oh, I know he's a weasel, but I have a hunch it's not him. If Doug really is dealing, both the competition and his accomplices have good reason to make sure he doesn't talk or that no one believes him if he does. Micki's a damn good lawyer and the local traffickers know it.

"Then again, maybe whoever had her followed is completely off our radar. Maybe it's that guy Novak. Micki's clearly worried about him. Doug is probably safe with the Bureau of Prisons, but Micki's another story. She's got to be reasonable about needing protection."

"Maybe Eric can make her see the light." Clovis deadpanned.

Micki walked back into the bar with Liz at her side, and we quit laughing. Liz looked cool and collected, almost a different woman. She had pulled her hair back into a low ponytail and wore ink dark, straight-leg jeans, a linen jacket over a silk blouse, and sandals. Heads at the bar still turned, but this time to admire pure class.

We rose to greet them, and Liz kissed me lightly on the cheek, whispering, "I'm balanced." I had no idea what her massage therapist had done, but I was ready to put him on the payroll.

"Where's my bodyguard, Clovis? I hear the boys are all chicken. So where is she? I hope she likes dancing and staying out all hours of the night. I'm ready to party." The vamp could return in a blink of an eye.

I guess we all looked worried. Liz punched Clovis on the bicep. "You need to lighten up, good looking. Seriously, where is she?"

"She's outside with Paul."

"Shit, Clovis," Micki frowned. "It makes absolutely no sense to have them sit outside. What if some kind of a bad guy is camped out in here? Besides, we want to meet her. Please ask them to join us. Paul can drive me to Eric's tonight, but that's as far as it goes. I refuse to let Dub Blanchard intimidate me. Understood?" She looked directly at Clovis.

"Understood." Clovis glanced at me. I shrugged.

Clovis punched in a text to Paul, and before long he was introducing us to Liz's new chaperone, Moira Kostov. Clovis had told me that Moira's parents and grandparents had emigrated from Hungary during the Cold War. Now in her thirties, she'd grown up in Nashville where she'd been a good student and a better jock, swimming and playing tennis. She went to Michigan on a swimming scholarship and joined Detroit's police force right after graduating. A bad divorce, Detroit's economy, and Clovis's job offer had brought her to Little Rock just a few weeks ago.

Paul wore thicker glasses than my friend Woody, but looks can be deceiving. He'd been a champion wrestler in college and was an expert in martial arts. Last year Clovis had told me, "If I had a child, I'd rather have Paul protecting her than anyone else I know."

Moira was dressed in a navy blue pants suit and white blouse that looked at least five years out of date. Her shoulder holster was in plain sight beneath the jacket, and she wore black athletic shoes. You almost expected a badge. Her coal black hair was pulled back into a severe knot, and her almond eyes were dark green and very serious. She wore little make-up: a little blush and lip-gloss accented her strong cheekbones and generous mouth. Her grave handshake impressed me, and she seemed, well, she didn't seem like a cop. I was fascinated with this paradox of a tough former Detroit policewoman who had such a soft smile and a softer voice. Paul pulled out a chair for her, and they both sat down.

Liz was direct. "You think you can keep up with me?"

"Yes, Ma'am, I think so." Moira replied evenly, and Liz exploded.

"I'm not a 'ma'am,' I'm Liz, and I wouldn't count on it." Clovis glanced at Moira with an "I told you so" look.

"I'll keep that in mind, Ma'am . . . I mean Liz. It's going to be hard at first. Your husband was one of my professors at Michigan."

"You went to Ann Arbor? You knew Doug?" Liz raised her eyebrows in apparent disbelief.

"Well, not exactly. I was one of several hundred in his basic chemistry class. He was a wonderful teacher, always had time for any of us even though the class was huge. I'm sure he wouldn't remember me."

"Small world," I commented. "Moira, we all go by our first names. I'm Jack. I hope both Clovis and Paul have told you how we work: if you have a thought or idea, speak up. We're in a strange situation. Clovis has already told you that Micki and I have both been followed. I don't know how much he told you about Liz and why she needs protection."

"I'd like to hear myself," Liz said pointedly.

"If Doug was involved in selling drugs, his partners or his competition might think Liz knows more than she does and decide, well—to keep her quiet. If the arrest isn't about drugs, whoever is behind it may want to use Liz to get at Doug. Right now, none of us knows exactly what happened, and we need to keep Liz safe."

"Jack, the drug charges are bullshit. Doug wasn't selling marijuana!" Liz jumped in. "I don't know about that other stuff, but I've been married to him for almost thirty years. All Doug cares about are molecules, the Razorbacks, and, to a lesser degree, me. You're supposed to be our lawyer, our advocate—how can you think Doug was a dope dealer?"

Before I could answer Moira put a gentle hand on Liz's arm and said, "Liz, Jack doesn't believe any of that. He's here to defend Doug. I was Dr. Stewart's student, and I'd believe the President of the University of Michigan was selling dope before he was. Jack's telling me all this so we'll both understand why you need me. I was a beat cop in Detroit and saw dope deals every day. The U.S. attorney's behavior doesn't make sense, and it's up to Jack to get inside his head. He can't do his job if he's worried someone's going to harm you. I'm here to make sure that doesn't happen."

Liz looked at me and back at Moira. "Thank you. I get pretty protective when it comes to Doug."

Micki glared at me. "You have every right; the thought of a bodyguard is very unsettling."

I felt like an ogre. Maybe I shouldn't have been so direct in front of Liz. Maybe I was the one being overly protective, but I didn't think so. My instincts told me there was a lot more to this mess than ginger snaps.

As the waiter handed us menus, I complimented Clovis for adding Moira to his team. She'd stepped in with Liz at the right time, already beginning to build trust. I caught myself watching Moira as they spoke.

"Was she here during Woody's hearing?" I asked Clovis in a whisper.

"No. She was in Detroit until just a few weeks ago. She was a real find. She went straight from school to patrolling the streets. I'm lucky she needed a job and was willing to come to Little Rock. Her credentials all check out. What you see is what you get."

During dinner we talked about tomorrow's logistics. Micki would take the lead, I'd keep quiet. This strategy went against my grain but, given Dub's animosity, was absolutely the right thing to do. Micki and

I hoped to meet with Doug early, but we doubted we'd have enough time to do more than get him into a clean suit when he walked off the plane.

The judge for tomorrow's arraignment was the Honorable Wade Houston. A former FBI Agent and assistant U.S. attorney, he'd been on the bench for eight years, his views and rulings consistently both conservative and pro-government. He believed in a "rocket docket"—no delays in hearings or trials. The government was usually given tremendous leeway in presenting its case, while many a defense lawyer threw up his hands after the first day. We were not only going up against the power of the U.S. Government; we were also facing a "hanging judge" as far as granting defense motions and sentencing. Micki said most defense lawyers who drew Judge Houston usually called the prosecution and took whatever was offered. Since we couldn't talk to either Dub or our client, we didn't have this option.

Micki warned Liz that that the eyes of the judge, the prosecutors, and the press would be focused on her as well as on Doug and that she should dress carefully for the part. Moira would sit beside her, sans weaponry. Dub had been drumming up press all weekend, so the courtroom would be packed. It would also be full of Doug's students and colleagues. I expected nothing less than a circus.

The last thing on tonight's agenda was for Micki to go over what to expect at a bond hearing. Micki figured Dub would try to punish the Stewarts by arguing for a large bond. If a defendant doesn't have the money to post bond on his own, he has to purchase a bond that can cost up to ten percent of the bond's face amount. A million dollar bond could cost the Stewarts one hundred thousand dollars, money they'd never get back. Fortunately, Liz had liquid assets in her own right, and her sizable trust meant she probably wouldn't have to go through a bondsman. The downside was that Dub was likely to use Liz's wealth as a reason to ask for an even higher bond, arguing that Liz had plenty of money to help Doug flee the country. Prosecutors love to put defendants and their families between a rock and a hard place.

After Micki finished, Moira asked, "Is there any possibility they won't produce Dr. Stewart tomorrow? If he's in Oklahoma City tonight, can they get him back in time?"

Liz looked at me, chewing on her bottom lip. "Can that happen?"

Micki answered, "Well, Liz, they can't have an arraignment without him. He still has some constitutional rights. I've already prepared a habeas if they try another trick like they did today. Frankly, I don't think he's in Oklahoma at all. Dub's just jacking us around."

What could Dub have up his sleeve?

MONDAY

April 21, 2014

16

I SPENT A restless night constantly checking the bedside clock, willing its digits to change. Just before seven, I finally put on jeans and went downstairs for breakfast, gathering the *Democrat* from the pile on the front desk. Egg yolk or pancake syrup invariably makes their mark on my shirtfront, so I try not to wear courtroom clothes to breakfast. Sure enough, the arraignment had made page one, all but repeating Dub's press release.

I had just ordered when Clovis sat down, bearing both a large plate of biscuits and gravy from the buffet and the printed e-mails Maggie had sent. Between bites he briefed me on the logistics for the morning. Liz and Moira would ride with us; we'd meet Micki in the courtroom. The deputy marshal in Dub's office had told him we couldn't see Doug until he was brought into the courtroom. *What was the point? Why deny me access to my client?* I knew Micki planned to file a protest with the judge, but I expected a less-than-sympathetic ear.

Plates clean, we finished our coffee and walked into the lobby just as Liz and Moira stepped out of the elevator. I was relieved to see Liz dressed very conservatively in a grey suit and fairly low heels. She had her hair pulled back with a scarf at the nape of her neck. Gone were her Rolex watch, her large aquamarine ring, and her showy diamond engagement ring. She wore only her gold wedding band and small pearl earrings. She gave a little twirl and said, "All ready for court, counsel."

"Perfect, absolutely perfect," I responded. She looked genuinely pleased, and again I wondered what made her tick.

ON THE WAY to the courthouse, I learned that Moira had set up a chair outside Liz's room for the night, but Liz would have none of it. She insisted that Moira sleep in the other bed, and they had stayed up late talking. Liz needed a friend right now, someone to talk to besides her lawyers. Families of the accused have a rough time. They're in a sort of limbo, no one's responsibility. Frequently, even when the lawyers win, the process itself causes permanent psychological damage to the family.

We arrived at the courthouse as Micki was stepping out of her car, Paul in watchful tow. Together we ran the gauntlet of the ravenous press and courtroom security. The sterile courtroom looked like most every other federal courtroom across the country: a large room with a judge's bench, seats for a jury, and two large tables, one for the defendant and one for the prosecution. Seating behind the rail allowed for about fifty spectators, if that.

Liz sat with Moira in the first row, which Maroney had reserved for family. They looked pretty lonely. Micki went back to the judge's chambers to tell his clerk we were there, and Clovis left to ask the marshals if we could meet with Doug for a few minutes. The press traipsed in, followed by a clearly frustrated Clovis.

"The deputy marshal was a real jerk, gave me the usual line: the prisoner is unavailable, and if we have a problem we should take it up with Dub. Of course, Dub is meeting with his 'people' and can't be disturbed."

"Why am I not surprised? Did he at least say Doug is here? Could you see Doug in the holding cell?" I asked.

"They wouldn't let me anywhere near the holding cell. I asked him specifically if Doug was here. He didn't even blink, and said 'All questions should be addressed to Mr. Blanchard.'"

Micki had returned in time for his last comments. I looked at her, silently willing her not to erupt. For the time being, she kept her cool.

The judge's clerks, court reporter, and bailiff filed into the courtroom, but still no Dub. As the clock hit nine o'clock the courtroom door opened with a flourish. In walked U.S. Attorney Dub Blanchard, a man of middling height, thinning hair that fell short of a high forehead, and a toothy grin. He wasn't actually fat—my daughter Beth had once called him the "Pillsbury Doughboy." He was followed by an army of assistants who took up the entire prosecution table and most of the row just behind the rail. They lugged in what looked to me like a lot of files for an arraignment. Dub strolled around the courtroom smiling and shaking hands. He finally glanced our way, turned his back, and joined his assistants.

As soon as the courtroom calmed down we heard, "All rise."

A fully-robed Judge Wade Houston entered the courtroom. He stood a little less than six feet tall, had a jutting jaw, and brown hair that looked like it had been razor cut, styled, and sprayed in place only moments earlier. Without a smile or a word to anyone, he sat down and frowned heavily.

"We are here in the matter of the United States versus Douglas Stewart. Who represents the United States?" His tone made clear that he thought this proceeding was a huge pain in the ass.

Dub jumped up. "I do, your Honor. Wilbur Blanchard, your Honor." He began to introduce his staff, but the judge waved him back down.

"Who appears for the defendant?" Judge Houston asked.

Micki rose and said, "Micki Lawrence and Jack Patterson, your Honor." I stood up.

Before Houston could say a word, Dub stood, paused gravely, and said, "Your Honor, before the court allows Mr. Patterson to enter his appearance, the United States would like to be heard. We object to his appearance and request that the court reserve any ruling on our objection until it can be thoroughly researched and briefed."

Oh, good grief. Dub really didn't like me, nor I him, but this was ridiculous.

The judge looked puzzled. I remained standing.

"Your Honor, I am aware that Mr. Patterson is a licensed lawyer in the District of Columbia, but the United States sees no reason why this court should allow a lawyer, not licensed in this state and not admitted to this court, to appear before his qualifications, integrity, and motives have been scrutinized. Ms. Lawrence can handle the matter before the court. She doesn't need some DC lawyer who's looking for publicity. To our knowledge, no motion has been filed requesting he be admitted by reciprocity and, when it is, it should be briefed. Might I suggest that if Mr. Patterson persists we delay this matter until the court sets a briefing schedule on this issue? The United States would need at least thirty days to respond to any motion for admission once it is filed."

Dub had played his first card. He wanted to delay my representing Doug for as long as possible, probably until the case was over. He was playing hardball. Fortunately, I knew how to play this game quite well.

"Your Honor, may I speak?" I said in my most respectful tone. The judge nodded. I didn't give Dub a chance to object.

"Mr. Blanchard remembers a time last year when I appeared in Circuit Judge Fitzgerald's court and had not yet been admitted to this state's bar. In that case, I had to enter my appearance by way of a motion supported by both my co-counsel and the prosecutor. Since that time, however, I have been admitted to this state's bar. My bar number is 2013-73. I have also been admitted as a lawyer in good standing in this federal district and in this circuit. I believe the respective clerks will verify that my dues are current. If the court will allow me to approach the bench, I have copies of those licenses. I apologize for not providing these to Mr. Blanchard prior to this hearing, but I had no reason to believe he would be so poorly advised."

After last year, I'd applied to be admitted on the off-chance Micki and I might handle another case together. Dub turned bright red and threw the papers I handed him at one of his assistants.

The judge took over. His face reflected his displeasure with both of us.

"Okay, that's settled. Let's get on to the business at hand. Bailiff, bring the defendant into the courtroom."

I sat down. Still no sign of Doug.

Dub, still standing, took a deep breath, almost busting his shirt buttons. "Your Honor, the defendant is not available."

I knew it. I knew it.

Micki was on her feet. The judge's gavel failed to quiet the gallery.

It took a moment to restore order. Finally, he said, "Sit down, Ms. Lawrence. You'll get your turn. Counsel, I hope you can explain."

Still miffed by my presence, Dub smirked at Micki, then turned to the judge. "Your Honor, as there are members of the press in the courtroom, I want to be careful what I say." Dub knew exactly how to get the media's full attention. "The defendant was in custody at the local jail, but was involved in an altercation Saturday evening that necessitated moving him to a more secure environment."

Micki shoved her chair back, but Judge Houston stopped her with a glare.

"That's all well and good, Mr. Blanchard, but why, pray tell, isn't he in my courtroom today? Where is he?" His scowl took in all of us, as though we were somehow in cahoots.

All eyes focused on him, Dub looked around and paused. I had to admit he had some natural acting ability.

"Because of certain facts which might jeopardize this case and even our national security, I cannot disclose his location in open court." I so wanted to wipe that smirk off his puffy face.

The courtroom exploded. Judge Houston let the crowd work off its surprise for a moment before gaveling them into silence. I kept my hand firmly on Micki's bouncing knee to keep her in her seat. Dub waited until the gallery had calmed down.

"Your Honor, the United States has filed its pleadings under seal to begin a process that is consistent with the national security interests of the United States. Your Honor has the requisite security clearances to review the pleadings. After you review them you'll understand why we're compelled to be so circumspect. I apologize for inconveniencing the court, but you will soon understand the need for secrecy."

Holy shit. We had gone from ginger snaps and marijuana to a full-scale national security alert. Judge Houston didn't blink an eye. He had probably been briefed in chambers and was ready for Dub's histrionics.

"Well, in that case, Mr. Blanchard, it appears there is nothing left for me to do today." The judge raised his gavel.

I removed my hand from her knee, and Micki shot up. "Your Honor. May I be heard, please?"

"Of course, Ms. Lawrence, but I'm not sure what, if anything can be done. The United States has taken Dr. Stewart into custody. They are holding him at an unidentified location as a national security risk and have filed motions under seal. What do you expect me to do before I read what they've filed?"

"Your Honor, we wish to file a habeas motion immediately. Dr. Stewart is a U.S. citizen and has certain rights. He is hardly a threat to national security," she said flatly.

"I'll consider your motion and the government's response and rule on it expeditiously. I'm not known for sitting on my hands." His face and voice were stone cold.

Micki replied, "Of course, Your Honor. But this case began as a simple drug case, and now Mr. Blanchard tells us it's a matter of national security. We've had no access to our client or to whatever has been filed under seal. Can we at least see what is so secret? I'll agree to any type of protective order the government wants, but I can't defend my client if I don't even know the charges. Surely I should be allowed to meet him."

The judge looked at Dub, "Well, Counsel?"

"I realize that Ms. Lawrence is frustrated, but this matter calls for specific procedures. Other federal courts have approved these procedures to protect the nation's interest. Among other things, the defendant's counsel will need to undergo a background check to receive a security clearance before she can have access to her client or what we have filed. She will have every opportunity to seek a security clearance, but until she does she can't see either her client or what we have filed."

"You're denying a U.S. citizen the right to counsel and the knowledge of the charges brought against him? Has the Constitution been torn to shreds?" Micki blew a gasket.

"Enough, Ms. Lawrence. This court is familiar with the procedures that have been approved in other jurisdictions. I've attended a training session at the administrative office of the U.S. Courts on this very issue. I'll read what's been filed and rule expeditiously. Mr. Blanchard is not out of line so far. I assure you that this matter will not sit on the corner of my desk. Is there anything else?"

I waited while Micki sat down, shuffling papers to cover her frustration.

"Your Honor, may I offer a suggestion?" I stood up.

"Mr. Patterson."

"I'm not privy to what Mr. Blanchard has filed, but he has just made it clear that defense counsel will be subjected to a thorough background check in order to receive a security clearance before we can proceed."

The judge said. "That's my understanding as well, Counsel."

"Thank you, Your Honor. In that case, I ask you to grant us immediate access to both our client and what has been filed. Ms. Lawrence and I already have the highest code word clearance given by the U.S. Department of Justice. We have a jet standing by to go wherever they're holding our client." A rising hum of surprise rose through the room.

"You're lying," Dub barked, his face dark red. "Your Honor, Mr. Patterson has not worked for the government in the last fifteen years, and Ms. Lawrence works strictly in Pulaski County. How could they have a current code word clearance? I suggest Mr. Patterson is in contempt of this court and should be permanently barred from representing Dr. Stewart."

Houston replied, "Mr. Blanchard, I'll decide who's in contempt in my court. Mr. Patterson, Counsel makes a serious charge."

I did my best to stifle a grin. Micki kept a poker face. This would be fun.

"Your Honor, with all due respect, once again Mr. Blanchard is mistaken." I handed the documents Micki had been shuffling to both Judge Houston and Dub. "I give you copies of a letter from the Department of Justice dated yesterday that affirms the current status and level of our code word security clearance. These documents should satisfy any concerns this court or the United States may have. I renew my request to see my client. His wife is concerned for his well-being."

For the first time, I saw Judge Houston smile.

"You came prepared, Counsel."

"Always best to be ready, Your Honor." I returned his smile.

Staring at the letters, Dub interjected. "This document is dated yesterday—a Sunday. I'm not prepared to stipulate to its authenticity."

The judge looked perplexed. I'd had enough.

"Your Honor, I have been a lawyer in the courts of the United States for over twenty years. I've never submitted a false document or a forgery to a court in my life, and I'm not about to now. I was promised access to Dr. Stewart yesterday by U.S. Marshal Bill Maroney. He told me yesterday that Mr. Blanchard had moved my client out of state. When I tried to contact Mr. Blanchard, his deputy told me he was unavailable, even though I could see him watching me through his office window.

"I suspected then that Mr. Blanchard was up to no good. At his press conference about this case and during his many television appearances Mr. Blanchard has used the words 'national security' every chance he could, so I called the attorney in charge of security clearances at Main Justice. Ms. Lawrence and I are both counsel in a matter that required us to obtain code word security clearances almost a year ago. The official at Main Justice agreed to send me verification of our status overnight, and as you can see, it came in to my hotel at eight o'clock this morning, central time. I don't lie, and I don't manufacture false documents."

Turning to Dub I said, "If Mr. Blanchard has evidence to the contrary, let him produce it here and now. These are games for children, Mr. Prosecutor." I felt Micki's hand on my arm this time. I was grandstanding, but it felt good.

Dub sputtered wordlessly. His face was very red, and I wondered idly if he should be taking blood pressure meds. The judge rescued him. "Cool down, Mr. Blanchard. I'll give you three days to determine the authenticity of this letter. If it is what it purports to be, I expect an apology to Counsel."

Fat chance of that.

"This turn of events is certainly unexpected. I'll review what has been filed under seal and rule on everything by the end of the week."

Micki began to rise, but he glowered her down.

"That includes any habeas you file, Ms. Lawrence. Mr. Patterson, I'm certainly aware of your need to speak with your client. Am I right in assuming that you're willing to go to him wherever he may be?"

"You are, Your Honor."

"This is not pertinent to my ruling, but do you intend to remain in Little Rock, Mr. Patterson, or should I contact Ms. Lawrence with anything that comes up? Does she have full authority on this case?"

"Your Honor, Ms. Lawrence is lead counsel. My role is only temporary." Houston raised his eyebrows, but let it go.

"Thank you, I appreciate that clarification. If there's nothing further, this court is adjourned."

17

WE REGROUPED IN Micki's office. Frustrated, angry, and totally disorganized, we tried to make sense out of what had just happened. Liz sat quietly at a small table by the window, idly twirling a strand of hair.

The office phones rang constantly with reporters asking Micki or me to comment. Clovis and Paul tried to keep the media off the front lawn and from coming around back. Micki's orders changed every five seconds.

Pulling a beer from the fridge in the kitchen, I returned to her office and sat down quietly across from Liz. It wasn't long before the mayhem played itself out. Micki looked at me expectantly.

I started. "Okay, we've got lots to talk about. Nothing will happen for the next few days, so we have time to get organized. So let's take a deep breath and regroup.

"First, Liz, I promise you we'll find out where they're holding Doug. His safety is our first priority. Neither Micki nor I will rest until we know he's okay. You need to focus on getting back into a daily routine. I know it's hard, but you can't panic."

Squaring her shoulders, she looked up. "Don't worry—I won't collapse. I think I'll go to Memphis for a few days, spend some time with my dad. I can be back in a couple of hours. Does Moira have to go with me?" She put up a good front, but looked exhausted.

"I think a visit with your dad is a good idea. Leave security up to Clovis," I answered, no longer surprised by her composure.

"Micki, you and I need to figure out how to divide the work, and I need to go to D.C. for a day or two while we wait on the judge. I want to talk to Peggy Fortson, in person. I also want to meet with a couple of lawyers I know who represent prisoners in Guantanamo. They'll know how the Justice Department uses the Patriot Act and the words 'national security' to avoid client access and, more to the point, how to get around such tactics. Clovis, I still need you to find out what you can about Little Rock's drug suppliers. Focus on that. Dub is threatening 'national security,' but right now we still have a drug case to defend."

Debbie walked in, handed Liz what looked like straight bourbon, and said casually, "Micki, Jim Bullock's on line one. He'd like to come by here in, say, ten minutes."

"Tell him to come on," Micki responded with a shrug.

Moira caught my glance toward Liz. Quick to catch on, she roused Liz, and they left quietly, Liz clutching her bourbon. I didn't want Liz anywhere near a prosecutor. They'd hardly gotten through the door when Deputy Assistant Bullock emerged from a black Buick that had quietly pulled up to the curb. His driver looked around lazily then lit a cigarette, and leaned against the car door.

Bullock shrugged off Micki's offer of coffee or iced tea, and we all sat down stiffly. After a few pleasantries, he got down to business, handing Micki a large manila envelope.

"This is a copy of a pleading we've filed under seal. Since it doesn't involve national security, I can let you have it. I'm sure it will come as no surprise. We're instituting civil forfeiture proceedings against all of Dr. and Mrs. Stewart's assets, or at least most of them—their cars, home, furniture, bank accounts, and his research at the University."

I blurted out, "You're going to take their home before Doug's even been charged?"

He seemed to find my naiveté amusing. "Micki will tell you we have a right to seize any asset that has any connection with illegal activities even if we never formally charge Dr. Stewart or anyone else. But he'll be charged all right. You needn't worry."

Micki managed a grim nod.

"I don't have to provide you with even this, since the proceeding is technically against the property itself, not the Stewarts. But I thought I might use this delivery to suggest that we are open to resolving the forfeiture proceeding without protracted litigation. I don't need an answer today, but I thought you and Micki might want to discuss it."

Micki's knee began to bounce, and I decided to intervene before she threw him out on his ear.

"What do you have in mind?"

"An argument might be made that the home belongs to Ms. Stewart if her money was used to acquire the real estate. The same goes for the art and furnishings. Of course, the land itself was used to grow a great deal of marijuana, and both the house and the out building contained plants and seedlings, so who owns the home and whose money was used to acquire it may not make any difference. As you know, even an unwitting owner can lose his property if it was used in an illegal enterprise."

Lesson learned—you'd better know your gardener.

"Anyway, I can't extend a formal offer, but I think the U. S. Government might be willing to see its way clear to letting Mrs. Stewart keep her house and furnishings if we can avoid any protracted litigation over the remaining assets."

The non-offer seemed to be too good to be true—there had to be a catch. Micki managed to control her face, didn't say a word. She knew this offer made little sense from the prosecution's standpoint.

"Is your proposal conditioned on some guilty plea by Dr. Stewart? How can we consider such a proposal without our client's willing participation and involvement?" I asked.

"No, this would be a settlement of the asset forfeiture case only. I know we're going to be at war for a long time over Dr. Stewart and his criminal liability. But I'm suggesting we might be able to settle the matters on the periphery. In fact, I think we can commit to no criminal charges against Mrs. Stewart, if that helps in your deliberation. You have to agree, she has some exposure." Bullock smiled.

He had just offered to let Liz keep her home and her belongings without requiring a plea from Doug. And he wouldn't charge Liz. Very generous.

"What's the catch? Dub won't give me the time of day. You have Doug hidden away under the blanket of national security. Yet you've made what appears to be a reasonable offer, one I will definitely present to our client if I ever get to see him. Why?" I asked.

"Our task force is focused on drug trade. Local law enforcement uses asset forfeiture to fund their office. We don't need to. Our funding comes from the Drug Czar's budget. We only use asset forfeiture to seize money and assets that either fund or provide logistical support for illegal activities. We don't use forfeiture to be punitive or to buy new radios or squad cars. Ms. Stewart's home wasn't a meth house or used to sell medical marijuana. You and Dub may have your personal differences, but our operation adheres to our mission. Like I said, I don't need your answer today, so talk to Mrs. Stewart and get back to me." He handed me a card with his cell number handwritten on the back.

Micki wasn't going to let him leave without trying to see Doug. Especially since we thought we might be dealing with a reasonable man.

"How can we make a deal on the civil forfeiture if we can't speak with our client? When can we see Dr. Stewart?"

He smiled, almost ignoring her. "My compliments, by the way, for predicting the need for security clearances. You impressed Judge Houston as well as most of the rest of us. Dub, well, not so much."

Turning back to Micki he continued, "My guess: the doctor will be made available as soon as Friday by the judge–but where, I can't tell you. Don't hold me to this, but if you really do have a jet, be prepared to use it. That's part of the reason I brought the pleadings over personally. When you see him, be ready to talk along the lines I've proposed."

Micki smiled and pushed a little harder. "While we're not at each other's throats, any chance we might be able to work out something on the criminal side? It is a first offense and contrary to what you may think, he wasn't selling. Maybe along the lines of a supervised release? He's going to lose both his job and his national reputation. Shouldn't that be punishment enough?"

Bullock didn't budge an inch.

"Don't start, Micki. You don't have all the facts. I'll be reasonable when it comes to his wife and her home, but when you get our discovery you'll understand why there'll be no bargains regarding Dr. Stewart. We have good reason to believe he's a threat to national security. I'll be straight with you, and from your reputation, I know you'll do the same. Dr. Stewart is going to prison for a very long time. Don't try to imagine any other outcome." The easy smile was replaced by a cold stare.

Micki appeared to be at a loss, so I stepped in. "I appreciate your candor."

I gave him my contact information, and we spent a few more minutes trying to be pleasant. Closing the door behind him, Micki sat down behind her desk, and I sunk deeply into a well-used armchair.

"Well, that was fun. What do you think?" I asked.

"Liz gets her home, furniture, and a deal not to prosecute. It's too good to be true, especially if they really have the goods on Doug. He gives up a Healy, a truck and personal possessions. Unless he has a lot of cash in the bank, I must be missing something. Let's get Liz to sign a power of attorney so we can access their bank and brokerage account records. I want to be familiar with their finances before we talk to Doug."

"Bullock seemed pretty reasonable. Why is Dub being such an ass? Surely it can't just be his well-known love of me. I'll see what I can dig up in Washington."

"So, you really are going to DC tomorrow?" Micki asked. I was surprised to detect disappointment in her voice.

"Not for long. Like I said, I want to run some traps at Main Justice. Dub is sure to try to get our clearances pulled. I have a feeling that once we've heard what Doug has to say, we'll have plenty of irons in the fire. Guess I'm going to need that desk after all."

She gave me a slow grin. "Sounds good to me, partner."

"Well, at least until we figure out what they've got on Doug. Since when do a few marijuana plants rise to the level of national security? Even a few hundred—either Doug has snookered a lot of people or we have a lot to learn."

"Jack, I don't trust any of them, but we can't ignore the offer. That home is worth a lot. With all that marijuana in the back yard, we don't have a prayer keeping it off the auction block without their offer. Besides, Liz told me it means a lot to her and Doug."

"Maybe so, but she may not feel the same way if Doug is never free to live in it again."

18

MICKI AND I spent the next couple of hours mapping out who would do what over the next few days. Her focus would be to get the appropriate petitions and motions before the court, and mine would be to learn as much as I could about Dub's task force and how to get around the "national security" roadblock so we could access our client and the case against him. In a normal criminal trial the prosecution is required to give the defense all the evidence against their client, including any evidence that might help prove the client's innocence. But this was hardly a normal case, and Dub was using every means in his power to keep us in the dark. All the normal rules of law seemed to have been suspended. We spent the last half hour talking about how to deal with Bullock's offer. I needed to plant the seed with Liz before she went to Memphis.

Moira had taken Liz to work out, and was making arrangements for her protection while she was in Memphis. Liz's plane didn't leave until eight, so I was going to meet both women at the hotel around five. I'd leave for DC in the morning, returning Friday, unless we got access to Doug earlier.

Micki asked if I could handle the meeting with Liz without her. She wanted to spend some time with Eric, who apparently was feeling a bit deserted.

"Sounds like Eric is a permanent fixture," I commented.

"It's getting pretty serious. We have the same interests, the sex is beyond great, and when I'm not with him I find myself wishing I were. He's too possessive though—you know I'm overly sensitive about feeling owned. Then again, I get jealous when some nurse flirts with him at the hospital, so, yes, it's getting serious." She gave me a wry smile.

"My advice—and, yes, I know you haven't asked for it—is to let this thing with Eric run its course. See where it goes. Allow yourself to be vulnerable." I cleared my throat a bit before continuing. "But enough with the personal stuff. I'm off to see Liz. Anything you want me to tell her?"

"She needs to take the Bullock deal. Civil forfeiture laws are the hardest part of being a defense attorney these days. The government can seize everything the accused owns, and even if the verdict's 'not guilty,' they don't give it back. I still don't get why Mr. Reasonable has offered to let Liz keep her home, with immunity no less. It doesn't make sense—nothing in this case does—but we can't look a gift horse in the mouth. The cars may have some strong sentimental value, but it's hard to argue about the rest. His lab equipment can't be worth much. If his research is about marijuana, we don't have a chance in hell of convincing anyone that it isn't part of an illegal activity.

"I say get her permission to accept it, and use it as leverage. I'll tell Bullock we have a deal subject to meeting with Doug. Maybe that will break things loose."

I'd been thinking along the same lines. "You're right; let's go with it. I'll explain it to Liz. I smell a skunk, but it's probably just Dub's . . . well, his aftershave."

Micki laughed. "You're starting to think like a criminal lawyer."

She walked me to the door, where Clovis was waiting to drive me to the hotel.

Liz and Moira were perched on barstools, Liz sipping on a large martini. She'd pulled her hair back loosely and was dressed casually in jeans and a crisp, white shirt.

"Any news? Is Doug safe?" Liz asked nervously.

No games this time, not even a hello. The bar was still mostly empty, so I pulled up a stool and ordered a glass of wine.

"Well, we know he's in a federal facility, and they're pretty good about protecting their charges. If he's in Oklahoma City, at worst he'll be in a cell with one other guy. They'll share a bunk bed, toilet, and a desk. During the daytime he'll be allowed to go out into a big central area with the other inmates. He'll have three passable meals a day, and as long as he doesn't get into an argument, he's safe—much more so than if he was in a county jail. The worst part is the boredom." Not exactly what my friend had told me about Oklahoma City, but there was no sense in worrying Liz at this point.

"Sounds pretty miserable," Liz said into her drink, absently poking the olive with a straw.

"It is, but he's safe, and that's the important thing."

Moira jumped in. "Liz, he'll be okay. If he has to be locked up, a federal facility really is a whole lot better than the county jail." Her soothing tones were out of keeping with her blunt appearance.

Time to change the subject. "So, Liz, you still have family in Memphis?"

Her face lit up slightly, and she gave me a hint of a smile. "Dad and my stepmother are still alive and kickin'. My stepmother plays a lot of mah-jongg with her friends and takes classes at the Culinary School—lucky Dad! He still goes to the Exchange every day, although what he does I haven't a clue."

Moira asked, "Does your dad know anything about what's going on here?"

"I'm sure they've read the papers. I feel bad–he's tried to call a couple of times. That's why I need to go back—they need to hear what's happening from me, in person. Dad will try to convince me to move back, but no way. Can you imagine what Memphis would be like? I mean, a woman whose husband is in prison for selling dope? Then again, it might be fun." Liz laughed and drained her glass. She seemed more at ease—I hoped it wasn't just the gin.

I hadn't really taken to Liz when I met her in DC. Having grown up in an old area of Memphis, I had a built-in prejudice about people from Germantown whose daddies were "in cotton," but she'd grown on me quite a bit the last couple of days.

She turned to Moira. "You're driving, right?"

Moira nodded.

"Good. I'm going to have another martini, then let's order something to eat. Jack's about to give me some bad news, and I want to hear it on a full stomach with something to ease the pain."

Nobody could say she wasn't perceptive. I didn't realize I tele-graphed my blows. We talked idly about life in Little Rock until the waiter finally brought her another martini accompanied by a trio of Texas Caviar, hummus, and deviled eggs as well as a dish of spicy Pimento cheese with crackers and flatbread.

"My father, Conner Flowers, is likely to call you after I tell him what really happened. He'll mean well. He and Doug always got along, although he still thinks I should have married Bud Potter, the full-back I dated in high school. Good thing I didn't. Bud came out of the closet about ten years ago. Dad still refuses to believe it."

"Of course I'll talk to him, Liz. I look forward to it. But you were right; we need to talk about something else that's come up."

"Here it comes. Shoot."

"As you know, an assistant U.S. attorney who works with Dub came by after you left. He suggested that, although they fully intend to pros-ecute Doug, they're willing to negotiate a deal regarding the asset forfeiture. They're willing to let you keep your house and furnishings and, better yet, have agreed not to bring any charges against you."

"Well, that wasn't so bad. What do I have to do? Give that weasel Blanchard a blow job?"

I wanted to hug her, but I pretended shock.

"Sorry, Jack. I forget how old-fashioned you are. Seriously, why wouldn't I take that deal?" She smiled. "I'm not ruling out the blow job if that's what that oily bastard wants. I'd just have to have a few more of these." She pointed to the martini and laughed loud enough that heads turned.

I shook my head. "Nothing like that. Actually, all they want are Doug's cars, his lab, and his research. We might have an argument over the cars unless they have pictures of Doug dealing out of the Healy or carrying plants in the pick-up. But if he did use the mar-ijuana in his research, it's hard to argue it's not part of the illegal operation. It's not like it has any value. He won't be able to continue his work even if we can get him a plea deal."

Her face softened as she reflected. "I bought Doug that Healy after he won the 'DeWitt.' I think he was more excited about the car than being named Outstanding Chemist in North America. He'll be heartbroken, but I'll buy him another one. Or would the government maybe sell it back to me? The pick-up isn't worth a thousand bucks, but he loved driving it to class and football games. What is it with men and pick-ups? They're uncomfortable as hell."

"Well, they're . . . well, honestly I don't know. But I do know that if they'll be content with a couple of clunkers and his research, we can't complain. Maybe Dub wants to look magnanimous, put away the bad guy without any appearance of overstepping."

She gave me a withering look.

I continued. "Sorry, but maybe that's what he wants the public to think. I don't trust Dub any farther than I can throw him, but we can't afford to let cynicism get in the way. Keeping you free of any criminal charges is a huge deal. As often as not, prosecutors indict the wife for the sole purpose of getting the accused husband to plead. Just think about it—we don't have to decide tonight."

Moira reminded us it was time to get Liz to the airport, and I invited her to join Clovis and me when she returned.

I walked them out of the bar and said to Liz, "I promise I'll be back to meet with Doug just as soon as they let me. I'll tell him about the deal they've offered, and if he's all right with it, we'll talk again."

She hesitated. "If Doug says 'yes,' go ahead. You don't need to ask me again. But, let's see what he thinks. The house has no value if Doug isn't there. The house, the furnishings, what happens to me—I'd swap it all for Doug."

On first meeting Liz, I wouldn't have figured loyalty to be one of her major characteristics. I usually trusted my first impressions, but in this case, I was happy to revise my opinion.

"Jack, talk to Doug, tell him I love him, and no matter what, don't let him compromise to protect me. If the government is up to no good, he'll know why. You don't know him like I do. He's much smarter and tougher than those bastards think he is, and the two of you make one formidable team. He told me things would get rough, but I didn't want to hear about it, didn't want to know. Well, my head's out of the sand now. I didn't marry him for the short haul; so if keeping him means losing a few sticks of furniture, so be it. No deals, Jack, without you talking to him. That's my bottom line. Got it?"

"Got it." I gave her a grin, a kiss on the cheek, and said, "He's got one hell of a partner. You be careful."

19

IT FELT GOOD to settle into my room at the Armitage and relax. Pondering the different faces of Liz, I had just opened the bottle of wine in the ice bucket when Clovis opened the door. He always had a key to my room, and this time, had no reason to knock.

"I'm not up for going out tonight. Get yourself something to drink. Let's order room service and talk about what's next." I tossed my shoes in the corner, plopped onto the sofa, and stuck my feet up on the coffee table.

Clovis grabbed a beer from the mini fridge and ordered us both guacamole and bacon cheeseburgers with extra crispy fries. I like to think I enjoy fine food as much as the next man, but sometimes nothing beats a good cheeseburger. He took a pretty good pull, looked at the bottle and said, "I guess you'll be busy trying to reach your client. So while Liz is out of town, I'll ask Moira to find out what sort of research Dr. Stewart was doing at UALR. Maybe there's another professor or a graduate student who knew what he was up to."

"You seem to have a lot of faith in Moira."

"Well, if she lives up to the recommendations from her superiors, she'll fit right in. Her immediate boss in Detroit said she's tough as they come, good instincts for her age. I'm happy to have Liz lie low in Memphis for a while—it'll be good for her and good for us. It frees up Moira and, well, Liz makes me nervous."

"I noticed."

He didn't take the bait, so I let it go. The cheeseburgers arrived and we wolfed them down. We caught up on Ben, the owner of the best barbecue restaurant in the South, talked about the NFL season, and how the Razorback baseball team seemed to have run out of luck again this year. Moira knocked on the door just as I was starting to yawn. She had changed out of her blue suit into a sweater and jeans. She glanced at our almost empty plates, and I offered to order her dinner.

"No, that's okay. I got a bite on the way back from the airport."

She smiled at Clovis. "Am I off duty, too?" He nodded, and I poured her a glass of Cabernet. She reached into the hobo bag hanging from her shoulder and handed her Glock to Clovis. She caught the look on my face.

"I have a rule. If I have a drink, I don't carry. And it's not often I get to have drinks with two handsome men, even if we are talking shop."

"Sounds like a good rule to me."

She'd let her hair down and put on a little make-up—I found myself looking at her curiously as Clovis took the gun and stowed it in his briefcase. The moment passed in a flash and we were back to business.

"We've got to get a handle on Dub's claim that Doug was selling to kids. If it's true, his distributor has to be local. Right? If you two can't learn anything on campus, dig deeper. If Doug is as evil as they say, he has to have made enemies, stuck his nose in somebody's business. Or maybe somebody's looking for a new supplier."

Clovis looked thoughtful. "Dub's brought in a slew of DEA agents. Agents usually don't talk out of school, but I bet they all hang out at a bar somewhere, and where there's booze, there's gonna be talk. I've got some guys who can get a story out of a rock. Lawyers are no different. They love to talk about themselves—you just got to get 'em going. Give us a few days, and we'll know if Dr. Stewart's the only target or if there's more to Dub's task force than the garden in the Stewart's back yard. It's not like we're dealing with a thousand acres in a national park."

I thought about it for a minute, picking at the last few fries on my plate.

"If Doug was sneaking marijuana onto the campus to perform experiments, somebody had to have known. Moira, talk to his students, and find out if he held seminars. Seminar students get pretty close to their professor. Maybe someone helped unload the stuff."

I handed Clovis a list of Angie's colleagues at NIH who had worked with Doug, asking him to work with Maggie to contact them. I made a mental note to ask my daughter if she and Angie had ever talked about Doug. Moira said she had a friend in Ann Arbor who could ask around. Ideas were coming quick now.

"Clovis, tell me a little bit about this Novak guy and his connection with Debbie. Could he have any connection to Doug? Is his operation something we need to worry about?"

"Novak is trash. He's evil, ruthless, and as immoral as they come. I hope you never meet him. He looks like what you might expect– big, burly, lots of bling around his neck, and bad teeth. Rumor has it he was an Olympic wrestler who ended up as a bodyguard for a Russian mobster in Miami. When his benefactor met an untimely death, Novak somehow landed in Arkansas. Who knows how or why? He pays a percentage to Miami, but otherwise he runs his own organization throughout the Middle South and Southwest. Why it's based here is anybody's guess. He's got people as far east as Atlanta and as far west as Amarillo. Rumor has it that something recently happened to his brother, and now he's trying to go legit. But I'm not buying.

"Your friend Sam can fill you in on his local connections—they're surprisingly good. Sam's been able to limit his activities a bit, but he's pretty much untouchable. His major sources of income are gambling and prostitution—he has an unlimited pipeline of girls coming in from Eastern Europe. His recruiters promise them work, husbands, and the American dream. When they get here, he makes sure they end up totally dependent on drugs and on him. He doesn't care how old they are or where they end up— they're just business to him. Makes the Godfather look like a fairy godmother.

"So, yeah, you should be worried about Novak. But I don't see any connection with the professor. Novak doesn't normally deal in marijuana except as an accommodation. If it were heroin, prescription drugs, or white powder, maybe—but not weed. Novak makes really good money supplying heroin to his patrons when they run out of painkillers. Any kid on a corner can get weed. It's not worth the risk to Novak, not enough profit."

Moira followed, "Novak will order a kill at the drop of a hat. He has a rep as far north as Detroit. You don't need to cross him, Jack."

TUESDAY MORNING

April 22, 2014

20

When I stepped out of the cab at Hodges Air Center early the next morning, Walter's plane was gassed up and ready to go. Clovis didn't approve of my transportation choice. He wanted one of his men to drive me to the airport—didn't like taking chances, but I insisted. No sense having one of his men get up that early. I dozed to the hum of the engines during the flight, and woke a couple of hours later as we landed in DC.

A twenty-minute Metro ride landed me in my office, drinking good coffee and going through my e-mails. Maggie walked in carrying a cup of tea, and I was about to fill her in on my week when Rose knocked abruptly.

"Clovis Jones is on line one. He said I should interrupt you." Rose looked worried.

"Clovis, what's up? I've got Maggie on speaker."

"Are you both sitting down? I mean it—I want you to sit down." Maggie carefully put her cup on the corner of my desk. We both knew this couldn't be good. "Micki's disappeared–we're not sure, but we think she may have been kidnapped."

Maggie put her hands to her mouth in shock. I heard myself yelling at Clovis, demanding answers, demanding action. He waited until I ran out of steam.

"Jack, you need to calm down. You need to listen. Here's what we know. Micki spent last night at Eric's. I had Charlie Yates, one of Paul's guys, watching the townhouse, figured Micki would never know. When Charlie didn't call in this morning, Paul went to Eric's place and found Charlie lying in the bushes, barely alive. Paul rushed into the house—the porch door was open. The place was a mess, no sign of either Micki or Eric."

"Okay. I'm calm now." Deep breaths. "When did all this happen?"

"Had to have been right after your plane took off. We found Eric working his ER shift at the hospital. He said Micki was in the shower when he left. He's being questioned by the police, but I believe him."

Clovis didn't sound all that sure about anything. "Charlie's going to make it, but we can't speak with him yet. There's no note. Looks like they grabbed her the moment Eric left. The shower was still on."

"Has anyone checked on Debbie? Could this be Novak's work? Hasn't he always said he'd get revenge?"

"Debbie and Mongo are at the office under guard. Sam definitely thinks it was Novak, and I don't have any reason to think it wasn't."

"I'll be there as soon as I can."

"Jack, there's nothing you can do here. The police and Sam are all over this—my people are working the trail, too. The FBI has been notified. We'll find her. I'll keep you updated."

I couldn't think. "Clovis, I want Debbie guarded twenty-four hours. No exceptions. Contact whoever is protecting Liz: make sure she's okay—don't let them leave her for a minute. I want to talk to Sam. Tell him to call. No matter what it takes, you have to find Micki. Got it?"

"Got it. Keep your phone by your side. Looks like it'll be a long day."

I put my phone in my pocket, determined not to forget it. Maggie eyes were wet, but her voice was firm. "We're going to Little Rock, right now."

"What? You heard Clovis. There's nothing we can do and what's with the 'we?'"

"Do you really think either of us is going to get any work done until Micki's safe? And does it matter? Micki's been kidnapped—if it's not that Novak character, it must be connected with Dr. Stewart. I don't know what we can do, but the answers aren't here."

She was right, of course. I canceled my lunch with Peggy Fortson, and Maggie phoned Walter's pilot. We agreed to meet in at the airport in an hour. I raced home, dumped my dirty clothes on the floor, grabbed some clean ones and was soon on my way back to National. Maggie and Walter, who had come to see her off, were already there. Sam called while we were waiting to board—his attempt at objectivity didn't wash. He sounded both angry and worried, but he couldn't or wouldn't tell me exactly what the police were doing.

Once we'd taken off, I tried to engage Maggie in what had happened at the office since I'd been gone, but neither of us could muster up much interest. My thoughts went to my first meeting with Micki and how we'd bonded as a legal team, playing off each other as we defended Woody Cole. Now she'd been kidnapped. It didn't do to think about what she might be going through, if she wasn't dead already. I put that thought out of my mind quickly.

THE PLANE TAXIED to the exact location it had been less than twelve hours earlier, and I saw Clovis standing by the Tahoe.

"Any news?"

"Not really. Sam is pushing Novak's people hard, but they swear they don't know anything. Novak's in Dallas and has been interviewed by the Dallas Police. No surprise—he's got an airtight alibi. If he's behind it, he's planned it well."

"I don't give a shit who's behind it, we need to find her. What about her boyfriend?" I found it increasingly hard to keep my voice under control.

"The police have been all over him. Yes, they spent the night together. No, they didn't argue or fight—they made love. He didn't do it, Jack. He would have had to get out of bed without waking Micki, go outside, attack Charlie, then come inside and subdue Micki. How would he even know Charlie was watching the house? You think he had the balls to shower while she was unconscious, take her somewhere and dump her, and then show up fresh at work with a big smile on his face? No, I'm sure he's telling the truth. That man's in love with Micki, he's not the kidnapper."

"Okay—I know you're right. This has all the makings of a well-planned abduction, not a lover's quarrel. I want to speak with Eric, but I need to talk to Debbie first. She's our only real link to Novak. It's not that I don't trust Sam, but my gut tells me our time is short, and the police can't move fast enough. Constitutional rights and proper procedures restrain them. I won't interfere, but I'm not going to wait until she's found dead."

My efforts to remain calm had gone out the window.

We found Paul pacing the front porch when we got to Micki's. He looked like hell. Micki abducted, Charlie in intensive care, Debbie almost comatose with fear—it was just too much. Maggie made sympathetic noises, and I suggested he should either go to the hospital or get some rest. He didn't budge.

"Leave him be—he's not going anywhere." Clovis answered for him. "He and Micki are good friends. He's the one who introduced her to Eric after the Pepsi 10K. This thing's as personal to him as it is to the rest of us."

Mongo came out to meet us, and I introduced him to Maggie. Apparently Debbie had gotten hysterical, and he'd given her a couple of Xanax.

"She's resting in Micki's private room–Moira's with her. She's awake now; I think she'll talk to you. But please be gentle—she worships Micki—this is really tough for her." Great—now Mongo was both her physician and her therapist.

I motioned Clovis to follow me. We found Debbie curled up in the day bed. Her face bore the evidence of smeared make-up and tears; you could almost smell her fear. She sat up, looking a little confused, tugging on her blouse as we walked in. From what little I knew, former victims of sex trafficking find it very difficult to talk about what had happened, what they had done. In order to live with the experience, they put it in a mental box and bury it deep. I needed Debbie to talk, to remember.

Before I could say anything, she gulped and blurted, "Oh, Mr. Patterson, I'm so scared. None of this has anything to do with me, does it?" Moira handed her a bottle of Mountain Valley water. She took a sip, shaking so badly she had to clutch it with both hands.

"No, Debbie, none of this is your fault. I know how much Micki means to you and you to her. But we think your old friend Novak may be involved. I need to ask you some questions."

"Oh, God, if it's Novak, it is my fault." Sobbing, she slumped back down onto the pillow.

"Debbie, please stop, please sit up," I said forcefully, and then scolded myself to be patient. I tried to take her hand, but she recoiled, pulling it away.

"Debbie, listen to me. I need your help. Micki needs your help. It could be Novak. We just don't know. We need to find her—that's what matters. Novak is our only lead. I need you to tell me what happened when you first got to Little Rock. How did they keep you in line, and most importantly, where did they take you? This is going to be hard. I know you've tried to forget it all, but your memories may be our best chance of saving her."

She mumbled, "I can't remember much about the early part, except that it was awful. It's just too hard."

"Debbie, I can't imagine how bad it must have been. But it's over now. You have to trust me. Would it be easier to tell me what happened to the other girls?"

Debbie steeled herself and sat up. "Well, Novak's recruiters promised us all pretty much the same thing: an education, a job, and a chance to meet eligible men. Most of us were around sixteen years old, our families were poor, and the dream of coming to America was more than we could resist. We wanted to meet American men, get married and send money home to our families.

"When we got off the plane, we thought we were going to the apartments we'd been promised, but instead they took us to what they called a 'training facility.' They took all our papers, our passports, and our visas, just for safekeeping. They said we needed to be trained for our news jobs and more importantly, how to act and behave like Americans. The rooms were mostly empty except for beds, and the windows were covered with dark shades.

"That first night we were all brought together for a party in the rec room. At first we just stood around, not sure what to do, but there was music, good-looking guys, and lots of food and booze, and they encouraged us to just have fun. They said it was part of our training. Americans partied all the time. So we relaxed, drank, danced, and the next thing I knew I woke up in my room with a big headache. I couldn't remember how I got there.

"Like I said, there was just the bed, a lamp, and a chair. My clothes had been folded on the chair, but that was it. Someone had dressed me in gym pants and a tee shirt. The door was locked. I yelled and banged on it until a woman in a nurse's uniform came in. She told me that the door had been locked for my protection. She said I had gotten out of control—they'd had to sedate me. She said it happened to a lot of girls their first night. I found out later on they'd given me a roofie."

I must have looked confused, because she gave a ghost of a smile and said, "You know, a date rape drug." I managed a weak smile in return, wondering how much Beth knew about "roofies."

"We spent that day in small groups learning to wait tables and flirt with customers, and that night there was another party. They were nice, even gave us manicures and new hairdos. I tried to ask a few questions, but the instructors just laughed, said we needed to get used to the American way of life: good times, music, dancing, booze, and food. Each morning for a week, I woke up in the same empty room. At some point I found an empty syringe on the chair, but by then I didn't care about anything but the next party."

Her story wasn't unexpected, but it wasn't getting me anywhere. She had slumped down with her elbows on her knees, staring at the floor.

"Debbie, are you okay? Can you try to jump ahead?"

She pulled her head up—I could see she was trying to focus. It wasn't easy to be patient.

"Sorry. I've tried so hard to put all this behind me." She took a sip of water from the bottle. "So, one morning one of Novak's men brought me coffee. He said they were going to have to send me back home. He said I had turned into an addict, that I wouldn't make it here and I owed Novak a lot of money. The thought of going back was worse than anything I could think of—how could I face my parents?

"I told them I'd do anything to stay. He gave me a hard time for a while and finally said he'd try to convince Novak to let me stay if I did exactly what he said. Novak knew some very rich and influential men who enjoyed the company of pretty girls like me. I could work as a cocktail waitress in the evening and some of the other girls would teach me how to make men happy. When I learned how to take care of Novak's customers, I could start paying off my debt and even make some 'real money.' I might even meet some rich guy who would pay off my debt to Novak and take me away with him. What choice did I have? "For weeks, I was trained by older girls and the guards how to please men. The vodka and the drugs made the training tolerable."

The room was chilly. She shivered and pulled up her knees to her chest. I didn't want to know what "training" entailed.

"Finally, they said I was ready. At first I worked at a casino in the south part of town, but I quickly graduated to the Quarter, where Novak's best customers gambled and were given 'special treatment.' I serviced some of the richest and most powerful men in Little Rock in that house.

"I never went down to the tables. The customers came to me, sometimes escorted by Novak himself. I was a quick learner and very good at my job. Novak was happy, but I wanted out more than I can tell you. I did my level best to stay off the drugs and booze, but sometimes after a bad night I went back to the drugs just to keep going. After a while, I became numb to what I was doing and what the men did."

Again she stopped, looking up at me. Her eyes were dull, like she'd quit feeling again. I felt like a heel.

"So maybe the rest doesn't matter, but Novak went out of town for a few weeks and he put a real jerk in charge. Novak protected his girls from the real sickos. I know you won't believe me but Novak really took good care of us. He was kind. This guy didn't care what the men wanted to do as long as they paid. What they made us do was awful and sick and before long I fell completely off the wagon, forgot my promises to myself, and didn't care about anything except the drugs and vodka. It didn't take long before my looks suffered, so I was booted down to the projects where for fifty bucks men simply had their way night after night. It didn't matter to me. I just wanted to die."

This was almost impossible to hear. How could this have happened to an innocent teenager hoping for a better life? I couldn't imagine what it cost her to relive it.

"In the projects I wasn't allowed a night off except during my period. At some point my friend Shannon gave me Micki's address. I don't know how I found my way to her doorstep, but I did. You know the rest. Twice since I've gone out with friends, had way too much to drink, and ended up back in the projects. Each time Micki found me and brought me back. I owe her my life."

I asked, "Where was the training center?"

"I don't know. The casino used to be in the Quapaw Quarter, but Novak moved them both after Sam got elected and turned up the heat. Now I hear the casino is somewhere in western Little Rock, maybe Maumelle, where the customers feel safe. Novak knows his best customers don't want to go into the projects at night. The new training center is somewhere near the airport."

"Debbie, try to think about the old training center. Do you remember any landmarks? Please try to remember."

"I remember seeing an old ball field. It was run over with weeds, looked like it hadn't been used in a long time, but like I said, Novak moved it several years ago." I begged her to describe as much as she could remember, and she did her best until she couldn't remember anymore. She looked miserable, pretty well done in. I wanted to fold her into my arms.

"Debbie—I've got to ask. If Novak's behind this, will he kill her?"

Her voice was now very matter-of-fact. "Oh no, Micki's too good-looking for him to waste. He'll treat her like every other woman he owns. He'll fill her full of drugs, brand her, and then offer her to his customers. Micki will draw a hefty price."

Clovis interrupted, his voice shocked. I'd almost forgotten he was there. "Brand her? Like a cow? What do you mean?"

Debbie didn't say a word. She lifted her hair off her neck to reveal a raised scar:

AN

Clovis closed his eyes, Debbie lowered hers, and my stomach turned.

"A plastic surgeon told me he can remove it, but it will be expensive—Blue Cross won't cover it. Micki's offered to pay for it, but I won't let her until I'm sure I'll never go back."

Blue Cross wouldn't pay? I wondered vaguely what sort of insurance plan would cover involuntary human branding.

Debbie brought me out of my fog, her voice rather matter-of-fact.

"If Micki fights back, they'll tie her up and let some of his sick clients have their way until she begs for the drugs. They're animals—believe me, I know. It's much better to cooperate, but knowing Micki, she'll fight, at least for a while. It will only turn the bastards on . . . poor Micki." Her face crumpled, and she began to cry. Moira wrapped her in her arms, muttering soothing sounds. Her eyes were full of pity and strength as she motioned me away.

Clovis and I stepped back into the hall, and I felt both relieved and guilty. I took a breath and let it out quickly. The very air felt lighter.

"Clovis, we've got to go—now. Tell Paul to come with us and get Sam on the phone. Will Debbie be safe with Moira?"

"Safe as houses—don't worry about her." He said a few words to Moira, grabbed Paul, and punched in Sam's number, handing me the phone as we got into the Tahoe.

"Sam, I don't have time to chit-chat. Do you remember a big dark green house around the block from Butler Field?"

"Sure, it's on Winkler—Mr. Kavanaugh's old home, remember? What's up? Where are you?" Sam asked.

"I'm headed there now. Look, I can't explain, just meet me there in fifteen minutes. No sirens. It's just a hunch, but I think the Kavanaugh house was Novak's old training center. It's worth a shot."

"Wait till I get there, Jack. Don't do anything stupid." Sam warned, but I'd already clicked off.

"Clovis, Winkler Street across from Butler Field. Let's get moving."

Clovis said, "It would help if I knew what you think we're up against. A whole gang of men or some isolated nut?"

"If I'm right, we'll probably have to deal with a couple of guys. But then again, it could be a dozen, or we might find just a nice family with three kids who bought the house without a clue."

Paul asked, "Why do you think it won't be a big group of Novak's thugs?"

"If Novak had come back to the neighborhood, with people and cars going in and out, someone would have called the police by now.

No, I'm betting there'll just be one or two men and Micki. The curtains will be drawn, no lights to raise suspicions. I sure hope I'm right about this, and God, I hope she's still alive."

We pulled up, followed immediately by Sam and two squad cars. I recognized the house—it had once been a stately Victorian with a manicured front lawn. Now the paint was peeling, sagging draperies shaded the windows, and there sure weren't any kids playing on the lawn.

We all stepped out of our cars, the uniforms holding guns at the ready, watching to see if anyone appeared. Sam spoke quietly.

"My office checked. Novak owns the house. Looks empty. What do you have in mind?"

"Thought I'd ring the doorbell, see if anyone's home." I didn't smile.

"We can't go in without a warrant, you know that," Sam cautioned. "But I guess it's okay to ring."

He waved the cops around back, but Clovis and Paul stayed with us, weapons drawn. I walked slowly toward the door, Sam right behind me. No doorbell. I knocked and listened for footsteps. Hearing none, I did what I'd seen a thousand times in the movies. I kicked the door right below the handle as hard as I could. It budged, but it didn't give way. My leg felt like it had kicked a tree. I was about to try again when Clovis shoved me out of the way and gave the door a huge sideways kick. The lock shattered, and we rushed in.

Sam's face reminded me of Billy's in *Beverly Hills Cop*, but like Billy, he followed me in. Clovis and Paul fanned out into the main rooms, but I trotted up to the second floor where Debbie said the women had been kept. We found a single, long hall with doors on both sides like in a hotel. Sam and I opened each door in turn. None were locked; all were empty except for a bed, a nightstand, and a lamp. We reached the end of the hall. No Micki.

"You know, you're in big trouble for breaking and entering. I'll catch hell as well," Sam said quietly.

"No, you won't. I'll swear you told me not to do it, not to come in. I rushed in, and you followed in hot pursuit." I didn't smile. Jeez, what did it matter? "Sam, she's here. I feel it. You do, too."

He nodded and pointed to the closet in this last bedroom. We rushed to the door, opened it, and Micki slumped out, pale as a corpse. I was terrified. Sam reached his hand to her neck.

"There's a faint pulse. I'll call an ambulance."

I yelled for Clovis, and he and Paul came running. They picked up her naked body gently and placed her on the bed. I ran to the adjoining room, grabbed a blanket off the bed, and covered her up. She was unconscious, barely breathing. I was afraid to touch her. We waited for what seemed to be an eternity for the medics to arrive. Sam begged us not to disturb anything. He ordered the policemen to search the house, but it was empty. Inside the closet were ropes that had been used to tie her up, syringes, and residue of what Clovis told me was top-grade heroin. Worse yet, we found a blowtorch and a branding iron under the ropes. When I covered her up, I noticed the angry burn at the edge of her collarbone—N.

Her wrists and ankles had been rubbed raw by the rope. Bruises covered her arms, legs, and body. Only her face remained untouched. Debbie had told me they wouldn't touch her face.

The medics arrived, as well as at least a dozen squad cars and a fire truck. Neighbors poured out of their homes. Clovis insisted that Paul should ride with her to the hospital, partly to protect Micki, and partly to be there for Eric.

I heard Clovis. "Jack, Sam needs you."

21

I SPOTTED SAM huddling with several uniformed officers. He waved me over, and the officers quickly dispersed.

"You gonna cuff me?" I tried, but couldn't manage a smile.

"No. I should chew your ass out, but I was right behind you, so I guess we're both guilty. Besides, what judge wouldn't let you off? You saved her life. How'd you figure out where she was?"

"Sam, I'm exhausted. I'm going to the hospital. If Micki's okay, I need to crash for a while. Can I tell you tonight over steak and a cold beer? "

"I'll take you up on the beer, but I can't let you see or talk to Micki."

"Why the hell not?" I shouted. Several police officers turned in our direction, but relaxed when Sam put his arm around my shoulder.

"Walk with me to your car and keep a lid on that temper of yours. In the first place, Micki's in no shape to talk to anybody. More to the point, when she is able to talk, law enforcement needs to be there first. I can't risk some hotshot lawyer saying you put words in her mouth before the police got her statement. I have to keep you two apart. This may be our best shot at Novak; I can't afford to fuck it up."

"I have no intention of fucking anything up, but what about Micki? This is one human being caring for another. If it were me in the hospital, you'd be there. Hell, if I remember right, you were–both times."

"She knows you care. Any idiot knows that. I'll make sure she knows why you're not there. She's been after Novak for years, for God's sake—she knows what's at stake. You'll see her soon enough, but stay away for now. I'm going to have a hard enough time keeping the lover boy away."

"I'll behave, but you've got to promise to hurry the hell up. I don't want her alone. Clovis will work with you to make sure she's protected, okay?"

"Okay." He sighed, his relief obvious.

We had reached Clovis's Tahoe. "Eight o'clock at The Faded Rose. I'll tell you how I figured it out. It wasn't Novak."

"Wha . . . ?" Sam's mouth was open.

"Thought that would pique your curiosity. Novak didn't do it. I'll explain tonight."

I hopped into the car.

Clovis asked, "I heard you tell Sam that Novak's not responsible. How do you know that?"

"I'll tell you both at dinner tonight. Let's go check on Maggie and Debbie. Sam won't let me see Micki."

The adrenaline was still flowing as we drove to Micki's office.

"Here's what I need right now: first, send Moira to Memphis to check on Liz. Second, call Marshal Maroney and schedule a meeting with him tomorrow. I want him to know how much danger Doug is in. Has the press descended on Micki's office yet?"

"I took a minute to call Mongo—he said a satellite truck just pulled up. He knows not to open the door or talk to anyone. Paul's at the hospital. The police have guards everywhere. He's already talked to Eric, who's about as happy as you are about Sam's orders to stay away. He wanted to supervise her care, but the hospital administrator stepped in at Sam's request." Clovis seemed almost out of breath.

"For the moment the police will watch Micki, but I don't trust them completely. I want Paul and his men at the hospital full-time."

THE SKINNY GUY had been sitting quietly in his car just down Winkler as Clovis pulled away. He'd watched the whole thing. They'd had just enough time to get out. The bastard Patterson was supposed to be out of town. Still, Lawrence was out of commission and wouldn't be able to identify a soul. Patterson's finding her had spoiled a little special fun his guys were going to have with the long-legged beauty. "Damn," he muttered to himself. At least, Patterson would pay for being so fucking smart—he was a dead man.

22

THE PRESS HAD set up a bank of microphones on the sidewalk leading up to Micki's front porch. A satellite truck was parked in the driveway so we couldn't drive to the back and park. I noticed Mongo had turned the lights out except for the porch light and a few in the back of the house. Smart guy.

"It's okay, Clovis. This one should be easy. Just be ready to clear a path." We got out of the car, and I shoved my way through the reporters.

"Prosecuting Attorney Sam Pagano has ordered me not to talk about what happened this afternoon because of his ongoing investigation. Sorry." I turned around, walked up Micki's porch steps, and through the front door, Clovis right behind me. The press was caught flat-footed. I don't get that lucky very often.

Maggie jumped up from Micki's desk and threw her arms around me with a sigh of relief.

"Are you all right? How's Micki?"

"I'm all right. Micki's another story. She was unconscious when the medics took over, and Sam won't let me near her. He's afraid I'll compromise his case, but I'm going to change his mind tonight. We've got a lot to do over the next few days. I thought Doug's case would go on for months, but we need to speed things up. Time is running out unless we change this game's momentum. Micki's alive, thank God, but . . ."

I was about to crash, but I had to do one more thing.

"Mongo, how's Debbie?" He was standing near the door to the bedroom.

"She's been in and out, but she's awake. It helps that you found Micki."

Debbie looked a lot better than when I'd left her. She was sitting up in bed watching The Cooking Channel, face cleaned up and hair combed: the resilience of youth.

"May I come in?"

"Yeah, sure. Paul told me you found Micki. I can't tell you how relieved I am." I was ready to be impressed by her newfound gravity, when she added, "In fact, this bed is giving me ideas. I'm ready for . . ." I frowned and turned to leave, but she'd seen my face flush.

"You're blushing!" She squealed and smiled like a coquette. "I'm teasing. I used to be a prostitute, remember? I talk about sex like you do about the law." I wondered how much it cost Debbie to keep up her brazen front.

My mind turned to my own daughter, Beth. She and Debbie were about the same age. I felt immensely grateful that Beth had lived a secure, almost pampered life, and yet oddly embarrassed that she would be totally unable to relate to the atrocities Debbie had experienced. I found myself wondering whether Beth could relate to Debbie at all.

"Debbie, look at me. You weren't a prostitute. I don't want to hear you say that ever again. You were a victim of revolting men who cheated and abused you. I came in to thank you. Micki is safe because of you. Thank you."

She flushed a little, and said "Well, I–I didn't . . . I mean, I really appreciate that. But what happens next? What are we going to do?"

"Until we get everything sorted out, Mongo and one of Clovis's men are going to stay here with you. Make a list of what you need—I'll send someone to your place. No texting or calls to friends telling them what happened or where you are. Please don't argue. It won't be forever. I don't want to scare you, but I'm still worried about your safety. I'll be back tomorrow morning. We have lots of work to do, and I need your help. I need to know I can count on you, okay?"

"When can I see Micki?"

"Sam Pagano won't let any of us see her for now. Besides, she's in no condition to see any of us. But as soon as Sam gives the okay, you'll be first on the list."

She squared her shoulders. "I need to know, was Novak behind this?"

"I don't know, but, honestly, I don't think so. From what you told me, I think someone has tried to set him up. Maybe we've landed in the middle of some sort of gangster turf war, but I don't think so. I have a hunch that Novak had nothing to do with Micki's kidnapping. Anyway, I want you to sit tight, mind Mongo and Clovis, and help me get to the bottom of all this."

23

MAGGIE AND I climbed into the back of the Tahoe. Clovis was already in the driver's seat. Moira joined us, riding shotgun. She spoke up as soon as the doors closed.

"I've already asked for Liz's security to be upgraded. My flight to Memphis leaves in a couple of hours and I'll be back in Little Rock tomorrow afternoon. How did you know where to find Micki?"

"Clovis will fill you in on the way to the airport. Hurry back, we've got a lot to do." Maggie gave me a quizzical look, surprised at my abruptness.

Clovis dropped us off at the hotel's door and left with Moira. I tried to call Beth. I knew she'd be worried about Micki, and even more upset if she heard it on the news or saw it online. When she didn't answer, I thought about texting, but somehow it didn't feel right. She'd have to wait.

Every part of me wanted to be at Micki's side, but she had Eric. She'd expect me to find out who was behind all this and, in her words, "neuter the bastard."

By the time Maggie and I had emptied our suitcases and cleaned up, it was time to go to dinner. The Faded Rose, housed in a nondescript building near the river, is famous for Rose's Creole soaked salads and mouth-watering steaks cooked in butter in cast iron skillets. You'd never find it if you weren't a local. Between rowdy families and armchair fans watching ESPN the place was already crowded–it was a good thing Clovis had called ahead.

We followed the waiter to a slightly quieter spot in a back corner. Maggie ordered a single malt scotch. I was tempted, but good whiskey would be wasted on me. Opening that closet door to an almost-dead Micki was going to haunt me for a long time. I settled for whatever Cabernet the waiter recommended.

"Thanks for getting me on the plane this morning, Maggie. I'm not sure Micki would be alive if we hadn't come."

She smiled. "You were in shock, you just needed a shove. Thank God you found her in time."

"Thank God is right. But I'm still more than worried for her safety. I don't think Novak had anything to do with Micki's kidnapping and torture. I'll explain my reasoning to Sam at dinner, no sense in repeating myself. Given that I think he didn't do it, I see two other possibilities. Either it relates to Dr. Stewart's arrest—somebody wants Micki out of that game—or it relates to her business, a former client or a case that went bad."

"That's more likely, don't you think?"

"Probably, so tomorrow morning I want you and Debbie to go over all of Micki's current files, see if you can find any leads. I know that's hard and boring work, but I've got to turn my attention to Doug. Even acres of marijuana don't justify the way the government is treating him."

"If it does concern Doug, what makes you think you won't be their next target?"

"Maggie, I'm not a threat to a flea, and what good does it to do to worry about it? We've got bigger fish to fry."

Ignoring her "who are you kidding" look, I said, "I'm more worried that Dub will try to pull some trick while Micki's in the hospital."

Clovis and Sam walked in together, turning a few heads as they walked to our table. Word had spread fast. Sam knew Maggie and greeted her as the friends they were.

"Plying me with liquor and food isn't going to get you out of telling me how you found Micki. But since you're buying, I'll tell you what I know first. We've put pressure on every area of Novak's business and come up empty. Novak has even agreed to let me interview him."

Clovis jumped in. "Well, why not? He's in the clear. He gives the order, but makes sure there's no way to link him to the kidnapping."

"You don't have to convince me. Novak's known for exacting revenge. He's made it clear that he blames Micki for losing Debbie, and he's sworn to get even. He may cry innocent, but I don't trust him further than I can throw him, which isn't very far." Sam responded.

"Suppose he's telling the truth–what then?" I interjected.

"All right, wise-ass, what makes you think Novak's not our man?"

"I'm probably wrong, but hear me out. Every piece of evidence points to Novak: the kidnapping, the use of his house, the drugs, and the branding—but it doesn't make sense. If Novak were behind it, surely he wouldn't be so sloppy. Why would he leave her to be found at his old training center? Why let her be found at all?

"Besides, if it were an act of revenge, he would never have left her to die. Debbie says Novak believes in using women, not killing them. She said he'd treat Micki the same as all his girls, getting her addicted until she was willing to do anything for a score. He's done it before. Sam, you have to admit, Micki would've been worth a lot of money to a man like Novak."

Maggie was rightfully horrified at my words. "That's terrible, Jack. How can you talk about Micki that way? She would never have agreed to be one of Novak's prostitutes."

Sam answered for me. "Maggie, it's not a matter of choice. The addiction takes over and controls everything. Thank God it didn't happen, but what Jack describes is exactly how Novak works. He gets very young girls addicted to the point they'll do anything to feed their habit. That's his business."

She was still glaring at me.

"Maggie, you know how special Micki is to me; you also know how much she means to Sam. Micki's not some piece of meat. I'm simply trying to explain the difference between what happened to Micki, as horrible as it was, and how Novak would've behaved. It's how I figured out where she was. It's just the facts."

Maggie understood my reasoning, but was still bothered by the discussion.

"Let's hear how you figured out where she was so I can mark you off my suspect list." Sam winked.

"You and Clovis were concentrating on where Novak might have taken her, with zero results. So I wondered–what would someone do if they wanted to frame Novak? It occurred to me they might take her to a location that was easily identified with Novak, but not currently in use—a place you wouldn't think of at first, but would get to at some point. It was a hunch and, fortunately, it turned out to be right."

Maggie reached under the table and squeezed my hand.

"Well, thanks to your hunch, she's alive." Sam smiled. "We've put her boyfriend through the wringer—he's not involved. The bad news is we didn't find a single fingerprint in that room except Micki's, not one. Not one hard piece of evidence to link the crime to Novak, and no real reason to suspect anyone else."

"Wait—you have a huge clue," I almost shouted.

Sam shook his head. "Okay, Sherlock. What did I miss?"

"The brand. That's not Novak's brand on her shoulder. Debbie's brand is different. It has two letters together: an 'AN.' The brand on Micki is a single 'N' with a different font, if you can consider brands to have fonts. Each of Novak's girls has the same brand on the back of her neck, not on her collarbone. Debbie confirmed that after I found Micki."

A low whistle escaped Sam's lips. "Nice work. Excuse me while I pass your reasoning on to my crack detective team. Order me a rib eye—bone in, rare. I'll be back in a minute."

I turned to Maggie. "I'm sorry. I had to be direct with Sam. His people are convinced Novak is guilty because it's easy. It's hard to get law enforcement to think outside the box unless you hit them up the side of the head, even Sam."

"I understand, but what happened to Micki is every woman's nightmare. I don't even want to ask if the bastards raped her." I hadn't chosen to ask either.

"Clovis, can you see if you can find a local source for branding irons? It's probably a wild goose chase, but it will take the police decades to follow up. If someone is trying to frame Novak, the iron itself will find its way onto one of Novak's properties soon enough."

Clovis replied. "Will do. Any other zingers?"

"Well, yeah, a couple. But I'm going to need your help to convince Sam."

24

SAM RETURNED, OUR steaks arrived, and it was time to get down to business; although the perfectly cooked rib eyes, smothered potatoes, and Creole green beans were a distraction. Even Maggie gave in, happy to forget her healthy habits for the evening.

"I know you don't know much about Dub's task force, but I think it's time you did," I began between mouthfuls.

"Why in the world would I want to get within a country mile of Dub or his so-called task force?" he responded.

"What if I told you they were involved in Micki's kidnapping?"

His fork made a loud clatter when it hit his plate—more than one head turned. Maggie and Clovis managed to keep control of their silverware, but were just as surprised.

"What have you been smoking? Why in the world do you think Dub has anything to do with Micki's abduction? Sure, she hates his guts, and I'm sure the feeling is mutual, as many times as she's cleaned his plow. But not even Dub would actually kidnap someone, much less leave them for dead."

I needed to be careful not to exaggerate or oversell.

"Look—as far I as I can see there are four possible abductors. First, there's the obvious, Novak. Second, there's some enemy of Novak who's trying to frame him. Novak's bound to have enemies, lots of them. Third, it could be one of Micki's clients. We're going to be all over that tomorrow. Finally, there's Dub, his task force, and whoever benefits from the Stewart case.

"Dub and his gang seem the most unlikely. But don't rule them out, okay? I haven't swum in your pool often, but it seems the least likely suspects sometime float to the top. It's the opposite of Occam's razor. Call it Patterson's shower if you like."

"I'd rather not, if you don't mind," Sam responded, downing his glass of wine. Maggie refilled it immediately.

"Bear with me while I tell you what little I know about Dub's case against Dr. Stewart." Sam leaned back in his chair, willing to indulge me for the time being.

He asked a few questions, but basically listened without comment. I hoped I hadn't given him too much wine.

Swirling his glass thoughtfully, he finally asked, "Okay—so now what?"

"You're not going to call me an idiot or a nut job?"

"Well my friend, I've learned not to discount your off-the-wall theories out of hand. I'm willing to do what I can, but so far I don't see how I can help." He gave me a forlorn grin.

"That's okay. It's enough that you listened, didn't pull me off the mound before the game even started. Next time I need something concrete like a search warrant or a subpoena, you'll know why."

"If you want a search warrant, you better have more than a theory, you better bring facts. No judge is going to touch a pending Federal matter without an ironclad reason and plenty of facts to back it up. But, I'll say something I wouldn't have a year ago. If you've got something–bring it to me. I'll listen."

"That's all I can ask for. Thanks." I meant it.

Sam put his fork down, deliberately this time, and gave me a hard look. "Jack, let me give you a bit of advice I know you won't take. Let me find Micki's kidnapper, and you concentrate on defending your doctor."

"Can't do that, Sam— I know in my gut they're related. If we find the kidnapper, we'll know how to defend Dr. Stewart. And if I figure out what's really behind Doug's prosecution, we'll know who kidnapped Micki."

I had planted a seed. That's all I could hope for out of one night's dinner. Sam was more than happy to accept Clovis's offer to drive him home. As he rose, he turned to Maggie.

"You'll be glad to know that no charges will be filed against Jack and Clovis for breaking and entering this afternoon. The deputies and I all agree that the front door was wide open when we arrived. We all thought we heard a scream, and Jack ran in." He winked, gave her a quick kiss, and turned toward the door, Clovis close behind.

Maggie and I lingered in silence over the last of the Cabernet. I watched the waiter serve bread pudding to the table next to us and wondered idly if Maggie had ever enjoyed real Southern bread pudding.

"Jack, you can't actually believe Dub is responsible for Micki's kidnapping." Her abrupt comment broke the reverie.

"Believe me, I hope not. However incompetent I think he is, he's still the U. S. attorney, and I'm not a conspiracy nut. Contrary to movies and blogs, our government doesn't kidnap defense lawyers, brand them, and leave them to die. But someone who stands to benefit from Dub's prosecution could be responsible. Or Micki could easily be collateral damage in a drug or mafia turf war between Novak and some other thug. What's important is that Sam knows what we're doing. He's not fighting us."

"Maybe he learned his lesson."

"No, the real reason is Micki. She rescued him once. He's on our team because we both want justice for Micki."

Our server offered the dessert menu, but Maggie declined, and I reluctantly decided to save bread pudding for another night.

"You're right, we should go—tomorrow's going to be a big day. I have to figure out how to see Doug. Let's not forget he's what brought us here."

WEDNESDAY MORNING

April 23, 2014

25

WHEN WE MET for breakfast, Clovis reported that Micki was still in ICU, but her condition had been upgraded to stable. Paul had stayed with Eric at the hospital all night, along with the two uniforms who sat outside her door and several others who weren't so obvious. Sam and Clovis were taking no chances.

I had to change shirts before we could leave for Micki's office–egg yolk on my cuff and the front of my shirt again. Two burly guards met us—Clovis still wasn't sure what to make of Mongo. Debbie showed no ill effects from the trauma of yesterday, and from the corner of my eye I caught Clovis admiring her tight jeans and tighter sweater. The entire time I'd known Clovis, I'd never asked whether he had a girl-friend; I was pretty sure he wasn't married. Angie would have known that and much more within the first hour of meeting him.

Moira had called to report that Liz's security was tighter than a drum. At my request, she had encouraged Liz to remain in Memphis until I either talked to Doug or had news from the judge. Maggie quickly took charge at Micki's office, reminding us that Marshal Maroney had agreed to meet with us this morning—we were due in ten minutes.

Security at the courthouse was tight, and we were a few minutes late reaching the marshal's offices on the fifth floor. I was surprised to see both Dub and Jim Bullock waiting in the reception area. We shook hands awkwardly, Dub's palm damp in my grasp. I fought off the instinctive urge to wipe my hand on my khakis.

He opened with, "I heard about Lawrence. How awful." His voice didn't convey an ounce of sincerity.

Jim was more sympathetic. "How's she doing? If there's any way we can help, please let us know. Any idea who's behind it?"

"The police believe a man named Novak is responsible. He's Russian mafia—you know what those guys are like," I lied. I was happy for everyone to think Novak was the guilty party.

Dub jumped in. "That guy's a piece of shit. I hope the police nail his ass. If it were my case, I'd be all over him. He wouldn't know what hit him."

Dub was showing off—he had no intention of crossing Novak.

"Technically, you do have the case. It's a kidnapping in this district. Maybe your office is already working it?" Butter wouldn't melt in my mouth.

I watched him squirm. I bet Dub hadn't talked to anyone in the U.S. Attorney's office in weeks. His pompous and self-centered little brain was focused entirely on "his" task force, not the kidnapping of an adversary.

"You might want to find out. The press might ask about your investigation," I suggested.

Dub glowered and looked relieved when Marshal Maroney opened the door to his office, waving us into wooden chairs as he leaned against the front of his desk. He asked about Micki, and I told him what I knew.

"Micki is good people. You tell Sam if he needs help keeping her safe, my people are available. I mean it."

After a pause, he reverted to his professional tone. "Mr. Patterson, I understand you have concerns regarding Dr. Stewart. That's why I invited Mr. Blanchard and Mr. Bullock to join us. I've been ordered by Washington to do nothing in this matter without their knowledge. I hope you understand."

Before I could answer Dub broke in. "The accused is no concern of yours at all, Marshal. Stewart is our responsibility. You got that?" He tilted his chair back with an insolent grin.

Maroney was pissed and let it show. "Well, he's my concern when he's in this courthouse, Mr. U. S. Attorney. You got that?"

"Of course, Marshal." Dub's tone made fingernails on a chalkboard sound pleasant.

My turn. "Since you called my client 'the accused,' do you mind telling me what he's accused of? To my knowledge he's being held in an undisclosed facility but has yet to be charged with a crime."

"Under the Defense Authorization Act of 2012, I can hold him indefinitely without charging him." Dub's chest puffed out, endangering his shirt buttons.

"Are you classifying him as a terrorist? Seriously? If so, you have to turn him over to the military. They'll probably be easier to work with." Now I was pissed.

Bullock stepped in before it got worse.

"Let's all calm down. Judge Houston will make his rulings soon enough. You must have some reason to be here other than to trade insults with us. You know we're not going to give you access to Dr. Stewart until the judge rules. . . ."

Dub interrupted again. "It'll be a cold day in hell before you see Stewart. If he rules against us, we'll appeal, so don't get your hopes of seeing Dr. Stewart any time soon." Bullock couldn't help but grimace. Dub had stupidly told me part of their strategy. Bullock had implied that we would have access in a matter of days. Now I knew better.

Since part of the cat was out of the bag, I toned it down.

"I asked to see Marshal Maroney both to update him on what happened to Micki and to reiterate my concern for Dr. Stewart's welfare. Marshal, since we've been denied access to our client, I need to know that whoever has him in custody is doing everything in their power to assure his safety, even if that means putting him in segregated housing. Micki is alive because of a lucky guess. I don't want someone to be more successful when it comes to Dr. Stewart."

His glasses slipped down on his nose a bit as his eyebrows shot up. "You think the kidnapping and attack on Micki are related to the Stewart case?"

Dub sputtered with impatience. "That's horseshit. Outrageous. Dr. Stewart's case has nothing to do with Novak. You're grasping at straws, Counselor."

Pointedly ignoring Dub, I spoke directly to Maroney. "Marshal, I'd feel a lot better if I knew where Doug is and could at least talk to him on the phone. It's not like he's going to escape or tell me where the crown jewels are hidden. His wife is worried sick about him."

Dub gloated. "Ain't going to happen. You're not playing ball with your old high school friends anymore, Mr. Big-time Antitrust Lawyer. You're dealing with me now." Dub looked at Bullock like he had set me straight. Clovis allowed himself a snort.

Maroney looked unhappy, but shrugged his shoulders and said, "My hands are tied. I honestly wish it were otherwise."

Dub shoved his chair back noisily, "Let's get out of here, Bullock." As he headed out of the room I heard him gloat, "Guess I showed him."

Clovis stepped between Dub and any reaction on my part. When the door closed, Maroney smiled.

"Pity they left so soon. If they'd stayed, I could have told you both that technically neither Dub nor I have jurisdiction over the prisoner at the moment. Once he was delivered to Oklahoma City, his care and welfare was transferred to the Bureau of Prisons. That means Warden Mitchell in OKC has the last word on whether or not you can speak with your client. It's his call whether Stewart can make or receive phone calls or confer with his lawyer. It's not up to the judge, the marshal, or Dub's task force. But since Dub's not here, I can't tell him that. Too bad—think I'll just keep it to myself."

I smiled in return, and we shook hands.

"You watch over Micki, you hear. She's special. Tell her as soon as she's ready for visitors, I'll be there."

As we walked to the Tahoe I mused, "Clovis, you may have to hold me back if I have to be in the same room with that asshole again. He's such an easy mark. I admit I enjoy baiting him, but it's distracting, gets me off my game."

"I think Dub protests too much and too loudly. Did you see how defensive he got when you suggested that what happened to Micki could be related to Dr. Stewart? You could tell Bullock was troubled."

"So you think there's a link?" I asked.

"Didn't say that. But I'm sure our U.S. Attorney knows a whole hell of a lot more about Micki's kidnapping than he let on. His face is an open book."

I opened the door to the Tahoe. "Hmm—I'll file that little tidbit away. It's time for us to go to Oklahoma City."

26

CLOVIS CALLED WALTER'S pilot, while I punched in the number Maroney had given me. The warden picked up immediately.

"Warden Mitchell, my name is Jack Patterson, and—"

He interrupted. "Bill Maroney told me you'd be calling and why. Don't waste your time talking."

My heart sank.

"Get your ass up here before somebody tells me not to let you see your client. Shit, man, I deal with the worst of the worst, but they still get to see their lawyers. We don't get many lawyers out here because we're basically a warehouse, in and out in a few days. But if you can get here, I'll let you in. Just bring ID, proof you're a lawyer—a business card will do—and be prepared for a search of your briefcase and your person."

"Thank you, Warden. I'll be there in a couple of hours."

"Look forward to meeting you. I checked with some friends at Main Justice. You get nothing but respect. Maroney warned me to expect a call from some jerk U.S. attorney named Blanchard. If he reaches me and orders me not to let you in, I'll have to comply; so if I were you, I'd get here quickly and quietly."

I thanked him, got the pilot back on the phone, and told him not to file a flight plan. Maggie was waiting for us on the curb, and Clovis sped to the airport. As soon as she was buckled in her seat, I told Maggie what had happened.

In the air, the pilot radioed ahead for a taxi, and we found it waiting for us on the tarmac when we landed. I could see the prison facility across the airfield, and within a matter of ten minutes we were being searched by the prison's security guards. I'll spare you the details. It's enough to know that prison searches are very thorough. Warden Mitchell was waiting for us in a small conference room.

"I apologize for the search, but sooner or later I'm going to have to answer to someone about your visit. It's going to be a lot easier on all of us if I can say the two of you were treated like any other visitors, regulations followed to the letter. Mrs. Matthews, I especially apologize to you, but you'd be surprised what people try to smuggle in and how. The rules exist to make sure nothing gets in, but one's privacy does suffer."

Maggie was still a bit red in the face and said tartly, "I don't suppose you have many women visitors." Warden Mitchell smiled and then got down to business.

"Dr. Stewart is undergoing a similar procedure as we speak. I seldom have inmates searched before they meet with their lawyers, but I'm following the book. Pick up your cell phones when you leave. Sorry, you're allowed only pen and paper."

"That's okay. Thanks for letting us see him on such short notice."

"Think nothing of it. Hell, I've never heard about not getting to see your own lawyer. What's this world coming to? In case you're interested, right now Dr. Stewart is in a cell by himself. The facility is fairly empty. He reads, eats his meals, and sticks to himself."

"That's good to know."

The Warden left the room, and in a few minutes a guard walked Doug through the door. I was relieved to see he wasn't in handcuffs or leg irons. Maggie and I teased him a little about his emergent beard, and he parried that it was a sign of his good health. The smiles didn't last long.

"Before you ask me what this is all about, tell me about Liz. Is she okay? And what else has happened? They won't let me make a phone call, and I don't understand why I'm here and not in Little Rock."

I assured him that Liz was safe in Memphis, updated him on the arraignment, the prosecution's offer not to charge Liz or seize the house, and a few other details. He was clearly relieved to learn that Liz had been given a security detail and assured me that no one had threatened him either in the county jail or here. Next came the question I was afraid he'd ask.

"Where's Ms. Lawrence?" I looked at Maggie, and Doug quickly picked up on my hesitation.

"What happened? What aren't you telling me?" Not a question, but a demand.

I lowered my voice and explained that Micki had been kidnapped, how we had found her and her current medical condition. Doug stared at me in silence, folded arms leaning on his knees, absorbing the facts. After a few seconds, he seemed to give himself a little shake and said firmly, "Okay, I don't know how much time we have. Someone is likely to bust in here any minute, so let me give you your marching orders, and then I'll answer all your questions. Okay?"

"Okay." I was reassured to find that his strength of character was seemingly unaffected by his circumstances, his will and thinking processes still strong. The treatment he'd received could break a man pretty quickly.

"First, thank you for arranging security for Liz. I'm surprised she agreed to it, but whatever happens, keep it up. She's in more danger than you know."

"Why?" I asked.

"I told you, answers later, instructions first. Micki's kidnapping is connected to all this." He gestured broadly at the small room. "Don't let anyone convince you otherwise. Second, you be careful. I'd bet my bottom dollar you're next." He looked at Maggie. "You should all have guards—every hour of the day. When they hear I've been talking, they aren't going to hang around and wait to find out what you know. They won't hesitate to take you both out. I'm sorry. I should have realized this earlier. I wanted to think I was the only one at risk."

Maggie asked, "What exactly do you know?"

Doug smiled. "Instructions first."

"Jack, take their deal. Make sure you lock in the 'no prosecution of Liz.' It kills my soul. A life's work gone, but I couldn't stand the thought of Liz in prison. You say the deal is too good to be true. That's because you don't know what they're getting in exchange. Take the deal. They can have my research—it's what they've wanted all along.

Once they get it, Liz will be safe, you and Maggie too. God, I hope Ms. Lawrence makes it."

You could feel the force of his pent-up energy lessen, and he began to ramble a bit. My brain swirled with too many questions to interrupt.

"Can you imagine, a nerd like me having Liz for a wife? She was so damn good-looking, and yet she chose to marry me. No one could believe it. She flirted with every boy on campus, occasionally went too far with a few, but always begged me to take her back. Can you imagine—me? They found my pressure point all right. They know I'd never let them harm Liz. If it weren't for her, I'd die before I'd give them my research." He put his hands over his eyes, almost overcome.

Maggie reached over to grip his shaking shoulder.

We hadn't gotten anywhere, from my point of view.

"Doug, I know how tough this is for you, but we don't have much time here. We need to decide how to deal with what's happened—right now. Listen to me. We don't have to agree to their deal today. I'll keep your agreement in my pocket. In fact, I've made it clear to them I can't agree to anything until I spoken with you. Since this is an unofficial visit we still have some time. You need to answer my questions now."

Doug removed his hands from his eyes, gave a sigh and nodded, but the door swung open and in walked the warden. He wasn't smiling.

"A word, Mr. Patterson."

I stepped outside and waited.

He began. "I just received a call from the Director of the Bureau of Prisons ordering me to terminate this interview immediately. Seems to me nothing much is a secret in Little Rock. Whoever's in charge down there pulled enough strings to get the director of prisons out of a meeting with the attorney general. I don't know who jerked her chain, but my instructions are clear."

I didn't know what to think. Dub wouldn't have that kind of pull, would he? And even if he did, how did he know we were here? Who else knew we were in Oklahoma? Whatever, it was clear I'd lost my chance to get any answers from Doug. I thanked the Warden, but he wasn't through.

"I'm going to catch hell for letting you in here, but I can handle it. I was also told to hold you here until the DEA agents arrived. I told the director I didn't have that authority, and she told me to do it anyway. Too bad—as it turns out, you were already gone before I could detain you." His smile brightened the room.

"So, don't let any grass grow under your feet. A bunch of DEA agents are on their way here right now to arrest you."

I went back into the room and said. "Doug, it's time for us to leave. In fact, we've got to hightail it out of here. You were right, the Feds are on their way. Much as I'd like to tell everyone to go jump in the lake, I don't imagine I can do you any good from a jail cell. I'll be back. Be careful, and don't give up. I've got a plan."

His look told me he thought I was nuts, but he was ready to clutch at straws.

"A plan?" He smiled. "Angie told me you were a little crazy."

I returned the smile and heard Maggie say, "Crazy like a fox."

"Be careful. And the answer to all your questions is the research. They don't care about the pot or my house. It's my research they want, and, yes, they'll kill for it."

"Maggie, call the pilot and tell him we'll be there in ten minutes and to get us in the air as soon as possible." Maggie was already punching his number.

Clovis was waiting for us at the car. "What's up? Why the rush?"

"We've got a problem. We've got lots of problems, but one is more pressing than the others." I told him what the warden had said, and I watched his face turn stone cold. I'd seen Clovis angry before, but I'd never seen this look—scared the shit out of me.

27

As we taxied down the runway, I saw several black sedans pull into the parking lot. Men in dark suits and sunglasses streamed out of the cars. Breathing a sigh of relief as we took off, I told the pilot to notify the guys at Hodges Air that various officers of the law were likely to be waiting when we arrived, and asked him to call a friend.

I explained to Maggie and Clovis that I was sure to be arrested. Maggie took a deep breath, but kept her usual composure. Clenching and unclenching his fists, Clovis was a silent image of fury. This I didn't need.

"Clovis, I can see how angry you are. I know you're second-guessing yourself, but I need you to let it go. Remember how on the football field the other team tried to get in your head? Don't let these guys get to you. The fact is they've tipped their hand. Now we know we've got a traitor in our midst. We have to figure out how to use what we know, how to use the traitor. Okay? Are you with me?"

"Why aren't you madder than hell?" Clovis barked. "Your meeting with Doug got cut short. Every move you've made has been thwarted. Dub's trumped up some charge against you, and this mole surely had something to do with Micki. I'll wring his neck when I find him."

"No, you won't. Come on, Clovis, get a grip. We've been handed a gift. Let's figure out who it is and use that knowledge to our advantage."

"Any thoughts on who it might be?" Maggie asked.

"Yeah, I think I know who, but if I told either of you, you'd be awkward around that person and tip him off. I'd rather you come to your own conclusions. Let's not focus on the traitor. Let's talk about what you need to do while I'm cooling my heels in jail. Maggie, I need you to call Beth right away, make sure she knows I'm all right."

"Of course, but don't you need a lawyer?"

"Already have one. If the pilot was able to reach her, I bet she'll be there when we land. Micki's not available, so I've got the next best thing."

As yet unrelenting, Clovis demanded, "Who?"

Maggie answered for me with a smile, "Janis Harold."

Clovis whistled and finally relaxed. "Dub's gonna wish he'd left your ass alone."

"That's the plan." I grinned.

I'd met Janis Harold during the Cole case. She had acted as both the senator and Woody's personal attorney, and had represented all of the senator's political campaigns. Janis was what my stepfather would have called a "little bit of a thing," not quite five feet tall. Her lack of height dominated any initial impression but, as they say, dynamite comes in small packages.

Sure enough, as we taxied toward Hodges Air, I saw her standing in front of the deputy marshals waiting for the plane.

As soon as we reached the bottom of the passenger stairs, a man wearing dark glasses identified himself as a Deputy U.S. Marshal and said politely, "Mr. Patterson, please come with me." He was fingering the pair of handcuffs attached to his belt, which wasn't so polite.

"On what charges?" Janis was in his face except for the two feet that separated them in height.

"Ma'am, I'm under orders to take Mr. Patterson into custody. Please don't interfere."

"I'm Mr. Patterson's attorney. I want to know on what charges my client is being detained and by whose authority."

"Ma'am, you'll have to take that up with Mr. Blanchard. I'm here to detain Mr. Patterson until he appears before a magistrate." Janis sputtered angrily. Since I'd known this was going to happen, I interrupted.

"Deputy, I'll come with you, but can you give me a minute with my counsel? If not, she's likely to have you in front of a judge in a matter of minutes. I promise I'll cooperate. Simply let me talk to her in plain view for a minute."

He knew he shouldn't agree, but he was already more afraid of Janis than Dub, so he nodded. "Well, just for a minute."

I pulled Janis aside. "Thanks for being here, Janis. Maggie will tell you what's going on. If I know Dub, he'll try to get me before Judge Houston, railing that I've conspired to get around the Judge's orders. Maggie has the transcript of the earlier hearing. Don't try to get me out of jail until right before tomorrow's hearing."

"I can have you in front of a magistrate before tomorrow."

"I know, but I think we can use Dub's arrogance to our advantage. I'll be okay overnight. Shoot, I'll actually have some time to think. You and Maggie have a lot to do. We'll talk again before the hearing." Janis looked a little flustered, but adjusted quickly.

We walked back to the deputy, and I extended my arms. He seemed a little embarrassed, but quickly took the cuffs from his belt and applied them to my wrists. My clients were right. They did pinch. Just then a cameraman hopped out from behind the marshal's Suburban and started shooting. Janis was furious.

"You bastards! Who notified the press? Tell that asshole of a U.S. Attorney, he better wear a cup. He's going to need one tomorrow."

I had a hard time not laughing, as did the deputy. The reporter with the cameraman was taking notes, but I knew the press wouldn't print Janis' tirade. I saw Clovis put his arm around Maggie, who looked a little lost. Going to jail was a new experience for both of us.

The reality of my circumstances began to sink in. Where were they going to keep me over night? Who else would be in my cell? A sobering thought.

The deputy spoke. "As I believe you already know, we don't have any overnight accommodations except at a safe house, and Mr. Blanchard specifically ordered us not to take you there. You're to be treated like any other prisoner. You'll spend the night at the county jail. We'll pick you up in the morning and deliver you to a magistrate."

I tried to keep my demeanor relaxed and unconcerned as the deputy put his hand on top of my head and shoved me down into his patrol car, but it wasn't easy. I sure couldn't smile.

I'd been to the county jail before when I was defending Woody, but had never made it inside a cell. The cuffs were removed, and for the second time that day I was strip-searched. The guards took my clothes and gave me an orange jumpsuit and cloth shoes, both too small, all the while talking about plans for their day off. I was just part of a day's work. When I was dressed, they led me to a holding cell where I was supposed to fill out various forms, including a questionnaire about my mental state. I wondered what happened to the guys who couldn't read.

The stubby little pencil needed sharpening—it didn't help that my hand shook. I felt the presence of someone outside the cell and looked up to the smiling face of Sam Pagano.

"You shouldn't wear orange—smacks of the Texas Longhorns."

"I'm not too enamored with it myself. Got an alternative?"

He laughed. "Maggie called to tell me what happened. You know there's not much I can do—Dub's running this show. But I've talked to Sheriff Barnes. They're going to segregate you from the other inmates. You'll be in the suicide watch cell. It's not comfortable, but you'll be safe. That's all I can do."

"Thanks. I figured Dub would put me in with a serial killer." Not funny. My words sounded hollow, even to me.

"How's Micki?" I asked, ready to talk about anything else.

"She's pretty weak, been through hell and back, but at least she's conscious. We decided not to tell her you're in jail. She'd want to deal with Dub personally. Better let Janis have that honor." His tone was light enough, but his face wasn't.

"Whatever she needs, make sure she gets it, okay?" Things kept getting worse.

"Don't worry about that. I think you need to worry a little bit about yourself."

"I'll be okay."

"I'm not so sure. Dub's had a hard-on for you from day one, and now you're interfering with his baby. Word has it he wants you arrested for aiding and abetting a terrorist. He's a jerk, but he's still the U.S. attorney. Fortunately, so far no one has taken him seriously. A night in here is hardly a walk in the park, but it looks to me like he wants you out of his way for good."

I thought about my response. "Sam, when I get out of here, it's time for a private chat. Okay?"

"Let's see you through the night first. The suicide cell is hardly the Armitage."

He was right. First, I was ordered to shower and wash my hair with lice shampoo. Then I was strip-searched again and led to a single cell, eight feet by eight feet. The bed was a solid concrete block with a paper-thin plastic mattress. No pillow, nothing to read, not even any toilet paper unless I asked. Dinner consisted of water, a slice of Wonder Bread, and something that resembled noodles with brown gravy. I had to return my plastic spoon after the meal. My friend Woody had been in solitary, but he'd spared me any details. This exposure to his reality made me wish I'd been more sympathetic.

I tried to sleep, and occasionally exhaustion allowed me to nod off for a few minutes. No dreams, no visions of beautiful women—mostly I just lay there. My attempts at rational thought and strategy were constantly interrupted by sounds of screaming and yelling coming from nearby overcrowded cells. How anyone slept in here was beyond me.

The loudspeaker blared a wake-up call at five-thirty, and pretty soon a guard came to lead me to a tepid shower, followed by another strip search more intrusive than I thought possible or legal, and a fresh orange jumpsuit still smaller than the first. Breakfast arrived, and the guard watched through the bars as I forced down oatmeal and soggy toast. Before long his cell phone rang, and he hooked me up to handcuffs, leg chains, and a chain belt that connected both. I was shoved into the back seat of a waiting Suburban, where I could see the deputy marshal in charge staring at me in the rear view mirror.

"I'm sorry about all the hardware, Mr. Patterson, but orders are orders. We'll have you at the courthouse soon enough. I got to warn you though; the press is there in droves. They're all dyin' to get a picture of you in irons."

"That's okay. You're doing your job." I said.

And it was time I started doing mine.

THURSDAY

April 24, 2014

28

NEXT CAME THE "perp walk," another new experience for me. The press surrounded the car—Dub's work, no doubt. The Deputy Marshals helped me out of the car and with each of them holding an arm. I slowly waddled toward the courthouse door, each step restricted by the length of the leg chain and the discomfort of metal digging into my ankles. I tried to look directly into the cameras, but it was tough— not because of any sense of shame, but because they were shoved right into my face. I was constantly bopped on the head by somebody's microphone as the reporters shouted inane questions.

Finally we were inside the building, and I shuffled my way into the elevator. We ended up in a third-floor conference room near the courtroom. The deputy unlocked the irons and cuffs and offered me a paper cup of water. Janis and Maggie appeared at the door almost immediately, relief at my safety obvious on their faces. Maggie gave me a quick hug and said, "Don't worry, I've spoken with Beth. She . . ."

Janis interrupted, "The deputy refused to let us give you fresh clothes. I've stashed them in a closet down the hall and, as soon as the judge's clerk gets here, I'll see if I can't get you out of those orange rags."

Straight from the prosecutor's playbook. Dub would be tickled pink if the lice shampoo turned my hair orange—happens as often as not.

"That's okay. Any idea what the charges are?"

"Not a clue. The only thing I know for sure is Dub insisted on Judge Houston's presence. He claimed a magistrate couldn't hear the charges."

I told her again to be ready for some kind of obstruction charge. We talked strategy for about thirty minutes, well aware that we were flying blind. A deputy whispered to Janis that the judge's clerk had arrived, and she left, soon returning with a clean suit and a tie. She also handed me a little comb. I quickly changed clothes and tried to smooth my rumpled hair. The day's stubble made me look like a middle-aged actor trying to look cool.

Maggie and Janis were already seated at our table when the deputy and I reached the courtroom. I smiled to see Debbie, Clovis, and Mongo in the front row of the gallery–the only family I had right now. The press and various rubberneckers filled the other rows. Dub hadn't made his entrance yet. The small army of lawyers crowded around the prosecution's table grew quiet as I walked in. Bullock nodded to me slightly, managing to look embarrassed. Sam and Micki's friend, Rodney Fitzhugh were sitting together in the back of the room. Sam caught my eye and returned my weak smile. If the night's screams were any indication of what could have happened without his influence, I owed him serious thanks. An ambulance had transferred two inmates to the hospital this morning. Their injuries hadn't been noticed until breakfast.

Dub came bursting through the doors, stopping along the way to shake several reporters' hands. Pausing at our table, he extended his hand to Janis, but she failed to return the gesture. Caught off-guard, hand hovering in mid-air, he turned to me. I wasn't as nice as Janis.

"You've got to be kidding."

"Just a gentlemanly gesture." He actually looked surprised.

"When you act like one, we'll think about it," Janis sneered.

Flushing a bit, he dropped his hand quickly and walked over to his table.

"Did you hear that?" he asked to no one in particular.

Maggie whispered in my ear, "I'd like to cut it off."

"Maggie, Maggie," I said. "Little Rock is making you irritable." That didn't even raise a smile.

"All rise," said the bailiff, and Judge Houston stormed in followed by two clerks.

He'd barely gotten settled before he fumed. "Mr. Blanchard, what is all this about?"

Dub rose from his chair, turned to the gallery for effect, and then responded to the judge.

"Your Honor, yesterday we apprehended Mr. Patterson at Hodges Aircraft after he violated both this court's order and my instructions not to contact Dr. Stewart. He flew to Oklahoma City specifically to meet with Dr. Stewart. Fortunately, I put a stop to the meeting. Mr. Patterson fled the scene, eluding apprehension at the airport. If we hadn't captured him here in Little Rock when he stopped to refuel, he might have fled the country. We ask the court to hold Mr. Patterson without bond until formal charges can be brought, issue a contempt order for his conduct, and remove him as counsel for Dr. Stewart." He fairly glowed with confidence.

I looked at Janis. We had expected the contempt request, but Dub had played his hole card early–what he really wanted was for me to be removed from the Stewart case. Janis stood up, although it didn't make much difference. She was as tall sitting down as she was standing up. Her tone was all business.

"Your Honor, if you please, my name is Janis Harold. I represent Mr. Patterson."

"Ms. Harold. Welcome."

"Thank you. May I speak?"

"Of course."

"I'm puzzled by the nature of these proceedings. If this is a contempt hearing, does the prosecutor base it on some motion or a Show Cause Order issued by this court? I've checked the record and can find no such pleading or order on file. If the charge is obstruction of justice, is this an arraignment? If so, what are the charges? All I know is that my client was taken into custody last night by a deputy marshal assigned to Mr. Blanchard, made to spend the night in the county jail, and then paraded in front of the press in chains and an orange jump suit. What exactly has Mr. Patterson done to warrant such treatment?"

Dub jumped up. "Your Honor, he met with Dr. Stewart in Oklahoma City."

"He's Dr. Stewart's attorney. Didn't you know?" Janis snapped.

"Of course, but he did so without receiving this court's permission." He looked at the bench for a sign of approval.

"He didn't need this court's permission. Your Honor, I've reviewed the transcript of the prior proceeding. At no time did this court say Dr. Stewart's lawyers couldn't contact their client. Your only statement on the subject was that you would review the government's pleading to determine whether the client should be made available to counsel. Mr. Patterson simply found another way to meet with his client once he discovered where Mr. Blanchard had hidden him."

Janis emphasized the word "hidden." Dub flushed again, this time a deep red. He really did fluster easily.

"I told counsel yesterday that he couldn't see Dr. Stewart."

"That's right, you did. Let me quote, 'It'll be a cold day in hell before you see Stewart.' You also said you would appeal any order from the court giving him access."

Dub hadn't expected to hear that. Neither had the judge, whose lips were set in a grim line. Dub rushed to add fuel to the fire.

"Your Honor, that's not what I said. I simply explained to Mr. Patterson the options my office has available." Janis was ready for the lie. She handed Maroney's affidavit to Dub and Bullock and turned to the bench.

"If Mr. Blanchard intends to make such a representation to the court, if he denies that he used the words 'cold day in hell' and 'we will appeal,' I will call both Mr. Bullock and Marshal Maroney to the stand to testify." I saw Bullock gulp.

"Your Honor, after my client's partner, Ms. Lawrence, was kidnapped and almost killed, he became concerned for the safety of Dr. Stewart. Having been denied access to his client, he did what any good lawyer would do—he hit the books. He determined that once a prisoner is detained in a federal facility, jurisdiction over that prisoner lies not with the court, not with the U.S. attorney, and not with the U.S. marshal. Jurisdiction resides with the warden of the facility where he is incarcerated. The warden controls any and all visitation." Janis handed the judge a memo outlining the law. "I might also add that Mr. Bullock recommended this precise course of action to Mr. Patterson last Sunday."

She continued, "Only then did Mr. Patterson contact the warden, obtain permission for a visit, and fly to Oklahoma to check on his client. To clear up the record, he did meet with his client briefly, but the meeting was interrupted. The warden told him that the he had been ordered him to curtail the interview immediately. Of course he flew back to Little Rock, but certainly not to refuel. A deputy marshal met the plane upon landing, and Mr. Patterson accompanied him peacefully. He didn't run or flee from arrest." She turned to glare at Dub scornfully.

The judge interrupted. "All right, I've heard enough. Mr. Blanchard, do you intend to charge Mr. Patterson today?"

"Not today, your Honor, although my office is still contemplating charges."

"All right then. First, since you have no charges, I see no reason why Mr. Patterson should be held. Second, Mr. Blanchard, if you wish to seek contempt charges against Mr. Patterson, you must file a motion. Furthermore, if you think disobeying your orders rises to the level of a federal crime or some form of contempt, I want to see some legal authority. Got it?"

No longer contemplating anything, Dub mumbled, "Yes, your Honor."

"I expect to issue my rulings on your motions very soon. I don't want you to read anything into what I say, Mr. Blanchard, but if I were you and didn't want Mr. Patterson to have access to his client, I'd be preparing my appeal." He smiled.

I felt almost giddy. We were finally going to get access to Doug— unless the Eighth Circuit Court of Appeals stayed his orders. Then Judge Houston turned to me.

"Mr. Patterson, I understand your hurry to see your client after Ms. Lawrence's tragedy. However, I get the impression you tend to play a little fast and loose. I won't tolerate any games in my court. I believe that justice delayed is justice denied. I know you are hampered by the loss of your co-counsel, but I will not accept her absence as an excuse for delay in either this case or the companion civil forfeiture case. I expect both sides to be ready within the dates I set in my order. Understood, counsel?"

I jumped up and said, "Understood, your Honor."

Dub couldn't leave well enough alone. "Your Honor, what about our request that Mr. Patterson be dismissed as counsel? He may not have violated an order, but surely his conduct warrants dismissal."

The judge appeared to be seriously pondering the request. I was beginning to worry, when, a slow smile spread over his face.

"Request denied, Mr. Blanchard. Your request would only delay matters." The judge banged his gavel and escaped the courtroom before anyone could say a word.

We remained in the courtroom for some time, relishing the moment. Dub and his troops left immediately, gearing up for an "impromptu" press conference. I had no desire to listen, and at my request Janis declined to participate. Too many battles were left to declare victory just yet. The opposition already had enough guns; I didn't want to give them any extra ammunition. No matter what, Dub would spin it his way, and I couldn't control how the press reported it. What mattered was that I was no longer under arrest, I was not in contempt of court, and I wouldn't spend another night in jail.

Normally, you don't just get to walk out of jail after being arrested. You have to be 'processed.' But since Dub and his attorneys had vanished, Marshal Maroney just smiled and opened the door.

So I walked out of the courthouse a free man. I'd spent one fairly safe night in segregated confinement—what would it be like to spend years behind those bars? Even if you were tough, made it through physically unscathed—what would it do to your soul? Laws in this country are unforgiving—where would you find a job? How could you support your family?

Janis and Maggie had decided to have a celebratory lunch, so I decided to wait for Sam who was just pocketing his cell phone. I started to thank him as he walked up, but he stopped me with an outstretched hand.

"That was Eric. Micki's out of ICU and wants to see you. Eric gave in, but insists on being there. I'm okay with it as long as one of my officers is present. You probably won't . . ." Clovis and I were already off like a shot.

29

Little Rock has the only Adult Level One Trauma Center in the state. The University Med Center had worked hard to attain the status and worked equally hard to maintain it. I'd known the director, Terry Collins, since we were kids. Terry met us at the door and told us to take the elevator to the third floor, the staff was expecting us. Clovis and I introduced ourselves to the two uniformed police officers standing outside Micki's door.

I knocked, and a tall, worried-looking man opened the door. He looked like the kind of guy who ate a lot of fish and spinach. He stepped out into the hall, and I offered my hand.

"You must be Eric. I'm Jack Patterson."

"Pleased to meet you. I—well, I feel like I already know you, but I sure didn't think we'd meet like this. Micki's asleep again, but I promised to wake her whenever you came. I don't think she's suffered any permanent physical damage, but she still sleeps a lot, and psychologically, I don't know. She'll need a lot of time and a lot of therapy. It's anyone's guess when she'll be back to normal."

"Jack—can I call you Jack?" I nodded, feeling my feathers ruffle just a little. He wasn't *that* much younger than me. "I know you have this big case together, and I know it's important to her, but she can't be involved. She made me promise to let you see her, but she's not ready to deal with you or some case or much of anything for that matter. She's lucky to be alive." He looked ready for combat, and I settled down. He really was in love with her.

"Listen to me, Eric. I'm here as her friend. I need to see her and assure myself she's all right, maybe to reassure both of us. I don't want to interfere with you or any of her other doctors. I just want her to get well. I'll only be here for a little while."

"Okay, but she's very fragile."

You've got a lot to learn about Micki. Fragile was not the word I would use to describe her, whatever the situation.

We stepped quietly into the room, and Eric pulled back the curtain. *Why is it that even orderlies barge in without hesitation, but visitors tiptoe?* Plastic bags dripped saline and medicine into IV catheters in her wrists. Her eyes looked like they'd been punched, and her skin was pale.

Eric said. "Micki, Jack's here."

She turned her head to look at me, eyes still bloodshot. I could still see a twinkle.

"Hello, partner," she whispered.

I took her hand gently, pulled the chair close, and sat down. Micki looked at Eric, Clovis, and the policeman who had trailed in behind us.

"I need to talk to Jack alone. I know I'm not supposed to, but I'm gonna do it. So everybody out."

Eric was the first to protest. "Honey . . ." but she interrupted.

"Out." She couldn't shout, but no one was about to argue with her. I continued to hold her hand, an innocent bystander, pleased as punch.

They all retreated, Eric scowling at me as he closed the door. "How'd you figure out where I was? Sam told me it was you who found me."

"Just a hunch." She looked so tired, so unlike the Micki I knew.

"Jack, I know I won't be able to stay awake very long, so tell me what's happening. I've got to know. I promise not to say a word, but please tell me what's going on." She leaned back, clearly expecting me to talk, so I did. Told her about going to Oklahoma City, spending the night in jail, and what had happened in court today. Her eyes remained closed, but I could tell she was listening and thinking.

I had just finished when Clovis stuck his head in the room.

"Jack, the policeman's getting anxious. Eric's gone, but if he comes back and you're still here he's going to have a cow." *I could easily grow tired of Eric.*

Micki tried to smile. "Just a few more minutes, please . . . c'mon Clovis, just a few more minutes." Clovis closed the door quietly.

I tried to interrupt, but she stopped me, sounding a bit like her old self. "My turn, Jack. It wasn't Novak. Somebody's trying to frame him."

"I agree," was all I could get out before she continued. "They all wore masks, but. . . ." The effort it took her to speak was heartbreaking.

"Sam will find whoever did it," I told her. "I think what happened to you is somehow related to the Stewart case. I haven't figured it out yet, but I will. What's important is for you to recover. Don't worry. You're my partner—we have a lot to look forward to."

She smiled, but was clearly about done in. Releasing her hand, I promised to return.

As I rose to kiss her on the check, she whispered, "Please, be careful. They're coming after you next."

"I know."

30

CLOVIS AND I thanked the two officers and drove back to Micki's office. I found myself sitting in her office chair, full of nervous energy, with nothing to do until Judge Houston issued his orders. Maggie and Debbie were going through all of Micki's current cases. Clovis seemed preoccupied, so I busied myself calling a couple of friends to let them know I'd be in Little Rock for a while. I also called Liz to tell her about my conversation with Doug, emphasizing his willingness to give up his research if the prosecution would leave her alone.

It wasn't yet the right time to press for the deal. Dub was bound to be pissed about this morning, and I didn't want to deal with Bullock until Dub had calmed down. Besides, I still had no idea what Doug's research pertained to or how marijuana was involved. Finally, I was at an extreme handicap without Micki. She knew all the pitfalls and tricks in negotiating a drug plea deal involving civil forfeiture. I only knew enough to be dangerous.

Liz said, "Jack, I'm not comfortable with any kind of deal until you get all the time you need with Doug. I know, I know, it's great for me, but it concerns the both of us, so until you're totally comfortable, don't jump the gun. That said, I trust you completely. In the end, do what you think is best."

"Thanks for the confidence, Liz. When the time comes I'll only have a short window of opportunity, so your trust means a lot. You doing okay, otherwise?"

"Actually, I've enjoyed spending time with my dad. We don't usually get along so well."

"Good. Take it easy. Something's bound to break soon. When it does, I'll need you here."

The last two days—and the night—were catching up. I needed some down time. I told Clovis I was going back to the hotel to take a nap. He had already pulled out his keys when Moira appeared and offered to drive me back. Clovis hesitated, but I waved him off, told him to relax and enjoy the afternoon. I was in good hands.

On the way back Moira and I chatted, and I took every opportunity to find out more about her. I'm sure Beth would have said I should have been more subtle. Maggie would say Moira was becoming a distraction.

I realized I hadn't had a bite to eat except for noodles and brown gravy in over twenty-four hours and asked Moira if she would join me for a quick lunch. The hotel bar was full of men in suits who stared at me like I'd just spent the night in jail. Even in decent clothes, I suppose I looked a little seedy. Or maybe these guys watched TV. Whatever—all I could think about was food and sleep. I decided against wine, opting for a Diet Coke. Moira and I shared an order of nachos covered in cheese, jalapenos, and chili. She easily deflected my questions about her background, peppering me with questions about the case and my theories about the link between Doug Stewart and Micki's kidnapping. I found myself enjoying her company.

Her fingers casually grazed my hand and shoulder more than once, and I couldn't help but wonder about asking her up to my room to share a bottle of wine. Fortunately I had the good sense to leave it to my imagination. This woman carried a Glock in her shoulder bag and worked for Clovis. Maybe after the case, when things settled down . . . .

While we were waiting for the check, she offered to walk me to my room. When I declined she looked me in the eye and said, "Are you sure you want to be alone right now? I can be pretty good company."

I won't deny it felt good to know her interest hadn't been all my imagination, but I managed to reply firmly, "Thank you, but yes, I'm sure—I'll be fine, I just need some rest."

Once upstairs, I showered to get the lice shampoo and jail smell out of my hair, turned down the thermostat, crawled into the bed and burrowed into the comfort of its soft covers. My eyes closed, and I was quickly dead to the world.

31

It's amazing that our sense of danger or preservation, or whatever you'd like to call it, works even when we're sleeping. I was dreaming about Micki when I woke up with a start, aware of another presence. Moira had slipped under the covers and was climbing on top of me. She quickly undid her hair, which fell abundantly to her shoulders. She wore only a sweater. I'll admit it: I was stunned, almost unable to react.

She smiled and said in a low voice. "You don't have much of a poker face, Jack. Don't be in a hurry now. I'm in charge."

Bending forward her lips brushed mine, a soft testing, and then another. She stretched upright and began to slowly rock back and forth against my lower torso until I was fully aroused. She reached behind her head and lifted her sweater exposing two very full and round breasts. Placing her hands behind her, she squeezed my thighs and began to slowly lean back, pressing her backside hard against my groin as her hands slowly slid down my legs.

She arched her back until her hair was brushing my ankles, her bottom swaying back and forth on top of my pelvis. Then slowly she came back up and bent forward from the waist. I felt her hands gliding their way up my torso until her mouth touched mine and her tongue began to probe. I arched my back to meet her, and she held my face to hers, lips open, tongue exploring. I felt her fingernails press deeply into the back of my neck as her other hand slid slowly down my chest. We met eagerly, and moaning softly, she began to rock her pelvis back and forth. I cried out in pleasure. Couldn't help it.

Her mouth slid to my ear and she whispered,

"Sweet dreams, Jack."

32

I DISTINCTLY HEARD a voice ask, "Was all that really necessary?" Moira responded, "A dying man's wish." I tried to clear my brain—had it all been a dream? Was I still dreaming? I hadn't opened my eyes yet, but I sensed I was no longer in the same bed, and my wrists and ankles were tied to something. I felt a tight band around my chest. What kind of game was Moira playing? What had I gotten myself into? I still felt pretty groggy, but now the man's voice was crystal clear. "You need to leave. It's time to finish this."

Her voice now heavily accented, Moira said, "I know, but I want to say good-bye. He isn't a bad man, you know? Besides what's the rush? They won't find him till we are long gone."

"Wake his ass up then, but get out of here. I need to finish, and we need to leave town."

I wasn't at all sure I wanted to wake up. Suddenly, I felt a heavy hand go to my groin, grab my testicles, and squeeze. I screamed, or at least tried to. My mouth was taped shut.

I heard the man say, "See, he's awake. Say goodbye, and get the hell out."

I looked up to see Moira hovering over me, this time fully clothed.

"It would have been fun to go another round, Jack, but Roger is running out of patience."

I tried to speak, but the tape kept me silent. I could only stare and strain my restraints.

"Sorry about the duct tape, but we can't have you screaming, now can we? Although, come to think of it, no one could hear you if you did." Moira mused. "Jack, you're just too damn smart for your own good. You found Micki before Roger could finish, and I bet you figured me out too, didn't you? Too bad you didn't tell Clovis what you suspected. Thought you could string me along—maybe seduce me like James Bond, you poor fool. Things don't work that way in real life. I kill people for a living, and you're a contract, nothing more, and nothing less.

"No one will miss you, at least not for a while. Everyone thinks you're taking a long nap after your terrible ordeal in jail. Roger and his friends botched Micki, but he's going to finish the job right this time, aren't you, Roger? I've given him very precise instructions."

Roger growled, "Don't tell him everything."

She turned on him with a sneer. "Don't tell me what to do, you moron. You're the one who blew it with the bitch. Listen—I need twenty-four hours before he's dead. Give him the juice slowly. Don't give him the final dose until I call, got that? Play your silly games if you must. I don't care how much he suffers, but don't leave any clues, and for God's sake keep him alive until I call. Fuck up again, Roger, and I'm coming for you."

Moira began to speak in some Slavic language. I had no hope of understanding. I watched her as if I was in another world, unable to process her words, but totally fascinated by her presence. Gone were the ponytail and frumpy blue pants suit. She wore tight designer jeans, Frye boots, and lots of bling.

What are you doing, Jack? Admiring your killer?

I forced myself to look at Roger. He was on the small side, skinny with a bad comb-over and a pencil thin mustache—reminded me of Fredo in *The Godfather.*

Moira turned back to me. "Roger wants to play a few games, but it won't be any worse than the night you got all these scars." Moira ran her fingernail down a long scar along my shoulder. "In fact, the heroin will kick in soon, and you won't have a care in the world. You should never have interfered, Jack. You're out of your league." Collecting her jacket and purse from a chair, she gave me a cool kiss on the forehead and left quickly, leaving only the scent of her perfume.

I sure knew how to pick 'em.

Roger smiled and busied himself with an IV drip on a stand next to the bed. I tried to thrash around, but he taped my elbow to the side of the bed. I could do nothing but watch as he inserted a catheter roughly into my vein. I noticed he hadn't bothered to swab my arm with alcohol, but I wasn't worried about dying from a dirty needle. A hypodermic lay ready on the tray table he had pulled up. I kept pulling against my restraints. Breaking them was unlikely, but maybe an adrenaline rush would give me superhuman strength.

When he turned his back I struggled as hard as I could, but the tape didn't give an inch. I couldn't hear what Roger was up to, but it didn't sound good.

"Moira said you wouldn't feel a thing, but she's wrong. I'm not going to set the drip until she calls. I want you to feel everything I do. I'm going to my car for a few instruments I forgot. Don't go anywhere." He giggled.

I tried not to panic, willing myself to come up with a plan. The space had been set up like a hospital room, but I could see metal rafters high above me—surely some sort of warehouse. Not much help. I felt sick to my stomach, but did everything I could to avoid throwing up into the duct tape. I might end up choking to death on my own vomit. Not a nice way to go.

I heard footsteps outside the door and steeled myself, dreading whatever Roger was bringing back into the room.

The door burst open and Clovis rushed in, followed closely by Debbie. Clovis jerked the catheter out of my arm, but couldn't undo the knots of the restraints. Debbie said, "You call the police and watch the door. I'll do this."

Clovis backed through the door and began punching in numbers and shouting into his cell. Debbie slowly untied me, talking smoothly. "Relax now. I'm going to take care of you." She carefully untied my restraints and slowly pulled the tape off my mouth. I could barely hear her—my teeth felt thick.

I watched her press a pillow over my arm. I could see it was bleeding, but didn't feel much of anything. Stroking my head gently, she said, "Lie back. You're going to be okay. The ambulance is on the way." Her tone reminded me of a dreamy-eyed nurse I'd met last year in an emergency room in Little Rock.

I might have dozed off. I wasn't sure of much anything. But at some point Clovis returned and threw his coat over me. "Sorry about the arm," he said looking at the bloody pillowcase.

"Not a problem. I . . . I just need a few minutes; I'll be okay, but. . . ." I sat up. Debbie and Clovis backed off a little while I tried to get my bearings.

I tried to make some sort of sense out of what had just happened.

"Where are we? I'm not sure what . . . I guess I'm still a little woozy. Clovis, get me my clothes. And how'd you find me?"

"It's a long story, but thank Debbie. She called Novak. And, um, Jack, you don't seem to have any clothes here." Now my memory was crystal clear—wasn't much I could say.

Debbie smiled, not the least bit flustered. I tried to change the subject.

"Oh, Jeez. Thank you, Debbie. I want to hear the whole story. It couldn't have been an easy call to make."

She lowered her eyes, still holding my hands. Then she looked up with a start. "Moira's been here."

Clovis protested. "Moira, no way—she's interviewing students and professors."

"I'd know her perfume anywhere. I asked her about it the first day I met her."

My eyes told truth to Clovis, who shook his head in denial.

"Sorry, Clovis, she's right. Did you get the other guy?"

"What other guy?" Clovis was instantly on alert.

"Moira left me with some guy named Roger. He went out to his car just before you got here—said he forgot something. " Clovis drew his gun and headed to the door.

"No!" I put out my arm to stop him. "He's either long gone or waiting to ambush you. Stay here until the police arrive."

Clovis hesitated, unwilling to face the truth. "Moira?" He already knew the answer.

"Clovis, don't feel bad, she fooled both of us. What's done is done—now it's time to end this."

33

I TRIED TO wave away the ambulance, but wasn't given any choice. Debbie rode with me while Clovis dealt with the police. The docs gave me a thorough inspection, but because Roger hadn't started the drip I really was okay. They fussed about shock and infection, gave me an antibiotic, and recommended I see a therapist. I took the antibiotics, declined therapy. Clovis appeared with some clothes and Maggie, who managed to look both relieved and disgusted. We sat in silence waiting for the discharge papers. To my surprise, Eric suddenly appeared in the doorway. He'd heard the story and had come to check on me. His news wasn't so good. Micki was back in ICU.

As Eric was leaving, Sam barged in without warning, and without a smile. "Jack, your nine lives are about to run out. I need you to give a statement to my detective. If Clovis has his facts straight, we have two killers on the loose. The hunt for Moira is on, but we've got nothing so far and we have no idea who her partner is and no idea why they were about to kill you. It's time for you to spill the beans."

"I'll talk to your detective, but I want Maggie and Clovis to hear everything, and I want Debbie to tell you how she found me. Sam, I need your help if we're going to put a stop to all this."

Exasperated, he drug his fingers through his hair, but relented. The detective came in, and I told them most of what had happened. I left out the intimacy at the hotel. My screw-up was none of their business. I told them Moira must have snuck into my room and knocked me out. I showed them the welt on the back of my neck and told them I'd woken to find myself tied up. I repeated what Moira had said about breaking cover and someone putting a contract out on me, and described Roger. The detective left immediately to put out an all-points for Roger, and I asked Debbie to tell us how she'd found me.

"We were still going through Micki's files, when Clovis called to ask if we'd heard from you. He was worried because you didn't answer your phone and you weren't at the hotel. Your bed had been slept in, but your room was empty. Maggie joked that you were probably flirting with Moira at some bar and had forgotten your phone. Sorry, Jack, that's what she said."

Maggie raised her eyebrows, clearly not by way of apology. Boy, was I glad none of them knew the whole story.

Debbie continued. "Thirty minutes later he came into the office looking like the world had come to an end. He couldn't find you anywhere. He was convinced you'd been grabbed, and while he was calling Sam, the police, and every spare body he had to look for you, I slipped away to make a call."

Sam interrupted "And just who did you call?"

"Novak."

Sam frowned harshly, but Debbie held her ground. "I know, I know. Micki will be pissed, but I couldn't think of anything else I could do to help. Look, I know everybody else thinks Novak grabbed Micki, but I don't and neither does Jack. Why would he kidnap Jack? It doesn't make sense. So I thought maybe Novak knew who was trying to frame him and where they might have taken Jack." She licked her lips, now a little unsure of herself.

Maggie leaned over to put her arm around her. "What you did saved Jack's life. You have nothing to be sorry for. Tell us what he said."

"He took my call right away. He was scary-angry, not at me, but at what had happened. He's not about to be anybody's fall guy. He told me to sit by the phone. About ten minutes later, he called me back with a few locations where Jack could be. I told Clovis and, thank God, we found Jack at the one he said was the most likely."

Hands on his chin, Sam mouthed a quiet "wow." "Debbie, have you talked to him since then?"

She looked at Maggie, who nodded her encouragement.

"I called him once we got to the hospital. He's in Dallas. You can contact him at the same number. He'll tell you everything he knows."

"You're damn right I want to 'contact' him. He led you directly to Jack. He's behind every bit of this. He put out the contract on Jack—I'd bet a million bucks on it." Sam shoved his hands in his pockets in frustration.

Debbie shrank back, finally unnerved by Sam's angry tone.

I thought a minute. "Debbie, how were you able to reach him so easily?"

She looked nervously at Maggie, who again nodded.

"After Micki was kidnapped, a girlfriend called me who still works for Novak. She told me that Novak was in a total rage that he could be on the hook for Micki. She gave me his cell number—in case I needed it."

Sam looked at me. I wasn't sure I wanted to ask the next question in front of Sam, but what the hell—I needed his help if I was ever going to figure the whole thing out.

"Did he say anything else other than what you've just told us?"

I caught her furtive glance at Sam.

"Sam's okay—he's on our side," I said.

Sam was "the law," and she still looked uncomfortable. "He wants to meet with you—just you, me, and him alone, when you can travel."

"No fucking way!" Sam burst out.

"Clovis, set it up," I replied with equal emphasis. "I'm just fine."

34

"Jack, I can't let you do this. Novak's a prime suspect in Micki's abduction and now yours. What if he told Debbie where to find you? Who better to know? He wants to get his hands on you—and Debbie, too."

I tried to interrupt, but Sam held up his hand.

"Hear me out. Novak is worse than a thug. He's been heavily involved in the sex trade for years. I'm talking about little girls being sold, raped, and abused. And not just girls he brings over from Eastern Europe—twelve year olds have been abducted right here in Arkansas. His guys target malls, concerts, and theaters—anywhere young teenagers are likely to hang out. This isn't some guy in a grey suit stealing money from other guys in grey suits. I'm talking about a murderer and a pimp—a man who would just as soon cut your throat as look at you. You'd be a sitting duck. Micki has been terrified he would snatch Debbie, and now you're going to hand her over on a silver platter? If something were to happen, Micki will kill you if Novak doesn't."

"Okay, I won't ask Debbie to go, but remember, it was Moira who just tried to kill Micki and me and frame Novak for it. I don't think for a minute that Novak hired Moira, but he might just know who did. Who better to know? Clovis has been all over town trying to find out who's responsible, and he's turned up zip. So it's time to go to the source. If he hadn't volunteered, I would have found a way to ask him. Novak's not stupid. If something happens to me, he'll be in jail for the rest of his life."

What could he say? He knew I was right.

"Clovis will be in charge of arrangements, and I won't go unless he's satisfied."

Debbie spoke up. She seemed to have gotten a second wind. "I'm going, too. He doesn't frighten me. He'd be a fool to do something in plain view, and Novak's no fool."

Clovis was ready.

"I'll coordinate everything with the Little Rock and Dallas police. Whoever is behind all this has no qualms about killing. Novak wants this meeting because, for once, he's scared. Someone is trying to set him up for a murder rap—most likely the same someone who's moving in on his operation. Micki and Jack are alive today because we got lucky twice. We can't risk giving someone a third bite at the apple." He paused and threw me a bone. "Who knows? Jack here is pretty good on his feet—maybe Novak'll slip, and you'll finally get him."

Sam twirled the pen in his hand, staring at the blood pressure machine. The tension was palpable. I heard a little noise, and realized that Eric had slipped in and was sitting silent and unnoticed in the corner.

Now he rose, his countenance one of both dismay and disgust. "Are all of you crazy? I feel like I'm in a bad dream." With that, he stalked out.

We stared at the door in silence and regret for a few seconds, before Sam recovered and said, "He may be right—we may all be crazy, but we can't just do nothing. And Clovis is right about one thing. So far, we've got zip. God help us all if something goes wrong. Jack, you get to deal with Micki—have fun."

Clovis and Debbie left to make the arrangements, Sam to worry some more. Maggie and I sat waiting while the painstaking hospital checkout process lumbered forward.

I looked at Maggie. "You've been quiet."

Maggie was too proper to cry in public, but her eyes were full.

"It's just you and me. Tell me what's wrong."

"What's with you and this death wish? If Beth were here she'd be going through the roof. First, it's Micki, and now you who've barely escaped death. And what's your response? You fly off to Dallas to meet with the head of the Russian Mob?"

"Do you have a better idea?"

"Leave Little Rock and never come back. Every time you set foot in this town you dance with death. We have a nice thing going in DC. Walter's foundation is doing good work. You have a thriving antitrust practice. Why come here and get yourself killed?" Now the floodgates were open.

I wrapped her in my arms. "Maggie, let's get out of here. I'll explain why this is all so important. I promise."

We'd been at the hospital for more than three hours, and I was ready to leave. I left the papers on the bed and walked through the doors of the emergency room to find Clovis and Debbie waiting.

"Wait a minute. Has the doctor signed the orders? Can you just leave?"

"He'll get around to it. Now he doesn't have to hurry. I've had a tough day, and Maggie and I both need a drink. You can stay, but we're leaving." I wondered idly why Americans feel so bound by hospital bureaucracy. I know it's all about liability, but, jeez, why does it have to take so interminably long?

Clovis looked rattled, but said he'd bring the Tahoe around. We drove to the Armitage mostly in silence, each of us occupied with our own thoughts. I gave Clovis the key card to my room and suggested he and Debbie continue to work out the details of tomorrow's trip. Maggie and I found a quiet corner in the bar. She ordered a Glenlivet, no ice. I had no idea what was in my system but figured a glass of pinot noir couldn't do it too much harm.

Maggie excused herself to "freshen up"—the correct English-woman had returned. I thought about what I wanted to say to my best friend, my business associate, and the one person I could always trust.

After she had settled back into in her chair I took a sip of wine and said, "The long and the short of it is that I came here because Doug Stewart was a friend of Angie's. I had no reservations about Micki representing him. I came more out of loyalty and the need for a little change of scenery, not because of some death wish."

"I'm sorry about that. I didn't mean it. But this thing's such a dog's breakfast—I admit I'm scared." I took her hand and gave it a squeeze.

"No apologies. I deserved it. I don't know why I'm not more scared. Yes, I got swept up in the circumstances and events until I almost got myself killed. Yes, I was careless–once again, I let bedroom eyes and a nice figure get the best of me. I had a feeling Moira was our mole, but I thought I could outsmart her. Maybe I thought I could turn her. Okay . . . I was a fool." She'd rolled her eyes in disbelief.

"I was wrong and foolish and almost paid the price. Thank God and Debbie, I didn't die, but I owe it to Doug, Liz, Micki, and Debbie not to run away scared. And I owe this to Angie. She believed in Doug, and she saw this coming. It mattered to her, and I wasn't paying attention. I've got to see this to the end, but I promise to be more careful. Believe it or not, I think I'm close. If I'm right, we've fallen into one hell of a mess. I need to hear what Novak has to say, and I need to consult Liz. If they confirm what I suspect, we'll know for sure what we're up against."

She sighed. "So tell me what you think is going on."

"Not yet. I need to know whether I'm right or whether we're back to square one. Maggie, either way, I hope you'll stay. I need you. Micki's out of commission and Clovis has his hands full just keeping us alive. So it's back to the old days—just you and me, kid."

"Should I ask Walter to offer Clovis some help?"

"Let's ask Clovis. Moira's betrayal has shaken him. I trust him with my life, but we're dealing with real pros. Moira must have been placed inside his organization weeks ago. The very existence of Moira suggests we're up against more than a drug charge and Dub's outsized ego. I certainly expect you to tell Walter what's going on. In fact, if I'm right we're going to need his help for more than security."

"Really?" She was suddenly excited.

"Really. Somebody with serious money is behind all this, and it may take Walter's help to flush him out."

"You really don't think it's Novak or some competitor?"

"The smart money is on those two, and they're probably right, but, no, I don't."

"Okay, I'll wait, but this time I'm right beside you every step of the way. Well, not to see Novak, but everywhere else. I don't want to be anywhere near a sex trafficker."

"On that point, we're in total agreement."

Clovis and Debbie walked into the bar, both looking a good deal calmer.

"We're on for tomorrow. We fly to Dallas in the morning. Sorry, but everyone gets searched. The three of you will meet for lunch at Fearing's in the Ritz-Carlton. I'll be in the lobby along with Novak's bodyguard, and Dallas's finest will be posted all over. I'm pretty comfortable this is on the up and up. Novak must feel pretty secure. He's agreed to meet with Sam and one of his detectives afterward."

"Clovis, I know this isn't a set-up. Novak has as much to gain as we do if we find the real culprit. Does Sam want to fly down with us?" I asked.

"I asked, but he didn't think it would look right. He and his detective are flying Southwest."

"Just as well. I want to go to Memphis to see Liz tomorrow afternoon. I assume you've already spoken to the people protecting her."

Clovis laughed. "I have. Apparently Liz is not the easiest person to protect. I also made sure they were on the up and up—after all, they were hired by Moira."

"Okay. Let's talk about security. You've got Paul and his team watching Micki. That means you've got me, Debbie, and now Maggie, full-time. It won't have gone unnoticed that Maggie was with me in Oklahoma City."

Maggie opened her mouth, but Clovis was ready.

"I'm not comfortable with Debbie staying at Micki's office tonight. I'd rather have everyone here, so my people aren't spread out."

"She can stay with me. I'm glad to have the company," Maggie interjected.

"Thanks. You saved me from asking. Jack, I'm sure you remember Martin, who provides security for Walter's company. He's agreed to help with some of his men. Moira made me question my procedures, and I need the manpower," Clovis said.

"Don't kick yourself over Moira. She was a professional sent here to do a job. You couldn't have seen this coming," I said.

"Clovis, look at Jack—he went daft the moment he saw her." Maggie kidded, not knowing half the story.

"You guys leave Jack alone," Debbie jumped in. "Men are easy to seduce, but Moira was a pro. It takes one to know one—I should have warned you. But I never imagined she was a hired killer."

None of us could come up with an apt response. I wondered . . .

I broke the awkward silence. "This has been one hell of a day—I feel like a big, juicy burger and a cold beer. Sam told me the Buffalo Grill has one of the best burgers in town and pretty good cheese dip to boot, so let's go. Clovis, you need some down time— let your men take tonight's shift. I need you at your best tomorrow."

His worried face relaxed into a grin. "A plate of extra crispy fries sounds good to me, too."

"You, too, ladies. Tomorrow I meet the infamous Novak. By the end of the day we may know who's behind this whole thing."

FRIDAY

April 25, 2014

35

Burgers, crispy fries, and cold beer hit the spot, but I was ready to crash the moment we got back to the hotel. My head felt like the inside of a Levon Helm drum. I threw back a couple of Advil, but sleep was elusive, and the few times I nodded off the nightmares were worse than my pounding head. It was hard to imagine I was about to meet the evil Novak. I got out of bed around five o'clock. Even a long hot shower didn't help much.

I managed some coffee and sourdough toast with a surprisingly talkative Debbie and, before long, my motley crew was buckled safely in Walter's plane, ready for Dallas. After take-off the pilot let Debbie come up front, exciting her to no end, and saving me from begging her to be quiet. Maggie knew my moods well enough to let me be, and I used the quiet time to try to will my headache away.

Sooner than I had hoped, we were on the ground and on our way to the Ritz with a friend of Clovis's, who had helped him iron out the day's details.

Now Debbie sat quietly in the back seat, twisting her scarf nervously through her fingers.

"Debbie, I'm sorry. Are you still okay with this? I know you must be scared, at least a little."

"Well, a little. But I'm okay. Maggie and I had a long talk last night. She's a very good listener. Novak will try to mess with my head, that's his way. But I've heard it before, and this time I'm ready. But you and Clovis need to be ready, too. He won't threaten us, and I don't think we're in any kind of physical danger, but he loves playing mind games."

We stepped out of the car and into the elegant tasteful lobby of the Ritz. I spotted Novak easily, slouching carelessly in an overstuffed chair. A surly bodyguard paced behind him. Novak looked nothing like my preconceived image of a Russian gangster. Thinning brown hair, slight build, pencil neck, and no bling or earrings. He stood a little less than six feet, wore a tailored business suit and Italian shoes.

I reached out to shake his hand, but his bodyguard stepped between us and grunted, "First, you're searched." His accent was straight out of the movies. We went to a small private room where we'd agreed to be checked for recording devices and weapons. After the door was shut, Novak's bodyguard pointed to me.

"Take off all your clothes."

This had not been part of the agreement.

Clovis spoke strongly. "He will not. This isn't a prison–hell, it's not even an airport. And what about Debbie? She's not going to take her clothes off in front of you or him." Novak remained silent. So this was one of his mind games.

"Take off clothes or no meeting." I was sure the bodyguard could speak better English, but he played his part well. I looked coldly at Novak and was turning to walk away, when Debbie unexpectedly pulled up her sweater.

Clovis said hoarsely, "What are you doing?"

Debbie responded with a bored shrug. "He's seen it all before. I don't mind if you don't. I'm not ashamed." Her sweater was off and on the floor, and she had started to unbutton her jeans when we heard:

"Stop. This is not necessary."

Debbie stood up straight, her well-rounded breasts directed squarely at Novak, almost a challenge.

"Put your sweater back on," he said brusquely. Debbie didn't move. Who was playing mind games now?

"Please, Ms. Kotrova. My apologies. This is not necessary." He turned to the guard, giving him a hard stare. I took the hand he offered me, a little gingerly, I admit.

"My apologies, Mr. Patterson. Yuri takes his job very seriously. Let us go into the dining room, have a little lunch, and talk."

Clovis was supposed to frisk Novak, but he had the good sense not to act. Debbie pulled on her sweater and we followed Novak, leaving Clovis and the bodyguard in the lobby.

"Please, call me Jack. What should I call you?"

Debbie replied for him. "His Christian name is Alexander Novak. He once told me that only his enemies called him Novak. His friends call him Alex."

Novak looked at Debbie in surprise. "You remember."

"I remember." Her tone was nonchalant, the words almost tossaway. I wondered . . . but Alex's voice brought me back to reality.

"Please call me Alex. We are hardly enemies; I owe you a great deal. But first, let us drink together. I understand you appreciate good wine. I've asked the maître'd for something special. If his choices don't meet with your approval, please ask for whatever you like."

Debbie had told me to expect this type of hospitality, but I certainly wasn't expecting the excellent French Bordeaux or the Flora Springs Chardonnay the waiter was carefully uncorking. "Alex" seemed pleased, and I wasn't paying for it, so why not enjoy the wine and go with the flow? We started with the Chardonnay. He spoke to Debbie in what I assumed was Russian, but she interrupted.

"Alex, we should talk in English. Jack must know everything that is said." Again, Debbie didn't seem to be intimidated. But as Novak lifted the wine bottle, I saw her swallow and look away for just a second.

He lifted his glass and said "My apologies. I haven't had the pleasure of Debbie's company in some time. It's my nature to compliment her, but she rightfully reminds me why we are here."

I raised mine to Debbie. "Debbie can indeed be a distraction, a very pleasant one. I wish we were here only to enjoy her company, outstanding wine, and a good meal. But, that's not the case. I hope you won't mind if I'm direct. You claim you're not responsible for the attacks on Ms. Lawrence or me and that someone is trying to frame you. Frankly, I hope that's true.

"The person who tried to kill me goes by the name of Moira Kostov, surely not her real name. Sam Pagano thinks you hired her. I don't. Why would you? You have the means to order an execution without hiring an outsider. Nor do I think one of your competitors tried to frame you. Little Rock isn't that big a market—sorry. I think the common denominator is Doug Stewart, a chemistry professor at UALR."

Novak regarded his glass with appreciation and took a generous sip. "Actually, her name really is Moira Kostov, although she's used different names in the past. Moira is a professional assassin, a very dangerous woman, and she doesn't come cheap. She's in Rio now, but when she hears you are alive, she will be very unhappy, as will the person she works for, and his client. She will come back to finish the job. She has a reputation to protect—sorry." He looked at me evenly.

"Well, I admit I find that prospect somewhat troubling. All the more reason to figure out who's behind all this."

Novak put his wine glass down abruptly. "When I find out who that person is, I will take care of that problem for you."

"Thanks, but I'd rather you didn't. Let me tell you what I think. You can tell me where I'm wrong."

"I'm listening."

"The Feds have pulled out all the stops when it comes to Doug Stewart—something not's right. Micki saw it first. Growing fifty plants, even a hundred, is small potatoes. The Feds have more or less decided to leave marijuana alone. So, normal procedure—they would have turned the case over to the local prosecutor or done nothing. Instead, Blanchard is all over the airwaves gloating about a major drug bust and terrorism. At first, Micki thought he was grandstanding, but when they moved Dr. Stewart to Oklahoma using the cover of national security, she knew something else was up."

Novak responded. "Dr. Stewart wasn't dealing drugs in any big way. I would have known. I've never heard of the guy. I've asked around and nobody, I mean nobody, knows of a single person who bought weed or anything else from him. No one is looking for a new dealer since he was busted. I, of course, do not engage in the sale of illegal drugs."

"So I've been told." Determined not to lose control, I allowed myself a swallow of the Flora Springs. It was a lovely wine, clean and almost effervescent.

"The events smack of smoke and mirrors, but Blanchard's prosecution of Doug Stewart is real enough. I told the court at what should have been his arraignment that Micki would act as lead counsel. Her reputation is to dig and dig deep. Someone decided he couldn't risk her discovering what lies behind the smoke. They decided to kill her and frame you for the murder. Everyone knows you have it in for Micki. You're the perfect scapegoat."

"Do you really think the government would do such a thing to win a case?" Debbie asked.

"No, I can't go that far. No, it's someone who stands to gain, big time and big bucks. I don't see Dub and his gang hiring Moira. I mean, how would they have found her and how could they pay her? The same people who planned Micki's abduction grabbed me after they realized I wasn't going to walk away. Moira all but told me that. She also said you'd be the dupe again."

Novak cringed at the word "dupe." He poured more wine just as the waiter delivered the first course. The crab cakes were superb, and we took a minute to appreciate them. The crab was fresh and succulent; the cakes contained only a hint of breadcrumbs. Novak was obviously thinking. After a few bites, he looked up.

"Why would I want to kill Micki? How would I benefit?" He turned to Debbie, who shrank back a little. "You were special, Debbie, one of a kind. My customers miss you. I miss you, *moy kotenok*. You made me good money. The man who ruined you is, shall we say, no longer with us. But I'm not stupid. If I killed Micki, nothing would stop Sam Pagano until I was under his jail. It may surprise you, but I'm getting out of the business. I've learned you can steal more money legally in this country than you can make illegally, with far fewer complications. I'll be totally out in a year. But I still have my sources. Moira's contract didn't originate in Little Rock. She was placed in Detroit to do another job. I have no idea why she was moved to Little Rock."

"Do your sources know the identity of the slimy guy she left me with?"

"His name is Jan Stosur. He is, you would say, a little fish." He raised his hands in a quick, dismissive gesture. "He has dug his own grave."

I felt a little bead of perspiration form on my forehead. Novak had confirmed my suspicions, but the details were more than a little troubling. I felt like I had a big fish on my line, and the fish was playing me. I tried to keep my face calm, resisting the urge to wipe my brow.

Novak asked the hovering waiter to decant the Bordeaux. Another waiter brought in pomegranate duck served over a mushroom risotto. I took a tentative forkful, surprised to find myself hungry.

Debbie excused herself to the bathroom, and I used the opportunity to ask a question I had hesitated to ask in front of her. Novak confirmed my suspicion, another tidbit to put in the bank.

After a few bites I put the fork down and regarded my host thoughtfully, "Why did you ask for this meeting?"

"You have encountered many obstacles. Most men with your intelligence would take their marbles and go home. You haven't. So, I've concluded you and I are not so different."

A compliment to me, or to him?

Novak took another bite of duck, followed by a swallow of wine, and continued.

"You and I are not fools, so I'm going to let you in on information I would normally keep to myself. Before I do, I must ask your pledge."

"I'm a man of my word."

"That I already know, or we wouldn't be enjoying lunch together. You must promise that you will do everything you can to protect Debbie. Moira will surely realize it was Debbie who found you. Debbie is a loose end, and Moira's employer doesn't leave loose ends. Debbie won't let me protect her, and I understand why. So, I want your word that you will protect her."

"You have my word. Without asking."

Debbie had slipped quietly into her chair just a few seconds earlier. She hadn't said a word.

Novak smiled and poured us each a glass of the Bordeaux.

"What else? You must want something more."

"You may never reveal the source of your information—to anyone. Not to Micki, not to your friend Sam, or anyone else. You may tell them what I am about to tell you, but you must never reveal your source. Only you and Debbie know the source."

"I agree." I had no idea what I was about to hear, but I was definitely interested.

Novak raised his glass, examined the wine's color, and said, "Dub Blanchard is dirty. I don't know what that means to you, but it's a fact you may wish to consider."

You could have heard a pin drop. I stared at this Russian thug, knowing I had heard the truth. He had finished his wine and signaled easily to the waiter.

"I will honor our agreement, but I must ask. How do you know?"

"He was a client. He was Novak's client for many years."

The small voice was Debbie's. I turned to see her bright red face. I admit my attempts at a poker face failed. How could she have not said anything earlier?

"Drink your wine, Jack. Debbie and I have a few things to tell you." Novak smiled grimly as the waiter filled our glasses.

36

For the next hour, Novak and Debbie told me about Dub Blanchard, his visits to Novak's gambling parlors, and his kinky preferences with the girls. He'd taken up gambling to relieve the pressures of law school and was quickly hooked. A trip upstairs and a good night at the tables helped restore his bruised ego. He was lucky at first, but soon was up to his ears in debts to the house. Twice he had to call on his uncle for help, the same uncle who would find him a job in Congress after he finally got his JD degree.

In the beginning, he didn't indulge his habit in Washington. He managed trips back to Little Rock as often as he could. But his needs grew, and Novak soon set him up with an associate in DC. Novak and his associate extended him credit, knowing Dub was a valuable asset. Debbie told me his sexual preferences became "weirder" over time, but he never hit a girl or asked her to do anything "really sick."

Not long after he was appointed U.S. attorney, he came by for a night at the tables in Little Rock. He drank more than usual, lost heavily, and took a girl upstairs. He was too drunk to perform, got frustrated and beat her senseless.

Novak said, "Because of his position I was called in. I sobered him up and told him I'd make it right with the girl, and that I'd overlook the incident. After all, his favor was worth a lot. He promised to pay me back, and I thought I'd seen the last of him for a while."

"How much did he owe?"

"Thirty-seven thousand."

I whistled, and he continued.

"Much to my surprise, he came in a few weeks later and handed me fifty thousand dollars in cash. He said, 'Now we're even. Give the balance to the girl. I won't be back, and it's in your best interest to forget I was ever here.' He hasn't set foot again in any of my places since, but he didn't quit playing the tables or enjoying the ladies. That much I know."

Debbie interrupted. "He was never my personal client. I knew about his fetishes from other girls, but only Alex knew who he was or what he did for a living. I'd see him at the tables, and once, a long time ago, he asked Alex about me, but Alex told him I wouldn't play the games he liked. Thank God."

I felt quite sure I didn't want to know what she was talking about.

She continued, "When I went to court the other day, I recognized him. He might have recognized me, I don't know. I knew I had to tell you that Dub was a customer, but Alex has an absolute rule about confidentiality. If I talked about his customers, he'd have no choice but to kill me."

I was learning more than I wanted to know about a world to which I couldn't begin to relate. Honor among thieves was hardly an apt analogy. But I understood. I gave it a little thought, and then spoke to Novak.

"Debbie called to tell you I was alive, that Moira was responsible, and that I thought it was related to Dr. Stewart's case. You put two and two together. You think maybe Dub's in the thick of this business. That's why we're here. But you need to be sure I won't talk out of school."

"Debbie told me you'd catch on fast." Novak almost smiled.

"If Dub's involved, he's got to be on somebody's payroll. Who's behind all this?"

"I don't know, I really don't. Otherwise I would have taken care of them myself. But I know it's not about a hundred or so marijuana plants."

"For sure. But I can't even speak with Doug Stewart, and he's the only one who can give me answers."

"I thought a man had a right to a lawyer here in the States. Maybe it's all rigged after all," Novak mused to no one in particular.

I slammed my hand down on the table, scaring Debbie and causing Novak to rise in alarm. "Damn, why didn't I think of that? I'm sorry, sit down, it's okay." Novak didn't realize it but the word "rig" had pushed a button in my antitrust mind.

"Think of what?" Debbie slurred a bit—too much wine. Novak sat down, but I noticed he kept his right hand under the table.

My right hand ran through my hair. I wanted to be precise, to be clearly understood. And I wanted Debbie to hear me loud and clear.

"Alex, thank you for helping Debbie find me. I owe you my life. But I need to ask you one more favor. In return, I promise you I'll do everything in my power to expose whoever is responsible for framing you. I'll do my best to protect Debbie, and I'll never reveal my source."

"Go ahead," he said, eyes narrowing.

"Leave Debbie alone, for good. Don't even think about trying to get her back." My face had turned to stone. "I want your word."

Novak looked grim, almost insulted, but he gave in gracefully.

"You have my word. I'm happy she is free from drugs and is once again a beautiful young woman. I am a ruthless and heartless bastard, but I keep my promises. Debbie and your precious Micki have nothing to fear from me or anyone in my organization. You have my word. Now I think it is time for us to part."

He offered his hand again, and I shook it firmly.

I pulled back Debbie's chair and took her arm—she wobbled a bit on her heels. We walked carefully out of the restaurant. I don't know who looked more relieved, Clovis or Yuri.

As we parted, Novak said, "Be careful, Jack Patterson. You face formidable adversaries who are not happy that you're still alive."

"Thanks for the warning. I plan to stay that way."

37

I WAS TEMPTED to quiz Debbie, but she'd had too much wine and stress, and before we were a mile down the road she'd fallen asleep. Clovis had some good news: Micki was improving, again out of ICU, and Martin had arrived in Little Rock with reinforcements. While Maggie and I met with Liz in Memphis, Clovis would meet with her security team to make sure they were as "top-shelf" as Maggie had said. He raised skeptical eyebrows when I told him Novak had given his word he'd leave Micki and Debbie alone. His job was to be skeptical. His brow lowered to a frown when he heard Novak's prediction that Moira would be back.

Clovis carried Debbie onto the plane, and she curled up in the back seat, fast asleep. After we'd gotten settled in, Maggie told me that the judge had given notice that his rulings would come down tomorrow in open court at ten AM.

Tomorrow was a Saturday. The judge was a hard worker.

"Maggie, when we land, I want you to call Janis Harold—see if she can join us in court. We're going to need all the help we can get. I also need to see Sam tomorrow, preferably after we get the court's decision."

"I'll see to it."

"One last thing. You and I need to go back home for a few days. Is the plane still at our disposal? At some point, doesn't Walter want his plane back?"

"It's not a problem. Walter's checking out the latest Falcon, looking for a new toy," Maggie replied, without a glimmer of approval.

"Will he be available when we get back?"

"Sure. What have you got up your sleeve?"

"Maggie, we need to find out what Liz knows. She holds the final piece to the puzzle, whether she know it or not. If I'm right, you'll see it right away."

"Okay, but it seems to me that you're simply jumping from one crisis to another."

THE FLIGHT FROM Dallas to Memphis took less than an hour. We left Debbie asleep in the back of the plane—I knew she'd be safe with Walter's pilot. Clovis rode in the lead car so he could talk to the head of Liz's security. Maggie and I followed in an Explorer driven by a guy who looked like he was a pro wrestler in his spare time. Before long we pulled into a circular driveway in East Memphis.

Liz threw open the door. She was back to the wild hair, exercise pants, and a sloppy grey sweatshirt. Maggie couldn't control her eyebrows, but did manage to keep the rest of her face straight.

On the way to the "solarium" Liz whispered, "Jack, I know Maggie doesn't approve of my hair or these clothes, but they drive my stepmother crazy. I can't resist."

I chuckled and was introduced to the perfect *Town and Country* couple. They were adorned in matching white pants, and Drew wore a polo shirt with a sweater draped over his shoulders. Cindy wore a flowered silk blouse, scarf, and lots of gold jewelry. Her hair was pulled back and tucked under, all perfectly in place. Tall glasses of iced tea waited on a tray in front of them, but I saw him swirling a martini and she was sipping straight bourbon over shaved ice.

After we spent an appropriate length of time introducing ourselves and playing "who do you know," I asked if I might have some time alone with Liz , and we left them happily chatting with Maggie. Liz asked the maid to bring drinks to her father's library. Most of the house was bright and airy, but here cypress-paneled walls enclosed a large, well-worn desk surrounded by brimming bookshelves and leather wingbacks. Not the sort of room you see too often today. Most men seem to want their private space to be equipped with a 52-inch TV screen and a beer fridge. Liz gestured to the sofa and took up the seat at the other end, sitting on her legs so she could face me.

"I heard you were almost killed by my former bodyguard. A bit off-putting. Are you okay?"

I gave her a truthful but understated version of recent events and explained that one of the reasons we had come was to assess her security. I told her I was still very concerned for her safety. She didn't bat an eyelash. I gave her a much longer version of my brief visit with Doug.

"I know Doug would do anything for me, but remember you promised not to make that deal for my immunity without consulting him. A few minutes in Oklahoma doesn't cut it. Doug's research is important, and I'm not sure he should agree so quickly."

"We may not have a choice. I won't play that card unless I absolutely have to, but the law isn't on our side when it comes to forfeitures. But civil forfeiture isn't the only reason I'm here. Liz, as your lawyer, you can tell me anything in complete confidence. Sometimes when the lawyer is a friend, you're reluctant to tell him everything, but I need you to tell me the truth. No holding back, okay?"

"Of course, silly. What else would I do?" Her eyes were very wide.

"No, I mean it. Not just about what you think is important, but everything."

"Jack, I'll tell you about my sex life if you want, although right now it's piss-poor. My bodyguards are starting to look hot." She smiled.

"Dammit, Liz, I'm not a fucking idiot! Enough of the act. Micki is lying in a hospital fighting death. I was almost tortured and thrown into a dumpster. Your husband is likely to be locked away for life with a bunch of rapists and murderers, and you're holding out. If I have any chance to get him off, I need you to quit pretending to be an airhead. I need the Dr. Liz Stewart who is as smart as her husband and much more street savvy. What in the hell were you two doing with a garden full of marijuana? What are you hiding?"

She toyed with her drink for a minute, and then answered in the same blasé manner.

"Jack, I'm not holding out on you. I promise I've told you and Micki everything. I just made some ginger snaps for my friend."

"Okay. Then tell me when you had your mastectomy." My voice was matter-of-fact, no smiles this time. Her face dropped, and her well-formed chest jutted out in reaction.

"How did you know? Did Doug tell Angie? He swore he never told a soul, but with what she was going through, I can see him telling her. There's no way you can tell. Dr. French is the world's best." She proceeded to show them off through her sweatshirt, arching her back.

I took hold of her arms and returned them to the couch, clasping my hands firmly over hers. "Liz, I don't know if he told Angie or not, and you certainly can't tell from looking. I actually know Dr. French—he has a well-earned reputation. I guessed because of the marijuana and the ginger snaps. But, Liz, none of this is about your perfect breasts. You've got to come clean. Do you really think whoever is behind this is going to let Doug or you live, if they're willing to kill your lawyers? Get real."

"You guessed. You had me showing you my boobs because you guessed. I should make you do a hands-on inspection for that bit of trickery, Jack Patterson."

Shaking my head, I succumbed to her thousand-watt grin. "Well it was an educated guess. From the way you described your friend who had breast cancer, the way you knew exactly how to handle the plants and mix them with the ingredients, and because of how proud you are of your body, which you should be. Yes, I guessed. I also guessed that the friend you described isn't the first person who's benefited from your ginger snaps."

Liz threw down her bourbon, got up from the couch, and poured herself another. She bit her lip and spoke with a Liz voice I had never heard.

"No, Jack, she's not, and I guess the reason you're asking is because you want to know if the recipe is Doug's."

"That and a whole lot more."

"I'll give you his formula, but you've got to promise to keep it to yourself. Doug made me promise not to share it with a soul."

I promised, and she slowly told me about learning she had cancer. The radiation left her weak and exhausted, and the chemo destroyed her hair as well as the cancer. "Losing your hair is so unfair. I mean, here you are, trying to fight this horrible disease with some sense of privacy and dignity, and then your hair falls out. Bald men are 'in,' bald women are not. It's like your body is screaming to the world, 'I have cancer.' I know my hair looks wild, but now that it's back, I just want to let it be.

"I went days without being able to hold anything down. Doug couldn't bear seeing me like that, so one night he made me a batch of ginger snaps. I didn't think I could manage even one down, but I did. The first batch was more than a little strong, and the trip was pretty wild, but over time Doug modified the recipe until he had it down to perfection. Without those cookies, I'm not sure I'd have made it."

"Did he teach you how to make your own?"

"Not at first. Not until I was fully recovered. We had a mutual friend who was going through a similar hell, and I begged him to let me make her a batch. He finally relented. They're not that much different from regular ginger snaps."

"So, exactly how many have you made?"

"I couldn't tell you. I always keep some in the freezer for friends in need. Do you have any idea how many women my age get cancer? But Doug watches me like a hawk. He wants to be sure he knows exactly where they're going. That's why he's going to be so mad at me for giving some to Sheila. This time I forgot to ask."

"Liz, don't start again. I need candor, not bullshit. He was growing hundreds of plants—how could he possibly know when you snipped a few for cookies?" I asked.

"He controlled the spice."

"The what?"

"That's what he calls it. Besides the marijuana, the recipe calls for a level tablespoon of 'spice,' no more, no less. He keeps it locked in a safe in the basement. Whenever I make cookies, he gets it out and gives me a level tablespoon. I don't mind. It takes a lot of work on his part to make the spice, and it's what makes the cookies taste so good."

I gave her a look. "Liz, the truth, remember? I'm not somebody you play bridge with."

"That's for sure. Doug says the spice helps with the actual cancer, not just the wasting and the pain. He made me promise not to tell a soul."

"Does it?"

"Well, the truth is, I don't know. I only know what it did for me. Doug tells me not to read anything into it, calls it an uncontrolled environment. But it did help, and my friends have said the same thing. They're very grateful."

"So that's why you don't want to give his research to the Feds, and maybe that's why Doug told me it's not about the marijuana."

"That's what I think."

"Did the Feds remove the spice from the safe?"

"No, I was lucky. I told him I was going to make a batch the night before the raid. He got it out and made me promise to only use a tablespoon. I forgot to give it back, just put it with the regular kitchen spices, and when they raided our home that was one of the few things they didn't take. Go figure. That's why I was so anxious to get back into the house, but I couldn't tell Micki. It's now in Daddy's safe. He has no idea what it is. Do you want it?"

"No. It's probably safer here with you than it would be with me. Liz, why didn't you tell Micki any of this?"

"Doug made me promise. Six months ago, he and I had a 'come-to-Jesus' talk. Usually it's about me spending too much money or my flirting. He worried about people talking and the cops finding out what was in my cookies—you know how people talk. But he knew how much they could help people, so . . . we agreed that if anyone asked about the cookies, I would play dumb in general and for sure not mention any special ingredient. He said if push came to shove, he had a plan, and that it included you. That was it. That was all he told me."

"Why was he was so worried all of a sudden?"

"I don't know—maybe because I had three or four sick friends with cancer?"

"Don't do it, Liz. Don't patronize me. I think you know exactly what his research is about. You may not know what kept him awake at night, or what his plan was, but you know."

"Why don't you tell me? You seem to know."

"I think Doug was working on a cure for cancer using some chemical compound found in marijuana. You told me about his grafting and pruning—I think he was experimenting with crossing the properties of other plants like kale that are known to have cancer-limiting effects. I think the special spice you talk about consists of ground seeds or other parts of hybrid plants he has been developing over time. I think his research precisely documents every step he has taken over the years.

"Everyone knows marijuana can help with the pain and side effects of cancer treatment, but Doug thought it might actually have curative qualities when combined with other plants. I may not have the science right, but I bet he was improving the marijuana in ways that nobody had thought of or tried. Most people grow different strains of marijuana to improve the high. Doug was developing different strains to find a cure for cancer.

"Despite the government banning this kind of research, Doug decided to forge ahead on his own, or maybe with Angie, at NIH, and his work here in Arkansas is just a continuation. But something got to him recently, really scared him. He couldn't stop because he felt sure he was close to a breakthrough. I think the Feds finally realized what he was up to and put the quash on it.

"He was ready to tell me, but the government wouldn't and won't let me communicate with him, and is determined to get his research and whatever else he has discovered."

The thoughts that had been swirling in my head had finally crystallized into sense. Now I really was scared.

Liz smiled like a Memphis Belle. "I told Micki it was all about the ginger snaps."

I couldn't help but laugh.

"Jack, it's time to relax. Where on earth is the maid? She's supposed to be bringing us wine. My folks are entertaining Maggie, and now that you've figured it all out, I can tell you a lot more about what he actually discovered and what his research has uncovered. It's a lot more complicated than marijuana, kale, and cross-breeding. Doug truly is a genius, but because it involves growing, testing, and more testing, the work is slow and tedious, and he needed lots of the actual plant.

"I'm sorry I played the dumb blonde with you. I promised Doug, but I was wrong to hold out on you and Micki. Doug wanted to protect me from the authorities as much as he could. We had no idea they'd go to such lengths to isolate him, not even let him talk to his lawyer. I resorted to the only thing I could think of: the clueless wife. Sorry."

I was ready for a little quiet, a little time to think about what she'd said. But she was quickly back in gear, chatting about the difficulties of furnishing a rental house on short notice. How she could turn it on and off on a dime was amazing. The maid finally arrived with a chilled and uncorked bottle of wine, two glasses, and a bowl of cheese straws. She set the tray on a table and left without a backward glance. Liz morphed back into Dr. Elizabeth Stewart and for the next hour she educated me with a lecture on cancer, biochemical research, and "ginger snaps."

I left her father's house feeling overwhelmed with knowledge. My head was spinning either with information or wine, maybe a little bit of both.

38

WE BUCKLED UP for the short flight from Memphis to Little Rock. I begged off giving Maggie, Clovis, and the now wide-awake Debbie a report. I needed time and rest to process what I'd learned, time to let my brain—my whole body—catch its breath, so to speak. So I insisted Debbie take the seat across from Maggie, and dozed for the short flight in the back of the plane.

We touched down safely and were back at the hotel within a few minutes. We were a silent, weary lot, each ready for a little solitude. I indulged in a hot bath before easing into my very comfy bed, but I couldn't get to sleep, couldn't help thinking about what Liz had told me.

I thought of Angie and those last few months–the pain, the weight loss, Beth and I trying to put a good face on the inevitable. Liz had told me that Angie's suffering, even more than her own, had a profound effect on Doug. As a chemist, his research and experiments had all been more or less theoretical, until he saw firsthand what Angie was going through. Then his research became a mission. Apparently he and Angie collaborated in experiments crossing marijuana with other plants, but, as Liz had said, his research soon became much more complicated.

To my surprise, Doug had offered ginger snaps to Angie, as well as a few joints for her pain and weak stomach, but she'd declined. She told him it would upset me and set a bad example for Beth. I wish she'd asked me. She would have been surprised.

So now I had a good idea what Doug had been up to since Angie's death, but proving it would be another matter, and growing marijuana was still illegal. As for Dub, he was a sleezeball as well as inept, but I could hardly walk into court and accuse him of being dirty on the word of a former prostitute and her pimp. Novak would have about as much credibility as a snake oil salesman.

Moreover, I had no evidence of any connection between Dub's obsession with this case and his personal habits. How could I get around all the plants in Doug's backyard? The plants may have been for medical research, but I faced proving a negative. The law presumes that if you cultivate that many plants, you are growing for the purpose of distribution. Medical necessity and medical research are not valid defenses, no matter how well intentioned. How could I rebut Dub's assertion that Doug sold to kids—call Novak to the stand to testify? I had to assume Dub had someone ready, willing, and available to testify against Doug.

Finally, who was behind all of this and why? Who had moved Moira from Detroit weeks ago just in case her special skills were needed? Who'd decided to raise the ante by trying to kill Micki and me? Who had that kind of money and what had they to gain?

SATURDAY
April 26, 2014

39

The alarm on my iPhone woke me up at six-thirty. It took me a minute to focus, but I was glad to be up. Better to be awake to face a new day than to be plagued by memories and bizarre dreams. After a long shower, I left the room with my day organized and my thoughts all in their appropriate boxes.

Maggie had convinced the manager to open a private space off the main dining room. We indulged in excellent eggs benedict, hash browns, and fresh berries I doled out assignments ending with a concern that had been nagging at me.

"Clovis, someone needs to check our hardware. I wouldn't put it past Dub to hack our computers in the name of 'national security.' I know you've already checked our rooms and phones for bugs, but the government uses more sophisticated tools than simple bugs. Debbie, does Micki have a guy who can deal with this? Maggie, what about our offices in DC?"

Maggie nodded, taking notes in shorthand. A lost art.

Debbie spoke up, a bit tartly. "As a matter of fact, we do, and she is not a guy. Her name is Stella Rice. She's a whiz, and it will really piss her off if the FBI got through her system."

"If she finds anything, tell her not to disconnect it, at least not until you've checked with me."

Debbie smiled. "You're going to like Stella. She's your type, Jack."

"I don't know what that means, but don't introduce me. No more Little Rock women."

"What about Micki?" Debbie produced a little pout.

"Micki is different. She was never a distraction," I lied.

Clearly irritated, Maggie interrupted, "When are you going to let us in on what you learned from Liz?"

"Plenty of time for that later. If the judge gives me access to Doug, we'll be on our way to Oklahoma City in short order. If he doesn't, you, Clovis, and I are going to DC to meet with Walter."

Debbie looked like an eager puppy.

"Okay, what's up?" I asked, smiling.

"No offense, everyone, but all this security is putting a huge cramp in my lifestyle. Clovis, can't you at least assign a cute, male guard to me? You know—someone to keep me from getting lonesome."

Remembering what we owed her, I tried not to frown—or laugh. Clovis's jaw dropped—first Liz, now Debbie—they just didn't fit into any niche he was prepared for.

"Clovis, I'll leave her request in your capable hands."

He wasn't amused.

40

Janis Harold was waiting on a bench outside the courtroom. The look on her face told me she had bad news.

"Jack, Maggie, you know I don't mince words. My husband received a call last night from one of our best clients. The client feels that my involvement with you is a conflict of interest. If I persist, he intends to file a complaint with the Supreme Court Committee on Professional Responsibility."

I asked, "Is he right?"

"No, but he's not someone who issues idle threats. Archie and I talked about it. We don't think he's bluffing, and we're going to drop the bastard as a client."

"Why drop the bastard as a client? There's no reason for that," I responded.

"Oh, yes, there is. Archie and I don't need any client, no matter how rich, who'd make such a threat. We're better off without him. Still, dropping him doesn't cure his perceived conflict, so I can't help you today or in the future. Totally pisses me off, but there it is."

"I understand and won't lean on our friendship to ask who he is."

Janis grinned. "I wish I could tell you. Believe me, I do. Be careful. I have no idea what hornet's nest you've stirred up, but it's a doozy, and it's clearly not about a few marijuana plants."

"No, Janis. It's about ginger snaps." I enjoyed the look on her face.

Lack of local counsel could be a real problem. I'm very familiar with the ins and outs of federal court, but every state has more than a few idiosyncrasies. A good lawyer should never venture into another state's courtroom without a local lawyer who knows both the eccentricities and the judge.

Maggie's lips tightened as Dub walked through the courtroom doors. This time he didn't bother to shake any hands. We had just taken our seats when a frowning Judge Houston strode in, robes flapping, brusquely motioning us to remain seated. He didn't waste any time.

"I'll post my orders online in a timely fashion. However, I thought it appropriate to advise counsel of the substance of my findings. First, Mr. Patterson, I hope you will convey our deepest concern to Ms. Lawrence for her well-being. However, I see no reason for her absence to delay our proceedings. My clerks have confirmed that you are what you represent—licensed in this state and admitted to the bar of this court. Despite these facts and without providing you a copy, the prosecution has filed a motion under seal to have you removed from this case."

I couldn't believe my ears, but before I could say a word the judge continued, "That motion is denied."

Dub fumed, and I relaxed.

"Mr. Blanchard, I have carefully reviewed your claim that by designating the defendant as a terrorist you have the right to hold Dr. Stewart indefinitely without charges. The problem with your argument is that the Defense Authorization Act of 2012 may give the military the right to do just that, but you're not the military. So you will either charge Dr. Stewart or release him.

"I also find that Mr. Patterson's security clearance is valid. You've not contested the documents he gave the court earlier, so I'm ordering that all the documents filed under seal be given to him under appropriate procedures, and that he be granted immediate access to Dr. Stewart."

So far so good, I was winning on every issue, but the judge wasn't finished.

"I understand you plan to appeal these decisions and seek a stay of my orders from the Eighth Circuit Court of Appeals. Is that correct?"

Dub jumped up quickly. "That's right, your Honor."

"That request will not be necessary. I will stay my orders pending a timely appeal by your office."

I rose as well, trying to keep a poker face. Staying his orders pending appeal meant nothing would happen for months.

"Your Honor, does the stay apply to access to my client?"

The judge's face was sympathetic, but his answer was not.

"Mr. Patterson, I understand your frustration, but the government's filings carry enough credibility that I'm confident the Circuit Court will grant a stay, so I'm going to save everyone the time and effort. You won your argument, Mr. Patterson. You will just have to wait until the government exhausts its appeal."

Meanwhile my client rots in jail.

Dub and his associates were having a hard time holding back their glee. I'd won the first battle, but was losing the war.

The judge continued, "As I understand it, technically no charges have been filed against Dr. Stewart, so the only thing before the court is the civil forfeiture case. Mr. Patterson, you have a few weeks to file a response to the government's complaint and seizure. As soon as you do, I'll set a civil hearing. I like to move my docket, so be prepared for a quick setting."

I had only a moment to make a decision. I'd hoped to get all my ducks in a row, consult further with Liz and Doug before I gambled their lives on a long shot. I looked at Maggie. She had no idea what I was thinking, but we'd worked together long enough that she had a sixth sense about my instincts.

She shrugged her shoulders with a discreet smile, and I took the plunge.

"Your Honor that may not be necessary."

I could almost hear ears perking up.

"With the prosecution's permission, I'd like to inform the Court of the offer the government has made concerning civil forfeiture and suggest a resolution."

The judge transferred his gaze to Dub, who was already conferring with Bullock. He asked the Court for a brief recess. The judge gave us five minutes, and I watched Dub make a beeline to a well-dressed man in the gallery who was surely not a lawyer. Bullock, who suddenly appeared directly in front of me, interrupted my line of sight.

"Okay, Jack, what's on your mind?"

"I'm suggesting we take your deal. You decline to prosecute Liz, you let her keep her house, furniture, artwork, etc., and you get to auction off Doug's cars, his lab equipment, his research, etc. I have only one condition: I want you to hold the auction in two weeks, with the judge present, and the right to bid on everything. Doug's wife wants the Healy for sentimental reasons."

Bullock rubbed the back of his neck and grimaced like he had a crick—maybe he was just worn out. "Okay, Jack. Here's the deal: no deal on Doug criminally, period. We won't let you talk to him before the appellate court rules, and we're going to fight you tooth and nail on the criminal side. We'll bring charges if we don't get to keep him under wraps as a terrorist. You have to understand, there's no deal concerning Dr. Stewart."

"You've made that point very clear."

"Why so fast? And why do you want Houston present?" He asked, showing a spark of renewed interest.

"Liz is disgusted by this whole mess, just wants it to be over. Right now we can prove Liz made the down payment on the house and the monthly payments out of her trust fund. It's the same for almost all of the furniture and artwork. I'm sure you knew that or you wouldn't have offered us the deal."

Bullock nodded.

"She has no idea what her husband was up to, but she doesn't trust Dub to keep his word, and neither do I. I know it sounds like she's living in *lala* land, but she still wants to host her neighborhood's cocktail party, and she wants her house back sooner rather than later. Look, she's more than a little weird, okay?" I hoped my nose wasn't growing.

"Why don't I just give her the Healy? Then there's no rush, and we don't need Judge Houston," he responded.

I couldn't let that happen. I needed them to hold the auction quickly before anyone could think through what I was up to. "I'd be inclined to do that, except you'd get back to the office and realize the deal isn't consistent with all Doug's assets going to auction, and you'd want to renegotiate. The Healy belongs to Doug. It's titled in his name. The cars, the lab equipment, and the research are all Doug's.

If some other lawyer later on down the line wants to attack the sale or the prosecution, he'll point to the Healy and argue that you let Doug keep it, so he should be allowed to keep the rest."

I was on shaky ground regarding forfeiture law, but I hoped to plant the seed that if they didn't go along with my plan, there could be legal title questions to everything sold at the auction. I felt sure they wouldn't want any issues concerning the legality of the auction to bite them further down the road.

"Your reasoning doesn't hold water, but she's your client. I can go along with the early auction and your right to bid, but the judge's presence? What if he won't do it?"

"If Judge Houston refuses to engage, Liz won't agree. I tried to reason with her, but she's adamant. Honestly, I don't get it, but Liz is a woman who knows her own mind. For her, the judge validates the whole proceeding."

I relied on an old stand-by. When you don't have a good explanation for something—blame your client.

"I'll try to get Dub to see reason." A man with a *loco* boss—I felt a twinge of pity for him.

It didn't take him long to find Dub, who was still whispering with the suited man. I sat down at our table and took Maggie's hand, trying to absorb some sense of calm. I was taking the gamble of my professional life.

Maggie whispered. "Whatever you're up to, I hope it works."

"Me too or we're in for a really hard landing."

She squeezed my hand in return, and I whispered, "Slip out for just a minute—see if you can get Clovis to photograph the man Dub's been talking to. He can't take photographs in the courtroom, but maybe he can get him as he's leaving."

"If he's not around, I'll use my iPhone." She murmured something about the ladies room and quietly excused herself.

Judge Houston returned, sat down, and said firmly, "Mr. Blanchard."

At a signal from Dub, Bullock rose slowly to address the court.

"Your Honor, we've consulted with defense counsel and would ask the court's indulgence. With regard to the forfeiture proceedings, the parties have reached an oral agreement that certain assets seized by

the government will be returned to Mrs. Stewart. Certain assets seized
by the government belonging to the defendant will be sold at auction with the consent of his counsel. This action will completely settle
the civil complaint against the property seized. In no respect will this
agreement alter our appeal of the Court's order or any further proceedings concerning the defendant."

The judge responded, "Then you don't need me."

He was about to strike his gavel when Bullock continued. "I'm
sorry, your Honor. There are a couple of wrinkles."

Judge Houston loosed a long sigh and looked pointedly at me.

"The first wrinkle is that the defense has asked us to hold the auction in two weeks in this courtroom." Bullock waited. Houston pursed
his lips.

"I see no problem with an accelerated schedule as long as Marshal
Maroney agrees, and you are comfortable that proper notice can be
sent out."

"We'll expedite notice and get all parties to waive any time require-
ments. The second wrinkle is that Mr. Patterson requests your presence at the auction."

This time Houston did not smile. "You want me to be an auctioneer?"
He barked.

I rose; it was up to me to convince the judge we needed him.

"Your Honor, I think you remember our first day in court. My client
couldn't be here, but his wife was present."

His face relaxed into a smile. "Yes, I remember Mrs. Stewart very
well."

"Well, Mrs. Stewart was pretty freaked out, if you don't mind the
phrase. Someone unknown to her used an axe to crash through her
front door, haul her furnishings away, pile her clothes in the middle of
the floor, and seal her home with yellow tape. Not only was she fright-
ened, she felt violated." I paused letting the image sink in.

"I've explained to her the law of civil forfeiture: that even if her
husband isn't charged, his assets can be seized and sold, but she's
not convinced that action is constitutional. She was impressed with
the Court's demeanor and fairness that first day in court. She has
agreed to the settlement and the auction if, and only if, you agree to

be present. She's not comfortable with the prosecution, and who can blame her? Dr. Stewart is God knows where, and she's all alone."

Maggie had slipped quietly back into the room. The judge looked at me for some time without comment. Finally he smiled. "Well, I can't see any harm in attending. It might be beneficial for me to watch one of these auctions first hand."

I said, "Thank you, your Honor. I know Ms. Stewart will appreciate your forbearance and courtesy."

Maggie whispered, "You ought to be ashamed."

The judge banged his gavel. "Assuming an agreement is reached in writing and approved by the Court on Monday, on a week from Wednesday at ten in the morning Marshal Maroney will hold an auction in this courtroom. Don't disappoint me, gentlemen. I expect everything to be signed, sealed, and in proper order." He rose abruptly and left. Bullock stopped by our table to say we could expect a draft agreement this afternoon.

The party was over and soon only Maggie and I remained in the courtroom.

"I take it, Jack, that you're way out on a limb. Do you have a safety net?"

"Not really. If truth be known, I'm further out on that limb than you know."

"What do you mean?"

"I've agreed to settle a civil case, believing I can outsmart an opposition that's been ahead of me the whole time. Liz and Doug trust me. I hope I can pull it off. I can't see another choice. I can't see any other way to save Doug and his research."

Maggie smiled and gave in. "Okay, what's first?"

"We pay a visit to Micki. Eric may kill me—though he may have to wait in line—but I have to talk to her. I need her help."

41

ERIC STOOD OUTSIDE Micki's door, clearly ready to defend it against all comers.

"Jack, please don't bother Micki. I know you mean well, but . . ."

"I promise I won't be long, and if I know Micki, she's been pestering you to get out of here so she can get back to work. All I'm going to do is tell her what's going on, reassure her that we're doing all we can, and encourage her to stay away."

Eric didn't believe a word, but knew he couldn't really keep me away from my partner and friend without both of us going ballistic.

He sighed and moved away reluctantly. "Okay, but don't take too long."

"Promise." I went through the door, closing it firmly behind me.

Micki was watching an old movie. Her eyes looked hollow inside dark circles. Her skin was no longer grey, but still pale and she was incredibly thin. The blue and black from the bruising was now pooling in her legs.

"Hi, beautiful." I gave her an unconcerned smile.

Her voice was hoarse. "If you mean that, come give me a kiss."

I bent over the bed to kiss her cheek, but her hand went to my head and she gave me a quick soft kiss on the mouth. I lingered a bit, reassured by the taste of the Micki I knew.

My eyes begged the question.

"Sorry, I shouldn't have asked, but I miss you, and he's got to loosen up, or it won't work. He's very sweet, but I don't need a mother hen." I assumed she meant Eric. "What I need is to get out of here." Her voice was strong and firm.

"When do they think you can leave?" I asked.

"Eric says in a few days, but I think he's just stalling. When I do get home, he says no riding horses and no work. I know he means well, but jeez, I've got a life—why does he have to be so controlling? Speaking of—what's happening? Bring me up to date. What's going on with Doug and Liz? I'm dying of boredom."

I pulled up the chair and filled her in. Eric stuck his head in the door a couple of times, but left when Micki scowled. Didn't he have his own patients?

I tried to tell her about our meeting with Novak, but she was clearly troubled—too much water under that bridge. She had no footing in our current reality. So I told her about Liz and her revelations and what had happened in court.

She had closed her eyes—I couldn't tell whether she was thinking or asleep, so unlike the Micki I knew. I rose to leave, but her hand pulled me back.

Her eyes didn't open, but her hand felt warm and strong. "When you get back from DC, you and Maggie stay at my place. Debbie too. That way Clovis can have us all in one place. What do you think?"

"That's part of why I'm here. I need your help, but not if it jeopardizes your health."

"I'm okay, I'm okay. I really am getting better, can't you tell? Anyway, Eric isn't going to let me out of his sight, especially if he hears you're spending the night." She tried to giggle, but it came out as a cough.

"You're bad, you know that? If I can convince Liz my plan is the way to go, we have less than two weeks to pull it off. I need your expertise on how this kind of auction works. I can't afford to screw this up."

"My brain still works, as far as I know. You know, it could work unless they see it coming. How are you going to keep it quiet?"

"Still working on that. I'm set to meet with Sam after I leave here, even before I see Liz. If he isn't willing to keep an open mind, I'll have to go to Plan B, and so far I don't have one."

"Tell Debbie to come see me. Tell her I'm not mad—I know she did the right thing. We'll have everything set up at my house by the time you get back."

I stood up.

"Micki, maybe this isn't such a good idea. You're already worn out, and we're just talking."

She gave me a dirty look. "Don't worry so much about me. I need to get out of here; I need to get off these meds. Talk to Liz, do your thing in DC, and hurry back. We'll be ready."

She closed her eyes again, and I knew it really was time to go. She fell asleep, and I lowered the back of the bed and left the room. Eric was right there, fuming. Didn't this guy ever take a break?

"Eric, you're a very lucky man." I smiled.

He looked confused, and I didn't give him a chance to regroup. Paul stood just a few steps away.

"Paul, she says Eric can take her home in a couple of days. She wants all of us to join her there when we return from DC. It will be easier to guard us if we're all in one place, but we'll make an enticing target."

He raised his eyebrows, nodded, and pushed the elevator button. Paul wasn't much of a talker. I turned to Eric, practically daring him to argue. He turned away with a sour look, and I walked into the elevator, relieved he had backed down.

I glanced at my watch. I was supposed to meet Maggie and Sam for lunch at the Town Pump, a cheeseburger dive down by the river; it was Sam's mom's favorite, totally unknown except by long-time locals.

Clovis had me there in no time at all. We all ordered cheeseburgers and fries—what else?—and got down to business.

"Sam, I know if I get out of line, you'll let me know in a hurry, right?"

"You bet. I've sure done it before," he grinned. "So, shoot."

"Here's the long and short of it. Dub is going after Dr. Stewart because he can use the forfeiture process to get Doug's research, and he's getting paid to do it. No, I have no proof, no solid evidence. But I will, and I'm going to need your help."

"Good Lord. Why in the hell can't you accept that they're going after this guy for the forest of Mary Jane growing in his back yard? Are you really suggesting our U.S. attorney is on the take? Even for Dub that's a reach. He's an idiot, but dirty? Can you prove anything?

Besides, it's out of my jurisdiction. If someone is actually paying him, it's a federal matter."

"Sam, hear me out. It's not just a federal matter if it also involves kidnapping and attempted murder."

"Are you saying Dub Blanchard was behind your kidnapping?" he asked incredulously.

"I didn't say that and, in fact, I don't think he was."

"Well, what's your point?" I had to admit my side of the conversation didn't make much sense so far.

"Doug Stewart was growing the plants for a research project on the cancer-curing effects of marijuana and other plants. Not pain relief, but the ability to cure. The federal government has known about his research for years. At some point, someone got worried he was getting close to a breakthrough, how I don't know, and Dub was paid to go after Doug. That same someone got even more worried when Micki and I agreed to represent Doug."

"Jack, you've been reading too many conspiracy blogs. You need help. Are you sure Moira didn't mess with your mind?"

I hoped he was kidding. I took a deep breath.

"Listen, Bullock made us an incredible deal, and Dub didn't put up a whimper—he won't prosecute Liz, and has agreed to give her house back in exchange for our not fighting the civil forfeiture of Doug's research."

"So take it!" he exclaimed. "That's a great deal. Don't look a gift horse in the mouth, my friend. Don't look for conspiracies. Take the deal and celebrate. Do you have any proof that the government knew he was growing grass for research? Which, for the record, is still against the law."

"No—as of now, I can't prove that."

"O . . . kay," he said patiently. "Any proof as to why somebody would care that Doug was getting close to a breakthrough?"

"No proof—yet."

"Any idea who might have ordered the hit on Micki and you, other than Novak?"

"Somebody sent Moira to Little Rock weeks ago. Who paid her and who ordered the hit, I don't know."

"And you don't think it was Dub?" He kept his tone serious, but couldn't control his face.

"No, although he may have known about it," I said, although my heart wasn't in it.

Sam laughed. "Any proof that leaving Liz alone, giving her back her home, and seizing what little Doug Stewart had that can be traced to his marijuana enterprise isn't as good a deal as it sounds?"

"No, but I believe his research is worth a whole lot," I answered defensively.

"Any evidence to justify that belief?"

"No."

"Jack, if I didn't know better I'd say you've been eating too many of Liz Stewart's ginger snaps." He winked.

"You knew about her ginger snaps?"

"Hell, everyone in town did. As long as nobody got sick eating them, I wasn't going to bust her bridge club. I've got bigger fish to fry. It sounds to me that when it comes to Dr. Stewart you've got nothing but vague theories. Possibly because you don't have a defense to his growing hundreds of marijuana plants in his backyard?"

"What about Moira? Who hired her? Someone did try to kill us." I knew I sounded desperate.

"That I don't know, Jack. I'd lay odds on Novak or one of his competitors. Or maybe it's someone from your past seeking revenge. Don't worry—I will find him, and I'll nail his ass to a wall. "

I seized on his words. "Okay, if I bring you hard evidence of who's responsible for the kidnappings, you'll keep an open mind to the rest?"

"I'll do more than that. Whoever it was, Novak, Dub, or the attorney general himself, I'll go after him with everything I've got. But Jack, I'm not buying theories. I need hard evidence."

"That's all I can ask." I finally smiled.

Neither Maggie nor Clovis had said a single word. Sam looked at them and asked, "What about you two? Are you buying this malarkey?"

Maggie glanced at Clovis and said to Sam calmly, "Jack could be wrong this time, but somehow I don't think so. And good burgers aren't worth much cold."

So we spent a few minutes just eating our burgers. They reminded me of the ones you used to get as a kid at the swimming pool snack bar: hot, full of flavor and just a little greasy. I had accomplished my purpose. I didn't have any proof, but I had planted a seed in the fertile ground of Sam's mind.

As we pushed our chairs back to leave, Sam commented, "Well, at least you have some time. Forfeiture sales don't happen overnight. If there's any proof out there, you've got plenty of time to find it."

In lilting tones Maggie began to hum "It's Now or Never" and Sam bit. "Okay, what?"

She dropped the tune, looking smug. "Jack managed to expedite the sale. It's in less than two weeks."

Sam looked incredulous. "Now I know you're crazy."

42

WE WERE ALL quiet on the way to the airport—in fact, we looked like three teenagers: Maggie updating her iPhone calendar, Clovis checking his email, and me—well, I admit to checking out yesterday's box scores. I knew they were waiting to hear what Liz had said.

"Maggie, you were great with Sam." I said. "Clovis, I promise I'm not crazy, at least I don't think I am. Here's the story."

Fudging about my source, I told them about the allegations against Dub and what Liz had said about Doug's research and his spice.

Maggie eyebrows shot up, "You mean Doug's discovered a cure for cancer?"

"I can't go that far. He must have found something important enough to get the government's attention. I think marijuana may do more than alleviate the pain of cancer and the side effects of other treatments. According to Liz, he experimented with hybrid strains, using other plants that have certain cancer-fighting characteristics, such as kale and flax, and breaking down their molecular makeup. He may have found something in all his cross-breeding that actually attacked the cancer. That's exactly why Dub has put him out of reach—he wants to destroy every ounce of Doug's credibility, leave him with no way to defend himself before he's charged. The accusations against Doug as a major dealer and a seller to children would turn off anyone who might be inclined to listen to an award-winning chemist.

"It's not unusual for someone with a valid story or information to be attacked on a personal basis to make sure that whatever he says down the road has little credibility. It's a hybrid form of killing the messenger when you don't like the message. Political operatives like Dub are especially adept at this tactic. A woman roughed up by a rock star, professional athlete, or rising political star is likely to have her character dragged through the mud to prevent anyone from believing what actually happened. A whistle blower is likely to be labeled a traitor and indicted, to prevent people from believing his or her allegations. It's a morally repulsive tactic, but one that's time-tested and proven to be very effective."

"But who would want to stop someone from finding the cure for cancer?" Maggie asked.

"Lots of people. Think about the drug companies that manufacture current drugs and treatments. Think about the thugs who profit from illegal marijuana sales. If you really want to be conspiratorial, law enforcement has gotten a whole lot richer by pursuing the war on drugs—a war on marijuana. Forfeiture alone fattens government coffers by over two billion dollars a year. That's more than loose change."

"So do you have any idea who our bad guys are?" Maggie was excited.

"Well, no, not yet, but they must be pretty damn influential. And I think I know how to bring them in out of the shadows."

"How?" They asked in unison.

"The auction. I'm relying on the auction to flush out the bad guys. But Sam shot a lot of holes in my hypothesis—and he's right, I don't have any proof, no hard evidence. A lot depends on what we can find out over the next week."

"More of a shotgun blast than a single shot, if you ask me," Clovis deadpanned.

"You're right. So I need you two to plug as many of those holes as possible, while I go about getting everything in place for the auction. We need evidence."

No argument from either. I knew I could count on them, even if they weren't yet convinced. If she were here, Micki would be my harshest critic, yet ready to charge the hill. I couldn't wait to have her back.

The flight was uneventful—always a relief. and one of Martin's men met us in another black Tahoe. I wondered if the security business was keeping Chevrolet in business.

We drove directly to the foundation offices, where I knew we'd be both comfortable and secure.

"Clovis, you've had people check for computer intrusions at Micki's office, the Armitage, and here at the Foundation. What else do we need to do?"

"We'll go over your house on Monday for bugs, and I've already talked to Martin about checking Maggie's house and everyone's cell phones again, as well as any portable devices like iPads."

"Once you're comfortable, let's go on the offensive. I don't want you to cross any lines, but if Dub is as dirty as Novak says, we need to find hard evidence. Find out what you can about gambling and girls without tipping him off. Okay?"

"Should be fun." Clovis winked and then his face set. "As long as we're here, I'm also gonna try to get a bead on Moira." I winced. I had enough on my plate without worrying about her impending return.

"Maggie, any luck finding the letter Doug wrote about his research?"

"I've come up against a stone wall with every agency I've contacted—the Drug Czar, FBI, DEA, Homeland Security, you name it. They tell me it will take months to process my request. They all hide behind one word—backlog. I'm convinced the Freedom of Information Act is used to prevent openness instead of providing it."

"Keep after them. And while you're at it, see what you can find out about Doug's research at NIH. Did you tell Walter I needed to talk to him?"

"Of course. You're meeting him at ten on Monday morning. Do you need me?"

"Yes. You forget—you're my boss. I need you both."

Glancing at my watch, I saw that it was almost five-thirty. We needed a little break before dinner, so I suggested we meet at eight at DeCarlo's, my favorite neighborhood Italian restaurant, where I knew we could both talk and hear one another. Locals love it because no matter how famous you are, you can count on both a good meal with your family and easy privacy. The food was genuine and the service was impeccable. I was sorry Walter couldn't join us. His participation was integral to my plan, although he didn't know it yet. We ordered drinks, and I asked the waiter to hold off for a while on the menus.

"So exactly how do you propose to spend the rest of your Monday while Clovis and I are working our fingers to the bone?"

"I'm having lunch with Peggy Fortson at 701. Then, I thought I'd take in a round of golf at Burning Tree."

Silence.

"Kidding—just kidding! After lunch I'll connect with some old friends who may know more about Dub's task force. Look, tomorrow's Sunday—let's all take some time off. Clovis and I are going to a double-header Nats game, and I'm sure you and Walter have plenty to do."

"Do we have that kind of time?" Maggie asked.

"I've been pushing pretty hard; we've been going non-stop for over a week. Once we get back to work, it's full steam ahead until the auction is over. We all need a break. Sometimes time away clears the head. That said, the Bolognese here is the best in the city, let's relax and enjoy it." The waiter arrived with a bottle of excellent Chianti. "We're all off duty. That's an order."

"I thought I was the boss," Maggie laughed.

We chatted easily about movies, politics, and our families. For a while it felt like a normal dinner with good friends. Clovis had arranged for Martin's men to be on duty tonight—that included driving us home. The restaurant's long-time manager came to our table as the plates were being cleared, and it wasn't long before he and Clovis discovered their mutual love of fine bourbons. They soon migrated to the bar and began sampling some very select bottles. Maggie and I were left to noodle over the day's events and how we planned to proceed.

"Jack, Sam has a point. Your reasoning is almost believable, but the conclusion does seem pretty far-fetched. I mean, really, marijuana curing cancer?"

"I know it's hard to imagine, but think how many people have been helped by marijuana—people dealing with chemo, crippling diseases, or suffering from migraines. So far, no one knows how it works. But it does work. Why couldn't it provide more than just pain relief? Besides, Liz says it isn't just the marijuana. Apparently, Doug has been developing strains of marijuana that can be supplemented with the natural ingredients of other plants. That takes time and careful documentation. Doug Stewart isn't some doctor making a little extra money peddling marijuana on the side. He's a world-famous bio-chemist, winner of any number of awards and, until Dub busted him, a man of impeccable reputation. His research might just be the key to unlocking a cure."

"Well, okay, but now his reputation is gone. And, before this week, you haven't spoken to him in years. You only have Liz's word and a few minutes with Doug. How are you going to find out what this is all about unless you can talk to him? You know Liz is an airhead."

"Well, in the first place, Liz isn't quite the airhead she chooses to portray. And I'm hoping you'll get lucky at NIH or with your FOIA requests. I have a back-up plan if we can't talk to Doug, but it's important to be able to prove the government knew what he was up to three years ago and exactly who knew."

"You just lost me," she responded, but as I was about to explain, Walter appeared in the doorway. Walter Matthews is almost as tall as I am. His well-cut suit and easy slouch turned every head as he walked in. He looked like he owned the place. He had founded Bridgeport Life Insurance Company straight out of college and through a cre-ative investment strategy, built it into one of the most admired compa-nies in the United States.

Walter isn't just successful; he is the most ethical businessman I've ever met. My old law firm used to represent his company, and we became good friends on the golf course. He met Maggie during the months before Angie's death and fell for her head over heels.

"Hello, dear. Hello, Jack," he greeted us. "I managed to close out my part of the meeting early so I could join you."

He kissed Maggie, shook my hand, and ordered a glass of port.

"I hear you've almost gotten yourself killed again. A word of advice—find another vacation spot."

"Or at least stay away from murderous Arkansas women," Maggie added.

"Wait a minute—Moira isn't even from the South, much less Arkansas," I protested.

Walter asked, "Want to tell me what you want to talk about Monday, so I can be giving it some thought?"

I did, but this was not the time or place.

"Take this beautiful woman home and let her tell you what we've learned. We should all be fresh after a day of rest. I'm going to ask you for a little blind faith, and I need you both to be in a good mood. Maggie's been a bear without you. Besides, I've got to pull Clovis away from the bourbon."

"I have not been a bear, you've been foolish. That woman was so obvious you should've seen it coming. I'd bet she had you wrapped around her finger the first night you met, just like that hotel manager," Maggie scolded.

"Okay, okay—but would you have me any other way?" We all laughed, and they walked out hand in hand. I went to the bar and tugged on Clovis's arm.

"Come on, big fellow, it's time for us to get home. We both need some sleep. We've got a big day of baseball ahead of us."

A SOLITARY MAN leaned against the telephone pole outside DeCarlo's, smoking a cigarette, watching and thinking. He knew Patterson had met with Novak and then flown to Memphis to meet with Liz Stewart. Novak would know nothing of their client's plans. And he had probably wanted to talk to the Stewart woman in person about the prosecution's offer not to prosecute her. Patterson had taken the bait just like they had hoped. The fact that the auction was going to happen in two weeks pleased the client to no end. But he wondered what brought Patterson back to DC. Whatever it was, it was his job to make sure Patterson hit nothing but brick walls, no matter what he was after.

MONDAY

April 28, 2014

43

IT FELT GOOD to sleep in my own bed for a change. Four years had passed since Angie and I had shared it. It was a queen-sized bed—we'd talked about getting a king, but couldn't quite bring ourselves to sleep that far apart. I smelled bacon frying and knew Clovis was up.

My house hadn't smelled this good in a long time. Not only was he frying bacon, but he'd made biscuits as well. Unknown talents.

"You're not even the slightest bit hungover?" I asked. Clovis had enjoyed a double-header's worth of beer yesterday and plenty of bourbon the night before.

"Slept like a lamb and feel great."

I made a mental note to ask him his secret someday. This morning he was already full of news.

"Micki gets out of the hospital tomorrow. Eric wants to keep her under glass, but she's going home. Debbie's at the ranch setting up a temporary office, and I've put Paul in charge of security until I get back."

"Clovis, what about Sam? Our friendship is pretty well known. Can we protect him, um, well, quietly?"

He gave me a cat's grin. "He can be as prickly as Micki, but I've had a little talk with Sheriff Barnes. His guys will watch him pretty close—he'll never know."

"Good thinking. But we can't maintain this level of security for long. And the cat's gonna get out of the bag sooner or later. That's one reason why we need to hold the auction so soon. Right now they think they're in control."

"Aren't they?" Clovis asked.

"Well, yeah, pretty much, but I've got a few wrenches to throw in the works." I poured a fresh cup of coffee from the pot and sat down with my thoughts.

Dub and his task force had thought out their strategy well, but they hadn't counted on me showing up to represent Doug. My security clearances had come as a surprise, but they'd adjusted quickly and successfully. Nothing seemed to faze them. That had to change.

"Clovis, when we get back I'd like to talk to Debbie and Paul. I've got an idea, but I need to make sure it's safe."

Clovis had worked with me long enough to figure out I'd explain my reasoning soon enough. "Any more shower thoughts?"

"Now that you mention it, is there any way we can get Moira's personal cell phone records? She wouldn't have used your company's cell phone to call her contact when we went to Oklahoma City. I'd like to know who she called and for how long."

"We must have taken the same shower. My people are already on it."

I finished breakfast and put on my lawyer's uniform, a dark suit and the requisite conservative tie. As I brushed off the jacket, it occurred to me that the dust meant I really didn't wear it that often any more—a very good feeling. Walter wouldn't care if I appeared in a golf shirt and blazer, which was about as formal as I got unless I had to appear in court. But I had arranged to have lunch with Peggy at 701, and I wanted our meeting to look official. A lawyer in uniform lunching with a high-ranking Justice official wouldn't turn a single head.

Clovis dropped me off at the foundation offices.

Maggie had chosen one of the fairly new buildings near the White House for our offices, modest in size and tailored to our individual needs. The focus of the space was a very comfortable conference room with a view of the White House. Location—it always counts.

Walter's primary business address was on E Street, but he kept a private office at the foundation. I could see him and Maggie in the conference room as I approached the door: private words and private smiles. How I missed that magic. The moment passed as I walked through the door. Maggie was already sipping on a hot cup of tea, and I poured myself a fresh cup of coffee from the pot on the sideboard.

"Jack, I hardly recognize you in a coat and tie! Totally unnecessary on my account." Walter looked very comfortable in a golf shirt, slacks, and docksiders.

"No offense, Walter, but it's not for you."

Walter laughed. "Maggie's told me about Doug Stewart, a thug called Novak, and a jerk by the name of Dub. Of course, I know what happened to you and Micki. Besides worrying, what can I do to help?"

"Well, maybe nothing, maybe everything. Has Maggie explained to you about the auction of Dr. Stewart's cars and research?"

"She has. I have to say: the concept of being able to take someone's belongings and sell them before being charged with a crime sounds downright un-American to me."

"Me, too. The reason I'm coming to you is that you are the well-known and well-respected owner of Bridgeport Life. In order for me to bid at this auction, I have to post a letter of credit amounting to ten percent of the amount I bid. So, for example, if I wanted to buy Doug's Austin-Healy 3000 for thirty thousand dollars, I'd have to post at least a three-thousand-dollar letter of credit to show I have the financial means to come up with the thirty thousand within a requisite period of time."

"Okay, but any bank would do that for you. Why are you coming to me?"

"Well, I want to smoke out the person who's behind all this, and to do that I may have to post a somewhat larger letter of credit."

"How much do you want to spend on the car?"

"I don't care a flip about the car. I want to buy Doug's research, his notes, his calculations, his papers, and his computer. If I'm right, that's what all this is about. Someone wants to take possession of all Doug's research through legal means. They want to have legal title to it, so they can patent it or destroy it."

"What if you're wrong? What if it's worthless?"

"Then I won't have to bid very much, and I'll be able to pay you back."

"What if you're right? What if it is a breakthrough toward a cure for cancer? What would that be worth?"

"You tell me. I don't think either of us could place a monetary value on something like that. What bothers me is that it might be worth more destroyed. I could be wrong, but I don't believe Doug hoped to gain fame and fortune through his research. I have a hunch he wanted to protect it through the patent system and then give it away—maybe even through open sourcing online."

"Sounds good, but Jack, where's your evidence? Maggie says what you've got is thinner than a Girl Scout's Thin Mint. Have you got anything stronger than a hunch?" Walter could be very direct.

"Maggie's right. It is thinner than thin, but I've got a few days to flesh it out. It still might come down to you trusting me. I won't be foolish with your money. If I don't think I've got the goods, I won't bid. But I have to make them think I'm for real."

"How much?" He at least asked.

"My opponents will surely bid enough for the research to make it look like a legitimate transaction. They won't want someone down the line to claim the auction was a fraud, that the government was gypped. If I were running the scam, I'd use two or three shills to run up the price. Remember, the government is the beneficiary of the funds. Dub will be able to gloat over how much money he's brought into the government coffers, and no one will be the wiser."

"Again—how much do you need?"

"They'll take the price up a little at a time, but they'll already have decided when to stop. My best bet is they'll shut it down somewhere around five million." I almost choked on the figure. Could I really ask Walter to risk so much money?

Walter whistled. "So, what you want me to do is provide you with a half a million dollar line of credit and be prepared to back it up by paying five million dollars for research that may be worthless."

"I don't think it's worthless, but, well, yeah, I guess I'm asking exactly that."

Walter looked at Maggie, who was studying her teacup. "What if they go higher, outbid you?"

"Then we'll know that Doug Stewart's research is the real goods. Five million isn't chicken feed. The government's had Doug's research for over a week now, and more than likely so has whoever went after Micki and me. It's surely been gone over with a fine-toothed comb by any number of scientists. If someone bids more than five million dollars for it, it's probably worth hundreds of millions."

Maggie asked, "What's to keep the government from destroying his research or handing it off to whoever is behind all this?"

"Good question. Knowing Doug, he has probably already applied which will establish prior ownership. His letter to the government, if we can find it, can help establish the same thing. If I'm right, they want to destroy Doug's credibility and at the same time obtain clear title to his research by means of the auction. Then whoever is behind this can control whether it's destroyed, or use it down the road, saying they bought the research fair and square. Walter, I hope to have a few aces up my sleeve, but it may come down to the auction itself. We need them to be at least a little nervous. I'd like to flush out my opponent, even if he gets the research in the end."

Walter's bland countenance had kept him at the table many a time. I had no idea how to read it. I always knew what he would do on a golf course, but in a business transaction he was hard to read.

I'd made my pitch. Now it was up to Walter. He was playing with numbers on a legal pad, deep in thought. Maggie still hadn't said a word. She was in a difficult position—it was her money, too. Finally Walter capped his pen.

"Jack, I think the chances are slim that you're going to be able to prove a single element of your conspiracy. More than likely you're going to be able to buy Dr. Stewart's research for a hundred dollars, and we're all going to have a big laugh. But, on the off chance that Dr. Stewart really has something, I don't want to be the fool who let it get stolen out from under his nose. I'm not afraid to lose a little money. But I think you're wrong about the 'how much.' If you're right, they're not going to let it go for five million. So I'll furnish our foundation a letter of credit that will satisfy the authorities. It will allow you to bid a little more than five million, and, if you should be successful, Maggie and I will figure out how to come up with the rest. It wouldn't be the worst thing if our little foundation owned the cure for cancer."

I rose immediately. A hug seemed out of order, so I stuck out my hand. "Thank you, Walter. You've put a lot of faith in me; I'll try not to let you down."

"Do more than try." He laughed, and the awkward moment passed. "I have some work to do with my bankers, but you'll have the letter of credit in plenty of time. I'd like to attend the auction if I may."

"Of course. At the least it should be entertaining."

"Jack, if the research proves to be worthless, that means someone else is trying to kill you. Have you thought about that?"

"Not until just now, thanks." The prospect was sobering.

"Well, if you two can do without me, I have to go meet with our bankers."

"That's what you always say when you're going to play golf," Maggie interjected.

"I didn't say where I was meeting them."

He was out the door before either of us could protest.

We sat back down. "Thank you, Maggie. What did you say to him?"

"I told him everything. He figured you needed to talk money. We trust you, as Doug and Liz are going to have to. He's not worried about the money. He's worried about losing his best friend. We both think it's your love of Angie that's driving you this time, that maybe you can't see or believe that someone she cared about could be a criminal. But I'm always amazed how you see things none of the rest of us can, so we trust you. That's the bottom line."

"Five million dollars is a lot of trust." I said, moved by her faith.

"Yes, it is. But I know you well enough to know you aren't going to lose five million dollars, any more than you're going to quit falling for pretty women—anywhere."

"Ouch, that hurt."

"I meant it to. You need to be careful." She raised her cup, giving my arm a light touch.

We sat quietly for a bit, each thinking our own thoughts, until she broke the spell. "Okay, so what's next?"

"I'm taking Peggy to lunch, and you're going to find that letter."

44

When I worked at Main Justice, 701 was my favorite spot for a meal. The atmosphere was classy, the waiters were discreet, and best of all, and it was right across the street. As a regular, they always found me a table for lunch, dinner, or simply meeting Angie for drinks before we headed home. The savvy owner ran several other DC mainstays, but I felt most comfortable at 701.

Peggy walked in as I was waiting for our table—she looked terrific. Her dark, curly hair fell casually to her shoulders, and she greeted me with an easy smile. I was a little taken aback by her unexpected glamour—Angie would have recognized the designer of her upscale suit. Disarmed by her physical allure and winning smile, many a man in the male-dominated Justice Department has underestimated her brains, but not for long. Her looks may have opened a few doors, but it was her intelligence and good judgment that kept her in the room. Now a career deputy in the Criminal Division, she and I began our careers at the same time. I moved to the Antitrust Division, but our paths crossed often, and we quickly became lifelong friends.

"I can't believe I'm actually breaking bread with my elusive friend Jack Patterson. I hope you don't think this counts as that dinner you owe me," she opened as we sat down.

"No way. That's one promise I look forward to keeping," I said truthfully.

Peggy was married when we first met, but the marriage hadn't worked because her husband expected her to follow his career path, rather than her own. After Angie's death we met for drinks on occasion, but it never went beyond that. She'd made it clear she was open to more, but at the time I needed her friendship more than romance. As I sat across from her and watched her smile at the waiter, I wondered if it was too late to change my mind.

"Wine at lunch?" I kidded, as she ordered a New Zealand Sauvignon Blanc.

"I'm not holding my breath for that dinner. Besides, I've got a feeling I may need something stronger than iced tea. So before you drag me into your latest pickle, I want to enjoy this lunch. I've signed out for the afternoon, and I intend to spend your money on a wonderful meal and enjoy this time. I'm going to take what I can get." Her eyes betrayed loneliness, and I kicked myself for cancelling more dinners than I care to admit.

We ordered a three-course meal and shared a really nice bottle of wine and easy conversation, both doing our best to avoid business. She brought up my kidnapping over dessert. She'd heard about it and called Sam for a brief rundown of the events, but she wanted my version. I told her the complete story—minus a few details involving Moira.

"Jack, when are you going to learn?"

There really wasn't much I could say. "Well . . ."

"Okay, what is it you want to talk about?" she asked, letting me off the hook.

"I want to talk about Dub's task force." I was entering safer ground for me, but not for her.

"I told you. That whole operation is hands-off. Nothing I can say or do." She was blunt.

"You may not have a choice," I said with emphasis.

"What do you mean?" I had her attention.

"If I'm right, your U.S. attorney is on the take, and he's involved in a conspiracy so big it makes the banking and mortgage scandals look like chicken feed."

"Oh, Jack. I hope you have some actual evidence. You can't just accuse a U.S. attorney of impropriety on a lark."

"My source says Dub has both a gambling habit and a penchant for prostitutes."

"Do you have a credible source, or is this someone trying to smear Dub? I know you don't like the man."

It was the reaction I expected. I waited for her to continue.

She shook her head. "Jack, you know I would never condone that sort of behavior. If you have any real evidence to back it up, you need to go to the Office of Professional Responsibility. But you'd better be damned sure. And I don't see how it connects him to a conspiracy. Don't forget that several senior attorneys from Main Justice have been assigned to his task force—it's not just Dub. They all report directly to the Drug Czar. Are you saying they're all corrupt?"

"Listen, Peggy, I admit I don't have any proof yet that anyone's on the take, or even that a conspiracy exists. Write all this off as evidence of my lunacy, but what if I'm right? You can't overlook it because you're under orders to let the task force do its job. I know you too well. What if I told you the task force's real purpose is to confiscate research that may lead to a cure for cancer?"

"What on earth has cancer got to do with dope dealing? Have you been diving off the shallow end?"

She might have been right, but I found her total incredulity irritating. I plugged away, told her my theory about Doug's research and why its destruction would be invaluable in certain quarters. I could tell from her expression, polite but bored, that I was getting nowhere. It would be a mistake to go any further.

"I'm sorry, Peggy, you're probably right. I shouldn't have bothered you with any of this. I'm really sorry." What I wanted to say was "so why in the hell did someone kidnap me and very nearly murder Micki?"

"If you hadn't bothered me, I wouldn't have enjoyed this lunch, and you wouldn't have found a realistic ear to bring you down to earth. It sounds to me like your Dr. Stewart is in deep shit, and he's doing what most marijuana dealers do—holler medical use, with a new wrinkle. I know he was a friend, but you need to leave Little Rock before you get yourself killed chasing rainbows or women." She squeezed my hand.

Well, shit, didn't that make me feel better?

Both Sam and Peggy thought I was nuts, that I'd lost all perspective. I didn't want to believe Doug was a criminal, therefore I had convinced myself that Dub was involved in a major conspiracy and two kidnappings based solely on the word of a Russian thug. Maybe I was delusional.

I changed the subject, and we chatted amiably about old friends, but our words were a bit forced, the tone a bit strained. We finished our coffee, I paid the bill, and we exchanged an awkward kiss, once again promising to stay in touch. She was still a friend, but watching her walk out of that restaurant, I suddenly didn't feel so bad about cancelling those dinners.

I tried to reach Maggie, but she was out running an errand. A text from Clovis asked me to meet him at the office at three-thirty. I walked past the Treasury Department and decided to kill some time in Lafayette Square. This tiny jewel of a park, originally known as Presidents' Park, is situated directly across Pennsylvania Avenue from the White House and serves as a perfect venue for protestors. I always enjoy watching them tromp up and down the green, carrying angry signs and enjoying the exercise of the First Amendment. This week they were railing against the evil of canned tuna. The park was never empty, but I found a spot on a bench near the statue of Andy Jackson.

The White House: home of the president of the United States, and the official office of the Drug Czar. The Drug Czar didn't rank highly enough to actually have an office in the White House. More than likely his offices were around the corner in the New Executive Office Building or in Jackson Square, but his mailing address was the same as the President's. Dub's task force reported to the Drug Czar, not the attorney general. What did that mean?

Although appointed by the president and confirmed by the Senate, the attorney general had to maintain some degree of independence from the political influences of the executive branch. The attorney general was also an officer of the courts and owes a duty to the justice system to make sure individual prosecutorial decisions are free from political considerations.

So did this independence carry over to the Drug Czar's office? The answer is an emphatic no. The office is a creature of politics, and I doubted that whoever reported to the Drug Czar felt the same ethical constraints that a career justice department employee might. That concern had led me to approach Peggy, but I'd botched it. She clearly didn't want to go near my theory.

Had Peggy's reaction been honest or had she been prepped?

No need to get paranoid. Peggy had always been my friend, and still was, I hoped. I had to trust someone, and Peggy had lived up to that trust in the past. Sam and Peggy were both right. If I believed in the truth of my hazy allegations, I needed hard evidence, not theories grounded only in my vivid imagination.

THE MAN WATCHED Patterson sitting on the park bench and grinned. He now had people watching Jones and Maggie, and he was tailing Jack. So far, so good. He'd figured Patterson would try to involve Main Justice. Fortson was a straight arrow, but any problems she might have created had been handled long ago. Jones would also strike out with his sources. Dub was too important an asset to let him leave tracks. A few rumors might still be floating around, but no hard evidence remained. Maggie would run up against a dead end at the federal agencies. Today she was knocking on the door at NIH, but the General Counsel had been alerted. She would come up empty again. He found it irksome that no one seemed to know or care why Patterson wanted to accelerate the auction, but the client said they had the auction covered. So he let it go.

45

WHEN I WALKED into the office, Rose told me that one of Martin's men had driven Maggie to NIH and Clovis had called to say he was running late. I sank into the chair behind my desk and decided to call Debbie and Paul. Why wait?

"Debbie, is Paul around? Can you get him on speaker?"

In a matter of minutes, I was talking to them both.

"Debbie, I've got an idea, but I want you to think it through. Paul, if you think there's any risk for either of you, you need to say so."

They agreed to be candid.

"Let's see if we can't shake things up. For the next week, every time Dub makes a public appearance, I want you both to be right there in the front row."

Debbie laughed. "That's easy, but why?"

"You're too cute to miss, and eventually he'll remember where he's seen you. Your smiling face will surely fluster him, make him nervous. Paul, you're there to protect her. Once he remembers, he'll want her to disappear—and I don't want her to end up as road kill." Tough words, but I really did want them to be careful.

Paul cleared his throat. "Do you want her to speak, ask questions, or just be visible?"

"Just be visible. It won't take long for Dub to spot her, and the press won't be far behind—but no talking or baiting, understand? Debbie, I know this is going to be hard, but I want you to tone down the short skirts and make-up. Pretend you're a sorority girl. If the press throws you a question, just smile and walk away. Don't try to make something up. Paul, don't let Dub's deputies bother her. Debbie, if they ask you to leave, you need to leave straightaway. Our only purpose is to make Dub sweat."

"A sorority girl? No way! Why can't I dress up? He'll be sure to remember me if I wear some of the same outfits I used to wear."

The thought of Debbie confronting Dub in a hooker's outfit had a certain appeal. The press would have a field day. I shook the thought away. I was already asking too much of her. Victims of trafficking have difficulty getting out after they've been rescued, but Debbie seemed to be made of special stuff.

"No, Debbie, I need you to be subtle, intriguing. I want him to wonder. Paul, until Maggie gets there to help, I leave her outfits up to you. Nothing that makes a story."

"Got it," Paul responded. I knew I'd given Paul an impossible assignment.

We talked for a little longer and, to my relief, Paul reported that Micki was improving steadily. I asked Paul to tell her I'd call later this afternoon. I still hoped that either Maggie or Clovis might come up with something positive I could tell her. Maggie returned, and I told her about my conversation with Paul and Debbie.

"What's the point?" She asked. She settled into a comfortable leather chair, still holding the file she had brought with her.

"Dub is surrounded by lawyers and law enforcement types giving him advice and keeping him under control. It's a pretty good bet he hasn't let them in on his secret life. I think he'll develop serious heartburn when he sees Debbie—maybe he'll make a mistake. Even if he doesn't, he'll be distracted. You have to admit Debbie can be a distraction."

"I take it you're finally learning?" Maggie grinned.

We had a laugh at my expense before I asked, "Any luck finding Doug's letter?"

"The FBI, DEA, Drug Czar, and Homeland Security all gave me the run-around—again. They won't acknowledge such a letter exists and, if it does, hell will freeze over before I see it. I've tried every trick I know. The FDA and CDC were more cooperative, but they insist they don't have any correspondence from our professor."

"Somebody has to have the letter. We know he wrote it. Aw, hell, I hope to God he wrote it!" I said in frustration. I noticed that Maggie's eyes were twinkling. "Rose said you went to NIH. What happened?"

"Well, I started with the general counsel. To say he was unhelpful is an understatement. He was pleased to inform me that anything related to Doug's research had been sealed by Dub's task force and was exempt from the Freedom of Information Act. The same went for any letters Doug may have sent the Director. Let me quote: 'I don't even have to go to the trouble to look. It's all been sealed.'" Her disgust was evident.

"I was afraid of that. It was worth a try. Thanks."

"Let me finish. Do you remember Dr. Jonas Ketcher? He was Angie's supervisor."

"Of course I remember him. Why?"

"As I was leaving the GC's office, Dr. Ketcher stopped me and asked why I was there. As soon as I mentioned Doug Stewart he smiled, took my arm and led me down the hall. I liked his smile, so I told him the truth. He chuckled and said, 'Nothing good ever comes out of a lawyer's office.' He told me that about three years ago everything that had Doug's name on it had been boxed up and removed—every computer purged. It created quite an uproar at the time, but all protests were ignored, and the issue died down.

"The timing agrees with what Liz said about Doug's letter, but it doesn't help in finding the letter." I sighed in frustration, but a smile still hovered on Maggie's face.

"I had exactly the same reaction, must have actually slumped, because Jonas put his arm around me and said, 'Walk with me.' When we reached his office, he closed the door. We just stood there for a minute—he seemed to be listening for something.

"I was about to ask, but he put two fingers up to my lips and spoke softly, 'When they purged everyone's files, no one thought to look in Angie's old office. We finally got around to cleaning it out and came across a box of unopened mail. Most of it was publications and flyers— junk. I told my assistant to give me anything that looked important and throw the rest away. She found a few letters. One was addressed to Angie and marked personal. I saw that it was from Doug's address in

Little Rock. I remember thinking how strange since Doug didn't leave NIH until after Angie died.

"He said, 'I kept that letter and a couple of others in a drawer—I meant to give them to Jack, but forgot all about them. Probably should have turned them over to the General Counsel but it slipped my mind.' He winked, unlocked his desk, and handed me a few envelopes. I thanked him, and he asked me not to tell anyone where they'd come from. I promised.

"I let him escort me from the building, and as he held the door to my car open he said, 'That letter might turn out to be just his Christmas list, but Doug never did anything without a reason. Give Jack my best and tell him that a lot of us at NIH are glad he's defending Doug.'"

"Finally!" I was suddenly excited. "Do you have it with you?"

She handed it to me with a flourish and came around to read over my shoulder. In the manila envelope I tore open, I found a note card and a copy of a letter. I read the note first.

Jack,

I sent this to Angie's attention knowing she was already gone, but hoping somebody would pass it on to you. It seemed like the best thing to do. I sent another copy to your house. Please keep this letter in a safe place. It is self-explanatory, and I hope you never need it. Angie was instrumental in encouraging me and helping me get as far as I have. She said if trouble came calling you would help. I hope it never comes to that.

Doug.

I didn't remember getting anything from Doug in the mail, but after Angie's death I seldom looked at her mail, except for the obvious bills, throwing them all away. *Idiot.*

I unfolded the letter. It was directed to the Federal Food and Drug Administration and the Drug Czar's office. It showed copies to the DEA, FBI, CDC, HHS, NIH, and Homeland Security. It neglected to mention this copy.

Dear Sirs:

My name is Douglas Stewart, PhD. I recently completed a fellowship at NIH and am now a professor of chemistry, occupying an endowed chair at the University of Arkansas-Little Rock. Over the past several years, I have become more and more convinced that besides its therapeutic benefits, marijuana in hybrid and modified form may offer significant curative benefits. I'm not talking about "medical marijuana" in its conventional understanding, but medical use derived from the chemical makeup of the plant altered by cross breeding and molecular alteration.

I hope that instead of writing me off as a "crackpot," you will review my credentials and study the attached summary of my research to date. Anyone familiar with chemical research will find my work exciting, especially as it relates to a breakthrough towards a cure for cancer.

I recognize that medical research using cannabis is currently illegal, but I believe that, given what I have found, such research is vital. I ask you to give me permission to continue with my work. I know there is an accepted protocol, but it is too cumbersome and the research is seldom approved. I grow a limited number of plants in my backyard for research purposes only. I welcome your inspection of my garden or my records to verify the truthfulness of my statements. I keep meticulous records so you can verify that the plants are only used for research, not for personal or any other use. Any restriction you wish to place on the source of the marijuana I grow is fine with me as long as I can use it in my research.

You should also know that I have no intention of profiting from my research. I have filed for patents on my discoveries, only to protect them from misuse or fraud. When the time is right, I will post my research on the Internet, much like open-source codes for computer programming, so it can be shared with the world. It is my fervent hope that this science will facilitate the development of cheaper, safer, and more effective treatments for cancer and other similar diseases using biochemically altered marijuana and other plants.

I welcome the opportunity to discuss my discoveries with a panel of experts of your choosing.

Sincerely,

Doug Stewart

Not only had Doug told the regulatory world what he was doing three years ago—he had invited them into the process. I felt sure that, given his reputation, his research had been carefully analyzed and had scared the shit out of law enforcement and those who profit from the disease. I also bet they had decided not to respond to his letter until their ducks were in a neat row and they could crash down his door with an axe.

Maggie gave a whistle. "So you were right!"

"Not so fast. A cynical lawyer would say Doug was just developing a convenient cover. We don't have proof that the letter was received, and we certainly don't have any proof that anyone took action on it."

"But you do have the letter, and we can prove its *bona fides* through the Patent Office. I'm already on my way to Virginia, as soon as I call Jonas to thank him."

"Go slow with the thanks to Jonas. Someone was bound to have seen you together, and he may be under suspicion by now. We'll find a way to thank him later. We need to find out who stands to lose the most if Doug's research proves credible. Want to bet his patent applications are sealed because of national security? But let's not tip our hand. The less anybody knows the better."

I called Micki on the secure line Clovis had created to tell her about Doug's letter. Her response pricked my balloon of optimism.

"That's nice, but it's not much help legally. In fact, it proves he knew he was breaking the law. If that kind of letter would let you grow over fifty plants in your backyard, the Drug Czar would be inundated with letters. I'd be more interested in the summary. I guess he didn't send that to you?"

"No, although I'll check at home just in case I didn't throw it out. How do you feel?"

"Better. By the way, Debbie and Paul just left for Dub's latest press conference. She looked—well, sort of like a college girl. Are you sure that's a good idea?"

"I hope so. There's a risk, but I'm trying to throw Dub off his game. Let me know how it goes."

She promised me a summary of what to expect at the forfeiture auction and a memo on forfeiture laws that would put me to sleep. After a few attempts at small talk, she asked when I'd be back.

"I'd say this weekend. Maggie has gone to the Patent Office. I'll know more when she gets back this afternoon."

I called a couple of Angie's former associates to ask if they'd heard anything about a new cure for cancer. They were polite, but no help. I called another old friend, an economist I'd used as an expert witness in antitrust cases. We made lunch plans, and I told him I'd buy if I could quiz him a little "off the clock."

THE MAN HAD circled the block three times to find a legal parking space in front of the Foundation's office—no sense in annoying the DC parking cops. His colleague had just phoned to say he was waiting for Maggie outside the patent office. Patterson was becoming a real pain in the ass. Good thing they had seen that inquiry coming and made sure she was stonewalled. He was always amazed at how many people the organization had co-opted. They did their jobs, never arousing suspicion, but at the right time they were ready to do whatever it took to accommodate the client, for a fee, of course. He had never asked how much this foresight cost the client. It wasn't his business, and he felt safer not knowing.

I WAS YAWNING at my desk when Clovis and Maggie returned. Maggie threw her purse down on the couch, looking hot and frustrated. She'd been shut completely out at the Patent and Trademark Office.

"All filings by Dr. Stewart have been placed under seal for reasons of 'national security.' I was referred to a Mr. Atkinson, who had a hard time even confirming the existence of applications. A total waste of time."

"No surprise, but thanks for trying. More than likely, Dub plans to sneak Doug's patent applications into what is auctioned. Even if no one will confirm they exist, whoever buys his research will certainly want them, so we should be on the lookout for a legal sleight-of-hand. We know a letter was sent, that Doug did exactly what he said he would. Now we have to prove they received the letter and acted on it."

"Oh, they got the letter all right." Clovis spoke up. "About three years ago, word went out to every agency that no one was to touch Dr. Douglas Stewart. Totally hands-off. I've now confirmed that a representative of the Drug Czar's office met with Pulaski County's sheriff,

Little Rock's police chief, and the Arkansas state police. They were told a special task force would handle all matters concerning Dr. Stewart. Under no circumstances were they to interfere, and Sam's office specifically was to be kept in the dark. Sam's going to be really pissed. I wouldn't want to be Sheriff Barnes when Sam finds out he held out on him."

"You're shitting me!" I'd suspected something of the kind, but not a total blitz.

"I am not. Apparently the attorney general and the FBI balked at the quarantine at first, but somebody got to them. The Drug Czar gave the task force total authority to handle the matter. Any time Dub or his associates step on someone's toes, that someone hears 'excuse me, national security,' and the bull keeps stomping in the china shop. I've never seen so many people looking over their shoulders." He frowned happily. Clovis loved a conspiracy.

"We're clearly way past ginger snaps," I mused. "What's more, we seem to be the only good guys standing in the way of the bull. We have evidence of Doug's intent, we know the government wanted him stopped and why. The question is, how do we stop it?"

46

WALTER JOINED US for dinner at Johnnie's Half Shell, home of the best crab cakes in the city, light and delicate. But I still miss their crowded, noisy DuPont Circle location. Angie and I used to enjoy sitting at the bar, eating tiny succulent oysters from Maine or Prince Edward Island, chatting with people waiting for a table. The Capitol Hill location traded atmosphere for space, but the oysters and crab cakes are almost as good.

The waiter brought us wine—Clovis opted for pale ale—and I brought Walter up to date. If he was going to give me a letter of credit, he needed to know as much as I did. He seemed mildly interested when Maggie told him about Doug's letter, more so when Clovis told him about the government's involvement in controlling how the government reacted to his letter.

"Jack, do you realize what effect a free cure for cancer would have on the economy?"

"Well, it's crossed my mind. I have an appointment with an economist friend tomorrow."

"The answer's simple—enormous. Medically, it would be more significant than the polio vaccine and possibly bigger than the discovery of penicillin. A huge segment of our economy is dedicated to the treatment of cancer. Think about it: drug companies, hospitals, insurance companies, treatment centers, and physicians . . . the trickle-down effect is enormous. I bet your economist pegs the number in the billions."

Maggie jumped in. "But we're talking about a cure for cancer. Who cares about the economic effect?"

"Well, sure, everyone wants to find a cure for cancer—beyond its invaluable worth to mankind, it's the proverbial golden egg. Big pharma, insurance, the medical community, the government—they all want to control any breakthrough, either for profit or to control its effect on jobs, profits, taxes, revenues, and the economy overall. The thought of Doug putting his research online as open source, free for all, has got to scare them no end. Make no mistake: this isn't about the illegal use of marijuana. The real issue is control of the bottom line. No wonder your friend Dub has been instructed to play the national security card."

Trust Walter to have seen the whole issue from a financial perspective.

"Walter, I can't believe my ears! We're talking about cancer. Think of all the suffering." Maggie always reacted from the heart first, a trait I dearly loved.

"My dear, on a personal level, I don't disagree. In fact, a cure for cancer would also mean hundreds of millions of dollars to our company alone. Life insurance companies love medical breakthroughs and life expectancy extensions. I'm sure any political administration would feel like you about a cure, but that doesn't mean they wouldn't want to control its timing and its protocol."

"Aren't you being a bit cynical?" Maggie flushed, now clearly irritated. Walter didn't lose a beat.

"Well, maybe, but look at the reality: I'm in the business of insuring lives. Every week I see how new drugs and medical breakthroughs are affected by profit and politics. Hardly a bill gets through Congress that doesn't contain some break for the drug or health insurance industry. You only have to look at how long it takes a new drug to get through the system—usually not until the patents on old drugs are about to expire. It's my business to know how quickly a breakthrough will be approved because it affects my bottom line."

"Well, okay, but I have a hard time thinking our government would try to stop a cure for cancer."

"Darling, you're probably right. Believe me, I hope so. But I wouldn't put it past some fairly senior politico to decide that any significant medical breakthrough needs to be in the hands of the people who've donated millions to their campaigns, not some chemist who's talking about providing invaluable research to the world for free. And you're right to be troubled by the facts—trouble is, they're true."

The waiter returned with hot crab cakes accompanied by really crispy fries and excellent slaw. No one said much of anything while we gave our food the attention it deserved. But I didn't stop thinking.

His point of view had proved my theory. "Walter, you've hit the nail on the head. It was Doug's reference to 'open source' that got them all riled up. No one wants to prevent breakthroughs in cancer research, but everyone wants to own it."

Clovis, who had been content to listen so far, carefully folded his napkin on the table and said, "You're forgetting that if marijuana is legalized, even just for research, folks in the liquor and cigarette industries as well as law enforcement will howl like banshees. Those guys have invested a lot of money in keeping marijuana illegal. They sure don't want anyone with credibility to claim smoking weed cures cancer."

Silence. I saw three troubled faces and tried to lighten things up. "Look at it this way. Even if we don't win, we'll have a great recipe for ginger snaps."

"Dub will probably claim the recipe is one of Doug's assets and auction it off," Maggie said, relaxing a little.

"Seems to me someone needs to give Dub a few of those cookies," Clovis deadpanned.

We tried, but our laughs were halfhearted. The waiter returned with dessert menus. No takers—no surprise. Maggie and Walter excused themselves, and Clovis and I were soon ready to go home as well. Clovis wanted to watch the Cardinals game, and I opted for a shower. As the warm stream massaged my back a thought hit me. I'd hoped that Debbie's presence would make Dub nervous, make him wonder why she was there, maybe cause him to screw up. What might help him slip over the edge? What would distract Dub even more than Debbie? What about a little unexpected publicity?

TUESDAY

April 29, 2014

47

I WOKE UP early and placed a call to Cheryl Cole, Woody's former wife, now the host of an evening talk show on Fox News. Cheryl had divorced Woody long ago, but the publicity surrounding the Senator's murder had given her the chance she needed to emerge from relative obscurity to her new status as host of the moment on talk news. Her ratings exceeded Bill O'Reilly's, and she used both her obvious charms and her newly unleashed moxie to trap guests from business, politics, and entertainment. To the delight of her audience, once she had lured them into her silken web, she sunk her teeth in; Cheryl had found her calling.

I knew it wouldn't be long before she returned my call. Cheryl had invited me to appear on her show several times, but I'd always declined. I'd known her in college, and she kept in touch because she was a beneficiary of a trust I administered. I sent her a check every month, but she always seemed to need an advance. It amazed me how much she could spend, knowing she was getting at least six figures from Fox.

Clovis appeared in the kitchen before long, silent and clearly out of sorts. I figured he was hungry and suggested breakfast at a favorite place of mine where you sit on stools and watch the cook deal with four orders at once, never mixing up bacon for sausage, scrambled for fried. His specialty was corned beef hash, which made us both happy. It wasn't long before we both felt better.

I'd given Clovis an extra office at the foundation to conduct his business. I wanted him to consult with Stella, Micki's IT person. She'd uncovered something peculiar in Micki's computers. Clovis knew enough to ask the right questions. I didn't.

Maggie was in the office before me, of course. I told her about my call to Cheryl, feeling lucky when she didn't throw anything at me. Cheryl was not included in Maggie's social register. But when I explained what I was up to, she agreed that Cheryl would be perfect.

"All right, but don't get too close. I don't buy for a minute that you're through with Little Rock women, and Cheryl Cole has them all beat by ten furlongs. She'd love to get her fangs into you. Why can't you go for a woman with a little class, like that schoolteacher in Vermont? What was her name?"

"Marion South. And it would take a stick of dynamite to get her out of Vermont. Believe me, I tried."

"You didn't try hard enough." Maggie almost never backed down.

"Yes, I did—how would you know? And what about Micki? She has class."

"She's spoken for, or have you forgotten?"

I was never going to carry this debate. Bless her; Maggie Hen was nothing if not protective, sometimes a little too protective if you asked me.

"Back to my point. You be careful around Cheryl." She smiled easily, knowing she'd won. She also knew how far she could push me.

We got down to business—foundation business. I had to reschedule meetings, take a first look at the new stack of proposals and grant requests on my desk, and an ominous-looking envelope from the IRS, which told us we were being audited. I wasn't worried. We relied on a good CPA firm who made sure we dotted every "I" and crossed every "T," but it would be a distraction. Walter had shown a sudden interest in meeting my economist friend, so we were set to join him for lunch at The Bombay Club. My afternoon was still free, but I hoped to hear from Cheryl.

THE MAN LOUNGING against the meter outside the Bombay Club kept one eye out for the parking cops. All in all he felt pretty good—Maggie was lunching with her friend from the FTC, but she would learn nothing. Patterson and Mathews were clearly engaged in foundation business—why else meet with an economist? Nevertheless, he had reported the meeting to his boss, and he'd soon know if the meeting had anything to do with Dr. Stewart. Jones was another story. He was a tough nut to crack. His boss had told him to pull out all the stops and spare no expense, and he couldn't help but wonder who was the client writing the checks.

48

I WAS LATE for lunch, couldn't help it. Tag Bettis was an economist I often called upon in antitrust cases. He and Walter were already engaged in a lively discussion about the current state of the economy, economic theory, and what role the Feds should be playing. They managed to order lunch and enjoy excellent tandoori trout with almost no interruption in their conversation. I waited until the waiter brought coffee to focus on the issue at hand.

"Tag, I want to pose a hypothetical. I realize this is new to you, and I'll be happy with an educated guess. What would happen to the economy if a reliable cure for cancer suddenly dropped into the marketplace?"

"Well, since you're buying, I'll give you an answer that's worth the price of this lunch. The answer is—very little. Whatever the drug companies lost on old cancer treatments would be offset by the cost of marketing and selling the new drug. Some companies would suffer, but others would reap the rewards of a miracle drug. Given the time it takes to bring any new drug to the public, the economy would have plenty of time to adjust. Is your question even feasible?"

"Probably not, but let me add to the hypothesis. What if the science was available to anyone, and the cure was free or relatively so, without the need for drug manufacturers, doctors or pharmacies—sort of like an aspirin or heartburn medicine?"

"The government won't let that happen. You're talking about drying up a huge sector of the economy. Clearly the world would be a lot better off, but such a discovery would have to be phased in over a long period of time in order to maintain stability. Otherwise, it could be an economic catastrophe." Tag looked troubled. "Jack, you're talking about trying to balance the value of life with the likelihood of economic chaos. The FDA makes these types of decisions every day, though they would never admit it. Economics are a major factor in their decisions, although they hide behind phrases like 'Protecting America's Health.'"

Walter asked, "Do you think a comprehensive study of Jack's hypothetical could minimize the uncertainty?"

Tag looked even more uncertain. "Well, to do it right would be very expensive—I'd have to create new computer models—but yes. The right study, done by the right people, would help significantly. I'd have to know how far along the company is in the drug's development."

I looked at Walter, unsure of where he was headed. He was way ahead of me.

"Technically, this is Jack's decision, but we want to hire you and your firm to produce such a study on behalf of Bridgeport Life and the Matthews Foundation. For everything you learn to remain within the privilege, my law firm will actually hire you. It's imperative for you to begin this work as soon as possible." Tag's eyebrows shot up, and his mouth dropped open.

"Wow. You don't beat around the bush, do you?"

"No, I don't. We don't have the time," Walter replied firmly. "If you're not interested, I'll find someone who is."

They agreed to meet again later that afternoon, and we all left, Tag still looking shell-shocked.

Walter dropped me off at the office, and I met Maggie walking in the door. She had lunched with a friend at the Federal Trade Commission, hoping to gain some insight into who might profit from a potential cure for cancer.

"How'd it go?" I asked.

"Well, we had a very nice lunch—you know, catching up on friends, trading a little gossip. Oddly, it was Ruth who brought up the business, not me. She said she'd heard her boss talking about how you'd gotten involved in a case that looked like a simple drug bust, but was actually a matter of national security. She told me very politely that we should butt out. The White House is handling whatever's going on, and everyone else had been told to stay away. Sounded to me like she knew a lot more than 'I heard my boss talking . . . '"

"And . . . ?"

"Well, I managed to change the subject, and she seemed to get more comfortable. I used one of your old tricks—kept her glass full. As we were about to leave she said, 'Maggie, be careful.' I nodded without thinking and asked for the check. Then, out of the blue, she leaned across the table, 'I understand Jack is involved in an antitrust investigation of Akron Drugs.' I assured her we weren't. She gave me a quick kiss and left before I could say a word. Jack, is there an ongoing investigation of Akron?"

"Not as far as I know. Think she was trying to tell you otherwise?"

"It certainly seemed so. Shall I handle it, or do you have any special instructions?" She knew I'd have to put my two cents in.

"Yes, don't go through normal channels. Call David Dickey and ask him to give you an opinion on Akron. He'll get it when you tell him you don't want our foundation's possible investment to raise any flags."

David handled all the investments for the foundation. He's Walter's favorite financial advisor and a great guy to boot. We'd have a full report on Akron Drugs within a matter of days, and no one would know we were interested.

Rose stepped into the office. "Jack, Cheryl Cole is on the phone. Says she's returning your call. Should I tell her the check already went out?"

"No, Rose, I really did call her this time. I'll take it." Maggie gave me a scowl and left to call David.

"Cheryl—how nice to hear your voice!"

"I hope you're calling to say you've increased my allowance."

"Nope, same amount. I need to ask you a favor."

"Jack Patterson is asking me for a favor? This is a first. It must be a whopper."

"I think you might find it intriguing," I replied, hoping to pique her curiosity.

"Hmm . . . then it's going to cost you drinks at a very public place." She wasn't above milking speculation. She was probably dialing the *Washington Post* as we spoke.

"I'm happy to buy you drinks, but our first meeting needs to be at least a little private. Surely you know a nice place where we won't be noticed until you decide to break the story."

"There's a story in this favor?"

"Only if you're intrigued."

"I know the perfect place. People will recognize me, but if they know who you are, I'll just say you're bringing me up to date on Woody."

Her perfect place was one of those new hot spots near the Newseum. It was hardly private, but Cheryl had a plausible story. We agreed to meet at six.

Clovis arrived and collapsed onto the office couch. He'd spent the whole day with "computer geeks" and was "just plain wore out."

"By the way, Stella puts Walter's geeks to shame. She's now got Micki and Debbie set up at the ranch with a system that should be impregnable. Apparently, everyone's been hacked, and Micki's phones were bugged, but the intrusions were so well disguised it was almost impossible to discover. She isolated the spyware in Micki's computer system in a way the hackers won't know we're on to them; same for the bugs. Walter's flying her here to do the same thing for Bridgeport and the Foundation."

"So who's behind all this? Who has this level of sophistication? And, sorry to ask, but Stella's not a Moira, is she?"

"No, she's not. Of that I'm sure. I don't think she can figure out who the bad guys are, but she can take care of our computer security issues."

"Okay, the sooner the better. I'm sorry—I had to ask," I said. "What about Walter getting the line of credit? Do 'they' know about that?"

"No. Walter is handling the letter the old fashioned way—in person."

"Okay, good. I'm off to see if I can stir up some trouble with Cheryl Cole."

"That woman's nothing but trouble. You sure you know what you're doing?"

"Not exactly, but I figure it'll come to me."

The warm sunshine of the late spring afternoon felt luxurious on my face as I walked down Pennsylvania Avenue. Washington is a beautiful city if you can ignore the traffic and don't fall prey to the intense backstabbing that's part of its culture.

I was the first to arrive—no surprise. If you're on time, that means you're not busy and therefore not important, the ultimate DC sin. A few heads turned as I was seated, but I was last year's news, so interest quickly died. I was content to enjoy an Oregon Pinot Gris I hadn't seen before on a restaurant wine list. Cheryl arrived twenty minutes later, and I had to admire the way she worked the room. It took her a good ten minutes to cross, stopping at every table. I first met Cheryl when she was Woody's college girlfriend. Back then her unruly hair had been as scruffy as her faded jeans. Now every bit of her package conveyed power. Her hair was perfectly coiffed, her skin was flawless, and her clothes radiated class. Her trademark silk blouse was always unbuttoned one too many. Cheryl couldn't be called beautiful, but she was attractive enough, and she could sell her song.

She greeted me with a kiss square on the lips that took me aback. Maggie's warning light was glowing. She beckoned to the waiter and smiled easily.

"Paul, I'll have my usual: a large bottle of Pellegrino, a glass of ice, and a cup of decaf."

Pretty soon the waiter returned bearing the Pellegrino, a glass of ice, and a coffee cup filled with bourbon. She noticed me staring as she dropped a couple of ice cubes into the cup.

"What one eats and drinks in this town is fair game to anyone who notices. If I were to order a bourbon and water, it would be all over town that I was soused on the air. Be sure to reward Paul well. Your tip will be in the *Post* tomorrow—heaven forbid—if you aren't generous."

The *Post* relishes celebrity comings and goings, whether they're movie stars or politicians. Come to think if it, everyone in DC does—in some ways it is a very small town.

"First, tell me what you know about Woody, so I won't have to lie if someone asks."

"Actually, not much at all. Micki sees him more often than I do. His quarters are pretty small, but you know Woody; he doesn't need much. Sam says he's doing well."

Cheryl waved across the room at someone. I could tell she was already bored. I needed to get her attention and keep it.

I raised my glass, smiling. "You look really good, Cheryl. I'm glad you're so successful. So is Woody."

I watched as she measured her response. "I'm tempted to turn on my charms and seduce you, Jack. You're still one good-looking man. But I have a feeling you're that rare breed of man who wouldn't take the bait. So let's cut the crap. You need a favor and, since I owe you about a hundred, tell me what it's all about. Let's say I'm intrigued."

No warm-up pitches. Lock and load.

"I want you to come to Little Rock under the pretense of doing a story about what has happened since Senator Robinson was shot."

"Could be a good story, but not my cup of tea." She lifted her cup in a toast and tossed down the liquor without a hiccup, signaling the waiter for a refill.

"I know it's not, but it's an excuse to interview Dub Blanchard, the U.S. attorney, and to get him to tell you about his task force."

"He's asked twice to come on my show, claims some chemist is abusing children or something like that. Disgusting man, your Mr. Blanchard. Besides, what's one more drug bust?"

"Nothing, but Dub's a star-fucker, ready to appear on every talk show he can to talk about his big drug bust. His pitch isn't what your show's about, but I want you to do it anyway."

"What's in it for you? More to the point, what's in it for me?"

I took a deep breath.

"Micki and I represent the defendant in Dub's drug bust. My client also happens to be one of the world's top chemists. Dub's gone all hard-ass, won't let me see him, claiming 'national security.' Next Wednesday, the U.S. marshal is going to conduct a civil forfeiture auction of Dr. Stewart's assets, and I thought you might want to be in the courtroom when it happens."

She took a sip of bourbon. "Jack, you never change. You aren't telling me shit. You want me to go to Little Rock, pretend like I'm doing a story, but in reality cozy up to Dub to find out why he's keeping you from talking to your client. To top it all off, you want me in the courtroom next Wednesday."

"I couldn't have said it better myself, except Dub can't know I asked."

She was quick. "Why in the world would I do this? You've got to give me more."

"I forgot to ask. We are off the record, aren't we?"

"Of course," she said easily. "Off the record" had gone out with vinyl.

"If I'm right, next Wednesday you'll be the only television reporter in the courtroom to cover the biggest story to hit the news in a very long time."

Her eyes widened. "Okay. I'll bite. Why me? Why aren't you going to Katie or Diane? Let's be honest, I can't be one of your favorites."

"Because any hint that the big-time press knows what this is about, and the story is blown. You're high enough profile to excite Dub, but not big enough to send up a warning signal to the people pulling his strings."

She didn't like the answer, though she knew it was true.

"Don't be offended, Cheryl. If you pull your part off, you'll out-score both *60 Minutes* and *World News Tonight*, or whatever it's called." I had her interest now.

"One last thing. Getting close to Dub can be extremely dangerous."

"Oh, come on, I've dealt with men far more dangerous than Dub Blanchard."

"Hear me out. Since we're off the record, and since I think you should know, someone kidnapped Micki, then me, and tried to kill us both. I got lucky. Micki's in bad shape, still recovering."

Now Cheryl's eyes practically bulged. She ordered her third bourbon. "You want me to believe a U.S. attorney is behind all this? Dub doesn't have the balls. He's a fucking weasel."

"You're right about that. No, this is way above Dub's pay grade. I think he was chosen to be the front man because he happens to be the U.S. attorney for the district and he's got skeletons in his closet. No, he's not calling the shots. I warn you because he does have a reputation when it comes to women. The more I think about this, it's unfair to ask you to get involved. I'm sorry. I promise to let you in on it when it's over." I might as well have waved a red flag at a bull.

Cheryl grabbed my wrist, practically panting. "No, you don't, Jack Patterson. I'm a big girl. Tell me whatever you can. I'm not as dumb as

I look, you know. I smell a story, a career-making story. Don't tease me."

She nursed her bourbon and listened as I told her how to play the part. She had her own ideas, and we finished with a pretty good game plan.

I asked. "Don't you have a show tonight?"

"If you mean the bourbon, I know my limit. You'd be surprised how many talk show hosts have more than water in those coffee cups." She smiled. "Tell me, Jack, how come you and I've never gotten together?"

"I was married, and you were married to my best friend—two very good reasons."

"Not for me," she laughed.

"I know, but for me they were both game stoppers."

"What about now? Angie, God rest her soul is gone, and I'm divorced."

"Not that any sane man wouldn't be interested, but you're still the former wife of my best friend, who's still in love with you—again, a game stopper."

"Jack Patterson, loyal to the core. You'll never change, but I'll tell you one thing—you are missing out."

"That I'm sure of, Cheryl. That I'm sure of." I raised my glass in a toast wondering who her guests were tonight. Boy, were they in for a hot time.

"I'll call Dub tomorrow morning and we'll go from there. I've got a feeling I just joined a gang of thieves."

In a sense, she could be right. I hoped so.

The skies were ominous, big thunderheads building up in Virginia, but Maggie was determined we should have dinner at the Lebanese Taverna in Bethesda, not far from my house—wonderful Lebanese food and great service. Clovis and Maggie were fascinated by my conversation with Cheryl, although Maggie wasn't happy with how I had roped her in. It was getting to be a bad habit, inviting others to put themselves in danger.

We stayed away from business, other than discussing plans to go back to Little Rock via Memphis in a few days. Walter wouldn't come down until the Tuesday before the auction, bringing the letter of credit with him.

Declining dessert, Walter rose to help Maggie with her jacket. "Well, Jack, we need a little luck, but you know what: I'm looking forward to the fireworks."

Clovis and I decided to indulge in a glass of port, not quite ready to call it a night.

"Maggie is right about Cheryl. I do worry about involving her."

"You should. You and Micki are lucky to be alive. Micki's office was bugged, and all our computers were hacked, including the Foundation's and Bridgeport's. Your foundation is under audit, and Walter's companies are being investigated. To top it off, whoever is behind all this sent an international assassin to Arkansas, just in case somebody got wind of their plans. I wouldn't say you're overly cautious. Maybe in over your head, but definitely not overly cautious."

I chuckled. "In over my head is hardly an adequate description."

The storm broke with a flash of lightening and a torrent of rain just before we climbed into the rented Suburban. Waiting until we had shaken the water off, our driver said calmly. "You guys have company. Those two followed you into the restaurant and now have followed you out. Want me to lose them?" He pointed to two other guys hastily climbing into an old Subaru.

Clovis answered. "No, just get us home. Better have somebody watch the house."

He turned to me. "I'll be glad to get back to Arkansas. I can spot a stranger there, but I'm useless in DC."

"Hardly useless, but otherwise you're right. I never thought I'd look forward to returning to Little Rock, but I do. I'm ready to play our hand, see if we can pull this thing off. I'm not optimistic—they haven't made many mistakes, and we're up against overwhelming resources. But we do have surprise on our side. That's got to count for something."

FRIDAY MORNING

May 2, 2014

49

THE ALARM CLOCK read four o'clock when I woke from a nightmare about Moira wielding a branding iron. I wanted nothing more than to fall back to sleep, but the prospect of another bad dream got me out of bed and into the shower. I relaxed for an extra-long time, letting the warm water loosen the knots from wounds old and new. I also began to rehearse my role in the upcoming auction.

I thought about how little evidence I'd been able to pin down. The rest of the week had been wasted on "sorry, I can't help you" and what seemed to be an avalanche of regulators descending on the foundation. So, I had to gamble on flushing my quarry rather than having the goods beforehand. I dressed for a day of travel, walked downstairs quietly, and made coffee.

I wasn't much of a cook, but I knew how to make a good breakfast. I pulled my grandmother's cast-iron skillet out from a bottom drawer and put the sausage on to fry. I found some frozen biscuits made by a little country store outside of Middleburg, Virginia and popped them in the oven. As soon as the sausage was cooked, I added milk, flour, and seasonings to the drippings, stirring constantly until my gravy was the perfect consistency. My grandmother used to tell me you had to listen to the scraping sound of the wooden spoon against the pan—that's how you knew the gravy was done. Wasn't long before Clovis came down. He drank his coffee in companionable silence, watching as I turned my attention to the eggs and to setting the table for our feast.

"What's the occasion?" he asked. "Not that I'm complaining."

"You know, I left Little Rock a long time ago, didn't think I'd ever come back. Now I've been there twice in as many years. And twice someone has tried to kill me. But thanks to you, I'm still alive. If history repeats itself, I figure this breakfast may be my last. So since I couldn't sleep, I decided to make us a good one."

We didn't talk much over breakfast. Clovis offered to clear and clean while I packed. I'd be gone for at least a week and would need court clothes. Angie had always checked my bag when we traveled. The right tie, the right shoes—now I felt good if I my socks matched.

We reached National without a hitch, found Maggie, and were in the air quickly. Liz was meeting us for lunch at the Peabody.

"Sleep well last night, Maggie?" I asked.

"Not really. When Walter's worried he tosses and turns. When Walter worries, we all should."

"Anything I don't already know?"

"I think more than anything, he's worried about Moira. He thinks the money is a good investment, but he doesn't think Moira will walk away from unfinished business. He said, 'Jack's got a big sign on his back telling the world Moira failed. If she wants to stay in her game, she's coming back.'"

Clovis had been listening. "For sure."

"Well, as you know I've had similar thoughts, but either she's coming or she isn't. I can't cancel her contract, and, well, it doesn't do any good to think about it."

One of Liz's bodyguards met us at the airport and drove us to the Peabody. She was waiting for us in the Lobby Bar and insisted breezily that we all have a drink. This time I held my ground and led her to our table where a waiter handed her a tall iced tea. I'd had about enough of her split personality. I told her what we'd found out regarding the letter and what little we knew about the government's reaction.

"Doug wondered why he never got a response from anyone, but decided not to push the issue. He figured the longer the government was willing to let him work in peace, the more he could accomplish.

"I thought as much. Actually, the summary he prepared caused some real excitement, but not in the way Doug hoped.

"So what happens on Wednesday?" she asked, looking glumly at her iced tea.

"I don't know," I admitted. "We're so close—I can almost feel it. But I don't have any hard evidence yet. I hope the auction process will smoke out the bad guys, providing us with exactly that evidence we need."

"I hope it works, but it would be a lot more fun if Doug were here," she plunked her glass down irritably. "Maggie, how can you drink this stuff? Somebody get me a margarita!" The entire room turned to stare.

I tried to contain my rising irritation—with Liz, with Doug, with the whole mess. Antitrust lawyers seldom have to deal with overwrought and devious wives. I took a deep breath.

"Look, Liz, if Doug were here, everything would be different. But he's not here, and I can't change that fact. Right now I have no idea when or if any of us will see him again. I'm sorry to be so blunt, but the fact is that we, and that means you, have got to move forward with that realization."

Now she had tears in her eyes. I felt like a lousy bastard, but kept going.

"I'm sure Dub and Bullock have taken the position that Doug's patent applications are part of the property to be auctioned. If someone can obtain his patents legally, he'll never be able to open source his research—even when he does get out of prison. And they intend for him to be there a very long time."

"Bastards," Liz murmured into her drink.

"Liz, wake up, it's time to get serious. I want you to come to Little Rock on Tuesday afternoon. You can stay with us at Micki's ranch. I'll feel better when we're all together."

"I am quite awake and quite serious. I get the picture. You don't need to shove it down my throat." She took a healthy swallow of the margarita that had quickly arrived, chasing it with a deep sigh.

"Okay, Liz. Are you ready to hear the plan? In a way it's a crapshoot, but I want you to know everything."

"No! I don't want to know a thing!"

Maggie was incredulous. "Why on earth not?"

"Because I can honestly say I don't know—that it's all in your hands.

It's safer that way. If the bastards think I know your plans, they could go after my father. People have been coming out of the woodwork to see Dad and renew my acquaintance. I can't tell you how many old boyfriends have shown up in the last week. It was flattering at first, but I figured out pretty quickly that most of them were trying to pump me for information. You should see their faces when I say in my best Scarlett O'Hara, 'I don't know a thing. Doug's lawyers are keeping me completely in the dark.'

"I want to see it unfold on Wednesday; knowing the plan in advance would be a mistake. Doug and I trust you. You say it's a crapshoot—well, so did Doug when he decided to take this course a long time ago. Everybody says they want a cure for cancer, but they want it on their terms. Jack, do your best, be safe, and I don't give a shit if we lose everything. Just get Doug back."

Liz dressed like a floozy, acted and talked like she didn't have a clue, and was completely irritating most of the time. Whenever I was ready to wash my hands of her for good, out came the real Liz.

We were ready to leave, but Liz said she wanted to stay for a while and watch the famous ducks. Why people get such a kick out of watching trained waterfowl march in and out of a pond is beyond me. Clovis grumbled. Without missing a beat, she morphed back into the old Liz.

"Clovis, you sure you don't want to stay in Memphis for a couple of days?"

Clovis rushed through the revolving doors, ignoring Liz completely. She was still laughing when Maggie and I left.

As we drove to the airport, Maggie mused. "Liz baffles me, and she certainly has Clovis's number. One minute she's a total tramp and the next minute, she's a lovely, loyal woman. I wonder what makes her tick."

"You know, I'm pretty sure it's Doug. The rest is for show and to shock, a form of self-protection, I think. Her love for him is the constant. He's a lucky man. But if I ever do get to speak with him again, I'd like to know why he puts up with her shenanigans."

Clovis gave himself a little shake. "Just keep her away from me."

I tried to keep a straight face.

50

I USED THE short flight to Little Rock to go over the notes I'd made earlier. After an uneventful and smooth landing, we drove directly to Micki's ranch. Nestled on more than two hundred acres of pasture bisected by a slow, lazy creek, it's hard to believe her home is only fifteen minutes outside of Little Rock proper. It had been extensively remodeled by the previous owner, and now the 70's style ranch consisted of open spaces, a big stone fireplace, and a large country kitchen, surrounded by enough bedrooms for all of us. Micki had just bought it when we were here last year. Now she'd given it her own character, using pottery and art by local artists to enhance her casual, comfortable furniture. Debbie, Paul, and Micki were there to greet us.

I kissed Micki gently on the cheek.

She whispered, "I've been waiting for you." My jaw dropped and she laughed. "Just kidding, Eric will be here tonight. He insists. I can't imagine why."

She was clearly on the road to recovery.

After we unloaded the car and settled our luggage, we gathered in her welcoming living room. She was curled up in an oversized chair, wrapped in an enormous quilt, looking uncomfortable. I said exactly the wrong thing.

"Micki, maybe you should get some rest. Let Debbie help you to your room."

The words were barely spoken before Maggie spoke sharply, "Be quiet, Jack. Micki is an adult who can take care of herself. Remember, she's lead counsel. So treat her as such."

I didn't pretend to be bothered by Maggie's scolding.

"I'm sorry, Micki. But if you get tired, let somebody know."

She didn't give an inch. "You do the same. If you need to go to bed, you know where it is."

Touché.

Debbie looked confused. She hadn't seen us banter like this before.

"Does anybody need coffee, tea, or something stronger? I made blueberry muffins," she chirped, trying to find the right note. The mood lightened, and Maggie went with her to the kitchen to brew a pot of tea.

"I'm sorry. You know it's in my nature to protect." I gave Micki a rueful smile.

"Yes, I've heard you say that before. Don't worry—I know my limits. While they're in the kitchen, tell me about your meeting with Novak. Clovis called to let me know you all were safe, but that's all I know."

I gave her a quick rundown including my impression of Novak. Maggie and Debbie returned as she gave a low laugh and said, "Dub's dirty? I'd love to believe that, but it seems pretty far-fetched."

Debbie handed Micki a glass of ice water.

"By the way, Debbie, were you spotted at Dub's press conferences?" I asked, accepting a cup of tea from Maggie.

"The first time we sat in the second row. Dub clearly recognized me because afterwards, a deputy asked me why I was there. I grinned and said 'I'm a huge fan of Mr. Blanchard.' I saw Dub watching me, but when I caught his eye he rushed out the door."

I laughed, relishing Dub's reaction.

"He's held two other press conferences this week. You should've seen his face when he recognized me the next time: he actually stopped in mid-sentence and had a hard time finding his place. Today, Paul thought he might try to keep me out. So while we were waiting to go in, I flirted with the *Democrat's* reporter, and when the doors opened we slipped past the deputy at the door. The look on Dub's face was pretty funny—he knew if he made a stink, the reporter would wonder why. I sat right in the front row with my *Democrat* friend. Dub was all nervous and sweaty. He ended up reading the press release the press already had and wouldn't take any questions. The deputy cornered Paul and me on our way out and asked for my press credentials. I told him I didn't have any, but I was a big fan of Mr. Blanchard. He told me not to come back."

I laughed. "Micki, do you have a friend who can get Debbie some press credentials?"

Debbie piped up eagerly. "My new reporter friend already gave me two and promised to save me a seat. He's hot."

"Be careful," I reminded her.

She pouted a bit. "Paul won't let me out of his sight."

"Good," I emphasized. "This isn't a game."

She rounded up empty glasses and returned to the kitchen. We turned our attention to the to-do list I had given everyone.

I remained silent, waiting for direction from Micki.

"Why don't you let me call Bill Maroney and work on the auction's logistics and details? Dub's people will think it's beneath them to actually handle the logistics. They may let Bill's people handle all the administrative arrangements and details."

"I'll leave it in your hands, but make sure we know if the letter of credit has to be posted before we bid, or if we just need to have it on hand in case someone questions our financial responsibility. And let me know whether it's public information," I responded.

"We'll know all that in plenty of time."

"Try to make sure they auction the Healy before the research," I added.

"What does it matter?" Maggie asked.

"I've made a big deal about the Healy with Dub and Bullock. I want to ride that pony as far as I can."

"When will you meet with Sam?" Maggie asked.

"That's a tough call. I want to give him plenty of time to get on board. At the same time I want to have as much evidence as I can. He wasn't buying the first time I pitched."

"Do you want me to call him, suggest he come out for a social visit?" Micki asked.

"No, besides, you and I have a tougher call to make."

"We do?"

"You told me last year that Rodney Fitzhugh's as honest as the day is long."

"Absolutely."

"Well, I need somebody from Justice, and Peggy Fortson told me to back off in no uncertain terms. I'm not sure how receptive she'd be to my call."

"That depends on why you're calling her," Maggie put in archly.

Micki raised an eyebrow. "I'd trust Rodney with my life, but let's wait. He'll be there if I ask. No sense getting him curious and asking questions before we are ready."

Maggie asked, "Aren't you getting ahead of yourself? We have a lot of work to do before you start calling Sam or Peggy."

"You're right. What do you think, Jack?" Micki asked.

"I think you're both right. You should work on the logistical details of the auction. Maggie will make sure we have all our ducks in a row financially. Me, I'd like to meet with your computer whiz. It would help if she could tell us who's been hacking our computers."

"Stella's really good," Clovis said, walking in on our conversation. "I'll ask her to come out tomorrow morning. Debbie and I are headed to the grocery store. Anybody need anything? I suggest the three of you give it a rest and relax for a while."

Debbie emerged from the kitchen with warm cheese puffs and a chilled bottle of wine. The cheese puffs were just that, golden puffs of cheese and pastry. Micki had gotten the recipe from her friend Marty, but cooking wasn't one of Micki's talents. We had many reasons to be thankful for Debbie.

"I'm cooking tonight, but these ought to tide you over until we get back."

I saw her glance at Micki and then back to me. "Jack, can you help me reach something in the kitchen?"

"Sure thing," I said, following her. We were alone, but she still spoke quietly.

"Jack, Novak called a few minutes ago. He wants you to call him as soon as possible."

Her reticence in front of Micki was understandable. "Use my phone. He'll answer. Just punch 'call.'"

I punched, put the phone to my ear, and heard a heavy accent.

"Novak here."

"Jack Patterson."

"Jack, you're a very sneaky man. Remember your promise to protect Debbie? I'm holding you to it. Let me tell you what happened."

I listened for the next ten minutes, never said a word. Debbie waited anxiously for my reaction, practically hopping from one foot to the other. I tried not to give her one, returning her phone with a mere "thank you."

51

ALMOST IN TEARS, Debbie blurted out, "Please don't tell Micki!"

"All right, Debbie, all right, but just this one time. It's time for you to trust Micki and explain your relationship with Novak. We are dealing with complicated issues here, and I need Micki's help. That means no secrets. But I owe you and Novak a lot, so I'm going to let you tell her in your own way. But be quick about it. Remember, everyone still believes it was Novak behind her kidnapping. We have no real proof to the contrary."

"I promise," she said.

"By the way, I know I told Novak I wouldn't tell a soul about my source, but Micki has to know."

"Oh, he knew you'd tell Micki, Maggie, and Clovis. Besides, I'm the one who told you most of the story. He just doesn't want any of his customers to think he might rat them out. Bad for business."

Eric came straight from the hospital. He clearly wasn't too keen about my staying at the ranch, but Micki had set him straight. I'd overheard her on the phone earlier. "Eric, Jack and I are law partners. You won't let me go to the office, so he's come to me. It's ridiculous for Maggie and Jack to drive back to the Armitage when I have plenty of room. So get over it."

He pouted for a while, but Debbie's stroganoff soon revived his good humor. Tomorrow we'd hit the ground running, but tonight we relaxed around the fire and told stories. Eric was soon bored and insisted that Micki needed her rest. Debbie excused herself as well, and Clovis and Paul left to make a tour of the grounds. Maggie and

I lingered by the fire to enjoy a glass of wine and reminisce about Angie.

It sounds corny, but I fell in love with Angie the moment I saw her after a class at Stafford State. She graduated at the top of her Georgetown Medical class, but immediately gravitated toward research. Medicine wasn't about money for her, and her passion for cancer research found a home at NIH. She used to come home exhausted from a long week of work, collapse, and say, "I know it's there, it's right in front of our faces. And when we discover it we're going to say, 'How could we have missed it all this time?'"

We both worked hard and preferred to spend our free time with each other. We enjoyed the company of close friends, but avoided the DC social circuit like the plague. She loved the real DC, the city itself: the pollution, traffic, even the sultry weather were only minor irritations for her. She scoured *The Post* for new ethnic restaurants, openings at the Smithsonian, or a reading at the Folger. Redskin games were a concession to me, although we could rarely get tickets. After Beth was born, a weekend trip with friends to the Virginia countryside or a week on one of the Carolina beaches was our favorite retreat.

When I couldn't join her, she turned to Maggie, dragging Beth with them until she was old enough to protest. Over the years she and Maggie became the best of friends, so much so that Maggie knew about Beth's diagnosis before I did. Her death hit us all hard. To this day she is the only one I can really talk to about Angie.

I said, "Can you imagine how excited she'd be if Doug really has made a breakthrough?"

"Oh, Jack, she would be bloody thrilled. Do you think it's possible?" she asked.

"Well, if it were anyone other than Doug, I'd think it was a ploy to disguise the sale and use of marijuana. But the Doug Angie talked about isn't some nutty professor type who's invented Flubber. Neither is the one Liz is in love with. Marijuana isn't opium or cocaine, despite what the government says. In fact, it's less destructive than tobacco or alcohol. And more to the point, for the last ten or so years its medicinal qualities have been pretty well-documented, despite the government's attempts to eliminate its production and use. Grass has certainly done a lot more good than harm. The government's only real argument against legalization is that it's a 'gateway drug,' but that's a lot of hooey. It doesn't rise to the level of alcohol as a 'gateway drug,' and it brings on passive, not violent behavior. If it has medicinal qualities when you smoke it, there's no telling what a chemist like Doug could do with the whole plant. Sorry—I didn't mean to make a lecture of it."

Maggie smiled. I knew enough about my right arm to know she had probably experimented in her younger days, just like most every other British kid. I was one of the few in my group who hadn't. My stepfather was a heavy smoker, and I didn't want to be part of anything he enjoyed, including smoking. I missed out on a teenage rite of passage but, on the other hand, I never smoked a legal cigarette either. Good thing I didn't know anyone in college who made special cookies, like Liz—I'd probably still be enjoying them today.

"Apology accepted. You know, I can just about believe in your premise," Maggie said as she poured herself a little more wine.

"Maggie, I feel it in my bones. Who has the money and power to initiate and then co-opt a Federal investigation, one that's top secret, to boot? We know it's there, we just don't know who, and I'll admit the 'why' is a little iffy as well." I topped off my wine. "I need a break."

"What exactly do we have?" Maggie asked.

"Surprise, I hope, and what should be more important—the truth." I raised my glass. "Oh, and the best team in the business."

"Thank you, but that usually doesn't win out against money, power, and time."

"Okay, maybe not, but it's worth the effort. Lost causes are still worth fighting for, and sometimes the good guys still win."

"Even if you get yourself killed?" She didn't smile this time. Maggie had every right to be concerned.

"Even if I get myself killed. For a while it was just fun being in the game again. Doug wasn't our usual client, but he was a client, just like at Banks & Tuohey. Now it's different."

Maggie came back. "Except you never lost at B&T, and no one tried to kill you."

"I never lost because I always settled the cases I couldn't win. But you're right: I never experienced an element of personal danger. At some point this past week I came to two conclusions. First, Doug Stewart may have actually made a breakthrough in the treatment of cancer. Second, someone, or maybe it's a 'they,' wants to make absolutely sure Doug's research never reaches the light of day until they're in a position to control production, access, and profits. They're ready to throw both Doug and Liz to the wolves. The rest of us are just collateral damage. Stopping that kind of conduct is worth a little risk, don't you think?"

"How could anyone be so cold-hearted? So selfish?" Maggie asked.

"For money, and by employing a million rationalizations: the research is illegal, any product that's untested could have terrible side effects, it needs to be controlled and regulated, its premature release could have a disastrous effect on our economy—the list goes on and on. Why try to think logically and unselfishly when you've got a perfectly good rationalization? Few people can go a day without at least two or three juicy rationalizations." I smiled, remembering my favorite line from *The Big Chill*. "Plus, Doug made it easy. He meant well, but his letter transformed his research into low-hanging fruit."

"So what's next?" Maggie asked.

"We get a good night's sleep and wake up ready to put our plan into action. The letter is evidence that the government has known about Doug's research for at least three years and has always been ready to shut it down before he made it public. What we don't know is the extent of the government's involvement or who else is involved. We need to gather hard evidence to supplement what we've found, and if that falls through, pray for a break or two, and roll the dice."

SATURDAY MORNING

May 3, 2014

52

WHEN I CAME down the next morning, I found Debbie in the kitchen making cranberry-oatmeal muffins. Clovis had already gone to pick up Micki's computer guru, and Eric had left for morning rounds. Micki had poured herself a cup of coffee and sat at the kitchen table in old sweats, wet hair wrapped in a towel. She looked great.

I took my coffee and muffin out onto the sunny patio and watched the Tahoe round the curve into the driveway. Clovis stepped out and opened the door for his passenger, Stella Rice. Micki had told me they'd met at a triathlon. She was a friend of Mongo's, and a computer whiz. I didn't have any preconceived notions, but I expected a more or less nerdy woman who spent her days and night in front of a computer screen. Boy, was I surprised.

In boots with four-inch heels she stood as tall as Clovis. She wore skin-tight jeans and a tank top that showed off her muscular arms, one of which was covered with a rose vine tattoo. She had twisted her heavy, dark blond hair up with some kind of comb. Bright purple nails and lipstick completed the picture. Debbie told me later that she owned a gym downtown and spent most of her time either in it or running with her constant companion, Blakely, a solid black retriever mix. Now the dog sprang out of Clovis's Tahoe, wagging and wiggling. He must've thought he'd died and gone to heaven when he saw the huge pasture.

Over her shoulder, Stella carried an obviously heavy bag filled with electronic gear.

"Hope you don't mind. I brought my office with me." She patted her bag with her off hand, as I shook hands with the other.

She greeted Micki and Debbie like long-lost friends, politely shook hands with Maggie, and began to set up her equipment on the dining room table.

Maggie stood staring until I pulled her into the kitchen to help me make a fresh pot of coffee. She gave me an appraising look and whispered, "Don't you get any ideas, Jack Patterson."

Debbie said, "See, Jack, I knew you'd like her. She's much more your type." I hadn't realized she had joined us in the kitchen.

My type? I had no idea what to think of this muscle-bound package who made Clovis look flabby.

We brought coffee into the dining area while Stella swept the house once again for newly planted bugs. It seemed to take quite a while; I was long through with the flimsy local paper before she returned.

"Sorry, but we can't be too safe," she said after she finished and gave us an all-clear.

For the next hour she told us what she'd discovered: in a nutshell, multiple attempts to hack both our office and personal computers by more than one source. She'd left the "hacking that succeeded" in place in case we wanted to send out false information, but had created a new firewall between the intruder and our reality. She asked us to reserve time for individual training after lunch.

I asked her about Liz's computers and phones.

"Liz was easy. She only uses an iPad to send e-mail and check Facebook. I told her to assume anything she did or said was being monitored. She laughed and said she'd be sure to be especially offensive from now on. Sounds like my kind of woman!" *Oh, great.* I tried not to think about what that meant.

Liz had called Maggie earlier to say she couldn't see us until Wednesday morning before the auction, something about an appointment with her hairdresser. *Her hairdresser?* I was irritated, but also relieved. Liz required a lot of energy.

Muttering something about what was really important, Clovis had slipped away when Stella began the debugging process. Now he returned with barbecue from Ben's— I couldn't believe it was already lunchtime. I had devoured my sandwich, and was eyeing a second, when Maggie asked the obvious question.

"How did you get so proficient with computers? The image of a tri-athlete doesn't exactly square with that of a computer nerd."

"I was good at math, one of the few girls who went to engineering school at Arkansas. I got hooked early on computer technology and worked for IBM fresh out of school. Then, on a bet, I entered a half marathon. I didn't make three miles. It pissed me off, and I started training for real. I found a new love and got into serious cross training. As you might have noticed, I gravitated away from IBM's dress-for-success look and mentality. I like glossy lipstick and turning heads. So I left IBM, bought a gym, and do computer consulting when I'm not doing personal training. I'm my own boss. If I want to take off to hike Mt. Magazine or bike in the Delta, I can."

"Have you ever married?" I was surprised by Maggie's probing.

"Never found a man who could keep up with me." She answered curtly, taking another sandwich and returning to her computers.

"I assume you've checked her out?" I asked Clovis, who was lin-gering out of her earshot.

"After Moira? What do you think? She's exactly what you see—former IBM, health nut, an independent woman with an attitude. An odd sense of style, but as smart as they come. You interested?"

"Not in that way. I'm not so much into muscles, besides Maggie would tan my hide. But she does seem to know computers."

"You should have seen Walter's IT guys. They were all giggly and snooty at first, but within thirty minutes, they were ready to hire her. She blew them off, but you watch, they'll make another run at her."

"I can't figure out how she stands up in those boots."

Clovis laughed. "I asked her the same thing this morning."

"And . . . ?"

"She said, 'Men admire my ass a lot more when I wear these. They hurt like hell, but I bet I can outrun you in them."

"Well, let's see how good she really is before we give her a gold star. I need a break. Maybe she can provide it." We wandered back into the dining room.

She and Maggie were huddled over Maggie's laptop.

I was blunt. "So, Stella, can you tell me who's been hacking our computers?"

"The short answer is 'maybe.' The problem is that more than one person is trying to get in there. She gestured toward Maggie's laptop. "The multiple hacking attempts make identification more difficult, but not impossible."

"Next question: if you figure out who it is, can you explain it to a judge?"

She didn't hesitate. "If I can discover who it is, I can make it so easy to understand, even you'll get it."

"I take it Maggie told you about my computer skills," I replied, not quite ready to be convinced.

"Micki and Maggie told me you have many talents, but computer proficiency is not one."

"Can you do it by Wednesday morning? We don't have much time." I caved.

"Well, again, maybe. No guarantees, but I'm willing to try, if you're willing to pay."

Micki interrupted. "What do you need? Money is not the issue."

"It would help if I could work from here. I'm likely to have lots of questions about who I'm looking for. I've got some idea what this case is about, but the more you can tell me, the better chance I have to discover the source. I'll need to run programs at night. Maybe I could crash on the couch and wake one of you on occasion?"

Micki answered before I could. "We've got plenty of room. We'll send someone to your place for clothes. You can start right now. If you have any questions in the middle of the night, you should ask Jack. He won't mind." She didn't give me a glance, didn't need to.

Paul beckoned me from the front door to let me know he and Debbie were leaving for Dub's next press conference. Holding a press conference on a Saturday afternoon . . . he was either clueless or desperate. I gave Debbie a little hug, followed by a stern warning.

"Be really careful, Debbie. Dub is a dangerous man. We want his mind focused on why you are there, but I don't want you to be in any danger. Okay?"

Debbie had chosen a very stylish dress by French Laundry. I recognized the brand from Beth's clothes. Her lips were bright pink, and she wore flashy crystal drop earrings. "Don't worry. He'll notice me, but we won't stay. I want him to wonder where I've gone."

I looked at Paul.

"Don't worry—I'll take care of her. I've got back up, just in case. It's the reporters I have to worry about," Paul said with a smile.

I wanted Dub to sweat, but I knew each time he saw Debbie the risk grew greater. She could be Moira's next target if we weren't careful. I was toying with Dub at Debbie's expense, and it scared me more than a little. Never mind my promise to Novak—Debbie was a keeper.

I returned to the dining room to find that Maggie and Stella had finished putting traps in place to catch the snoopers and were about to change into walking clothes. Micki came in from the kitchen and we walked out onto her patio. Winding wisteria covered the pergola, and the late afternoon sun crept in and seemed to embrace us with its warmth, allowing my brain to relax, to wander from the business at hand. After a few minutes of reverie, my thoughts turned to words.

"Ah, Micki, this moment feels so good—I don't want to force my mind to connect with reality. Sitting on your porch, watching the sunset, sipping on a glass of good wine . . . it all feels so natural. Maggie, Stella, and Blakely are tromping through your property; they look like they don't have a care in the world. It's nice to forget all this chaos and just enjoy the peace—and being with friends."

"You know you're welcome any time," Micki responded quietly.

"I'm glad you're feeling better." I reached across to take her hand.

She left it in mine. "I'm glad to have some company. Eric means well, but he's such a wet blanket. I wish he'd give it a rest."

"If you were my girl, you can bet I'd be protective, too."

"You had your chance," she snickered. "But I'm serious, Jack. It's nice to have you all out here. Having Stella here is a special treat—she's such a kick."

"I'm not interested," I said, surprising myself with my automatic response.

"Really. Could have fooled me," Micki retorted.

"Listen, Maggie reminds me constantly that women here can literally be the kiss of death." I paused.

"There isn't much that gets past Maggie."

AT THAT VERY moment, Eric walked onto the patio, still in his morning scrubs and obviously tired.

"What are you two up to?" he asked as he bent down to kiss Micki.

MONDAY

May 5, 2014

53

MR. KIM, HEAD of the organization's North American operation, had called Mr. Smith to DC for a meeting with the client. He gave them both a full report on the activities of Patterson and his team. The ensuing discussion affirmed his presumption that their success depended on the upcoming auction. Mr. Kim recommended eliminating Patterson before the auction, but the client was concerned that his death would result in further unwelcome publicity, again delaying the long anticipated return on their investment. Mr. Kim agreed that loose ends could wait until after the auction. Smith's assignment was crystal clear.

AS EXPECTED, DUB had finagled his way onto the rounds of Sunday talk shows and public appearances. Debbie and Paul managed to be part the gallery, usually right up front, at each event. Debbie wore increasingly provocative attire, and Dub became increasingly uncomfortable with her presence. It was time to throw him another curve.

"Your gig is up. No more press events for you." I had said to Debbie Sunday afternoon.

She was clearly disappointed. "Why? I enjoy messing with his mind."

"I want him to loosen his guard, feel safe again."

"No more waving and watching him sweat?"

"I didn't say that. You'll be front and center Wednesday in court and, if Cheryl lures him onto her show, you'll be in the front row."

"You mean I could be on TV?" Debbie squealed like a child.

"Well, I hope so, but for now, let's make Dub wonder where you are."

Cheryl had booked a room at the Armitage and was enjoying her celebrity status to the hilt. The local TV stations had interviewed her and would broadcast her show all week from the auditorium at the UALR. Her theme was a return to Little Rock, one year after the murder of Senator Russell Robinson. She'd asked Dub to appear on Tuesday night, but he demurred. Ever persistent, Cheryl had convinced him to meet her for drinks after tonight's taping. I wasn't worried—Cheryl would wrangle the interview.

At Micki's urging, Marshal Maroney had agreed to personally supervise the auction. She managed to finesse the arrangements so the cars were available for inspection at a marshal's lot. Doug's files, computers, and lab equipment could be seen, if not actually examined, in a spare room at the courthouse. Dub's office insisted that Maroney keep a list of exactly who requested access to either. Several car dealers had inspected the cars, but so far no one had asked to see the items in the locked room.

I decided against asking Stella to inspect Doug's computer—too much of a heads up. Clovis drove me out to look over the cars. It gave us an excuse to go to Ben's for lunch. The Austin Healy 3000 was in mint condition. I was dying to drive it, but was told it couldn't leave the lot. Bad luck. It was a beautiful car.

Maroney told Micki that as soon as Dub's staff heard I'd been out to inspect the Healy, two of his marshals showed up with a mechanic who went over the car from stem to stern.

Part of Maroney's responsibility was to insure the financial integrity of the auction. I spent some time becoming familiar with the rules. As evidence of ability to pay, he had decided to require cash, a certified check, or a letter of credit worth ten percent of the winning bid. Maroney was to be the final arbiter of financial ability. Of course, there were many more rules, but that was the one that mattered most to me.

All of Doug's research files, his lab, equipment, the patent applications, etc, everything except the cars, would be sold in one lot. That too worked in our favor. Liz had asked her bank in Memphis for a separate letter of credit to bid on the truck and the Healy. In response to my skepticism, she'd said, "A pick-up's a handy thing to have around. Besides, men love a girl with a pick-up."

I spent a good deal of time shooting baskets in Micki's driveway. We were all a little antsy, nervous about the auction, unsure what would happen next. Sam called two or three times—he was nervous, too. Moira had been spotted in Brazil, confirming Novak's intelligence. Her assistant, Roger, had turned up in New Jersey—unfortunately for him, face down in the Passaic River. As yet, New Jersey authorities had no idea what had happened.

I debated whether to invite Peggy Fortson to attend the auction. I don't know why I dithered—I'd known her my whole working life. If I couldn't trust Peggy, who could I trust? But she'd been so negative. An innocent slip on her part might give away our strategy. I finally decided against it, afraid her appearance might spook Dub.

Maggie and Stella were hard at work trying to discover the identity of the computer prowler. Maggie had come full circle with Stella. When Stella was unsure who or what was important, either Maggie or Micki could walk her through it without consulting me.

The three women worked well together. I put Debbie in another category, not that she wasn't constantly busy. She enjoyed cooking for us, was happy to do almost anything we asked, and kept us all in stitches, her bubbly personality infectious.

"Do you think Debbie and Paul are enjoying each other's company?" I asked Clovis as we watched them saddling horses for a ride.

"Can't blame him, can you?" he said with a grin.

"No. Can't say that I do."

Once again, my defense team had become quite the family. We all felt the tension, the awareness of danger, but, well, I guess we just shoved it away somewhere. Micki enjoyed walking the grounds with Stella and Maggie. She was becoming visibly stronger and feistier, enjoying her independence from Eric.

I felt a twinge of regret when I heard her comment, "Eric feels better about going to the hospital with us all here together. We were getting on each other's nerves—now things are smoothing out."

I tried to keep my mind on the task at hand, but I freely admit that I enjoyed watching Stella's workouts. I sure wouldn't want to arm-wrestle her. Imagine watching a woman almost my age lifting heavy weights, and then running at top speed around a two hundred acre pasture. After a cool down, she was back at work at her computer in boots and tight jeans, laughing with Maggie over some private joke.

When Debbie finally got up the courage to speak to Micki about Novak, she got a surprise. Micki had realized long ago there had to be more to their relationship than drugs. I think it helped that Debbie's continuing contact with Novak had saved both our lives. Micki heard her out, but gave her a clear warning: not only was Novak still the prime suspect in our kidnappings, he was also the source of the brand on Debbie's neck. Even if he were completely exonerated, they would need to establish boundaries. Novak was still scum in Micki's eyes. I knew that victims of abuse sometimes become unnaturally dependent on their abusers, but neither Micki nor I could quite figure out the seductive pull Novak maintained over Debbie.

I had time on my hands while my team worked, but they cut me some slack—they all knew my part in this drama would become center stage soon enough.

I decided to pay a visit to Woody's mother, Helen. She plied me with gossip, cookies, and questions and, as always, understood when I couldn't answer. It felt like coming home again.

Clovis had remained in the Tahoe, and as we drove away he said, "We've got company."

I turned and saw a black Lexus sedan a few cars back. *What had my life become that I could spot a tail so easily?*

"Should I be worried?"

"No, they're keeping their distance. We think everyone who leaves the compound is followed. I've let Martin know. You'd think they'd be bored by now, but it proves they haven't eased off one bit. Doesn't bode well for us having the element of surprise," he said with a shrug.

I rolled down my window and flipped them the bird. They were too far back to notice, but the car right behind us gave an angry honk.

"Jack . . ." Clovis frowned.

"I know, I'm sorry. That was childish, but someone or some corporation is working with my own government to stop the discovery of a cure to a horrible disease. Think how many people might be alive today, including Angie, if scientists had been able to research the medical benefits of marijuana."

Clovis didn't react at all, just drove.

"My own government—your government—is conspiring to prevent a lone chemist from telling the world what he's discovered. Fuck the guys in the car behind us, and fuck the guys they work for. What are they so afraid of? Maybe they won't make as much money or maybe they won't get re-elected. How can they look their wives and children in the face when they ask, 'How was your day, dear?' And the honest answer is, "Oh, I kept the world from learning about a cure for cancer."

I leaned back, totally spent. "Sorry, Clovis. Guess I needed to vent."

"That's okay. Save some for the judge."

We lost our tail when we pulled through Micki's gate, but I was still apprehensive. Walter was scheduled to arrive with a letter of credit that would enable me to bid on Doug's research. I wondered who knew that, other than Maggie and me.

MR. KIM LEANED back in his office chair, idly drumming its back with a pencil. *Why had Walter Mathews flown to Little Rock? Surely not just to meet his wife.* Their recent attempts to penetrate his company's computer security had been blocked. And he knew that Matthews had recently engaged the services of a well-regarded economist. Mr. Kim placed a single phone call—no sense getting caught off-guard.

WE KNEW THE rules of the auction, but to a certain extent I'd have to fly by the seat of my pants. Stella still hadn't been able to pinpoint the bad guys. She thought she was close, but time was running out. Cheryl hadn't been able to get Dub on her show, much less get her camera in the courtroom, and Sam had cold feet about showing up on Wednesday. I hoped something positive would turn up in the next twenty-four hours, but right now our prospects looked pretty dim.

Clovis pulled to a stop, and I had just reached to open the car door when my cell phone rang. Novak.

I listened for a minute, clicked the phone off and put it back in my pocket.

Clovis looked worried. "What?"

"Moira's back in town—came in through Miami. Apparently she's cut and colored her hair, but was recognized by one of Novak's cohorts. Clovis, will you call Sam's office?"

Clovis nodded silently. There wasn't much he could say.

TUESDAY

May 6, 2014

54

I GAVE UP on sleep around six, showered, and went downstairs to make the coffee. Stella was already well into her run. The morning was chilly, but held the promise of a glorious early May day. I put on a jacket and with coffee in hand walked out to the porch to watch. The horses had gathered at the fence and seemed to be watching, too. She waved, but never broke stride. She finally completed the circuit, wrapped her streaming face in a towel, and gulped thirstily from a large bottle of cool water.

"You make me tired, just watching."

"When you played ball, I bet your workout was similar."

"That was in high school and, you're right: two-a-days in August were pure hell. But we didn't do anything compared to what you just did."

"It's all in your point of view," she shrugged. "Mind if I ask you a personal question?" she asked cautiously.

"No, ask away. But I don't promise an answer." I winked.

"Is this normal for you? I mean all this security, people trying to kill you, high stakes, and big drama. Is this your normal life?'

I choked on my coffee.

"Thankfully, no, it isn't. For twenty-five years I practiced antitrust law, the most boring law you can imagine, except for maybe tax or patent law. IBM is excitement personified, compared to antitrust law. My practice involved poring over thousands of documents and deposing conflicting economists and corporate executives."

"But you seem so . . . well, unfazed by all this, even used to it."

"About a year ago, when one of my best friends shot Senator Russell Robinson, I came home to see how I could help his mother. I learned high drama the hard way. But one case certainly hasn't made me 'used to it.' This mess started the same way. Dr. Stewart was a good friend of my wife. When he was charged with growing and distributing marijuana, I came down to see what I could do to help and landed in the middle of a firestorm."

Her mouth curved up a bit. I waited for her to say something but she didn't.

The silence was just beginning to linger a bit too long, when Debbie called me into the kitchen to take a call from Cheryl. She had finally managed to hook Dub for her show.

"Jack, we met in the bar, and after a few drinks, he'd have agreed to anything. He kept trying to slide his hand up my skirt. Gross. I mean, my producer was sitting right there."

"Cheryl, don't get caught alone with him. Promise me."

"I'll be careful, especially after last night. Now that I have the sleaze ball coming on the air, what do you want me to ask him?"

"I'll email you some questions. Better yet, I'll have them delivered to your hotel. Here's the main thing: try to get invited to tomorrow's auction. I can get you in if he doesn't bite, but it's better if he invites you."

"He already has. He's arranged the whole thing with my producer. I sure hope whatever you've got is worth all this shit."

"I hope so, too, Cheryl, I really do. Listen, you'll see a pretty young woman sitting on the first row tonight. Dub tends to get nervous when he sees her. Don't ask him anything on air, but off the record feel free to ask all you want."

"Is she someone I know?"

"Nope—but Dub does."

"Promise me the story."

"If things go as planned, you'll know everything I know tomorrow."

She agreed to stay in touch, and I repeated my warning. "Cheryl, don't be foolish. I know you. Dub's dangerous. Be careful."

"I'm surprised you care, Jack. Maybe you and I can have drinks tonight after the show."

"I do care, Cheryl, but no drinks tonight. Tomorrow's a big day."

"I'll give you a rain check."

The others were waiting quietly in the living room.

"Debbie, Paul, you're on for Cheryl's tonight. Maggie, please give Debbie some extra pointers on conservative dress—no short skirts or unbuttoned blouses. Tonight, you exude class." Debbie looked irritated.

"I don't think I own anything that boring," she pouted.

Micki smiled easily. "Sure you do. You have a court suit, and I've got some pearls. We'll have fun dressing you."

"Debbie, I need you to be on your best behavior tonight, looking every bit the attractive, well-mannered and self-possessed young lady you can be. People will wonder who you are; I don't want any sneers or snide remarks. You are not to play the hooker. Remember what I've told you." I knew I had overstepped, but I also knew how important this might be.

Rounding her arm around Debbie and shooting me a dirty look, Maggie walked her toward the bedroom saying, "Debbie, Jack is only trying to protect you."

"Paul. Be especially careful tonight. No telling what Dub is apt to do. And we can't forget Moira." Jeez, I wished we could forget Moira!

Paul gave me a thumbs-up. Suddenly it came to me how we might protect Debbie and upset Dub even more in the bargain. I picked up my phone and punched in a familiar number.

"I need a favor."

55

After dinner, we settled in to watch the show, aptly named *Cheryl! Live!* Cheryl had texted Paul that she'd reserved seats for them in the front row. I wondered whether she would use the questions I'd given her. Dub was her last guest, so first we were treated to some "fair and balanced" propaganda from Cheryl's panel of experts on the subject of gun control.

After the commercial, the camera zoomed in on Cheryl and Dub. He licked his lips nervously. She had exposed more cleavage than usual for this episode. They sat side by side on a small couch. God bless her, she had no shame.

"Ladies and Gentlemen, our next guest tonight is United States Attorney Wilbur "Dub" Blanchard. Mr. Blanchard will tell us about his role in the Cole investigation as well as the other important investigations his office is handling. Welcome, Mr. U. S. Attorney—may I call you Dub?"

"Absolutely, all my friends do."

"Well, I'm certainly an admirer." Cheryl reached over and stroked the top of his hand. The poor sod didn't have a chance.

"Tell me, Dub, a lot of people thought the murder of Senator Robinson should have been your case. I understand you did try to intervene. What happened?"

"Well, let me just say it was a travesty of justice. Cole's lawyer was an old friend of the prosecutor. Then there was the judge . . ."

Cheryl interrupted. "Well, maybe we can ask the prosecutor about that? I understand he's in our audience." The camera cut immediately to the audience to focus in on Sam Pagano who happened to be sitting next to Debbie, looking very chic in pearls, hair pulled back demurely at the nape of her neck. The camera lingered on the two briefly before flashing back to Cheryl and Dub. Cheryl was all smiles, but Dub's face portrayed a mixture of anger and panic.

"Wha. . . What are they doing here?" Dub let slip. He pulled out a handkerchief, passing it nervously over his brow.

Cheryl didn't miss a beat. "Prosecutor Pagano is a friend of mine from college. I'd hoped he might join us on air, but he declined, noting that the assassination investigation is still pending. Am I right, Sam?"

Sam nodded, smiling serenely.

"I don't know the young woman sitting next to him. Do you? Should we ask her to come forward?"

Dub almost shouted. "No . . . I mean I have no idea who she is. I'm sorry. I just . . . just wasn't expecting Mr. Pagano to be here. I thought we were going to talk about my ongoing drug investigation."

Cheryl said smoothly. "Of course . . . of course. Tell me about this exciting new case you're working on."

Dub couldn't have been more relieved and swung into his full spiel about how terrible drugs were and how after a long investigation, he'd arrested a major dealer, a college professor. He appeared to get more comfortable as Cheryl continued to play with his hand, occasionally placing her hand on his arm.

"I understand there's a hearing tomorrow."

"Well, not exactly a hearing. Part of our goal in going after these drug terrorists is to take away their financial network, so they can't continue to endanger our children. Tomorrow we intend to auction off everything that was funded by Dr. Stewart's sale of drugs to Little Rock's kids. It's not a real hearing."

"Well, maybe so—but isn't it strange that the same Jack Patterson who represented Woody Cole now represents Dr. Stewart? I hear you forced him to spend a night in jail."

Now Dub was able to smile easily, turning his eyes on the audience. "We don't think in terms of pay-back, but . . ."

"Oh, come on now. It's got to feel good to know you bested Jack Patterson—made him wear prison stripes. I tried to get him to come on tonight's show, but he flat-out refused. I think he's running scared. Tomorrow's gotta be sweet for you. It has to be hard for him to watch all his client's assets auctioned off, knowing there's not a thing he can do." Cheryl had him going.

"Well . . . I admit tomorrow will be the end of a very successful investigation by a lot of hard-working people. It will be a great day for our country. Jack Patterson thought he'd come back to Little Rock and pull off some home cookin'. Turned out, we're about to eat him and his client for lunch." Clovis gave a big whoop at that one.

Cheryl took his hand in hers. "I'd love to be there—live, with cameras."

Dub seemed more focused on where his hand was. "I don't see why not. Like i said, it's not a hearing. In fact, I've already cleared it with the marshal."

Cheryl dropped his hand abruptly and turned to face the camera. "Ladies and Gentlemen, tune in tomorrow for a Fox News exclusive: the dramatic end to a major drug bust as U.S. Attorney Dub Blanchard reaps his revenge on Jack Patterson. We'll be with you live inside the courthouse at ten. You won't want to miss the climax of this investigation."

The cameras cut away for a commercial. I later watched the video Paul obtained of what had happened next. Cheryl had leaned over and whispered to Dub. "Are you sure you don't know the woman who's sitting next to Sam? She sure seems to know you."

Dub went from glowing to glowering. "Sorry, I don't. I'll see you tomorrow. Uh, thanks for having me on your show." He stomped off the stage to berate his deputies, slamming a stage door when he finally noticed the cameras following his every move.

Sam called almost immediately, said he'd be more than happy to escort Debbie to the auction.

"Throw me in that briar patch any time. I'll be there tomorrow. Don't *you* disappoint." He was laughing as he hung up.

Cheryl was holding on the other line.

"You better have the goods, Jack. Your U.S. attorney actually tried to get me alone in the coat room!" She was not amused.

"He's not my U.S. attorney, and I'm sure you know exactly how to handle him. He's in for a few surprises tomorrow and, if I'm right, you'll have a huge story either way."

"Dub's pretty confident, Jack. Are you sure? And when are you going to tell me about the girl sitting next to Sam? Dub about shit a brick when he saw her. She's way too classy for Dub."

"I'll pass on the compliment. You'll meet her tomorrow. Let me keep a few surprises in my bag of tricks."

Paul and Debbie came into the house on a high.

"Dub blew a gasket when he saw me. What a jerk! But let Paul tell you about it. I've got to get out of this outfit."

"Cheryl Cole said you were classy. I want you dressed the same way tomorrow. Cheryl may want to interview you."

"Classy? Me? No way!" She flounced out without another word. I wondered what she had against "classy."

Paul was full of himself. "Jack, it was great. We made an entrance at the last minute. Two of Dub's deputies showed up and asked us to leave, for 'security reasons.' Sam walked in at almost exactly the same time. He kissed Debbie on the cheek and said, 'Thanks for saving my seat, Paul. Gentlemen, these seats have been reserved, and this lady is with me. Is there a problem?' Sam loved every second of it, and the deputies backed down pretty quick. You should have seen Dub chewing out those guys. He was hopping mad. After the show the deputies tried to detain Debbie for 'questioning.' But once again Sam intervened, accompanied by two deputies of his own. This time the gloves were off. 'This lady is a witness in an ongoing investigation. If you wish to interview her, have one of your superiors call me.' He walked her out to my car and said, 'I'd be honored to be your escort any time. Tell Jack I'll see him in the courtroom tomorrow.' He even kissed her hand.

"Debbie was speechless, glowed the whole ride home. I hope we didn't telegraph too much." Paul wasn't speechless, but he was out of breath.

"You and Debbie did just fine; you got exactly the desired effect. Make sure you stay close to her in the courtroom. Dub is going to be livid when he sees her." Paul nodded happily. Debbie emerged in comfortable sweats and big bunny slippers, plopping down on the rug near Micki.

"Jack, everyone's here—hadn't you better tell us what to expect?" Maggie suggested.

"I'm not sure I can. If the auction is cancelled, we'll know they've figured out what we're up to. We'll be back to square one. I don't think that will happen, but they always seem to be one step in front of me. What's more, we may win the battle, but lose the war."

Stella asked, "What does that mean?"

"We're going to have a half-million dollar letter of credit, meaning I can bid up to five million. If someone bids more than that, we may know who the culprit is, but they'll still have Doug's research."

BACK IN DC, Mr. Kim was shouting into the phone, "Tell that stupid fool to keep the hell off TV and do his job. We have too much riding on this!" He threw the phone across the room blindly, managing to hit the cat, who flew from the room with a yowl. Feeling a little better, he wondered if perhaps Dub Blanchard had outlived his usefulness.

WEDNESDAY

May 7, 2014

56

I WANDERED INTO the kitchen around six the next morning, roused by the smell of fresh coffee. I could see Stella outside flipping some tractor tires she had found in Micki's barn. Flipping tires, big tires—my eyes were ready to believe, but it took my mind a little longer. Clovis joined me on the porch, and soon we heard the clatter of Debbie's skillets in the kitchen. Either the prospect of court or Moira had given everyone insomnia.

"Any Moira sightings?" I asked.

"Nope, not even a possible. We're all on alert. You nervous?" he asked.

"Not nervous exactly, but definitely on edge. It's like pitching a ball game. You start to warm up not knowing which pitch will work and which won't. It can be the fastball, curve, or slider, but until you get a feel for the game, you just have to throw and adjust on the fly. This morning I know I've got the pitches, but which one will work, I won't know 'til we begin."

We sat in silence watching Stella, admiring her energy, strength, and physique. She caught us looking and came onto the porch.

"Don't you two throw tires every morning?"

"Well, actually, no." I laughed. "You ready to make our case?" Late yesterday afternoon Stella finally discovered who had hacked into our computers.

"Ready as I'll ever be. Think I'll get the chance?"

"Honestly, I don't know. All I can tell you is to be ready. At least it's not a trial where potential witnesses have to sit outside the courtroom unable to hear anything else. You'll have a front row seat."

"Do I have to dress conservatively, like Debbie?"

"Wear whatever makes you comfortable, but don't turn off a conservative judge," I answered.

Just then a car pulled up into the parking area. Clovis went out to meet it and came back with a package. I opened it and smiled. It was a digital recorder.

"Stella, after you shower and clean up, I want you and Clovis to go over the contents of this package and give me a summary. If it's what I think it is, I'll figure out the best way to present it. You have less than an hour."

Micki emerged from the kitchen with a steaming cup of coffee, finally looking healthy and very stylish in a red suit I'd seen before. I gave her a slight bow.

"Once again, Ms. Lawrence, I'm just proud to be part of your fan club."

"You are so full of shit." She laughed.

"I can't tell you how happy it makes me to see you strong enough to join us. I've been worried."

"I know you have, and you've been doing all the heavy lifting. Any chance you can pull this off?"

"You mean success? Or just making a fool of myself?" I quipped.

"Aren't they the same thing?" The verbal jousting felt good to us both.

Pretty soon we were all ready to meet the day. Clovis gave me the high sign, and Micki and I joined him and Stella in the living room. After Clovis summarized what was on the recorder, Stella turned it on and we listened intently. Micki gave me a wide smile and a thumbs-up. I returned the gesture, knowing I had a long way to go before I could use this gift from such an unlikely source.

I usually preferred to appear in court with only Maggie by my side, encouraging the visual of a lone lawyer with one assistant against a team of antitrust lawyers. This time I had my own team: Maggie, Micki, Walter, Clovis, Debbie, Paul, and Stella. I halfway expected to see Eric—and where was Liz?

We arrived to a packed courtroom. Fortunately, Micki had asked the bailiff to reserve the row right behind the rail for our team. Dub and his entourage hadn't arrived yet, of course. The usual tables had been reserved for attorneys, but the atmosphere was totally different from that of a normal day in court. Along with the usual courthouse junkies and curious on-lookers, I saw a group of silent, impeccably dressed men in custom-tailored suits: the enemy, no doubt. I also caught sight of several less refined gents, probably car dealers, arguing among themselves. Cheryl's camera crews had organized themselves in the back of the courtroom, and Cheryl was barking orders. Marshal Maroney sat at a table in front of the judge's bench along with a court reporter.

Liz sailed in at the last minute, nodded to a couple of people she knew, and sat down next to Maggie. To my relief, she looked every inch the aggrieved party.

Sam had gotten permission to sit in the jury box along with several curious clerks. Sitting next to him were Assistant U.S. Attorney Rodney Fitzhugh and Peggy Fortson. After we'd gotten settled, I walked over, offering my hand to all.

"Peggy, you're a sight for sore eyes, but a complete surprise. To what do I owe this pleasure?"

"When I told the attorney general about our lunch conversation, he asked, 'What are you doing here?' I told him you were dreaming, that there was nothing to your theory. He cocked an eyebrow and said, 'I've agreed not to interfere, but that doesn't mean I'm going to turn a blind eye. If you don't think it's worth the trip, I'll send someone else.' I decided I'd better hightail it down here if I wanted to keep my job. Rodney and Sam have filled me in on what's happened so far. If you're wasting my time, Jack Patterson, you owe me two dinners."

I smiled and left them to confer. Peggy and Sam were still working on the aftermath of the Cole case, so they had plenty to talk about. I hoped I wouldn't need them again.

All smiles, Dub's team strode in and seated themselves at the table next to ours. Dub confidently took the chair closest to mine, pointedly turning his back to me. No handshakes on this day. At the strike of ten, Judge Houston entered the courtroom. It occurred to me that the clock, or to be precise, timing, could be a useful tool in the game of power. The size of the crowd seemed to take the judge aback. He looked a little uncomfortable in street clothes, and it seemed odd not to hear the "all rise." He shuffled some papers on his desk and cleared his throat loudly. The chattering voices ceased expectantly.

"All right. Let me say for the record that this is not an official court proceeding. The U.S. marshal is here to conduct a sale of assets pursuant to federal drug forfeiture laws. I am here at the request of defense counsel. My role is entirely that of an observer." Liz jumped up on cue.

"Actually, Your Honor, it's at my request. Thank you. I feel much better knowing you're here." Liz played her role perfectly. She was well-dressed in a cream Escada suit and Cole Haan heels. Judge Houston looked a bit flustered, but pleased just the same. Dub's crew radiated a collective look of disgust.

The judge continued. "Thank you, Mrs. Stewart, but perhaps you should take your seat. Mr. Blanchard's office has asked me to allow cameras in court for this auction. Against my better judgment, I've granted his request. I take it you have no objection, Mr. Patterson?"

Micki rose. "We have no objection, Your Honor. We don't understand the media's interest, but have no objection."

"Ms. Lawrence. I apologize for not calling on you to begin with. Welcome back. Do I take it you are acting as counsel?" The judge seemed genuinely glad to see Micki.

"Thank you, your Honor. Actually, I'm lead counsel in Dr. Stewart's criminal case, if I can call it that, since he has yet to be formally charged with anything. Since my co-counsel, Mr. Patterson, made the agreement with the prosecution regarding this auction, he'll represent Dr. and Mrs. Stewart solely for this purpose." I knew this would cause a buzz from Dub's team. We hoped to make them wonder if Micki and I'd been fighting about the agreement to auction the assets.

On cue, Bullock was on his feet. "Your Honor, we have a deal with Mr. Patterson regarding the sale of assets belonging to Dr. Stewart. I hope counsel for the defense doesn't intend to renege. Whoever buys the assets needs to know they have clear title."

He fell right in, and Micki pounced.

"Your Honor, our clients have every intention of honoring the agreement. Nothing has changed in that regard. I assume the government will honor its commitment as well. The winning bidder walks away with clear title. For example, if Ms. Stewart is the high bidder for the Healy, the car is hers regardless of how low the bid. Am I right, Mr. Bullock?"

"Absolutely." Bullock seemed relieved.

"All right, counsels. This is an auction, not a hearing. Marshal Maroney, you may proceed. Again, I'm only here to observe." Judge Houston sat down heavily.

Maroney stood up and said. "As you all know, the rules have been published. In summary we will auction by lots. As published, the winning bidder must present to me cash, a certified check, or letter of credit for at least ten percent of the bid and has thirty days to come up with the total amount. At any time a bidder may require another bidder to provide evidence of his ability to meet this requirement. Traditionally, I'm the judge of the sufficiency of a letter of credit. In this case all proceeds go into the U.S. Treasury. Any questions?"

Maroney looked around the room. No questions. "The first item is a 1965 Austin Healy 3000. The automobile has been available for inspection. Do I have an opening bid of five hundred dollars?"

Liz waited until the bidding from a couple of auto dealers reached three thousand dollars, and then raised her hand, just as planned.

"I bid five thousand dollars."

There was a murmur from the crowd, but no response from the dealers.

"Sold to Mrs. Stewart for five thousand," Maroney announced. "Mr. Patterson delivered a letter of credit from Ms. Stewart's bank to me yesterday. It establishes proof of her financial responsibility."

Liz had also insisted that we buy the old pick-up, and she was able to get it for two thousand dollars in record time.

The gallery grew restive as they waited for the papers to be signed. Maroney finally looked up, and you could feel the tension grow.

"The next lot includes Dr. Stewart's computers, his research, his files, as well as his patents and patent applications."

I noticed that Dub and all his deputies now sat literally on the edge of their chairs—why bother to conceal their interest at this point in the game? Poor coaching.

"Do I have an opening bid of, say, five thousand dollars?"

A balding man sitting in the front row stood up and bid one hundred thousand dollars. Almost immediately a man sitting on the second row stood up and called out two hundred thousand. A third sitting in the back offered three hundred thousand. I couldn't tell who was conducting this performance, but you could hear a pin drop. Both the judge and Cheryl were paying rapt attention.

Bids continued to bounce back and forth for a while. Maroney didn't need to ask for a raise until the bidding stopped abruptly at two million from the man in back. I noticed Dub trying to stifle a grin. I decided to find out who the man was.

"Marshal, on behalf of Dr. Stewart I'd like to know who offered the last bid and whether he has the where-with-all to bid such an amount."

Bullock jumped up quickly, almost as if a spring had propelled him forward.

"Marshal, my understanding is that only a competing bidder may make such an inquiry."

Maroney looked at me and said, "I'm afraid that's correct, Mr. Patterson."

"No problem. I bid two million, one hundred thousand dollars. I now request to know the identity of my opponent."

Pushing back his chair as he rose, Dub said gravely. "Your Honor, Mr. Patterson is playing games. He doesn't have that kind of money. He can't bid just to force someone to disclose his identity." The gallery tittered as Judge Houston rolled his eyes.

All eyes turned to me.

"I repeat my bid: two million, one hundred thousand dollars. I also repeat my request regarding the previous bidder."

Dub looked like a bump on a pickle. Apparently he couldn't figure out what to say. The three bidders looked at each other. I had taken them off script. I watched as the well-dressed man in the second row scowled at the man next to him, and raised a finger slightly. He was the same man we had seen in the courtroom the other day. Clovis had learned his identity: Ed Thompson, a senior VP at Akron Drugs. The other—I supposed he was an assistant—nodded to the man in the back.

"Two million, two hundred thousand dollars." He raised the bid and sat down quickly.

"Marshal, I am a legitimate bidder, and I demand to know the identity of the man bidding and whether he came prepared to present the proper security," I said sternly.

Fortunately, Micki had let Maroney know this might happen, so he said. "Sir, I must ask you to identify yourself and present the security for your bid."

"What about Patterson, where's his security?" Dub said loudly.

Maroney smiled blandly. "As you previously pointed out, Mr. Blanchard, only a bidder may make such a request." Dub sat down with a thud.

The bidder walked to the front and said. "My name is Robert Mangum. I'm a vice-president of Akron Drug Company. Here's my letter of credit."

Maroney looked it over carefully and announced, "Mr. Mangum's security is adequate to secure his bid."

Dub relaxed, that is, until I spoke.

"Thank you, Mr. Mangum. I bid three million dollars."

That brought a murmur from the gallery loud enough for the judge to instinctively bang down his gavel and bring Dub back to his feet. Thompson, clearly Mangum's senior, pulled out his cell phone, but Maroney was ready.

"Sir, no cell phones are allowed in the courtroom. Please turn it off, or I'll have to excuse you."

Thompson scowled.

Mangum was of cooler stock. "Marshal, I'd like to know if Mr. Patterson brought security adequate for his bid."

I rose and handed my letter to the marshal. He took his time and then looked up with a slight smile.

"Mr. Patterson's security is adequate to secure his bid."

Dub almost blew a gasket. "How high can he bid?"

The marshal said calmly. "Mr. Blanchard, that information is clearly confidential. You'll note I have not disclosed Mr. Mangum's information either. Mr. Mangum, do you have another bid?"

Dub wasn't satisfied. "Your Honor, Mr. Patterson is making a mockery of this auction. I don't know what he handed the marshal, but there's no way he could come up with such an amount."

Judge Houston said serenely. "Mr. Blanchard, the marshal knows what he's doing. What's your problem? The higher the bid, the more the government recovers."

Dub had no answer. The judge was right. Dub should be overjoyed by how much the assets he had seized would fatten the U.S. Treasury. I glanced at Peggy. She clearly didn't know what to think.

We waited in silence until Thompson in the second row nodded to Mangum, and I heard, "Five million dollars."

"Six million," I came back quickly. Micki grabbed my arm and said "Jack . . ." I turned to her and whispered, "Trust me."

Mangum asked. "Marshal, is that bid secured?"

"Yes, Mr. Patterson's bid is secured."

Last night Walter had pulled me aside and given me an envelope. "The opposition may have to bid a little higher than five million," he'd said with a grin.

"What's this?" I'd asked.

"A letter of credit in the amount of fifty million dollars. You can go as high as half a billion dollars for Doug's research and patents." Maggie walked up quietly and put her arm around him.

"If Doug has discovered even the basis for a cure, our foundation will be honored to own his patents and put him back to work. I have no idea if you can pull this off, Jack, but we didn't want you going up against a Sherman tank with a popgun. At least you know you can draw them out."

I was dumbfounded. "Walter, what can I say? You're taking a hell of a risk."

"No, I'm not. There's no way the government is going to let us own that research, but we are damn well going to scare the hell out of somebody, maybe expose a few bastards. That letter of credit is real, but it will never be called on. You and I know that, but nobody else does. On the other hand, if the one in a million shot does come home, we'll be able to change the world. Isn't that why I started our foundation in the first place?"

"One in a million—not very good odds." I smiled, again impressed by the foresight and intelligence of the man I worked for.

Now we had met the enemy.

Mangum looked at his boss, who again nodded.

"Seven million," he said clearly. No pins dropped, but the air was thick with anticipation. I paused for a minute until the marshal turned to me. "Mr. Patterson?"

I faced him squarely. "Ten million dollars."

Now I could hear Liz gasp. Dub's table was in full whisper, and Mangum seemed lost. Thompson's face wore a furious scowl.

"Marshal, is that bid secured?" Mangum sounded less sure of himself this time.

"Yes, sir, it is." Maroney was having fun.

Mangum asked for a minute, and Maroney said, "One minute." Magnum walked over to Thompson, and they began a heated conversation in whispers. I signaled to Cheryl, and she had the camera zoom in on the two men talking. They caught sight of the cameras and turned away. Maroney began to gather his papers, but Mangum slowly straightened.

"Twenty-five million dollars," His voice was barely above a whisper.

I was ready with "twenty-six," but Maroney said in a firm voice. "I'm sorry, Mr. Mangum. Your letter of credit doesn't entitle you to make such a bid. Do you have a different letter?" He turned to me. "I know you wanted to bid again, but until we clear up Mr. Mangum's bid, you still have the high bid at ten. You don't have to bid against yourself, Mr. Patterson."

Everyone now knew that I was prepared to go higher and had the security. Dub was beside himself, Mangum seemed lost, and Thompson sat in stony silence. Their well-laid plans had gone haywire.

"Well, Mr. Mangum, do you have additional security for your bid?"

"If we can postpone this auction for a day, I'll present whatever collateral you require."

Maroney shook his head. "I'm sorry, that's not permitted. Unless I hear another secure bid, I will award the assets to Mr. Patterson."

Dub's voice rose. "You can't do that. I'll vouch for this man's ability to bid up to any amount he wants."

The marshal said, "Thank you, Mr. Blanchard, but, again, your, uh, 'voucher' does not fall within the rules of our agreed upon procedure. Mr. Patterson, I . . ."

Dub interrupted. "I am the legal representative of the United States Government, and on its behalf, I demand that you accept this man's bid."

Maroney was in his element. "I too am a legal representative of the U.S. Government, Mr. Blanchard, and I will not accept an unsecured bid."

Dub was beside himself. Thompson glared at him, drawing his hand across his neck. The implication was clear.

Dub almost shouted, "On behalf of the United States Government, I cancel this auction. I will immediately open an investigation into whatever fraud Mr. Patterson is trying to perpetrate in these proceedings. He's attempting to make a mockery of this Court and American Justice. Your Honor, I hereby ask you to convene a grand jury and to dissolve any agreements we may have reached with counsel in this matter."

Proud of himself and his outrage, Dub turned to face the camera and smiled broadly.

How could such an incompetent jerk be so cocky?

I rose to my feet. My turn.

"Your Honor, I'm not the one perpetrating a fraud—that honor goes to Mr. Blanchard." Off the board and into the deep end, I thought, gulping a little. Jail, here I come.

Dub was livid, almost apoplectic with rage. The courtroom had let out a collective gasp and was about to erupt when the judge brought down his gavel.

"Mr. Patterson, you've made a serious allegation against an officer of this court. I hope you're prepared to back it up."

"I'm ready, your Honor, right here and right now."

57

HAD I LET myself go too far? Probably, but it sure felt good. The success of the auction had gone to my head a bit, although not many would've considered it a success. What no one yet realized was that I had effectively put a cloud on the transfer of Doug's research and patents to Akron Drug. I could tie up any further attempt to sell the research and patents for a good while by claiming I was the successful bidder. It would throw a monkey wrench in the works, but it wouldn't further research into a cure for cancer or get Doug out of prison. Those results depended on what happened next.

Dub was bursting at the seams and let it show.

"Your Honor, Mr. Patterson has accused me of fraud. His allegations are as baseless as his bid for Dr. Stewart's research. I demand he be held in contempt. He's making us all look like fools."

Micki muttered loud enough for everyone to hear, "Well, you, for sure." Maroney tried to hide a smile.

Judge Houston wasn't happy with anyone. He kept shifting his glare to Cheryl's cameras, still recording every sound, every movement.

"Mr. Patterson, were you serious when you said you could prove your allegations? I could be sympathetic if you merely spoke in the heat of the moment—after all, he said the same about you. Could you perhaps bring yourself to apologize to Mr. Blanchard?"

I looked at Micki, expecting her to urge caution. Her eyes telegraphed, "Go for it." I turned to Maggie, normally the very soul of logic and reason. She mouthed, "Don't hold back."

"Judge, it pains me to say this about Mr. Blanchard," I paused, "but I meant every word. I'm prepared to prove he's involved in an unconscionable fraud of the American people."

The audience in the gallery couldn't be contained. The judge rose and lowered his gavel, calling for order.

"All right, all right. Marshal, under the circumstances, I hope you won't mind if I take over here. You may consider your duties with regard to the auction to have been well performed and now absolved. By the way, the uncontested sales during the auction will remain in force. I think we should take a break for lunch. We probably all need to regroup a little. When we return, Mr. Blanchard, I will conduct an expedited hearing as to why Mr. Patterson should or should not be held in contempt. But I caution you to be careful what you ask for, because I intend to give Mr. Patterson some leeway."

I spoke before he could rap his gavel again. "Your Honor, in order to make my case, I ask that you subpoena Mr. Mangum and the other two men who bid on Dr. Stewart's research, as well as Mr. Thompson, who has been signaling both Mr. Magnum and Mr. Blanchard throughout the auction. I intend to call them as witnesses."

Both Dub and Bullock began to speak, and panic appeared on the faces of the men I had singled out. I had noticed that all three were edging toward the door.

Dub let Bullock take the lead. "Your Honor, these gentlemen are either bidders at an auction or merely observers. They couldn't have any knowledge of Mr. Patterson's allegations. Once again, counsel is trying to create a circus, to the point of harassing ordinary citizens. His tactics have no place in your court."

"I'll be the judge of what does or doesn't have a place in my court. Mr. Patterson may be digging himself a deeper grave, but he's entitled to subpoena witnesses. Since Mr. Blanchard wants immediate relief, I'll not deny Mr. Patterson the opportunity to defend himself. Gentlemen, you're all under subpoena. I expect you to appear in my court at one o'clock this afternoon. This . . . uh, auction, is adjourned."

I signaled our crew to leave quickly so Dub could confer with his people and the bidders in full view of Cheryl's ever-rolling cameras. I figured they'd notice the cameras were on eventually. Clovis hung back.

We'd optimistically arranged for a conference room close to the courtroom.

I looked at Maggie and Micki. "I thought you two were going to tell me to sit down and shut up."

"No way. Isn't this what you wanted? Micki will either keep you out of jail or get you out." Maggie answered.

"I suppose it is, but . . ." My fool's bravado was beginning to fade.

Micki grinned at me. "I'm going to go work on getting you bail, just in case. Walter, I may need your checkbook. Can you come with me?"

Walter rose, but before they left I said. "I may have to put you on the stand to authenticate the letter of credit. You ready?"

He nodded curtly and left with Micki.

Thankfully, Liz had been a silent observer so far. Now she asked, "Jack, do you think they'll let me have the cars today?"

Why in the hell was she worried about the cars at a time like this? I was irritated, but determined not to lose my patience.

"You'll need to catch up to Micki—get Paul to go with you. She'll get Maroney to let you have the cars, but how about waiting until this afternoon? You're not under subpoena, but . . ."

"Jack, I know you think I'm being ridiculous, but I need those cars. Trust me. Thanks to Cheryl, I can probably watch whatever happens this afternoon on my iPad. Let's go, Paul."

Debbie left to get sandwiches, and Maggie and I began to prep Stella for her testimony. Clovis finally sauntered in, a smirk on his face.

"I got to watch Dub get one ass-chewing from Thompson until they realized they were still on camera. It's a safe bet they'll try to get those cameras turned off for this afternoon."

"Let's hope Cheryl took my advice. Clovis, while we're working with Stella, y'all figure out how to replay the tape of their confab after court recessed. We may want to introduce it as evidence."

Micki returned with her arm through Walter's. She gave me a wink. "Well, you may have to spend a few days in jail, but I'll get you out in the end."

"That makes me feel so much better." I turned to Walter. "For a minute I thought we'd actually purchased the patents and some very valuable research. How high do you think they were willing to go?"

"They were never going to let you win. The product is too valuable. They didn't come prepared, but now they'll fight you forever. That's why you have to follow this through today. Otherwise Doug's research will be lost forever."

Nothing like a little pressure.

"I know, but it would have been nice to get it fair and square," I said. "Okay, Micki, get ready to rescue me. I'm about to commit professional suicide."

We returned to the courtroom. A whole new set of lawyers sat at the opposite end of the prosecution's table, pointedly ignoring Dub. Dub glanced at Debbie just before we sat down and on cue, with no coaching, she blew him a kiss. His reaction was worth my going to jail. Ed Thompson gave Debbie a cold stare and spoke quietly to his bulky companion.

Judge Houston strode into the courtroom and quickly called the hearing to order. We all sat down, and he looked at the new lawyers at the prosecutor's table.

With just a hint of a taunt, he asked, "Well, Mr. Blanchard, have you called up the reserves?"

Before Dub could answer, a very tall fellow with thinning razor cut grey hair rose to his feet.

"Your Honor, we are not with the prosecution. My name is Gerald Monday. I'm a partner with the law firm Monday, Williams, and Jones. These men are my associates. We represent the gentlemen who have been subpoenaed. We filed a motion to quash the subpoena a few minutes ago and request you rule on our motion before proceeding. I took the liberty of delivering a copy to your clerk, and I'm now prepared to argue our motion. If the court pleases, this. . . ."

The judge interrupted. "Has Ms. Lawrence or Mr. Patterson been given a copy of this motion?"

Monday didn't flinch, "We couriered a copy to Ms. Lawrence's office after we filed it. We had no idea where they might have gone for lunch."

I was ready to respond, but Judge Houston was well ahead of me. "Well, they're right here now, and after you give him a copy and they've had time to review it, I might consider taking up your motion.

As of now, we're in session. Your clients are here, and in a few hours your motion will be moot. So I suggest you and your five associates take a seat."

Monday and his group look offended, but knew when to be quiet. The gallery had swelled to its full capacity.

Bullock rose. "Your Honor, we can't help but notice that television cameras are still recording this event. Since the nature of the proceeding has changed, I ask the Court to order the cameras to be turned off and taken away."

"May I be heard," came a voice in the gallery. There was no mistaking the strong voice of Janis Harold. Thankfully, Cheryl had taken my advice.

"Your Honor, I represent Fox News. The other networks that are now carrying this broadcast by feed have also authorized me to speak for them. We oppose the closing of the courtroom. Mr. Patterson is a well-known attorney, both in this state and in Washington. His representation of Woody Cole made national headlines, and the possibility that he may be held in contempt is of national interest. Mr. Blanchard asked for these proceedings to be carried live, and Fox News went to great expense to accommodate that request. This matter involves Mr. Patterson only. I suggest he's the only person with standing to complain."

Micki rose carefully. "Mr. Patterson has no objection to the cameras, your Honor."

Judge Houston seemed perplexed, but waved Bullock down before he could speak.

"Mr. Bullock, I have to agree with Ms. Harold. Only Mr. Patterson has standing to object and, although I don't like cameras in my courtroom, it was your idea. The cameras can stay. Now, Mr. Patterson, what do you have to say for yourself? You have accused Mr. Blanchard of perpetrating a fraud. Do you have any evidence?"

I was ready, but Dub beat me to the punch. He looked sideways at Thompson who nodded. "Your Honor, I have to believe that Mr. Patterson was speaking in the heat of the moment. I'll withdraw my accusation of contempt. I think we've all cooled down. Surely this hearing isn't necessary."

His very body seemed ready to explode; I worried fleetingly about his blood pressure. But I could hardly hear his muttered sentences. Clearly, his bosses had told him to shut it down and live to fight another day.

I thought this might but I hadn't decided how to respond. I didn't have to. The judge did it for me.

"Mr. Blanchard. Contempt is for me to decide, and although you may be willing to let things go, I'm not. I want to hear what Mr. Patterson has to say. Mr. Patterson, it's time for you to speak up."

Clearly things weren't going as anyone had expected. Monday stood slowly.

"Your Honor, we must object. Mr. Patterson's intent is to harass my client. He's disrupted a legitimate auction of patents and chemical research and now intends to slander my clients and a respected U.S. attorney under the protection of a lawyer's privilege. You simply cannot let him get away with this travesty."

I think ye protest too much.

The judge finally gave vent to his irritation.

"Mr. Monday, I'm trying to make sense out of what Mr. Bullock unkindly referred to as a circus. First, Mr. Blanchard wants to hold a public auction on national TV, and now it appears he wants to cancel it, remove the cameras, and forgive Mr. Patterson for accusing him of fraud. I think it's time we heard what Mr. Patterson has to say because, frankly, I'm interested. What is it that Mr. Blanchard doesn't want me to hear? Mr. Patterson, can you shed some light on the subject? And let me warn both of you. Mr. Monday and Mr. Blanchard, it's time for you to sit down and be quiet. Mr. Patterson is currently the subject of this contempt hearing, but I can expand it if you continue to interrupt." He turned to me, actually smiling. "Mr. Patterson, why shouldn't I lock you up?"

"I'm happy to tell you, Your Honor."

58

"YOUR HONOR, THE fact is that our government, represented by Mr. Blanchard, and certain private interests, probably Mr. Monday's clients, are involved in an effort to appropriate Dr. Douglas Stewart's research and patents, using our criminal process to perpetuate their scheme. Their scheme is a bold attempt to prevent Dr. Stewart from giving the world a major breakthrough in the search for a cure for cancer."

Another collective gasp rose from the gallery. I felt sure it matched the judge's look of incredulity. Dub and Monday were visibly seething.

I continued, "Even more disturbing is that this unholy alliance is willing to stop at nothing, including illegal wiretapping, kidnapping, and even attempted murder to accomplish their purposes."

"Whoa." The judge sat up. "Mr. Patterson, I can't let you use this court to make scandalous charges without proof."

"Your Honor, I'm prepared to defend my statements."

"Including attempted murder?" he questioned.

"Yes." I didn't hesitate.

Monday and Dub had both risen angrily to their feet, but the judge thundered. "Sit down, gentlemen." He then turned to me. "What's the nature of this proof?"

"Your Honor, if you will allow me to summarize, I will then call witnesses."

"Go ahead."

"It all began several years ago when a world-renowned chemist sent a letter to our government informing numerous officials that he was working on a major breakthrough in cancer research." I handed a copy of Doug's letter to the judge.

Bullock tried once more. "Your Honor, again, I must ask you to remove the cameras. Mr. Patterson is getting into an area of national security."

Judge Houston raised an irritated hand as if to brush him away while he read the letter, then looked down from the bench. "I take it from your objection you already know of the existence of this letter and its authenticity."

Bullock realized he'd screwed up. "I am aware of its existence, but I'm curious how Mr. Patterson could have obtained a copy. That letter and the attached research outline are classified and should only be in the possession of the government."

"Are you suggesting Mr. Patterson stole the letter?" the judge asked.

"Uh. . . ." Bullock didn't know what to say, so he dug the hole deeper. "I hate to use that word, but I can't draw any other conclusion."

"Mr. Patterson?"

"Your Honor, when I attempted to obtain this letter through the Freedom of Information Act, I was stonewalled time and again by the government. Dr. Stewart's wife told me of its existence, and I believed her. Fortunately, Dr. Stewart sent a copy of the letter to my late wife, who was his colleague at NIH. I can give Mr. Bullock a copy of the envelope in which it was sent and which reflects the addressee, the sender, and the date it was mailed. Perhaps he'll also allow me to put my client, Dr. Stewart, on the stand. His testimony could possibly be pertinent."

Dub couldn't control himself. He jumped up. "Judge, don't you see this is just a ruse to get access to his client?"

"Mr. Blanchard, sit down or I will hold you in contempt. I'm warning you for the last time." Dub sat down abruptly, still seething. "Mr. Bullock, are you satisfied with Mr. Patterson's explanation? Do you wish to refute it?"

Bullock was smart enough to say. "No, your Honor, I trust he's telling the Court the truth."

Judge Houston smiled. "Good. Please proceed, Mr. Patterson."

"As Mr. Bullock implied, the letter must have caused quite a stir. The government doesn't put a letter under lock and key, classified under the blanket of 'national security,' as Mr. Bullock just admitted, if it's a hoax or the work of a crackpot. Our government moved quickly to monitor Dr. Stewart's progress and devised a scheme to suppress his work if necessary. I'm also prepared to prove he and his wife's phone calls, e-mails, and computers have been under government surveillance for the last three years."

"Why would our government want to suppress a breakthrough in the cure for cancer?" Judge Houston asked.

"Because in this letter Dr. Stewart signaled his intent to offer the results of his research to the public at no cost, free to anyone. This action would create economic havoc, especially for Mr. Monday's clients, who make billions annually off anti-cancer drugs. These same drug companies work hand-in-glove with our government in hundreds of ways. They have opposed marijuana research for decades, notably with regard to its hypothesized medical benefits. Every year our government spends billions fighting not only the illegal recreational use of the drug, but also any effort to legitimize it for medicinal purposes."

"Counsel," the judge said, "I don't have time to get into a philosophical argument on the pros and cons of medical marijuana. I find it hard to believe that our government would be involved in some conspiracy to prevent a cure for cancer, but that's not the point. You have accused Mr. Blanchard of fraud. Please explain the basis for that charge."

He didn't get it.

"Judge, our government has conspired with a major drug company to prevent Dr. Stewart's research from reaching the light of day. This company intends to use that research for private gain. That is why I intend to put Mr. Monday's clients on the stand. Sadly, Mr. Blanchard's purpose and role in all of this goes way beyond our government playing footsie with a drug company. From my point of view, Mr. Blanchard is small potatoes, but I'm prepared to go forward with that proof first, if you prefer."

Dub sat in stony silence. Bullock had actually scooted his chair away from Dub, and Monday clearly wished he were almost anywhere else.

"Proceed, counsel. But I've got to say I'm skeptical of your whole story about Dr. Stewart's research."

"I understand, Your Honor, but ask yourself one thing: why is a major drug company here today bidding millions of dollars on Dr. Stewart's research if it's worthless? Mr. Magnum's last bid was twenty-five million dollars. While I'm happy to know I won the bidding for the research at ten million, I was prepared to go to half a billion dollars. I'm sure given the chance Mr. Mangum would have matched my bid dollar for dollar."

The gallery erupted. Dub shouted, "Your Honor, he's lying. Where on earth would he get half a billion dollars?"

Judge Houston had raised his gavel, but I wanted to make my point.

"Marshal, what is the dollar amount authorized in my letter of credit?"

Maroney almost purred. "Fifty million dollars." Now the gallery went ballistic.

"Your Honor, the president of the company backing my bid is in the courtroom today. He is prepared to testify of his willingness to pay half a billion dollars for Dr. Stewart's research. I suspect that when I'm allowed to cross-examine Mr. Monday's clients, they'll admit that they too would be willing to pay that amount or more. If they tell the truth, that is. "

Monday didn't object. Judge Houston couldn't ignore either what I'd said or Monday's silence. The gallery now sat in stunned silence.

Houston spent a minute in thought, and then said firmly, "I don't think you want to go further with your objections, Mr. Blanchard, or I will have to question your actions at this morning's auction. Mr. Patterson, enough about your client and his research. What about your allegations against the U. S. attorney?"

"Your honor, I'm prepared to present expert testimony that after Dr. Stewart was arrested and Ms. Lawrence first appeared as counsel, the computers and other electronic equipment in her office and in the offices of the foundation I work for, as well as our personal hardware, were all breached and compromised by Mr. Blanchard's office."

Both Dub and Bullock looked uncomfortable, but remained silent.

"In violation of the Fourth amendment, Dub's office also wiretapped our phones and planted listening devices in Ms. Lawrence's office without a search warrant. We all know that hacking an accused individual's equipment with a warrant occurs, but hacking the lawyers of the accused without a warrant? Akron Drug, represented today by Mr. Monday, also engaged in the same scope of illegal surveillance."

Monday rose half-heartedly to object, but Judge Houston motioned him down with a glare, saying, "Mr. Monday, I'm going to let Mr. Patterson continue. Don't worry. Your clients will have their chance for rebuttal." He nodded at me. "Continue."

"As the court is aware, the government has not charged Dr. Stewart with any crime, but under the rubric of national security, he is being held without access to counsel. Mr. Blanchard has used this opportunity to seize Stewart's computers, his research, and his patents, attempting to auction them off before Dr. Stewart has the chance to appear in public to defend himself. If I hadn't shown up with a letter of credit, those assets would have been sold to Akron Drug for as little as two million dollars when they are worth at least a hundred times that amount. Furthermore, when it was clear that I was the successful bidder because Akron didn't come prepared for competition, Mr. Blanchard attempted to shut down the auction. That's because Mr. Blanchard has a private arrangement with Akron Drug."

Now both Monday and Dub were on their feet, but Bullock remained seated, glancing toward Peggy and Rodney Fitzhugh.

Monday made a feeble attempt. "Your Honor, I warned the court that Mr. Patterson would make desperate allegations, dreamed up entirely out of wishful thinking."

Dub was also emboldened. "Your Honor, first it's kidnapping and murder, now it's some conspiracy to defraud the government. Where's his proof? " He looked to Bullock expecting support, but Bullock avoided his gaze.

"Your Honor, just because I said the words in an opening statement, doesn't mean I don't have proof."

"Well, let's hear it," the judge said. It was time to fish or cut bait.

I shuffled some papers, and Dub watched as Maggie removed the digital recorder from my briefcase and placed it on the table. His face went pale. I was about to make it much paler.

"Your Honor, sitting before you in the front row is Ms. Debbie Kotrova. I came to know Ms. Kotrova because she is employed as

Ms. Lawrence's office manager. In a previous life, she was under the control of a man named Alex Novak, a member of the Russian mafia deeply involved in gambling and prostitution. Mr. Pagano, the local prosecutor, is also present in this courtroom, and I believe he will confirm Novak's reputation as a rogue and racketeer." Debbie smiled sweetly at the judge. God bless her, she just couldn't help herself. "After Ms. Lawrence and I were both kidnapped and almost murdered, I asked Ms. Kotrova to attend certain public appearances where Mr. Blanchard was a participant to monitor what he was saying. Her appearance must have upset our U.S. attorney because he repeatedly asked his marshals to remove her. Isn't that correct, Mr. Blanchard?"

Dub's expression was rewarding.

"I also chose her for this task because she had told me that for a period of time Mr. Blanchard frequented Novak's establishments—she was sure he'd recognize her from her previous employment. I have to admit I thought her presence might upset him."

Dub couldn't help himself. "I went to Novak's establishment as part of an undercover operation. I wasn't doing anything wrong," he said, whining to the judge.

I wasn't about to let him off.

"What I didn't expect was that Mr. Blanchard himself would give me the proof I needed to establish his involvement in the attempted murder and kidnapping of Ms. Lawrence and myself, as well as a conspiracy to defraud the government."

Dub turned toward me, clenching his fists, but visibly sagged as Maggie pushed the recorder across the table and I picked it up.

"Your Honor, I would like to play for the court excerpts from conversations Mr. Blanchard had with Novak over the last couple of weeks. I am fully prepared to produce evidence of their authenticity."

Dub lunged suddenly toward the recorder, but I held it securely.

"Sit down, Mr. Blanchard. Proceed, counsel." The judge smacked his gavel down and Dub slunk down into his chair.

"Your Honor, one of the voices in this conversation is that of Novak. I feel sure you'll recognize the other." The voice of Dub Blanchard blared across the courtroom.

"Why in the hell are you sending that whore to harass me? I paid you all I owed and something extra for roughing up the girl. You said we were good."

Novak's heavily accented voice responded. "It isn't me. I have nothing to do with it."

Dub spit back. "Yeah, right. Listen, I've got a sweet deal working. Don't mess with me, Novak, or I'll have you locked up for life."

Novak remained calm. "I'm telling you I have no control over Ms. Kotrova. She's doing this on her own."

Dub ended. "Well, you figure out how to stop her. I'm holding you responsible."

Dub sat still. His goose was cooked and he knew it. I waited for the judge to react.

"Mr. Patterson, the conversation we have just heard is certainly disturbing and will most certainly provoke further investigation, but I don't see that it implicates Mr. Blanchard in murder."

"I agree, your Honor. Let me fast forward to the last taped conversation Mr. Blanchard had with Novak, one which occurred only last night."

Dub's face mirrored his panic; he knew he had no escape.

I forwarded the tape to the last conversation.

We heard Dub speak first: "I told you to keep that whore away. She showed up at the TV studio tonight."

Novak replied, "And I tell you again: I had nothing to do with it."

Dub again, "Listen, the people I work for have hired a professional to take care of anyone who gets in our way. I'm going to turn her loose on your little tart if she shows up again."

Novak responded, "It must be that lawyer Patterson. He must have put her up to it."

"Patterson is a dead man. I've made sure of that, and if you want your whore alive, you'll convince her to stay away. If not, she'll end up as dead as Patterson and Lawrence are about to be. All I have to do is say the word. My partners and I can't afford any loose ends. Do I make myself clear?"

Novak finished the conversation: "Yes, certainly."

Complete silence.

Dub shoved his chair back violently, causing papers to scatter and Jim Bullock to back away in alarm. Judge Houston barked, "Marshals, guard Mr. Blanchard." Maroney and one of his deputies stepped forward quickly, and Dub fell back into his chair, head slumping into his hands.

I waited, as did the rest of the shocked spectators.

The voice that finally broke the silence was that of Peggy Fortson. "Your Honor, may I approach?" Judge Houston nodded, looking relieved.

"Your Honor, my name is Peggy Fortson, Deputy Assistant Attorney General for the criminal division of the U.S. Department of Justice. I'm compelled to intervene in these proceedings and request that they be postponed immediately. I've been here all day and, like you, I'm greatly disturbed by what I've heard. The Justice Department was asked not to interfere with Mr. Blanchard's task force, but I'm convinced we must do exactly that."

"What exactly is it that you want me to do, Ms. Fortson?" The judge asked.

"Well, for the moment, simply adjourn. The local prosecuting attorney, Mr. Pagano, and Deputy U.S. Attorney Fitzhugh have been observing these proceedings as well. I'm sure they join me in requesting you to detain Mr. Blanchard and turn over Mr. Patterson's recordings to us. We'll also want to confer with Mr. Monday about the continuing availability of his clients. Otherwise, we will have to take them into custody as well. But I'm hesitant to proceed while this hearing is in session." I'd never known Peggy to hesitate before.

Several of the Akron Drug people had sidled quietly toward the door, but they found it blocked by two very serious deputy marshals.

"Ms. Fortson, I understand your concerns. I've never been in a situation like this either. I also find myself more than a little concerned about our government's alleged involvement in the conduct Mr. Patterson has described." I took his concern as a request for my help, which I was glad to offer.

"Your Honor, this may be a first for all of us. I won't argue with the detention of Mr. Blanchard, and I will certainly turn over the recordings. They contain other interesting conversations that will shed further

light and confirmation of the conduct I've alleged. I also wish to reiterate my claim that we were the successful bidder for Dr. Stewart's
research this morning. Regardless of the outcome of that part of the
auction, I still have a lot of faith in our system of justice and specifically in Ms. Fortson and Mr. Pagano. Perhaps, as part of that process,
the court might consider ordering the release of Dr. Stewart to Mr.
Pagano? Furthermore, the court might advise the representatives of
Akron Drug that they are still subject to my subpoena. Other than
that, I guess I'll have to wait for your ruling on the contempt charge."
I couldn't help but grin.

Monday seemed about to respond, but chose instead to wave his
clients back to their seats. They didn't need a contempt charge on top
of everything else.

Judge Houston looked relieved.

"Okay. I'm going to hold everything in abeyance. We'll reconvene
in one week. Ms. Fortson, I expect a full report as well as your presence
in this court next week. All potential witnesses, and you know who you
are, should consider themselves under Court order to appear in this
courtroom one week from today. Failure to appear will be met with at
least a contempt of court citation, and very probably arrest and time
in jail. I promise you won't like it. Marshal, take Mr. Blanchard into
custody."

Maroney clearly didn't mind slapping the cuffs on the wretched
Dub, who was shaking like a leaf. I could almost feel sorry for him.
Judge Houston hadn't responded to my request for Doug's release,
but I felt pretty good about his chances.

"Mr. Patterson, under the circumstances, you will not be held in
contempt, but next time you appear in my courtroom, please try to be
a little less dramatic."

59

THE GAVEL CAME down sharply, and now the courtroom broke into pandemonium. I watched as my team broke into rampant hugging. The Akron Drug people looked lost. Monday was silently packing his briefcase. The cameras were still rolling, and Cheryl was talking a mile a minute into a microphone. Time to leave.

I signaled for Clovis. We still had lots to do, including getting Doug out of jail, but from now on we'd be dealing with reasonable people. Peggy walked over, hand extended.

"When am I going to quit doubting you?"

"Probably never."

She laughed. "You've handed me one hell of a mess—a dirty U.S. Attorney, a whole slew of government officials to investigate, congressional investigations and, with your friend Cheryl milking this for all its worth, a media nightmare. Someday you're going to have to explain how you figured it all out."

"Over dinner?" I asked.

"I won't hold my breath." She raised her brows and turned to confer with Sam.

Micki and I embraced, and she said, "Nice work, partner—not bad, not too bad at all."

We all agreed to meet at Micki's for a celebration. I told them I had an errand to run and they went ahead, chattering about the day. Clovis followed me slowly to his Tahoe.

"What's the matter?" I asked.

"Moira's employer is going to be pissed, and she isn't going to quit. We haven't seen the last of her. We need to be careful."

"Aw, come on, Clovis, let's at least enjoy this day. Besides, Moira's your problem. That's why I pay you the big bucks," I joked. I'd have been more than concerned if I'd noticed the solitary figure slinking out of the courtroom.

I hesitated a minute, then opened the door to the Tahoe. "Clovis, I promise to worry about Moira tomorrow, but not today. Let's go to City Park. I want to talk to Angie."

"Why am I not surprised?" Clovis laughed.

After the Cole case the last place I had gone before leaving town was City Park. Little Rock's City Park was an oasis of green on the outskirts of downtown: ball fields, walking paths, green space, playgrounds, tennis courts, picnic tables, all sheltered by woods of towering oaks and hickories. We pulled into the parking lot, and I told Clovis to wait. He was reluctant, but I told him I'd be in plain sight less than a hundred yards away. Both the dogwoods and the azaleas were in in full flower, and the warm spring sun felt good on my face. I strolled to a tall oak tree shading the creek. I had proposed to Angie under this tree and we used to come here on Sunday mornings to imagine our future. I leaned back against the solid oak and let my body slide to the ground, my mind sliding into the past.

I conjured Angie's image, closed my eyes, and silently began to tell her about what had happened. I could almost hear her say, "Now do you see why I wanted you to defend Doug?"

Within my reverie I could sense approaching footsteps. I felt relaxed but sort of heavy, it took real effort to open my eyes. A man in a dark suit was walking toward me. Oddly, I recognized him from the courtroom. He'd been sitting next to Ed Thompson, Akron Drug's senior vice-president. I wondered idly why he was here, whether he was looking for me. He looked friendly enough, but my brain was sounding alarm bells. I knew I should stand up, but I saw that he had taken a handgun out of his coat and was aiming it directly at me. Before I could even breathe, I heard a loud 'thump,' and the man crumpled to the ground. I looked around wildly to see a figure with short red hair emerge from behind a nearby tree. Now I couldn't move a muscle.

Moira walked casually toward my tree. "Mind if I join you?" She asked.

I gestured mutely and she sat beside me, her gun returned to a small clutch now resting on her lap. I couldn't think how to respond.

"I came back to finish the job I was hired to do, but when I saw Max sitting next to Thompson this afternoon, it really pissed me off. He had obviously been hired to do my job. He would have killed you, Micki, and Debbie, all the while laying the blame squarely on me. No way. And you know what? I didn't like what I heard in court today. Withholding a cure for cancer is really . . ." She shook her head. "Well, it's despicable. I even thought about walking away from the contract, leaving you alone or maybe even kidnapping you and taking you back to Brazil. Could be fun, don't you think? But Jack, if I did that, my boss would send somebody to kill us both. Besides, a girl's got to make a living, and I have a reputation to maintain." She gave me a forlorn smile and said, "Sorry, Jack. I hope you can understand."

She kissed me on the cheek, stood back up, and slowly began to back away. I was beyond any reaction, oddly frozen in the moment.

"Most of the people I kill deserve to die, but you don't. You knew I'd be back, and you forged ahead anyway. You've got guts, and we might have . . . but . . ." She paused, closing her lips and I braced myself. She reached into the small bag. She could hardly miss.

I don't know what happened first, hearing the explosion or seeing Moira drop to the ground in a heap. Her blood flew everywhere. I tried to wipe it off my hands and face, but I couldn't escape it. I saw Clovis, as if in slow motion, walk slowly toward her body, his gun still held warily in both hands.

"I hoped you'd show up. I . . . well, thanks." I hadn't moved from my seat against the tree. I seemed to be glued to it. My brain seemed stuck as well. After removing the gun from her hand and checking her pulse, or lack thereof, he sunk down beside me, handing me a handkerchief. Paul was off in the distance holding off a growing number of onlookers.

"You okay? Let's sit here for a few minutes. The park's a busy place today. Martin's holding the two guys who were supposed to keep me out of the way until she killed you. She wanted me to die knowing I'd failed to protect you. But I don't get fooled twice very often. And don't you be fooled, Jack. All that talk of hers was just that, talk. She was always going to kill you. You, me, then Micki and Debbie."

"What if you had missed?"

"I don't miss." He wasn't laughing. In fact, I thought he might be a little shaky himself. "Besides, Paul had her in his sights the whole time. She was never going to squeeze that trigger a second time. I have to admit we didn't plan for a second assassin—that guy was a surprise. Guess we owe Moira for handling him so efficiently."

"Yeah, right, you go ahead and thank her, not me. I've had enough of her. How'd you know I'd want to come here?"

"You've told me a lot about Angie over the last year or so, how much this park meant to the two of you. Didn't take a law degree to know you'd need a little time to wind down. Where else but here? Martin, Paul, and I have spent a good portion of the last few days trying to figure out what to do about Moira. Good thing you're so predictable."

Finally able to laugh, he eased up the tree to his feet and called Sam. The adrenaline had kicked in, and I was trying hard not to shake. He offered me a hand up, and we stood leaning against the big oak, waiting for the police to arrive. Neither of us said another word; we didn't need to.

60

SAM AND THE Little Rock Police wheeled into the park, sirens blazing, and took charge. Clovis gave him a brief version of what happened, and Sam suggested we return to Micki's. He put a firm hand to my shoulder, walked me to the Tahoe, and told me to get some sleep. I guess he could tell I was pretty much done in. Clovis called Micki to give her a quick rundown of what had happened. I dreaded having to retell the story a hundred times when I got to her place.

When we pulled into the drive, I was surprised to find a celebration already in full gear. Apparently my attempted murder hadn't put a damper on the evening. Micki looked almost like her old self. I asked if she felt well enough to take over Doug's defense. The wheels of real justice had been set in motion, and it was time to get Doug out of jail.

Eyes alight, she responded, "You bet—I'm back!"

I found Walter engaged in deep conversation with Liz. I was a little surprised to see her laughing and in such good spirits, but glad to see she'd dropped her alternate personality. I cautioned them it would be a long tough fight before we got our hands on Doug's research.

Liz giggled a little. "Oh, Jack, don't be a wet blanket—we won! And admit it: I bet you think I was crazy to spend any time or money on Doug's cars."

"Of course not. I looked at them myself. Both engines run just fine, and the Healy's in great shape." Liz smiled broadly and Walter gazed at the ceiling, whistling a little tune. "Wait a minute—what?"

"I don't really care about the cars, silly. But I do care a lot about two zip drives—one in each basin of the windshield wiper fluid, all packaged to stay nice and dry." She reached into the pocket of her jeans and handed one to me.

Walter was beside himself. "Each drive contains all the information on Doug's computer: all his research, his patent applications, and the latest recipe for his special spice."

I gave a whoop and turned to Liz. "You knew all . . ."

Walter interrupted me mid-sentence. "Wait, Jack, wait till you hear the rest. There's also a note from Doug—the computers hold only part of his research and the spice recipe is missing key ingredients. The government and Akron Drug may think they can stop us, but what they have is worthless. The foundation will pay Liz for these hard drives and give Doug all the support he needs, even if we have to do it in another country."

Liz kissed me on the cheek. "Doug will be working with you and the foundation just like he used to work with Angie. It won't ever be the same without her, but he'll be happy and so will I."

Overjoyed by our good fortune and Doug's good sense, I gave her a heartfelt hug and shook Walter's hand vigorously. But the day's events had finally gotten the best of me. I just wanted to curl up in my bed and sleep. I was out before my head hit the pillow. I understand the celebration lasted far into the night.

THURSDAY

May 8, 2014

61

Over coffee the next morning, Maggie and Walter told me they were flying back to DC that afternoon. For a moment, I thought about joining them. I felt sure Akron's lawyers would file an avalanche of motions, making it next to impossible for Judge Houston to convene court next Wednesday. Sam would be working night and day on the mess I'd handed him. Little Rock wasn't home, hadn't been for years. But I wasn't ready for DC yet, either. I knew both Sam and the Feds would need a complete explanation of the two dead bodies in City Park. Clovis came up with the perfect solution. We would do our civic duty, then spend a long weekend at his fishing camp on the White River. The weather was beautiful and the fish were biting. Just two friends fishing, eating, drinking, and swapping stories.

Mr. Kim sat quietly in his office with a view of the White House. Once again Patterson had gotten the better of him. Cleaning up the mess would be expensive and time-consuming, and it would be difficult to replace his two best assassins. A weaker man would order quick and certain retaliation, but he had decided against it. His organization didn't need the scrutiny that would follow if Patterson disappeared now; better to devote his attention to the client's rehabilitation. Besides, he held no personal grudge against the man. Surely Patterson realized that he had twice come very close to death; surely he wouldn't cross the organization again. If not, well, Mr. Kim would be prepared.

Epilogue

MICKI QUICKLY WORKED out a deal with Fitzhugh to get Doug released and the charges dropped. Doug had violated the law but, given the government's actions, Fitzhugh decided that prosecuting Doug would do more damage than good to the much bigger issues facing Peggy and Sam. When he was released from jail, Walter's plane was waiting to whisk him and Liz away for two weeks at a house on Pawley's Island in South Carolina. They'd return in plenty of time for Doug to cooperate in the upcoming investigations.

Akron Drug went into full damage control mode. Within a matter of days they landed a full crisis management team on the ground, headed by a former deputy FBI director and the recently retired White House Director of Legislative Affairs. They chose to blame everything on "rogue low-level employees." Several officers, including Thompson, quietly resigned, well protected by the legal team as well as by handsome retirement benefits. Sam and Peggy are up against Akron's bottomless pocketbook and an army of lawyers and former legislative aides. I still have my money on Sam and Peggy.

Dub posted bail and pulled strings to get admitted to the Betty Ford Clinic. Facing probable charges of conspiracy to commit murder, he is also all lawyered up, and refuses to talk. Rumor has it that Akron is footing his legal bills. Bullock, however, has agreed to fully cooperate with Peggy and Sam's investigation. The other members of the task force have tried to bury themselves in the woodwork.

White-collar criminal defense lawyers are in big demand once again in DC, and a large number of high-ranking individuals in the U.S. government have resigned in order to "spend more time with their families." For a change, no one in Congress has called for an investigation. Lobbyists for the drug companies are counseling all concerned not to open a "can of worms."

Cheryl's ratings have gone through the roof. She has a fat new contract and is milking the Akron Drug scandal for all it's worth. I have refused to appear on her show despite her pleas that I owe her.

Micki reports that Debbie and Paul are constant companions. They jog together, and she's teaching him how to cook. I had dinner with Sam and Peggy last week at Othello's, off DuPont Circle. It's clear they enjoy working together. For once, Peggy didn't ask when I was going to take her to dinner.

I stepped down as president of the foundation. No surprise. I told Walter and Maggie we needed someone who knew the world of medical research and could help Doug take his work to the next level and beyond. The reality, finally faced, is that I'm a lawyer first and last and belong in a courtroom. I'd prefer fewer attempts on my life, but I enjoy the rest. Walter insisted I remain on the board and I have a nice advisory contract with the foundation. My law office is still located in the foundation's headquarters. I can't afford to lose Maggie, and she feels the same way.

Doug and I had a long talk about Angie's involvement in his research. He wants her to be given equal credit for their discoveries. He told me that she was intimately involved before she got so sick, but didn't want me to know. She told him that I would make her quit because of her legal exposure. Again, I wish she had asked, but then again, she was probably right.

The foundation held a retreat at the Cloisters on Sea Island in Georgia. Angie and I had enjoyed a couple of beach trips there when Beth was a child; now it's gated and very, very swanky. Too bad.

Doug and the new president of the foundation, Dr. Rohit Catlett, gave us an overview of their plans for his research. Liz didn't attend. The retreat conflicted with a two-week wellness session in Peru with her "balancing guru." Only Doug missed her presence.

I asked the board to consider a project that had been rumbling around in my brain since Little Rock. To a certain extent Novak had come out smelling like a rose, a result I couldn't let go. On a hunch, I asked Clovis to research Moira's background. It turned out she came to the U.S. when she was just twelve years old, lured by Novak's organization. I said it was a hunch, but it wasn't really. Just before we left the Ritz-Carlton in Dallas, Novak had confirmed that Moira had once worked for him. I remembered Debbie's words: "It takes one to know one." Moreover, I thought I had noticed a brand when Moira and I were otherwise engaged.

It doesn't take a genius to realize that Novak didn't tape his conversations out of some sense of altruism, or a desire to save my life. He did it to protect his own ass. He knew I would use the tapes to stop Dub and whoever was trying to frame him.

He also had good reason to think Moira would complete her contract to eliminate Micki and me, leaving him free to lure Debbie back. Of course, I have no proof of that, but I do know that Novak is ruthless and morally bankrupt, not some sort of good Samaritan.

UNICEF estimates that more than two million children are exploited yearly in the sex industry. Debbie, and to some extent Moira, brought this atrocity home to me. Debbie's experience wasn't the exception, it is the norm. The recruitment of young girls, the drugs, the branding, and the torture—it's all real—not in some far-off place with a name you can't pronounce, but right here in America's cities and towns. I wanted our foundation to contribute towards the efforts already underway to bring this unconscionable activity to the light of day and to help pursue justice for its victims. The board unanimously approved my proposal. Not surprisingly, Walter insisted that we double the funds I requested.

Maggie had encouraged Stella to join us at the retreat, thinking, I'm sure, that we might click. She had that matchmaker look about her. But for once Maggie misread the signals. Clovis had already fallen for her, and she had eyes for no one but him. You could have knocked both Maggie and me over with a feather. Then again, Clovis was the only man I knew who could toss tires with her.

Micki and Eric seem to have worked out their issues, although every now and then Sam reports that Micki has gone on the warpath about something. I'm beginning to believe she just enjoys the make-up sex. Who knows with Micki?

As for me, I'm on my way to Vermont to see that schoolteacher, Marion South. Maggie's right; I haven't tried hard enough.

ACKNOWLEDGMENTS

Someone famous has said, "It takes a village," or maybe it was a title to a book. I have the best village one could imagine, and I am grateful for their love and support every day, and in this instance, for their willing and unending help in bringing *Ginger Snaps* to reality.

Peggy, Terry, and Caroline each read the early drafts, giving me valuable insight. My wife Suzy spent endless hours reading and editing every draft. My children and their spouses gave me input and encouragement. My Charlotte and Arkansas friends continue to be my biggest supporters and cheerleaders. My home state, Arkansas, once again provides a vivid background, wonderful memories, and constant inspiration.

My daughter Caroline and her colleague Sarah Byrne offered legal advice and tremendous insight into the world of illegal sex trafficking in the United States. Keith Stroup, founder of NORML, shared his extensive knowledge of the ever-changing laws governing marijuana and asset forfeiture. My sister Terry keeps me straight when it comes to medical issues.

Beaufort Books has my deepest thanks and appreciation. Publisher Eric Kampmann believed in me from day one. Megan Trank, Michael Short, and Felicia Minerva have given me invaluable help in editing, cover design, and publicity. No author has a better or more patient team.

Every day I remain eternally grateful to George and his family.